## "SIR—BEHIND YOU!"

Fraser spun in time to see one of his sappers reeling back from the Sandcastle's rampart with a bolt embedded in his shoulder. The other legionnaire swung his FEK and fired downward.

A *whoosh* and a thunderclap silenced the FEK as an explosive-tipped rocket projectile caught the second sapper square in the chest. The man flew backward, trying to save himself, but he slipped and fell. He landed in the mud below and lay still.

A dozen bulky, inhuman shapes clambered onto the parapet, their ill-assorted weapons gleaming in the light. One of them pointed a rocket rifle at Fraser and fired. . . .

# THE FIFTH FOREIGN LEGION #2

## *Honor and Fidelity*

---

Andrew Keith and William H. Keith, Jr.

---

A ROC BOOK

ROC
Published by the Penguin Group
Penguin Books USA Inc., 375 Hudson Street,
New York, New York 10014, U.S.A.
Penguin Books Ltd, 27 Wrights Lane,
London W8 5TZ, England
Penguin Books Australia Ltd, Ringwood,
Victoria, Australia
Penguin Books Canada Ltd, 10 Alcorn Avenue,
Toronto, Ontario, Canada M4V 3B2
Penguin Books (N.Z.) Ltd, 182-190 Wairau Road,
Auckland 10, New Zealand

Penguin Books Ltd, Registered Offices:
Harmondsworth, Middlesex, England

First published by Roc, an imprint of New American Library,
a division of Penguin Books USA Inc.

First Printing, September, 1992
10 9 8 7 6 5 4 3 2 1



Printed in the United States of America

# Prologue

**Soleil Rochemont:** Distance from Sol 138 light-years . . . Spectral class G1V; radius 1.006 Sol; mass 1.02 Sol; luminosity 1.102 Sol. Stellar Effective Temperature 5900°K . . . Four planets, one planetoid belt. There is only one habitable world, the innermost, designated "Polypheme". . . .

**I Polypheme:** Orbital radius 0.90 AUs; eccentricity .0136; period 0.845 solar years (308.8 std. days) . . . One natural satellite, Nonhomme, mass 0.004 Terra; density 0.6 Terra (3.3 g/cc); orbital radius 130,269 kms; period 5.16 std. days (123.8 hours) . . . an airless, waterless body notable only for its significant tidal effects on Polypheme . . .

Planetary mass 1.1 Terra; density 0.85 Terra (4.675 g/cc); surface gravity 0.93 G. Radius 6950.4 kilometers; circumference 43,670.54 kilometers . . . Total surface area 607,054,524 square kilometers . . .

Hydrographic percentage 82% . . . Atmospheric pressure 0.9 atm; composition oxygen/nitrogen. Oxygen content 18% . . .

Planetary axial tilt 17°40′57.4″. Rotation period 46 hours, 14 minutes, 28.9 seconds . . .

**Planetography:** Polypheme's close satellite produces tidal stresses which have shaped many facets of planetary development. The planet is more seismically active than Terra, with a consequently more rugged surface. . . . There are ten continents. . . . Tides cause broad coastal tracts to be regularly inundated and then exposed. . . .

Equatorial temperatures have been recorded as high as 45°C. . . . Polar temperatures rarely rise above freezing but are too warm to produce permanent ice packs. . . . There is a moderating influence exerted on the planet by the oceans, and humans find the climate tolerable outside the tropics.

The low planetary density is indicative of a general lack of worthwhile ore deposits, but there is an unusually high concentration of minerals in the planetary oceans, possibly caused by widespread undersea volcanic activity. By Commonwealth standards Polypheme is poor, and were it not for the twin interests of scientists studying tidal effects and miners lured by the high mineral content of the seas Polypheme might well have been ignored. . . .

Although the usual variety in terrain and ecology is present on Polypheme, of greatest interest are the many adaptations to the tidal conditions. . . . The tidal plains have become home to many species uniquely evolved for this strange environ, including the planet's sapient race. . . .

**Biology:** Intelligent life arose in the tidal flats, in a species originally adapted to a dual existence built around the ebb and flow of the tides. . . . Equally at home as swimmers or clinging by sucker-like appendages to rocks exposed on the flood plains, this species found intelligence useful both to cope with the fast-changing conditions of their unique ecological niche and to handle certain swimming predators. The latter further spurred adaptation to a dry-land environment. . . .

The sophonts of Polypheme, the *drooroukh,* are a bilaterally symmetrical, bimodal race with four limbs all equally well-adapted as hands, feet, or fins as circumstances warrant. A highly sophisticated pseudogill system can extract oxygen from air or water with equal proficiency, with membranes in the gill outlets serving as speech organs. They generally stand upright on land but can move on all fours very quickly and are superb swimmers. A flat, heavy tail provides propulsion in the water and balance ashore. . . . They are homeothermic, producing live young. The juveniles of the species cannot leave the water on their own, and they normally swim free except when feeding. . . . The young are parasitic, clinging to an adult and drawing nourishment from its blood. Although humanoid in gross appearance the *drooroukh* have little in common with Mankind. . . .

The average local measures 1.7 meters in length, not including the tail, with hairless, slick skin which ranges from gray-green to black in color. . . . Although possessed of two sexes and a fairly typical reproductive cycle, the *droor-oukh* have little concept of family, regarding child care as the collective responsibility of the group. . . .

**Civilization:** Several thousand years ago a schism developed among the inhabitants of Polypheme. Part of the population began spending more and more time on land, except as necessary for child-rearing and mariculture. . . . The process led to the development of a civilization along patterns similar to Terra, with metalworking, cities, and the rudiments of scientific thought. . . .

The second group, however, remained closely tied to the seas in a nomadic existence unchanged over a period of 50,000 years. . . . The nomads have enjoyed mixed relations with their land-dwelling cousins, sometimes trading with them, at other times in conflict. . . . Most researchers see them as locked in a cultural dead-end. . . .

**Commonwealth Contact:** Prior to the Semti War Polypheme was nominally a part of the Semti Conclave, but the Semti had little interest in the planet and leased development rights to the neighboring Toeljuk Autarchy. . . . The Toels found conditions on Polypheme familiar and applied many of the techniques invented in their own climb to power to exploiting the new world. . . . Though poor in metals ashore, Polypheme offered resources in abundance at sea, where a species of small aquatic grazer, the "shelljet," was found to extract and concentrate metals in its shell. A number of large harvester ships, and bases to support them, were established by the Toeljuks on Polypheme. . . . The project was abandoned about the time of the Semti War due to the collapse of the Autarchy's economy in that period. . . .

For close to a century Commonwealth contact was limited to a few scientific teams and the missionary work of the Uplift Foundation. . . . Three years ago Seafarms Interstellar put forward a proposal to duplicate Toel harvesting techniques, using the abandoned Toeljuk facilities as a basis for new operations. . . .

Excerpted from *Leclerc's Guide to the Commonwealth*
Volume VI: *The Toel Frontier*
34th Edition, published 2848 A.D.

# Chapter 1

Is it how a soldier lives that matters? Isn't it how he dies?

—Colonel Joseph Conrad
French Foreign Legion, 1835

Legionnaire Second-Class Alois Trousseau shielded his eyes against the dazzling light of the setting sun. Twilight on Polypheme was the stuff of romantic poetry, long, lingering, with brilliant hues of red and orange illuminating the low-lying cloud banks and reflecting off the vast empty stretches of the Sea of Scylla. The light caught the crescent shape of Nonhomme, Polypheme's satellite, as it loomed overhead looking close enough to reach out and touch, and reflections from the water rippled and danced everywhere.

But Trousseau paid little attention to the beauty that was Polypheme as he crossed the docking platform and knelt near the water's edge.

Displacing just under a hundred thousand metric tons, *Seafarms Cyclops* was a huge vessel. There were four of these docks spaced around her wide hull, but this was the best one for Trousseau's purposes. Designed to accommodate smaller ships with stores and equipment destined for the engineering spaces, this platform was rarely used or even visited.

And the setting sun would help hide Trousseau as he left the vessel in the raft he held bundled under one arm. By the time anyone noticed he was missing, he would be far from the confines of the huge harvester ship.

He'd planned his desertion carefully. Even the time was perfect. Not only would the sun help obscure his movements, but it was close to 0400 by standard ship-time. Polypheme's 47-hour rotation didn't mesh well with the cycles of bodies evolved for Terrestrial conditions. Most of the ship's personnel were asleep, and those on watch were likely to be slow responding.

In another few hours they would be leaving the Cape of Storms behind, and with it their last contact with solid land for a month or more. He had to act tonight if he was to escape.

Trousseau pulled the ring and listened to the hiss of the raft's inflation with a satisfied little smile. Once ashore it would be a long, hard march before he reached the native city of Ourgh. But it would be worth it to be quit of the Foreign Legion.

He knew some starport workers who would smuggle him aboard the next ship out for the hundred sols he's been hoarding for the last few weeks. Once they put in to the systerm on the outermost planet of the system he'd be able to come out of hiding. Maybe a ship would need an electronics technician. He'd put in enough time as the platoon's $C^3$ operator to get a job handling any commlink or computer a small ship could mount.

The raft slid slowly into the water. Trousseau lashed it to the cleat and ran through a last mental checklist.

Free! He was finally going to be free of the Legion, of the martinet NCOs, of the overbearing officers. Free of the boredom. He'd never imagined it could be so boring until he joined the garrison on Polypheme.

With a last glance around, Trousseau turned his back on the *Seafarms Cyclops*—on the Fifth Foreign Legion.

Something splashed at the forward end of the dock, and Trousseau's trained reflexes made him spin to face it before he was even consciously aware of the sound.

He found himself staring down at a bulky figure with smooth gray-green skin. It seemed to take forever for the legionnaire to register it as one of the Polypheme sophonts, a "polliwog" to use the slang of humans living on the planet. By the time he realized what it was it had already climbed free of the water to stand on the platform, its stalked eyes focused on Trousseau with an unfathomable alien expression.

It—no, *he*—was one of the planet's ocean-dwelling nomads, clad in nothing more than a loose harness that held an assortment of primitive weapons and implements. An intricate pattern of tattoos on his chest identified his tribe, but Trousseau had never taken adchip instruction on nomad symbols or tribal signs, so it was unintelligible.

The wog was large for his kind, nearly two meters long without the flat tail that balanced his slightly forward-leaning posture.

But Trousseau was only vaguely aware of the creature's size. His attention was focused, instead, on the small device clutched in one long-jointed, web-fingered hand. A slender tube mounted atop an alien pistol-grip . . .

The alien raised the tube to point at Trousseau's chest and squeezed the trigger.

The impact of the 5-mm rocket projectile made Trousseau stagger back. His duraweave coverall—and the short range, which kept the rocket from building up to full impact velocity—had saved his life, but the legionnaire was stunned. He struggled to keep his balance, but couldn't.

Suddenly his feet weren't on the solid deck anymore. Salt stung his eyes and made him gag as he fell into the dark water. Trousseau came to the surface spluttering, gasping for air. Long fingers closed around his throat, pulling him down again.

Trousseau knew he would die.

He let himself go limp, then kicked away again as the grip relaxed. Wincing at the pain, he took another breath and let himself sink, his fingers operating the keys on his wristpiece computer. He couldn't outfight the nomads in their own element, but at least he could warn the others they were here before it was too late.

An artificial voice whispered in his ear. "Please give the password for computer access."

*Damn! What was the password?* Trousseau twisted away from another wog and broke the surface again. "Nightwing!" he spluttered, gasping for air. "Nightwing!"

"Access accepted. Please—"

"Security code India!" Trousseau shouted. A knife blade slashed through his coverall, and pain lanced through his back. "India! Intruders on Deck One, En—"

The knife struck again, and again.

And Legionnaire Alois Trousseau bobbed to the surface, staining the water with his blood.

Subaltern Toru Watanabe rolled out of his bunk as the ululating alarm shrieked through the bowels of the *Seafarms*

*Cyclops.* The metal was cold under his bare feet, but the shiver that ran up his spine had nothing to do with the temperature.

Watanabe had hoped for a cruise as boring as garrison life back at the Legion's base, in the installation the humans on Polypheme called "Sandcastle." But the security alarm meant there was trouble aboard the harvester ship—serious trouble.

Still groggy, Watanabe crossed the cabin and slapped the call button on the intercom mounted above the desk. Like all the human equipment aboard *Seafarms Cyclops* the intercom had an improvised, unfinished look that stood out in contrast to the flowing lines and exotic patterns of the original vessel. The contrast reminded him vaguely of the blend of high-tech and traditional styles of art and architecture his Japanese ancestors had brought with them from Terra to his native world of Pacifica.

He forced himself to concentrate on the problem at hand as the heavy features of Sergeant Yussufu Muwanga filled the viewscreen. "Operations," the sergeant said gruffly.

"What have you got, Sergeant?"

"Computer just sounded the alarm, sir," Muwanga replied. "We're trying to find the source now. It wasn't any of our lookouts."

"A false alarm?" he asked hopefully.

Muwanga frowned. Watanabe rubbed his forehead absently. He knew the answer the man would give. Why had he let himself show his uncertainty so plainly?

"*Someone* put through an India code, sir," the sergeant said slowly. "The computer can't just come up with one on its own."

"Then get Trousseau down there and ask *him,*" Watanabe snapped. "Meanwhile, order Sergeant Gessler to assemble the men in Hold Two. I'm on my way down."

"Yessir," the sergeant replied. The screen went dead.

Watanabe slumped into the chair behind the desk, feeling drained. *Why can't I keep a lid on my temper?* he asked himself bitterly. A year ago he'd never have lost control like that. Toru Watanabe had the reputation for being quiet, soft-spoken, calm in any crisis—a competent platoon commander.

Since then, though, Toru Watanabe had changed.

He dressed quickly in duraweave fatigues, boots, and a

beret, his mind on the past year. First, the excitement of getting his assignment. It was rare for a top Academy student to request the Fifth Foreign Legion, but Watanabe had gone after the posting with a single-minded determination to follow in his father's footsteps and be a part of the Legion tradition. He'd made it, too, earning a platoon command.

But then came the fighting on Hanuman, the long overland retreat through hostile territory after a coup d'état had cut his company off from outside aid. And at the climax of the campaign the legionnaires had been forced to make a desperate stand against overwhelming odds, and Toru Watanabe had watched as his precious platoon was all but destroyed. Somehow he'd come through the fighting alive, but he knew he'd never be the same again.

War wasn't like the stories you saw on the holovid shows, or the textbook accounts of maneuvers and countermaneuvers. It took courage to command men in battle; not just personal bravery, but the kind of resolve that would let an officer order his men to their deaths. Toru Watanabe wasn't sure he had that kind of courage anymore.

But if the alarm was genuine, he might soon have to find that kind of courage again.

His mind was still grappling with doubts as Watanabe left his quarters and sought out the Operations Center, a windowless cabin two decks below his quarters near the heart of Legion country commonly known as "C-cubed." *Seafarms Cyclops* was a huge ship, originally designed to carry a crew of several hundred gregarious Toeljuks on an extended cruise. Since her refit for human personnel she needed less than fifty men for a crew, and there was more than enough space for a thirty-four man Legion platoon to have private quarters, rec facilities, drill spaces, a secure armory, and everything else they could possibly want to make a three-month tour at sea bearable.

Sergeant Muwanga looked up from a control console as Watanabe entered. "Sir, Trousseau won't answer. And he didn't assemble with the others."

Watanabe crossed the cramped room and bent over a computer terminal beside the sergeant. "Did you check his quarters?"

"Empty, sir," Muwanga said with a gesture at a viewscreen. It showed a small, spartan cubicle. There was no one visible, and the bunk was neatly made up. A locker stood open nearby, obviously empty as well.

"Goddamn . . ." Watanabe said softly. He punched up a code that would allow the computer to trace the legionnaire's helmet communications gear.

"No response from beacon," the computer voice said. "Helmet has been damaged or disconnected."

Muwanga and Watanabe exchanged looks. "Desertion," the black man said. "Has to be."

Watanabe sank into a chair. "Damn stupid place to desert," he said.

The sergeant shrugged expressively. "*Cafarde,*" he replied.

Watanabe nodded. *Le cafarde*—the expression meant *cockroach*—was a disorder that had been a part of Foreign Legion lore from the very beginning. A compound of boredom, instability, and confusion, it caused men to react in bizarre ways. Some committed suicide, some deserted, some picked fights, a few just went mad—all from *cafarde*. Some superstitious legionnaires talked of it as if it really was an insect, a bug that crawled into their ears and whispered to them in the night.

*Cafarde* was becoming a problem on Polypheme, as boring a duty station as any legionnaire was likely to see. But Trousseau had never seemed like the sort to crack under that particular pressure.

Muwanga turned away to operate another console. He held a headpiece speaker to one ear. "Sergeant Gessler says the men are ready, sir," he said. "What are your orders?"

Watanabe stared down at the monitor, eyes locked on the empty cabin. Trousseau had been with him on Hanuman, one of the handful who survived. He'd picked the legionnaire to be his new $C^3$ technician personally. It was like a betrayal. . . .

"Sir?" Muwanga insisted.

He looked up at the sergeant. "Didn't Trousseau like to go out on one of the docking platforms to get away from everyone?" he asked quietly.

Muwanga hesitated. "Yeah . . . Yes, sir. I'm not sure which one."

"Check the monitor cameras on all four of them, Sergeant." Excitement was putting a sharp edge in his voice. If he was right . . .

Muwanga's fingers skimmed over a keypad. "Nothing . . . nothing . . . Hell! Port-side aft platform doesn't have a camera feed. Must be out."

Watanabe leaned past him to stab at the intercom button. "Sergeant Gessler! Take the platoon to the docking platform, port-side, aft. I'll meet you there!"

Sergeant Muwanga stared at him. "Not much to go on, sir. . . ."

"*Someone* set off that alarm, Sergeant, and Trousseau's the only one not accounted for. And if he really was making a break for it, he would have knocked out the camera so you wouldn't see him." Watanabe ran from C-cubed, hoping inwardly that his guess was right.

Corporal Dmitri Rostov dropped to one knee and peered cautiously around the corner. The broad corridor leading to the docking platform was empty, and the door beyond was sealed tight. He hoped they weren't chasing shadows. That warning siren was sweet music, promising action, and action was just what he needed right now.

He glanced over his shoulder at his lancemates. "Vrurrth . . . Slick . . . Corridor's clear. Move up and flank the door."

Legionnaire John Grant—"Slick" to the rest of the lance—nodded and slid past Rostov noiselessly. Vrurrth, the hulking legionnaire from Gwyr, followed more slowly. Rostov had a grin at the contrast between the slender teenager and the big alien. The three of them had been on Hanuman together and made a tight-knit team.

The other two members of Rostov's recon lance moved closer. They were new to the unit. Legionnaire First-Class Judy Martin was a veteran who handled her laser sniper's rifle like she'd been born with it, but he still didn't know much about how she was likely to react. As for Legionnaire Jaime Auriega, he was a nube, a newcomer fresh out of training at the Legion's depot on Devereaux. As such, Rostov thought with another suppressed smile, he was the lowest form of life. He'd remain so until he proved he could cut it with the Legion.

"Cover 'em, Martin," he said. "Nube, when I move, you move. Got it?"

Auriega nodded dully. He wasn't bright, but he was willing, and that often counted for more in the Legion.

Rostov leaned around the corner again and gave Vrurrth a curt hand signal. The Gwyrran gave a ponderous nod and undogged the hatch. Like most of the fittings on the harvester ship it was of original Toeljuk design, manually operated and made to accommodate their squat bodies. Vrurrth pushed it open with a grunt, and Slick, his FEK gauss rifle held at the ready, rolled through the hatch with a smooth motion that looked like a move in an intricate ballet.

Slick came up on one knee, spraying autofire at unseen targets.

"Recon!" Rostov shouted, springing to his feet and pounding down the corridor to support the young legionnaire. Auriega's heavy footfalls echoed just behind him.

Slapping the helmet control that operated his radio, Rostov cut in the channel to Platoon Sergeant Gessler. "We got bad guys, Sarge! Better send some help!"

Watanabe heard the call from the recon lance over the commlink in the helmet he had donned in place of his uniform beret. He speeded up, ducking his head to avoid the low overhang of a Toeljuk hatch. Without a helmet he could walk through shipboard doorways without any trouble, but the extra communications and computer gear in a command helmet made it bulge up in back an extra three centimeters, just enough to be a problem.

Platoon Sergeant Karl Gessler turned to meet him. "You heard, Sub?" he asked.

Frowning, Watanabe nodded. "You could've sent more than one lance to check it out, Gessler," he said sharply.

The sergeant shook his head. "Rostov's boys were the first ones to draw their weapons. I sent them on ahead—per your orders, sir." His tone was cold. Gessler obeyed his platoon leader, but Watanabe knew there was no respect there. The sergeant had seen Watanabe struggling with minor decisions too often lately.

"Let's get some more men up there now, dammit!"

"The rest of Light Section's already on the way," Gessler said. "And I was *about* to get the rest moving. . . ."

"Then do it!" Watanabe turned away from the sergeant, cutting the conversation off.

"All right, you sandrats! By lances! Let's mag it!" Gessler's voice sounded even colder and harsher than usual.

Watanabe followed the legionnaires, trying hard to ignore

the growing conviction that he deserved every bit of the sergeant's contempt.

Rostov ducked through the outer hatch, swinging his FEK to the ready. The wind was starting to rise on the exposed platform, probably a sign of one of Polypheme's fierce storms moving into the area. He ignored the weather as he sized up the situation with experienced eyes.

Slick and Vrurrth were crouched side-by-side a meter from the hatch, spraying FEK fire across the platform into a small group of natives clustered at the forward end of the dock. Several locals already lay sprawled on the deck, their bodies shredded by the tiny gauss-propelled slivers that were the primary ammo of the Legion assault rifles.

He heard a sound behind and above him and whirled.

A large-eyed alien face leered down at him from the smooth sides of the superstructure. The polliwogs were equipped with sucker-like appendages on their arms and legs, which helped them cling to boulders and cliffs in the tidal flats that were their primary ecological niche.

This native clutched a knife in the feeding tendrils curled below its mouth. It seemed to move in slow motion, freeing one arm, taking the knife in a flat, long-digited hand, raising its arm to strike. . . .

Rostov's finger tightened on the trigger of the FEK and the face disappeared in a mass of blood and torn flesh. The knife clattered to the deck beside his boot.

"Look out, Corporal!"

Rostov barely had time to register Auriega's voice before the big legionnaire slammed into him, shoving him to the deck. There was a bright flash and a hiss of burning propellant.

Then Auriega sagged to the deck, his own face ruined. Beyond the dead legionnaire Rostov saw another wog clinging to the superstructure. It clutched an unfamiliar-looking pistol in one hand. He fired before the alien could shift aim and shoot again.

More men burst through the door from inside the vessel, led by a pair of figures clad in armor from head to foot and carrying onager plasma rifles in their bulky ConRig harnesses. The unbearably bright flash of a plasma bolt was like an extra sun shining on the deck. A nomad gaped down at the leg the shot had severed before falling over backward into the sea.

A native surfaced nearby, opening its mouth to give an eerie, deep-throated cry that Rostov couldn't translate. Suddenly the rest of the natives were diving into the water of their own free will, escaping.

Rostov stood slowly, checking his magazine and surveying the cramped battlefield. Much as he craved action, he wasn't about to follow those things into their own element.

Watanabe followed Gessler through the hatch and onto the dock. A pair of legionnaires were busy pushing native bodies over the side, but the splatters of blood were still plain testimony to the savage little fight.

Corporal Rostov met them and gave a sketchy salute. "One man dead, Sub," he said, pointing to a still form under an improvised shroud on the deck nearby. "Auriega. The new man."

Watanabe noted that Rostov avoided using the legionnaire's scornful "nube." The man had proved himself, and paid the highest price for doing so. "What about Legionnaire Trousseau?" he asked quietly.

"We found some of his gear on that raft, Sub," Rostov replied. "No sign of him, though."

"Then it's almost certainly *two* dead, corporal," Watanabe said wearily. They couldn't have helped Trousseau, but if Gessler hadn't sent the recon lance in ahead of everyone else Auriega might not have been killed.

But Gessler wasn't to blame. Watanabe was the platoon leader, and responsible for every death.

"Found something else I thought you'd want to see, Sub," Rostov went on. He held out a pistol of some kind. "Some of thc lokes were carrying these."

Watanabe examined the weapon. It was small, looking more like a child's toy than a real pistol, and made almost entirely of some lightweight plastic with a peculiar rubbery finish. But it was clearly an autoloading rocket pistol, more primitive than the FE-PLF he carried on his hip, but using the same principles.

Principles none of the natives of Polypheme were supposed to have mastered, not even the most civilized of the shore-dwelling cultures. Crossbows and blowguns were the limit of native technology.

Until now, it seemed.

He handed the pistol to Gessler. "Have this thing scanned and analyzed. I want to know what the owner of this thing had for breakfast!"

"Yessir."

"Corporal, did you see anything else that looked out of place, unusual?"

Rostov shook his head slowly. Another legionnaire, the kid they called Slick, looked around. "Uh . . . Sub? I saw something that struck me kind of funny."

"What?"

"Well . . . uh, our briefings said the natives were highly aggressive when they got into a fight, and swarmed on an enemy until one side or the other was dead. But these wogs broke off the attack when things started to go sour. Looked like an officer down in the water was giving them orders, sir."

Rostov nodded. "He's right, Sub," the corporal agreed. "I didn't really think about it, but Slick—er, Grant—put his finger on it. Those bastards were fighting like they knew what they were doing."

Watanabe looked away, staring at the choppy sea.

High-tech weapons and a new style of fighting. The nomads of Polypheme's open oceans were definitely becoming more of a threat than anyone had imagined was possible.

Captain Fraser would have to know about this.

# Chapter 2

> A new planet is just another place for legionnaires to die.
>
> —Colonel Maurice Lequillier
> Second Foreign Legion, 2238

Captain Colin Fraser squeezed through the throng, dodging around a pair of polliwogs arguing over the price of a bolt of plush cloth. The bazaar at Ourgh was a riot of color and sound, a scene that might have come straight out of Medieval Terra had it not been for the alien forms of the shopkeepers and passersby who filled the narrow streets. The noise they made was an assault on the ears as they haggled, individual voices blending together in an unearthly cacophony.

Here and there among the wogs there were even stranger forms as well. Some were company employees, like the majority of the humans on Polypheme, but Fraser was startled to note a party of squat Toeljuks waddling awkwardly on thick, stumpy tentacles, hampered by gravity twice what they were used to. Once the Toeljuks had been virtual masters of the planet. Now only the occasional trading ship kept up the contact between the Autarchy and Polypheme.

"Slow down, Colin!"

He turned back to see Kelly Winters struggling to push past a local who was busy unloading goods from the back of a stubborn-looking *groogh*, one of the oversized beasts of burden the land-dwelling wogs used for hauling heavy loads and plowing fields ashore. She finally got around wog and beast and joined him, out of breath.

"I thought you said you wanted a rest," she accused.

He grinned. "After two weeks behind a desk this *is* a rest, Kelly." It was hard to think of her by her new name, her Legion name, Warrant Officer Fourth-Class Ann Kelly.

She had been a combat engineer with the Commonwealth Navy, stationed on Hanuman, when he was still a newly posted Lieutenant serving as Exec with a Legion company there. Then came the rebellion and the long march out of hostile territory. Fraser's CO had died, forcing him to assume command of the unit; Kelly, the only survivor from outside the Legion, had accompanied the troops. At first she had shared the scorn for legionnaires most "decent" people felt, but over time she had come to respect them.

And in that final harrowing battle, when her own Navy people had left the legionnaires standing alone against horrible odds, Kelly had fought alongside Fraser's men. Her expertise in combat engineering had contributed to the victory they had somehow wrung from seemingly certain death. But when it was over, she'd made her contempt for the Navy clear. Instead of returning to duty, Kelly had volunteered to join the Foreign Legion, and Fraser and his superior had contrived to arrange her "death" in the official records of the fighting.

Sometimes Fraser's conscience gave him a twinge of guilt over his involvement in her desertion, but his unit owed Kelly Winters too much to refuse her. Signed on as a warrant officer specializing as a sapper and pioneer, Kelly had accompanied Fraser's men when they went back into hostile territory to put down the rebellion. Now she commanded a platoon of Legion sappers attached to the garrison on Polypheme.

They spent a lot of time together. Shared experiences, common interests, a similar way of looking at things . . . Fraser wasn't sure yet if it was love, but it was certainly a friendship that made life on Polypheme a little more bearable.

"Wish you my wares to see, *Ukwarr*?" a vendor asked. Fraser had chipped the principle local tongue, but there were many dialects and variations. This native seemed to be speaking one of the nomad tribal languages, but Fraser wasn't sure.

He glanced down at the blanket the native had spread on the ground, then knelt for a closer look. Being bimodal, the wogs found it perfectly comfortable to drop down on all fours whenever they had to, though most of the merchants in the bazaar had carts or tables. That confirmed Fraser's suspicion that this was a nomad. They didn't use carts—

there was little call for the wheel in their oceanic lifestyle—and a nomad wouldn't be likely to be carrying a table in a pouch on his harness.

"Take a look at these, Kelly," he said, picking up one of the delicate pieces. It was a piece of bone, intricately carved with symbols and designs that seemed to bring out natural patterns in the material.

Kelly dropped to one knee beside him. "It's beautiful, Col." She took it from him and held it up, letting the reddish rays of sunset play across the ornate surface.

*"Akurg muuin ghoourak?"* Fraser asked the vendor. "Free Swimmers carving made?" He hoped he was interpreting the curious dialect correctly. The sentence structure was quite different from what he had learned for dealing with the citizens of Ourgh, and nomads could be touchy.

The native's eyestalks twitched with pleasure. "Yes . . . yes, tusk from *woorroo* Free Swimmers carved. *Woorroo* hunt most difficult."

Fraser glanced at Kelly, who continued to examine the tusk. She seemed to share his fascination with the alien artist's ability to blend the natural appearance of the bone with the delicate strokes of a knife.

He smiled. There weren't many humans on or off Polypheme who could appreciate the nomads' art. Even the people who had to work regularly with the locals—scientists, and the businessmen from Seafarms Interstellar—were inclined to dismiss the nomads as worthless savages.

"On Terra about a thousand years back there were humans making carvings like that," he commented in English. "Scrimshaw, I think it was called."

"Who, primitives?" she asked.

He shook his head. "Sailors. Navy men on the old surface ships with too little to do on long sea trips." He held out his hand, and she passed the carving to him. Turning back to the vendor, he went on in the nomad dialect. "Barter for this would we."

The nomad held up a feeding tendril. "One *drooj*, *Ukwarr*," he said.

That would be at least ten times its real value, Fraser thought. The nomads understood money well enough from centuries of trading with the land-dwellers, but it didn't stop them from carrying on their own traditions of barter and hard bargaining.

"*!!ghoour,*" he replied, not quite getting the double clicking sound at the start of the word. "No. One *vroor!* is too much."

They bargained until Fraser was sure the nomad's sensibilities would be properly satisfied. It took a careful touch to keep from offending the sea-dwellers in transactions like this one. Offering too much for an item was almost as serious an insult as paying too little. He handed over four *vroor!*, small iron coins that were legal tender here in Ourgh. Then he turned back to Kelly.

"Looks like old Navy customs die hard," he said, handing her the carving. "A little scrimshaw to take your mind off the boredom."

"You saw it first, Col. Don't you want it?"

He shook his head. "It's yours. Take it, before I change my mind!"

She grinned and slipped it into her shoulder bag. Her full-dress Legion uniform looked out of place in the bazaar, but the Seafarms management had made it clear that they wanted legionnaires to show a high profile in the town. The uniform certainly did that, with a khaki jacket and slacks, a blue cummerbund, red and green epaulets, and a kepi. Kelly's headgear was white with a broad black stripe, while Fraser, a Legion officer, wore the traditional *kepi noire.* It was a needlessly gaudy uniform, but it traced its history through all of the units that had counted themselves as "Foreign Legions" all the way back to the original French Foreign Legion of pre-spaceflight Terra.

Fraser suspected that the company was probably insisting on high visibility as a way of overawing the locals with Commonwealth military prowess, despite the fact that there was no more than a platoon of legionnaires on duty in town at any one time, and their sole purpose was to act as military police to look after the legionnaires who could turn a town into a small-scale war zone while enjoying an overnight pass.

It was galling. There were exactly two combat companies, plus a few specialist troops, stationed on Polypheme, but Seafarms treated them like a full-fledged garrison. Nor was it comforting to know that the company regarded the legionnaires as their own private corporate police force.

But Seafarms Interstellar was a wholly-owned subsidiary of Reynier Industries, and even a subsidiary of the company that held the monopoly over the Commonwealth's production of interstellar drives commanded a lot of clout—at least enough to get Colonial Army troops assigned as glorified security guards on this worthless backwater world.

"You're getting that look again," Kelly commented as they left the scrimshaw vendor behind. "What's wrong?"

Fraser shrugged and pointed to her bag. "I guess that thing reminded me of boredom. It's a topic I've been running into a lot lately."

"More trouble with *cafarde*?"

He nodded. "Somebody in Alpha Company hung himself last night. And we've had three attempted desertions in the past week." He shook his head. "One of them was Gates—one of the Hanuman vets."

"It's getting pretty bad, then." It was more of a statement than a question.

"Yeah. These men are combat soldiers. Sticking them in a garrison is begging for trouble." He paused to dodge an aggressive shopkeeper hawking his wares. "They say the only real cure for *cafarde* is a loaded rifle and plenty of targets. Not much chance of that here."

She pulled him into an empty alley mouth. "You can't keep blaming yourself, you know," she said.

"Yeah. Right. The damned Commission is breathing down the neck of every Colonial Army unit in the sector. And I'm the hot potato no CO wants to be stuck with!"

Fraser didn't even try to keep the bitterness out of his voice. For a while there on Hanuman, it had looked like his luck was turning. . . .

He had been a rising star in the Commonwealth Regulars, son of the hero of New Dallas, General Lovat Fraser of Caledon. Posted to Intelligence with a lieutenant's commission and a spotless record, Fraser should have been set for life. No struggling for recognition like his father, no long career with nothing but Citizenship papers and a few distorted holovid stories to show for a lifetime's dedication, not for Colin Fraser!

That was before Fenris, though. The rebellion on Fenris had taken everyone in the Commonwealth by surprise, of course, but once it had erupted it should have been easy enough to put down. But Major Richard St. John, the officer responsible for overseeing the planetary intelligence-gathering effort, had turned out to be incompetent, and men had died. A lot of men, and Commonwealth Regulars at that.

Colin Fraser had been St. John's aide, and in the inevitable inquiry that followed the disaster he gave the evidence that sealed the man's fate. The major resigned the service . . . but the story hadn't ended there.

Major Richard St. John was the nephew of Senator Warwick, and Senator Warwick was an important man on the Commonwealth's Military Affairs Committee. Warwick had pulled a few strings and contrived to take down the man who had ruined his nephew, and Colin Fraser's promising career had evaporated overnight.

Volunteering for the Colonial Army had been the only real option open to him short of court-martial or resignation. The Colonials weren't as glamorous as the regular Terran regiments, but they offered more action, more opportunity to really *do* something for the Commonwealth. General Fraser had risen to command the Caledon Watch in the Colonial Army.

But General Fraser's patronage was no match for Senator Warwick's displeasure, and it turned out that the Fifth Foreign Legion was the only haven left open. The rising star of Intelligence had ended up as exec in an infantry company—that seemed somehow inevitable, military organizations being what they were—posted to Hanuman.

Bravo Company, his new outfit, had pulled off a miracle in the jungles of that primitive planet. After bringing his men across fifteen hundred kilometers of hostile territory and winning the battle that stopped the native insurrection cold, Fraser had suddenly seen new opportunities opening up. Promotion to captain and command of his beloved Bravos, a key role in the pacification of Hanuman, favorable notice from his superiors in the Legion . . . notoriety like that could have put his career back on track.

*Should* have put it back on track.

The Commonwealth Senate had chosen the wrong time to start one of its periodic witch hunts for corruption in the Colonial Army. Members of the Military Affairs Committee—including Senator Warwick—were on the prowl through the frontier sectors searching for someone to nail to the cross. Suddenly, notoriety and a promising future were the last things Colin Fraser needed. As a bona fide hero, Fraser was likely to attract the Senator's attention, and no one wanted to risk being caught in the fallout if that happened.

His previous CO, Commandant Isayev, had explained it carefully to Fraser. "Don't get me wrong, son," he had said. "The Legion looks after its own. But you know how the Commission does its business—none better, I'd bet. What we need to do is get you out of sight for a while. That's better for you, and it's better for the Legion."

When Seafarms Interstellar requested Colonial troops to safeguard their harvester project on Polypheme, the Legion had responded by forming a provisional battalion. Fraser's company had been one of the first units picked for the new formation, and so far only one other outfit had been posted to Polypheme.

He realized that Kelly was still watching him with a worried frown. "I could have asked for a transfer. Or resigned. That's what I should have done in the first place."

"You wouldn't be Colin Fraser if you ran from a fight," she said. "There were a dozen times you could have taken the easy way out on Hanuman, but you didn't. This is the same thing."

He tried to smile. "Yeah, that's me. I don't know the meaning of the word surrender."

"Right," she agreed, the frown melting into an impish grin. "Too many syllables for a legionnaire to handle."

"I'd stop knocking the Legion if I were you, Warrant Officer Kelly," he said, happy to keep the conversation in a lighter tone. "Of course, everybody knows you aren't really a Legion sapper."

"I've told you before, I'll work on the beard," she protested. Like the uniforms, that was an old Legion tradition. Sappers and pioneers almost universally wore long, full beards, except for the obvious exceptions like Kelly.

"You do, and you'll have to find someone else to go to town with."

Her response was cut off by a shout from the street. Fraser turned, craning his head to see the source over the milling locals.

The shout was repeated, and Fraser spotted the source. A native—a large, menacing female with an infant clinging to her back—had just thrown a piece of *kwuur*-fruit at a Terran girl in the coveralls of a Seafarms port worker.

"Where are your offworld promises now?" the native shouted.

Another local took up the call. "Fifty young carried off last night! Seventy more in the past six-day!"

Muttering spread through the crowd, and Fraser could almost *feel* their mood, like a sudden shift in the wind, turning cold and nasty.

"Kelly . . ." He paused, sizing up the situation. "When you see their attention on me, circle around and get her out of sight. And use your 'piece to alert the ready platoon. We don't want to hang around."

"I'll say," she concurred. "Be careful, Col."

He edged clear of the alley as the crowd started to close in on the girl in the Seafarms coverall. Whether at sea or on land, natives responded aggressively to any perceived threat, and it was hard to distract them once they fixed on a target. According to the chip he'd studied on early Terran contact with Polypheme, entire nomad tribes had thrown themselves at a handful of Terrans with autoweapons, refusing to run or exercise the most rudimentary tactics until the entire band was slaughtered.

Sometimes it had been the Terrans who had died, though. Mob tactics were messy, but they had a way of working when the mob didn't care about casualties.

He squatted down to pick up a loose piece of tile that had fallen from a roof. Hefting it in his hand, he gauged the natives carefully before throwing it at one of the largest males on the fringe of the crowd. The wog gave a bellow that was more surprise than pain and focused his eyestalks on Fraser.

"Over there! Another one!"

"A soldier!" someone shouted. "Soldier! What about the young?"

"Why can't you stop the swimmers?"

It had been a problem simmering for a long time, far longer than Terrans had been on Polypheme. The land-dwellers had built themselves a fine civilization ashore, but their life-cycle made it necessary for their young to spend most of their time swimming. They could cling to an adult for a short time, sucking blood for nourishment, but they needed to swim. No native city was very far from the sea where juveniles could swim aimlessly, supervised—"herded" was probably a better word—by a few adults.

But the nomads, who recognized no bounds of territory or property, often raided around cities to capture juveniles who could be raised as slaves for the tribe.

The company policy of high visibility, of pushing the power of the Commonwealth military forces, was bound to collide with the slave-raiding problem sooner or later. There was no way for two companies of legionnaires to police hundreds of kilometers of tidal flats and coastal waters against slavers, even if the job was part of their mission on Polypheme. But pressure had been building ever since the Legion started arriving, and a raid the night before apparently had been enough to set the whole thing off.

"What good are your guns, Terran, if you won't use them?" a voice called out.

"Your friendship is as empty as your faces!"

The mob was focusing on him now, allowing Kelly to reach the girl. She was speaking urgently into the microphone on her wristpiece computer. It would relay her message to the main computer at the Legion barracks here in town, and help would be dispatched.

He hoped it would come in time.

# Chapter 3

I'd rather face an army in the field than a mob in the streets.

—Captain Guillaume St. André,
speaking of the Aberdeen Massacre
Third Foreign Legion, 2398

"Spear! There's trouble over on the north side of the canal!"

Legionnaire First-Class Spiro Karatsolis cut the power to the vidmagazine he was wearing and removed the holovid viewer. Corporal Selim Bashar was buckling on a rocket pistol, his face grim. "What's wrong, Basher?" he asked.

"The call—it's from Miss Kelly. She's with the captain, and there's a riot brewing." Bashar picked a rifle from the weapon rack by the door.

"Goddamn!" Karatsolis was out of his seat in one fluid motion, his magazine forgotten. "What'll we take? Floatcar?"

Bashar shook his head. "They're warming up a veeter for us now."

Karatsolis grabbed an FEK riot rifle as he followed the corporal out of the old Toel warehouse that served as barracks for the legionnaires posted to duty in Ourgh. Outside, two legionnaires were just stepping clear of the veeter.

It was a small vehicle, barely big enough for two men and a weapons mount. It lacked the range and endurance of the floatcars and magrep APCs the Legion normally used, but the veeter had one tremendous advantage over those: It was a true aircraft, propelled by powerful tilt-rotor turbofans mounted on either side of the tiny fuselage. It was intended for scouting and short-range battlefield use, but the veeter was also ideal for fast movement through crowded or built-up areas.

Bashar took his place at the control console. Karatsolis mounted in front of him and ran through a quick check of the gun in the bow of the craft. It was a kinetic-energy cannon modified for riot work, firing anesthetic slivers, instead of conventional needle ammunition, at relatively low muzzle velocities. It wouldn't be worth much in an ordinary fight, but it was perfect for crowd control.

"Ready, farm boy?" Bashar asked from behind him.

"Any time," Karatsolis replied. "Just make sure you steer clear of the buildings!"

The fans whined, building to a crescendo that made the veeter shudder. Bashar pulled back on the stick and the craft rose slowly, kicking up clouds of dust. Nearby more legionnaires were clearing the way for an armored magrep APC, floating slowly out of the motor pool on a magnetic cushion.

The driver, Corporal Sandoval, had his hatch open. He flashed the veeter a quick thumb's-up.

Karatsolis returned the gesture, then checked the weapon again—just to be sure.

The crowd surged down the narrow alley like a snake striking at its prey, shouting unintelligible epithets and hoarse-voiced exhortations. Colin Fraser ducked behind a garbage bin as a stone struck the masonry a few centimeters to the left of his head. He drew his FE-PLF and chambered a round. He didn't want to use the 10-mm rocket pistol unless he absolutely had to. It wasn't much use for crowd control, and a Terran killing native civilians in a nominally friendly town would only make the difficult political situation that much worse.

But the mob didn't look like it planned to give the Terrans much choice.

Kelly had her Navy-issue laser pistol out. She waved it as she urged him toward the door niche where she knelt beside the other Terran girl. The laser was even less suitable for this situation than his own sidearm.

He sprinted from cover in a crouching, zigzag run. A thrown bottle shattered against the corner of the bin behind him. Kelly squeezed off a shot, angling her fire over the heads of the crowd. The beam was invisible, but the crackle of superheated air and the tang of ozone were unmistakable. Fraser dived and rolled, coming up beside Kelly and facing the advancing mob.

"Your charge'll last longer if you use a low-intensity beam!" he said as she fired again.

She flashed him a quick grin. "Any lower and I'd be holding them off with a flashlight," she answered. "I'll cover you two."

"You go—" he began.

"Go!" she cut him off sharply. "Save the male heroics . . . and your ammo!" She fired into the trash bin he had been hiding behind, nodding in satisfaction as something inside caught fire. A few natives shied away from the flames, but the mob continued to press forward.

Fraser pointed down the alley. "Run!" he told the girl in the Seafarms coverall. He noticed that the nameplate said K. VOSKOVICH. "I'll be right behind you."

She nodded and scrambled to her feet. Fraser hesitated a second longer, reluctant to leave Kelly to face the mob alone.

But Kelly Winters knew how to take care of herself. She had led a charge into the middle of overwhelming enemy forces at the climax of the fighting on Hanuman. Fraser forced himself to follow the civilian, Voskovich. She was the one who needed protection right now.

Behind them a native screamed as Kelly fired straight into the crowd. On low-intensity a laser pulse was rarely deadly, but it could cause a serious burn. Most opponents would be quick to run from a weapon that struck invisibly, but the wogs only seemed to become more aggressive. They sensed a threat to the community, and instinct was beginning to overwhelm reason.

The narrow alley opened onto a major street. Fraser caught up with Voskovich a few meters from the intersection. He grabbed her elbow and pushed her against the nearest wall. "Wait!" he hissed.

A curious crowd was already gathering there, attracted by the shouts from further up the alley. Fraser could sense their growing agitation as they picked up something of the urgency of the other mob.

The Terrans were trapped.

Kelly Winters fired again and glanced over her shoulder nervously. Were the others clear of the alley yet? The charge indicator on her pistol showed that the power cell was almost exhausted. Two or three more shots was the best she could hope for.

The mob surged forward again.

She fired twice, then lunged from the shelter of the door, running. Something wet and smelly hit her square in the back, but she ignored it and kept sprinting. Angry shouts followed her.

"Terran liar!" a native yelled.

Again something hit her, in the leg this time, a heavy, jagged stone instead of a ripe fruit. Pain lanced through her calf, and Kelly stumbled. She caught herself by grabbing at the nearest wall, then pushed off to run again.

She fell, the impact against the cobblestones knocking the breath out of her for a moment. Gasping for breath, Kelly rolled over into an awkward sitting position and raised the laser pistol. But it was empty now, useless.

The natives advanced.

Then Fraser was there, standing over her, his PLF rocket pistol leveled in a marksman's brace. He fired three times with scarcely any pause between the shots. Each one found its mark, but it slowed the natives only for a few seconds.

Fraser helped her to her feet. "The alley's blocked!" he said, firing again. "More natives!"

It took Kelly long seconds to realize what he had said, and what the words meant. The mob was sure to finish off the three Terrans before they worked their bloodlust off.

It took her even longer to react to the explosion of noise that erupted from the sky.

"There! There they are, Bashar!" Karatsolis shouted over the roar of the veeter's engines. He pointed at the narrow alley off the left side of the little flyer's nose.

"I see them, Spear," Bashar acknowledged. He angled the aircraft down toward the three Terran figures, then let off a string of curses in his native Turkish. "Can't get near them while they're in that strakking side street." Small as the tilt-rotor was, it couldn't operate in the confined space between those close-set native buildings.

Karatsolis leaned forward and flipped a switch on his control panel. The public address speaker slung from the bottom of the veeter crackled. "In the open, skipper!" he said into the mike. "Get into the open so we can cover you!"

"Hang on to your lunch!" Bashar called. The veeter

dipped and swerved alarmingly, and buildings flashed toward them until Karatsolis was convinced they would crash into one. He forced himself to ignore everything but his gunsights, swinging the weapon to fire into the smaller of the two native mobs hemming the Terrans in on the ground.

The stream of narcotic rounds cut a swath through the locals. A few fell immediately, but it took time for most of the natives to go down. Karatsolis kept gripping the firing stud on the gauss gun as the little aircraft pivoted again for another pass, fighting a wave of nausea from the violent maneuvering. The buildings that blocked the veeter were hampering his line of fire, but he could see the locals scattering as the strafing continued.

"Birdman, Birdman, this is Cavalry," the radio announced, using the call signs Subaltern Leonid Narmonov had assigned to the mission as they had scrambled for action.

"Cavalry, Birdman," Karatsolis replied. "Go."

"ETA your position is six minutes," Sandoval, the APC's driver, told him. "Longer, if these damned crowds get any heavier. Can you hold until we get there?"

"We have a choice?" Bashar muttered behind him.

"We'll do what we can, Cavalry," Karatsolis said. "But you'd better mag it if you don't want to miss the party."

"Roger that. Cavalry clear."

The veeter hovered for a moment, and Karatsolis pumped narco rounds at the largest clump of natives. He hit the PA switch again. "Work your way clear of the alley, skipper, so we can give you some cover!"

He saw Fraser waving an acknowledgment, and the three Terrans pressed through the path the strafing had opened up. Karatsolis fired again, keeping a worried eye on the ammo indicator. Veeters didn't carry as much of an ammunition reserve as most combat vehicles, and he was burning up rounds too fast.

Without some fire support, the captain would never hold out long enough for the APC to make it.

They broke from the alley entrance at a dead run, with Fraser in the lead and Voskovich supporting Kelly, who was favoring her injured leg. A native lashed out with an improvised club, but Fraser shot him at close range and he reeled backward, clutching at his wounded arm. The roar of the veeter rotors overhead swelled again as the aircraft dipped low over the alley mouth, its heavy MEK gauss gun keeping up a steady stream of fire, keeping the mob at bay.

The way they were using up ammo, though, they wouldn't be able to maintain their support much longer.

Fraser pointed at the open market square, signaling for the veeter to land. It would be a tricky approach, but Bashar—that *had* to be Bashar at the controls, nobody else in the outfit handled a vehicle with the same combination of skill and stark insanity—could handle it. He kept repeating the hand signals until he was sure the crew had seen him.

The veeter settled slowly to the cobblestones, still firing. Fraser grabbed the civilian girl's arm and pulled her toward the aircraft as the forward hatch popped open.

Legionnaire Karatsolis rolled out of the gunner's seat, dropping to one knee and raising a Legion riot rifle to cover the alley mouth. Like the veeter's MEK, the riot rifle was a modification of the basic gauss rifle design which fired narco rounds. Unlike the MEK, or the standard-issue FEK battle rifle, the riot-control weapon wasn't set up for full-auto fire.

"Get aboard!" Fraser shouted at Voskovich over the noise of the rotors. "Move it!" With more hand signals he ordered Bashar to get the veeter, and his new passenger clear.

Bashar opened his hatch long enough to toss another riot rifle out. Fraser caught the weapon with one hand and helped the girl close her hatch. He rapped twice on the canopy and laid down cover fire for Karatsolis, then followed him to the shelter of an abandoned vendor's stall. The rotors revved louder.

"Kelly! Grab on to the outside and ride it out. It'll carry the extra weight!"

She shook her head. "Forget it! I'm sticking this one out on the ground!"

The veeter stirred slowly, then lifted, turning north and climbing fast.

He'd taken care of the civilian, his first duty here. Now he had to keep three legionnaires alive until help arrived.

Fraser raised the rifle and started firing.

The M-786 Sandray plowed through a native stall as Legionnaire Second-Class Enrique Sandoval gunned the motor and turned onto the wide street that led to the Square of the North Gate Bazaars. With its broad manta shape the APC was ill suited to work inside a wog city, where only a few of the main avenues were large enough to accommodate the vehicle, but it was the only way to deliver a large number of troops to a trouble spot quickly. With only a platoon to cover the entire city, the legionnaires needed the speed. And the Sandray was also large enough to hold several prisoners. The usual problem that would require a Legion response was a brawl at one of the bars or the Company-sponsored brothel on the riverfront near the port complex.

Dealing with major native riots in the heart of the bazaar district hadn't been a priority—until now.

"ETA?" Subaltern Narmonov stuck his head into the driver's cabin to ask the question. It was the fifth time he'd asked since Bashar's report that the veeter had recovered one civilian and then withdrawn, out of ammo.

"Two minutes, Sub," Sandoval replied. He slowed the APC as a cluster of natives ran into the street in front of the vehicle. "Maybe longer, if these stupid lokes don't stay out of the way."

"Make some revs, damn it!" Narmonov told him.

"Yessir." Sandoval responded, hiding a grimace of distaste. Narmonov was frantic at the thought of Captain Fraser facing the native mob.

Fraser wasn't even in command of Narmonov's company, he thought, but he sure had everyone worked up. Bashar and Karatsolis, for instance; like Sandoval, they were in the demi-battalion's Transport Section, not part of either of the two regular combat companies. They'd served with Fraser before, of course—but with Narmonov it was different.

Sandoval shrugged. Captain Fraser was the one running things here on Polypheme. Alpha Company's CO, Captain David Hawley, was the senior officer of Demi-Battalion Elaine and thus the commander of the whole Legion force in the system, but everyone knew that Hawley was incompetent. As the garrison's second-in-command, Fraser ran virtually everything while Hawley remained in his own private fog, a useless dreamchip addict and alcoholic.

Maybe Fraser was the indispensable man on Polypheme. Sandoval doubted it. As far as he was concerned, officers hardly ever pulled their own weight. Not even in the Legion.

He gunned the engine again and grinned as wogs scattered ahead of the Sandray. All it took to keep these lokes in their place was a little force, a little willpower. Nothing else mattered.

Fraser checked his magazine and swore softly. Even without full-auto capability, the hundred rounds it carried were being consumed entirely too fast, and there were no refills available. The crowd wasn't making much headway against them, but neither were they breaking up the way a human mob would have under such steady firepower. They were still gathering, growing more enraged as the Terrans held off the attack.

He could feel the air throbbing with subsonics. Like the urge to swarm and overwhelm a threat, that was a legacy of the natives' aquatic origin, the use of low-frequency sound as a method of communication. It wasn't much use out of the water, and even in the seas they couldn't send more than the most basic of signals, but it was still disconcerting.

"How's your ammo?" he asked Karatsolis.

"No good, Captain," the Greek replied. He spat expressively as he picked out another target and fired. "Damned popguns!" His contempt for any weapon lighter than a turret-mounted plasma cannon was well known among the Hanuman veterans.

Behind them, pressed up against a wall, Kelly made a sour noise. "You think you've got problems?" She clutched Fraser's rocket pistol, empty now.

"If they rush us, sir, ma'am, keep behind me," Karatsolis said. "I'm better equipped."

"Are you talking about size or armor?" Fraser asked, trying to keep his tone light. The big legionnaire was wearing his Legion battledress without a combat helmet. He'd be slightly better protected against the mob, but still vulnerable.

Karatsolis didn't have time to answer. With a roar of powerful propulsion fans, a Sandray rounded a corner and drove into the square, gathering speed. Its stern ramp was dropping as it plowed through a stall and slid sideways, placing its armored bulk between the thickest part of the crowd and the three legionnaires.

Soldiers in battledress ran down the ramp and fanned out on either side. A subaltern waved urgently to Fraser. "Get aboard, sir! Get aboard!"

"Go!" Fraser shouted at Kelly. She started forward, limping. "Help her, Spear!"

The big Greek sprang after her, gathering her in his powerful arms and running for the APC. Fraser followed, clutching the riot gun. The thin cordon of soldiers fired into the mob with measured precision, holding them off.

As Fraser mounted the ramp, the subaltern was already shouting orders for the legionnaires. "Mount up! Mount up! Let's go!"

They remounted the Sandray smoothly, moving by the numbers without confusion or wasted effort. "Secured, Sub," their section leader told the subaltern. The officer slapped the switch that controlled the ramp and passed orders to the driver through his helmet commset. Stirring on magrep fields and fans, the Sandray lifted slowly and turned.

Rocks and bottles beat an uneven tattoo on the armored hull, but nothing in Ourgh would stop the APC. Fraser sank to a bench in the stern compartment, waving away a medic.

He realized vaguely that he was exhausted.

The subaltern sat down beside him and pulled off his helmet. He was young, fresh-faced, with the blond good looks that would have been perfect for a Colonial Army recruiting poster. But the handsome features were marred by a worried frown.

Fraser nodded to him. "Good job, Mr., ah . . ."

"Narmonov, sir."

"Good job, Narmonov." The man's platoon was a credit to Alpha Company. Captain Hawley's unit wasn't noted for efficiency, like their commander. It was good to see that some of them still took their soldiering seriously. "I'll be glad to get back to the city barracks."

Narmonov shook his head. "Sorry, sir, we've had orders to head back to the Sandcastle."

"Orders?"

"Yessir. From Citizen Jens."

Fraser winced. Sigrid Jens was head of the Seafarms operation on Polypheme. She had the habit of treating the legionnaires on the planet as her own personal corporate security guards. "What does she want this time?" he asked wearily, picturing another stormy meeting over the question of further thinning out the garrison to handle another of the company's schemes for a wider presence on Polypheme.

Narmonov swallowed. "There's been an attack on the

*Cyclops*, sir,'' he said slowly. ''Nomads. Watanabe reports they were carrying high-tech weapons.''

Kelly, nearby, looked up from where the medic was examining her ankle. ''If the nomads have high-tech weapons . . .''

''Then we've got trouble,'' Fraser said grimly.

He felt more exhausted than ever.

# Chapter 4

> The French, a people of etiquette, imagine that the Legion is full of criminals and barefoot savages.
>
> —Colonel Fernand Maire,
> in a letter from his deathbed
> French Foreign Legion, 1951

Officially it was known as "Cyclops Project One," but workers and legionnaires alike called the huge complex "The Sandcastle." It rose from the tidal flats a hundred and fifty kilometers southeast of Ourgh, a squat, ugly, starkly functional compound surrounded by a fifteen-meter high fusand wall. Even from a distance the base's nonhuman origins were plain.

The Toeljuks had constructed the Sandcastle as part of a chain of similar installations when they leased the world from the Semti Conclave centuries ago, and their characteristic architectural style was stamped on every building enclosed by those massive parapets. The walls, composed of a fused sand compound developed by the Toels, made the base look like an elaborate military fortress, but in fact their main job was to hold back a natural enemy, the water that coursed across the plain at high tide.

Tides on Polypheme were like nothing Colin Fraser had encountered before. They could raise the water level along the coast by as much as ten meters—more, during the fierce storms that boiled out of the equatorial latitudes during the *bhourrkh* season. In the space of an hour a stretch of open plain could be completely covered by water.

At high tide the Sandcastle became an island, and those walls were the only barrier to the lashing force of the flood tide or a raging *bhourrkh.*

The base had to be located on the tidal flats. When the waters closed in, it could become a port for the huge ore-extraction ships the Toeljuks had introduced to these seas. The corrosive content of the oceans here made frequent maintenance essential, so the Sandcastle was fitted with massive seagates which opened to flood the center of the complex and allow vessels to enter. Then the water could be pumped out, turning the compound into a dry dock where the ship could be unloaded and serviced.

At their peak, the Toeljuks had operated a fleet of thirty giant extraction ships, each one with its own home base. Since the Commonwealth had acquired Polypheme, most of the bases had fallen into ruin along with the ships. But Seafarms Interstellar had cannibalized the old Toel fleet to put the *Seafarms Cyclops* back in service, and the Sandcastle had become a port facility once again, all part of a pilot project designed to explore the possibilities of large-scale oceanic mineral extraction.

The tide was at the flood stage now, just beginning to rush in around the walls of the base. Fraser had moved into the driver's cab beside Legionnaire Sandoval, where he had direct access to the vehicle's communications gear. Glancing at the video monitor that showed the terrain ahead, Fraser tried to gauge the time left before the water would crest. About forty-five minutes, he thought. When the waters were at their highest the nomad threat would be greatest. If the nomads really were a threat . . .

Watanabe's report from the *Seafarms Cyclops* didn't leave much room for doubt. He'd spent the trip reviewing the computer file, trying to evaluate the implications of the subaltern's observations.

Any combination of high-tech weaponry and the kind of ferocity he'd seen for himself in Ourgh would be deadly. Moreover, Watanabe was suggesting that the nomads were using tactics more sophisticated than anything seen on Polypheme to date.

It all pointed to an outside influence. And odds were that the confrontation wouldn't stop with the abortive skirmish aboard the *Seafarms Cyclops*. . . .

"We're here, Captain," Sandoval said quietly.

Fraser looked up to see the massive seagates swinging slowly open to admit the APC. Water swirled into the center of the compound, turning the parade ground into a sea of mud.

The gate closed behind the APC as Sandoval guided it

across the complex toward the motor pool. Like the rest of the habitable part of the base, the motor pool was built into the inside of the wall, with doors that could be sealed tight when the interior was open to the sea.

A cluster of figures were waiting there, tension plain in their stances.

Sandoval guided the APC up a ramp and into the structure, then cut fans and magnetic fields to allow the Sandray to come to rest. Fraser turned in his seat to call orders to the legionnaires in the rear.

"Mr. Narmonov, keep your men ready to return to the city. I think it would be a good idea if we kept you as an escort for the company people, in view of what happened this afternoon."

"Sir!" The response was crisp, parade-ground correct.

He glanced at Kelly Winters. "Kelly, if this is going to be a full staff meeting, I'll want—I mean, Captain Hawley will probably want you there."

"I'll come with you, Captain," she replied formally. The medic had pronounced her fit, beyond a nasty bruise on her leg and a few abrasions from her fall.

He opened the hatch and clambered out of the vehicle.

"Captain," the smooth, cold voice of his Executive Officer greeted Fraser as he crossed the wide fusand floor. Lieutenant Antoine DuValier was tall, lean, and aristocratic, and Fraser still found him something of a mystery. His disdain for his surroundings was all too clear, and Fraser thought he sensed a personal dislike behind the young officer's aloof manner. He did his job efficiently enough, but Fraser was uncomfortable relying on DuValier as XO.

But because Captain Hawley needed his help running the demi-battalion, Fraser had been forced to leave Bravo Company almost entirely in DuValier's hands.

The man in Legion battledress beside DuValier was the only reason Fraser could allow the lieutenant to oversee his company at all. Gunnery Sergeant John Trent was another Hanuman veteran, an experienced NCO Fraser was willing to trust with his life. Without Grant, Fraser knew, Bravo Company would never have escaped from the jungles of Dryienjaiyeel or survived the desperate fighting in that last battle.

"Glad to see you in one piece, skipper," Trent said, genuine relief playing over his craggy features. "When the reports came in I—"

"Time for congratulations later." A small woman with short blond hair and wearing a conservative business coverall stepped forward. "Fraser, we've got problems on the *Cyclops.*"

"I know, Citizen Jens," Fraser said, keeping a tight rein on his temper at her abrupt manner. Sigrid Jens was said to be the youngest Project Director in the Seafarms hierarchy, and also the most aggressive. She was, so everyone said, destined for great things at Seafarms, maybe even in the parent company, Reynier Industries.

She was also, Fraser thought, a royal pain.

"I've been looking over the report," he went on, still trying not to betray any emotion. "From the looks of things you've got a hell of a security problem, Citizen, and I think we're going to have to reevaluate the entire setup on Polypheme if we're going to handle this mess."

The woman's assistant, Edward Barnett, stepped forward belligerently. "If you people had done your job, the nomads would never be able to threaten the *Cyclops,*" he said. "I recommended more troops for the ship right along, Fraser, but you and your precious Captain Hawley overruled the suggestion."

Fraser turned an angry glance his way. "Good thing, too," he said. "You wanted a whole company on board the *Cyclops,* and that would have stretched our resources way past the limit."

"Nonsense!" Barnett exploded. "You don't seem to realize how important the security of that ship is."

"Gentlemen," Jens said, holding up a manicured hand. "We need to take action, not pass out blame."

"Yes, ma'am," Barnett said quickly. He shot Fraser a sour look. "But I want to go on record as saying that we should have had more support from the Legion."

Fraser ignored him, turning to Jens. "This situation could get out of hand fast, Citizen," he said quietly. "I hope the corporation will be willing to work with us. Unless we deal with the nomads now, we could all be in serious trouble."

Warrior-Scout !!Dhruuj of the Clan of the Reef-Swimmers relaxed and let the flow of the tide carry him closer to the Built-Reef-of-the-Strangers. There was danger in swimming the tides so close to the massive stone walls, but !!Dhruuj felt no fear. He was a Warrior-Scout, and the best in the Reef-Swimmers apart from old Soor. He had claimed the honor of this swim, since Soor was still recovering from the wounds he'd suffered in the fight with the fangmouth three ebbs ago.

He felt no fear, just as his hand would feel no fear of its own even if he was to reach out to grasp a stingfloater stranded in a tidal pool. !!Dhruuj was a Hand of the Clan now, performing his function.

The water was already more than a head deep around the Built-Reef-of-the-Strangers, enough to keep him hidden. The Strangers-Who-Gave-Gifts had warned that the Strangers-Who-Lived-Within-Walls had powerful charms that allowed them to see clearly in the dark of the open air, and others that could chart the depths even more plainly than a Warrior-Scout, but the Stranger-Who-Betrayed-Clan had sent word from within that no such underwater magic was at work here. !!Dhruuj would be safe as long as he remained in the water.

He reached out to grasp the wall as the tide carried him toward it, then used his suckers to attach himself to the uneven surface. Inching slowly upward, !!Dhruuj raised his eyestalks and snorkel out of the water cautiously, and settled in to watch.

The Clan would need whatever information he could gather before they arrived to assail the Strangers above.

"You have to admit, Captain Fraser, that two companies of legionnaires was not what we were promised for the garrison here. We understood an entire battalion was to be stationed on Polypheme."

Fraser looked at Sigrid Jens and then shrugged. "A provisional battalion, Citizen," he replied carefully. "That isn't necessarily the same thing."

"A battalion's a battalion, isn't it?" Barnett said with a sneer. "Or doesn't your Foreign Legion use the same military units as the rest of the Colonial Army?"

"A provisional battalion is formed from scratch, Citizen Jens." Fraser went on, as if Barnett hadn't spoken. "To put one together, the Legion takes whatever extra companies happen to be handy and puts them into a unified command. Two companies plus support troops isn't unusual, especially for a hurry-up job like this. More companies are scheduled to join us later, unless something else diverts them in the meantime."

"Meaning we get whatever nobody else wants, I suppose," Jens muttered darkly.

"What else could you expect with the Legion?" Barnett asked her. "Criminals and screw-ups . . ."

Across the table from him, Gunnery Sergeant Trent made a low-voiced comment. "Criminals and screw-ups who might just have to save your ass from the nomads, Citizen."

Fraser broke in to keep the exchange from going any further. "If you would reconsider the plan I submitted last month for native auxiliaries, Citizen Jens, we might be able to police things the way you want without any more Legion troops."

"Native auxiliaries!" Jens laughed. "Get into orbit, Fraser! You've seen the locals. Lazy, shiftless . . . what use would they be as soldiers?"

"I think you're underestimating them, Citizen. I've . . . seen the townies at close range, and they'd make good enough fighters." He rubbed a bruise on his left arm as he spoke. "The nomads are even better material. They have the local knowledge we need to really make ourselves effective on Polypheme."

"You'd trust the nomads? I've seen the xenopsych reports, Fraser. They don't think anything like us. No concept of loyalty to anything higher than their own Clan . . . no understanding of tactical coordination . . ."

"We all know how you Legion types like to set up native armies so there will be plenty of soft billets for your legionnaires to fill as officers and noncoms," Barnett said. "But the whole idea of arming and training the wogs . . . that's ridiculous."

"Someone doesn't think so," Fraser commented. "Someone's equipping them with high-tech gear, and they're discovering tactical coordination fast enough, too."

They were sitting in the conference room set aside for the garrison staff, adjacent to the suite of offices and living quarters that housed Captain Hawley and his small staff. Formal discussions wouldn't begin until the captain joined them, but that hadn't kept anyone from airing his views.

Fraser studied the two civilians. They shared the common attitude most outsiders held for the Legion, but that was nothing unusual. More surprising was the contempt they directed at the natives. It was fashionable for the idle rich back on Terra to spout human-supremacist nonsense, but out on the frontiers those attitudes were usually rare.

Barnett, especially, puzzled him. The man had been doing field work on Polypheme for three years. How could anyone research a culture for that long and still hold it in such low regard?

DuValier spoke up from further down the table. "Actually, Captain Fraser has already shown that nomads can be used in conjunction with our troops, at least as native scouts," he said in his flat, toneless voice. "He has been training twenty of them for several weeks now."

"On what authorization?" Jens asked sharply.

Fraser glared at his Exec before answering. "Captain Hawley and I agreed it would be a good idea to look into the possibility," he said. "Nor do I think that Seafarms can overrule the military command on this kind of point." Inwardly, he was seething. As if he didn't have enough trouble with these civilians, now his XO was complicating things.

What the hell was DuValier's problem, anyway?

The door at the far end of the room slid open with a complaining whine. Gunnery Sergeant Istvan Valko and Lieutenant Susan Gage strode briskly through the wide, squat doorway. Valko, Alpha Company's senior NCO, marked out a brisk "Ten-hut!"

The legionnaires in the room, including Fraser, stood as Captain David Hawley followed the others. As Hawley took his place at the head of the table, Fraser watched him sadly.

A phrase Father Fitzpatrick, Bravo Company's chaplain, was particularly fond of ran through Fraser's mind. "There, but for the grace of God, go I."

Hawley was old for his rank, well past fifty, and looked even older after years of hard drink and the neglect that went with dreamchip addiction. His expression was vague, his eyes empty, a sure sign that he had been in dreamland when Gage and Valko roused him for the meeting. The man spent a lot of time in the living dreams of his habit, feeding fantasies directly into the brain by way of the computer implant in his skull.

Almost thirty years ago, David Hawley had been the hero of the fighting on Aten, when marauding Ubrenfars had nearly plunged most of the frontier into war. A lieutenant in the Legion, Hawley had stopped the Ubrenfars cold with a perfectly executed ambush by the survivors of his company. Promotion and recognition followed, but somehow it had all gone wrong. Hawley was shunted from one dead-end post to another, his brilliant mind wasted in minor administrative jobs and routine garrison duty. He turned to dreamland for stimulation, but the mock battles he fought in his mind proved more real to him than his waking life.

The classic pattern of dreamchip addiction . . . with the inevitable aftermath. Hawley lost out on promotions he might have earned, and gradually slid into obscurity.

*There, but for the grace of God* . . . Fraser was all too aware of how similar his career was to Hawley's early days.

He could end up like David Hawley, a superannuated Legion captain, grasping at memories and might-have-beens. The thought made him flinch, made his skin crawl.

"Ah . . . Mr. Fraser, why don't you, ah . . . take things in hand," Hawley said, blinking vaguely.

"Yes, sir," Fraser replied. He knew a lot of officers who treated Hawley with contempt, but he had vowed never to be one of them. Somewhere under the drink and the chip addiction, the hero of Aten remained.

He touched a stud on the table to call up Watanabe's report on the monitor screen mounted on the wall behind him. "*Seafarms Cyclops* was attacked around sunset by a strong force of nomads armed with high-tech weaponry and employing tactics that are far beyond anything previously credited to the locals on this planet." He manipulated a computer pointer to indicate specific features on an image of the captured alien weaponry. "This is a five-millimeter rocket launcher. The design is unfamiliar, but as you can see here the grip is obviously intended to accommodate hands not unlike a wog's. The whole mechanism is covered in a substance similar to duraplast. Subaltern Watanabe believes it is intended to insulate the weapon from the effects of corrosive seawater, and Warrant Officer Koenig, my Native Affairs specialist, concurs."

"Wait a moment, Fraser," Barnett said. "Are you trying to tell us that these things are manufactured locally? The wogs don't have that capability, and you know it!"

Fraser shook his head. "My people think that these are being brought in from off-planet, but they've been designed specifically for conditions on Polypheme." He paused a moment to let the implications of that sink in. "Someone is not only running guns to the natives, they're doing it as part of a consistent policy involving a long-term manufacturing commitment off-planet."

"Who?" Lieutenant Gage asked. "Any indications?"

"I'd put money on Semti renegades," Trent growled. The Semti, once the rulers of a vast interstellar sphere, had lost control to upstart Terrans after the destruction of their capital by a human battle fleet nearly a century ago. Semti administrators now worked diligently for their new overlords, but more than one plot had been uncovered in the decades since the end of the war. The fighting on Hanuman had been inspired by Semti agents, and probably the Ubrenfar campaign Hawley remembered as well.

"Could be Semti," Fraser agreed. "Or the Toeljuks. They leased the planet from the Semti, and I'm sure their leaders would like to get it back. Or we could be talking about human gunrunners, you know." He glanced at Barnett and Jens. "There's a lot of profit in instability, after all."

Barnett looked away. Jens met Fraser's stare with a level gaze of her own. "Surely it's a moot point, Captain," she said. "I would think we'd be better employed talking about security measures, not picturing plots and revolutions."

"What, ah . . . what do you have in mind?" Hawley asked.

It was Barnett who answered. "Obviously the first imperative is to protect the *Cyclops,*" he said. "I would say our first priority should be the dispatch of at least one more platoon, preferably two more, to the ship."

"Unacceptable," Fraser snapped. "We have no idea what kind of reach the opposition has, or what their object might be. Diluting our defenses would be the worst possible thing at this point."

"What do you recommend, then, Captain?" Jens asked.

"Recall the *Cyclops* to port at once. Keep her here where we can concentrate all our forces until we know what we're facing. Shut down operations in Ourgh, too, and bring all Terran personnel out here. Right now we're spread too thin."

Barnett started to make an angry response, but Jens overrode him. "I'm sorry, Captain, but that's equally unacceptable. The corporation is on Polypheme to make money, and we can't do that crouched here in the Sandcastle. The Cyclops Project can't be jeopardized at this stage. We have to show that it can operate at a profit, or the whole concept will be abandoned. And that would be a disaster, not just for Seafarms but for this whole planet. Without something like the mineral extraction operation, the Commonwealth will pull out entirely."

Fraser leaned forward in his chair. "I think you should reconsider, Citizen," he said quietly. "If you want the Legion to provide security, you're going to have to let us do it right. Otherwise . . ."

"You know as well as I do that your unit is answerable to civilian authority—my authority—as long as it is deployed on Polypheme," Jens said flatly.

"Except in cases where Commonwealth security considerations are stronger."

She smiled without humor. "I'd suggest you have some pretty powerful proof before you go invoking that clause, Captain. Unless you're planning an early retirement? I'm sure Reynier Industries can arrange it . . . if you fail to show the proper spirit of cooperation."

Fraser bit back an angry reply. He glanced at Hawley again.

*There, but for the grace of God . . .*

# Chapter 5

We are nothing now but Legionnaires, and Legionnaires die better than any men in the world.
—Captain Jean Danjou, at Camerone
French Foreign Legion, 30 April, 1863

Legionnaire First-Class Angela Garcia hated the Sandcastle. She hated the big horseshoe-shaped computer and communications desk in the base command center that was her standard duty station, and she hated Polypheme and Seafarms Interstellar and even, she was beginning to think, the Legion itself.

*Le cafarde* . . . the symptoms were easy enough to recognize, but harder to ignore. A lot of soldiers would have given anything for this kind of duty—a quiet backwater garrison, comfortable quarters, no threat of combat—but Garcia couldn't see beyond the routine. The boredom.

Somehow she hadn't really pictured boredom as going together with her posting as chief $C^3$ technician under Colin Fraser. Garcia had handled the command, control, and communications position for Fraser throughout the fighting on Hanuman, and by the time the long march was over she had learned to respect him. But he was different since the company had shipped out to Polypheme—more aloof, more concerned with administrative detail than the needs of the company.

It felt like a betrayal.

She shuddered at the thought, remembering how her husband had deserted her years ago. She'd only been eighteen at the time, a poor colonial without any living relatives, no skills, no hopes, her life shattered by the way Juan had treated her. Angela Garcia had joined the Legion to find a home, people who would always stand beside her.

Now the bug was inside her head, whispering hate. She tried to put those thoughts aside.

A buzzer brought her out of her reverie. She tapped the intercom button.

"C-cubed. Garcia."

"This is the main gate," a bored-sounding voice said. "We have a Company floatcar approaching."

"So? Let them in."

"Funny, Garcia," the legionnaire replied. "They say they've got a wog bigshot on board to see Citizen Jens. You want to lay on a formal reception, or what?"

Garcia muttered a curse in Spanish. "All the brass is in conference," she told him. "Call out the officer of the watch. Better get Mr. Koenig down there as well. I'll let the captain know we've got visitors."

She cut the intercom and patched in another line, a private channel that hooked up to the earpiece receiver Sergeant Trent was wearing. "Gunny? Main gate reports a Company floatcar coming in with a native VIP on board. I'm having Reynolds and Koenig do the honors. You'd better find out if the captain wants to see the wog now, or keep him on ice for a while."

Her message delivered, Garcia turned her thoughts back to Polypheme. Trouble aboard the *Cyclops* . . . the riot in town . . . now a native leader coming to see the Project Director.

Legionnaire Garcia had a feeling that her boredom wasn't going to last long. The favored treatment for the cafarde was said to be a loaded rifle and plenty of targets. From where she was sitting it looked like the prescription was about to be filled.

"If this project fails, the corporation will hold you personally responsible. I don't think either of you wants that."

Fraser glanced at Captain Hawley, but the older man just shrugged at Barnett's comment.

At this point in his career, Hawley had little to fear. No matter how much influence Seafarms or Reynier Industries wielded, it wouldn't make much difference one way or the other to David Hawley.

But it could be the final death-blow to Fraser's future.

He glanced down at the recessed monitor screen in the desk in front of him. Gunny Trent's memo stared back at him "COMPANY FLOATCAR WITH NATIVE COUNCIL REP HAS CLEARED MAIN GATE." That was the last complication he needed in the situation right now. The riot in Ourgh was still fresh in his mind.

"If I might suggest," Kelly was saying reasonably, "I think it would be better to concentrate on ways to *keep* the project from failing, instead of trying to hand out the blame in advance."

"Which is precisely why we have to send more troops to the *Cyclops*," Barnett shot back. "The ship was attacked, and we have to take steps to protect her."

"Not at the cost of weakening us everywhere else," Trent said. "Unless you're ready to give us the native auxiliaries we need, we just don't have the strength to waste."

Fraser cleared his throat. "I think we'd better wait. A native VIP from Ourgh is on his way up. He may have something to say that will have a bearing on all this."

Jens and Barnett reacted as he expected. "From Ourgh?" the woman said, plainly surprised. "What's he doing out here?"

"Perhaps lodging a protest over the way the Legion acted in the disturbance this morning," Barnett responded smoothly.

"Your own people sent him out in a floatcar," Fraser told Jens. "Presumably he came from your office in town."

She frowned. "Then it must be important. Damn." She seemed about to go on, but a chime from the intercom cut her off.

"Elder Houghan!! of the Governing Council of Ourgh, to see Citizen Jens," Legionnaire Garcia's voice announced.

Fraser glanced at Jens, who nodded. "Send him in," he replied, leaning back in his chair and trying to look more relaxed than he was.

Houghan!! was old for a wog, his skin dark and wrinkled, especially around the eyestalks, which looked stiff, even brittle. He was fat, and wheezed as he sank uncomfortably into an empty chair near Hawley's seat at the conference table. The Elder was dressed in brightly colored robes and carried a satchel slung over one shoulder.

There was nothing old about the native elder's voice, though. "The Council has sent me to discuss the issue of defense against the nomads," he said bluntly, the sound coming from the lower gill-slits exposed by gaps in his robes just above his hips. "In the past three moon-cycles we have suffered five raids, and you Terrans have given us no aid whatsoever."

Jens held up a hand, a very human gesture. Houghan!! swiveled his eyestalks slowly to look at her. "Elder," she said carefully. "Elder, we have been over this before. Terra is here to trade, not to fight. We still feel that it would not benefit anyone if the Commonwealth took on so much responsibility . . . not if you wish your government to remain sovereign."

Houghan!!'s feeding tendrils twitched in disgust. "Words!" he said. "You hide behind words! When the Toels traded here, they enforced the peace."

"And had most of their dealings with the nomads," Jens pointed out. "Your town, all the cities ashore, depended on nomad traders for everything."

"But the nomads who traded with the Toels had no need for raids. Since the Sky Lords and the Toels left, the nomads have become impossible to tame. And your people do nothing to discourage them."

"You know the size of our garrison here," Jens said quietly. "Do you really think we could patrol hundreds of kilometers of seacoast effectively? Your own troops cannot cover the waters-of-raising. How do you expect the Terran garrison to do it?"

The Elder blinked. "But . . . your achievements are so far beyond ours. All know that you have instruments to see in the dark and through the waters, and artificial voices to carry over great distances. Weapons that can kill a foe you cannot even see. Your garrison could guard our shores so easily. . . ."

Fraser spoke up for the first time since the Elder's arrival. "Our soldiers can do many things, Reverend Ancient," he said smoothly, using the most respectful mode of the local dialect. "But we cannot be in many places at once. There are too few of us to do everything we would like to do on your world, or we would surely provide the protection you desire."

The words earned him an angry look from Barnett. Seafarms Interstellar and Reynier Industries, like most corporations developing the Commonwealth's new frontier worlds, were forced to balance carefully between enough protection to ensure their own safety and the kind of full-scale Colonial

Army presence that would turn Polypheme into a Terran Client, with a Resident-General appointed by the government and safeguards built in to ensure that the locals were protected from exploitation.

Inevitably Terra's corporate interests tried to hold the government at arm's length, and keeping garrisons weak was one way to keep the Colonial Office from getting too involved on planets like this one. But it was those selfsame corporations that screamed loudest when their holdings were threatened and the Commonwealth couldn't instantly field enough troops to deal with the danger.

Houghan!! regarded Fraser with interest. "You are the commander of the soldiers?" he asked.

Fraser shook his head, then remembered that to the natives the gesture connoted agreement. "No . . . sorry, no, Reverend Ancient. I am only the deputy here." He indicated Hawley with a gesture. "But I believe I speak for the Reverend Ancient Captain Hawley in this."

The other captain looked up. "Ah, yes . . . yes, Captain Fraser is my deputy here. Yes."

The native made a gesture Fraser wasn't familiar with. "Then if you cannot aid us directly, you could certainly supply us with these weapons and devices for our own soldiers to use. We would pay well, very well. In food, or labor, or whatever else you need."

Before Fraser could reply, Jens took charge of the conversation again. "That, too, is something we cannot do," she said. Unlike Fraser, she was using the mode of speech reserved for equals. "At least not until I have time to refer back to my superiors on Terra. We must see how this would influence our agreements with your Council."

"Agreements!" The Elder's feeding tendrils writhed. "There will be no agreements unless we receive aid! Or is this a part of your plot against us?"

"Plot? What are you talking about?" Jens asked sharply.

The Elder set his shoulder bag on the table ponderously and drew something out of its depths. "This was found after the nomad attack yesterday. It killed six of our soldiers before they were even aware there were nomads in our waters." Houghan!! tossed it on top of the satchel with a contemptuous flourish.

Trent picked it up carefully, and Fraser watched him turn the weapon over in his hands. It was a larger, heavier version of the rocket launcher in Watanabe's report, plainly designed for conditions on Polypheme but far beyond local technology.

More proof of outside meddling.

"Deny that this is an offworlder device," Houghan!! said with a sneer. "Deny it!"

Fraser replied. "Yes, Reverend Ancient, this must have come from offworld. But my people and I have nothing to do with it."

"This I cannot believe," the Elder said. "You Terrans have control of the trade. Even the Toels who still visit must do all of their business through your company port. These would not be here unless you wanted them here."

Jens looked worried now. "Believe me, Reverend Ancient," she said, now adopting the supplicant's mode. "Believe me, these are not here with our approval. Smugglers . . . enemies . . . someone is bringing these in without our knowledge."

Biting off a comment, Fraser made a quick note on his computer terminal to check security on incoming cargoes. In theory everything was carefully checked and cross-checked, but there was ample room for corruption at a port as poorly staffed as the Polypheme facility. Were these weapons coming through the terminal, or was someone conveniently failing to notice incoming ships that landed away from Ourgh and contacted the natives directly?

Another note appeared below his own: LEGION STAFF ON APPROACH MONITORS? Fraser glanced up, his eyes meeting Trent's. The sergeant had put the weapon down, and his fingers rested on the keys of his own terminal. Fraser nodded slightly, and Trent responded with a quick nod of his own. It was always gratifying to find Trent's thoughts running so close with his own.

He focused his attention on Houghan!! again. "If your enemies are doing this," he was saying, "I cannot see why you will not protect us. Give us some proof of your good intentions, or we will follow our own currents henceforth."

"Your Council signed the agreements. . . ." Barnett began.

"They will not be honored," the Elder broke in. "Not until we see some proof of your good intentions." He rose slowly, his massive bulk suddenly very alien, hostile.

"When you are ready to deal fairly, contact the Council and—"

His words were cut off by the wail of warning sirens.

Karatsolis threw down his cards in disgust as the siren sounded. The other legionnaires clustered around the improvised table looked startled, not quite grasping what the ululating warning meant. *Not surprising,* Karatsolis thought wryly. *They haven't even grasped the basics of poker yet.*

"Look alive, you apes!" he said, reaching for his rifle. "That's the perimeter security alarm!"

"Jesus!" one of the legionnaires muttered. He was a nube, part of a draft of replacements for the demi-battalion's transport section who had arrived straight from the Legion depot on Devereaux only a week ago. His name was O'Donnell. "Jesus Christ, Spear, what the hell's going on?"

"When I know I'll tell you, nube," Karatsolis snapped. "Grab a rifle and get moving!"

The legionnaire looked confused until a more savvy comrade thrust an FEK battle rifle into his hands. Karatsolis waved toward the parade ground. "Let's mag it!"

The five legionnaires followed him as he ran down the motor pool ramp and across the parade ground. Shouts and the whine of FEK fire were coming from the western side of the compound near one of the gates, and in the absence of higher direction Karatsolis led them in that direction. Off to the left he spotted Narmonov's platoon turning out. More legionnaires were racing into the compound from other parts of the perimeter wall.

"Come on!" he shouted as he reached a stairway that led up to the scene of the fighting. There was a scream up above, and a body came tumbling past him to lie in the mud. He recognized the man as Subaltern Reynolds, one of Alpha Company's platoon leaders. The body was clad in a Legion dress uniform, but much of the officer's chest had been blown away.

Feet pounded up the fusand steps behind him. Karatsolis raised his rifle, his thumb groping for the selector switch to go to full auto before he remembered that he was still carrying the riot gun from the encounter in Ourgh. He cursed, and kept cursing as he noticed that there were less than twenty rounds left in the magazine.

A native, bare-skinned but marked with the elaborate tattooing of the nomad tribes, heaved himself over the wall, brandishing a pike and shouting a hoarse battle cry. Karatsolis fired twice at close range, and the wog toppled backward. Nearby a second nomad was waving a pistol. O'Donnell let loose with a full-auto salvo. Dozens of needle-thin slivers tore through the native's torso.

Karatsolis ran to the wall and looked over the edge. "God in Heaven . . ." he muttered, reeling back.

A half a hundred or more natives were climbing the smooth fusand wall, and more shapes were visible in the water around the base of the fortress.

O'Donnell pushed past him. "What is it, Spear?" he asked, leaning over the edge with his battle rifle at the ready.

Suddenly he jerked back, dropping the rifle. It clattered on the rampart next to Karatsolis's boot.

O'Donnell's hands clutched feebly at the native crossbow bolt that protruded from his neck. The legionnaire staggered and fell, Karatsolis dropped to one knee beside him, but it was too late for first aid, too late for anything. Legionnaire Third-Class O'Donnell was dead.

Karatsolis had never even known the kid's first name.

He grabbed O'Donnell's FEK and snatched the magazine pouch from his belt.

As he rose, the natives swarmed over the wall all around him.

# Chapter 6

> There is the tradition which is so strong that a man cannot be for long in the Foreign Legion without wanting, like his comrades, to do better than the soldiers of any other regiment.
>
> —Legionnaire Adolphe Cooper
> French Foreign Legion, 1933

"Lights! Get some lights on out here!" Fraser was shouting, as he buckled on a plasteel chest plate over his tattered dress uniform jacket.

They were clustered on the wall above the headquarters complex. The civilians—Jens, Barnett, and the native Elder—had followed the legionnaires, despite Fraser's orders to remain in the conference room.

He didn't have time to deal with them now. There were too many other things to be done first if the defense was going to pull together.

"Why not use infrared?" Hawley asked, as Trent passed the order to light up the compound.

"Native eyes are better adapted to darkness, sir," Fraser said. "Especially the nomads, who spend so much time underwater. Twilight is an advantage for them—probably the reason they decided to attack now. Bright lighting inside the compound might dazzle them enough to give us an advantage."

Hawley nodded slowly. "Good . . . very good, Captain. Use their weaknesses. Yes."

"With your permission, sir," Fraser went on, "I'd like to deploy Alpha Company and the support troops to the walls, and get Bravo Company together as a ready reserve."

The senior captain looked indecisive for a moment. "That's a pretty big reserve," he said slowly, closing his eyes for a moment. Fraser felt impatience rising within him.

Why couldn't Hawley *act?* "All right, Captain. Do it. You know how to handle this."

"Thank you, sir," Fraser said. Before he turned away he could see relief spreading over Hawley's features. The other captain was plainly happy to be able to turn the responsibility over to someone else.

Floodlights started coming on all around the central well, turning the gathering gloom day-bright. More lights were coming on along the walls. Fraser saw the fighting on the far wall by the gate clearly now. Nomads, taken by surprise by the sudden glare, seemed to be wavering, but there were all too few Terran figures up there to take advantage of the moment.

"Garcia! Garcia!" Fraser swung around in search of his $C^3$ technician. She was just emerging from the building, still settling the field computer and communications pack on her shoulders. "Commlink! General command channel."

Cursing his lack of a helmet with its built-in commo gear, Fraser took a handset from her. "This is Fraser. Alpha Company platoon leaders, Defense Plan Four. Perimeter deployment. Wijngaarde, Bartlow, assemble your platoons near the center of the compound."

"On the way," Subaltern Vincent Bartlow responded over the radio.

"Acknowledged," the First Platoon CO, Subaltern Henck Wijngaarde, added an instant later.

Fraser turned to the others. "Lieutenant DuValier, take Gunny Trent and join the rest of Bravo. You're in charge, but don't commit the men without my orders. Kelly, I want your sappers to take the west perimeter, You'll have to spread them pretty thin. I want Alpha Company to be able to concentrate around the gate. That's where most of them are."

"As you wish, Captain," DuValier said calmly. He managed to look like he was on his way to a social engagement instead of a battle.

"I'm counting on Bravo Company," Fraser told Trent quietly. "I know you won't let me down."

Trent gave him a sharp salute and headed for the stairs. Kelly hesitated a moment, then nodded and followed him.

Fraser turned his attention to Susan Gage. "Lieutenant, take charge at the gate." He pointed across the compound.

"Clear those natives away. If they can plant explosives or get to the gatehouse controls . . ."

She nodded grimly. If the legionnaires lost control of the gates, the nomads could open the whole compound up to the waters lapping outside. That would give them easy access to the interior. . . . Gathering up Gunnery Sergeant Valko with a look, the lieutenant followed the other staffers.

He turned back to Garcia. "Pass the word to seal all the inner doors once our people are deployed. I want this place shut up tight."

The $C^3$ technician nodded curtly, then frowned. "I can get through to our own people," she said, shooting a look at Jens and Barnett. "It'll take longer to get the civilians to cooperate."

The Seafarms technicians stationed at the Sandcastle kept their distance from the Legion. Even their computer and communications facilities were segregated. Jens and Barnett had made it clear many times over that they wanted no interference in corporate activities by the Legion garrison.

Before Fraser could answer Jens broke in. "We'll take care of our end, Captain."

Houghan!!, the native Elder, wheezed self-importantly. "I will remain here to observe how you deal with these nomad scum," he said in the dialect of Ourgh.

Fraser hesitated, wanting to order him away, but knowing the Elder would refuse to obey. Maybe it would help if Houghan!! saw the Legion in combat with his enemies. Nodding, he responded in the supplicant's mode. "As you wish, Reverend Ancient," he said. "But I pray you will be heedful of your safety and remain away from the walls. The nomads may wish to eliminate so vital a member of the Council of Ourgh."

The Elder didn't answer, but Fraser saw his eyestalks studying the walls with an expression that might have been apprehension.

That left Fraser, Hawley, and Garcia to deal with the battle. Fighting the temptation to join in the fighting, Fraser helped Garcia take off the backpack and set up the portable command/control unit. Hawley joined them after a moment, his eyes distant. *Probably getting the computer feed direct through his implant,* Fraser thought. It irritated him that Hawley had one of the rare computer interfaces hooked directly into his brain, when the captain couldn't or wouldn't put it to practical use. Hawley used it mostly for his battle simulations.

Something like that would be damned useful for fighting a real battle, Fraser knew, but implants were expensive off Terra, and only a privileged few colonials ever had the operation.

Hawley was plugged in to the information but obviously didn't plan to do anything with it. Fraser bent over the computer's small monitor screen and watched as Garcia called up a battle map. Data from individual helmet sensors and the larger surveillance systems mounted on the base walls was interpreted on the screen to give a fairly accurate picture of the unfolding battle. Of course, the computer might not pick up all the legionnaires out there who weren't in battledress, and the count of the nomads was necessarily vague, but it was enough to give Fraser an overview of the fighting that would be invaluable in deploying his defenders.

He only hoped it would be enough.

Warrior-Scout !!Dhruuj listened to the voices of the deep, his senses extended to their fullest. Already his clan-brothers were swarming over the Built-Reef-of-the-Strangers, and the sounds of their struggles pulled at the innermost core of his consciousness. The pull of the Clan was hard to resist, but !!Dhruuj willed himself to remain still. He could serve his clan-brothers better by remaining clear of the fighting, watching, listening.

It was less tangible than the Weapons-of-Far-Death, but !!Dhruuj wondered if this new teaching, this discipline and division of duties, might not be the greatest of all Gifts. Better weapons meant power, true, power even over the city-dwellers and their perverted ways. But the knowledge that instinct could be mastered by will was something that would outlast the War-Leader-of-Clans and all his works.

The knowledge would certainly be with them long after the Strangers returned to their distant homes and left the Free Swimmers to their endless realm.

He heard the Voices echoing through the deeps, far-off, faint. !!Dhruuj strained his senses to hear the Words-That-Were-Not-Speech.

The message repeated twice. When he was sure he knew what the Voices had said, he shouted the orders through the water in ordinary speech.

It was time to launch the second stage of the attack.

* * *

A pair of bearded sappers in full Legion battledress rushed past Fraser, their FEK gauss rifles catching the harsh spotlights on gleaming barrels. Fraser watched them unfolding bipods and positioning the weapons to cover the angry sea.

"Keep a sharp eye out, lads," he told them. "Those loke bastards can climb right up the walls."

One of them, a grizzled corporal with a beard that would have done a Biblical prophet proud, flashed him a quick thumb's-up. "Dinna worry, cap'n," he said, his words thick with the familiar accent of Caledon. "Ye can count on us."

That dialect was like a taste of home. "What's your name, Corporal?" Fraser asked him.

He beamed proudly. "MacAllister, sir," he said. The sapper paused to check his magazines carefully before he went on. "I was with yer auld feether, sir, back on Geryon."

"With the auld Watch?" Fraser asked, unconsciously lapsing into the dialect himself. "Why. . . ?" He choked back the question that would have violated one of the oldest codes in the Legion. *Never ask about a man's background. He is a legionnaire—nothing more, nothing less.*

The man grinned at him through the beard. "Long time it's been, cap'n. But you remind me of him, and that's nae mistake, sir."

Fraser turned away suddenly, overcome with emotion. What had made this Caledonian soldier seek refuge with the Legion?

"Sir," Garcia said quietly. "Sir, most of First Platoon Alpha is pinned by heavy fire near the gate. The wogs are setting up heavy stuff everywhere they've got a foothold."

"What about our own heavies?"

"Still kitting up, sir."

"Damn," he muttered. Legion heavy weapons—onager plasma guns, Fafnir rocket launchers, and semi-portable CEK gauss cannons—were too big and bulky for routine use and weren't issued for normal watchstanding duties. But it took time to prepare them, especially the onagers with their full-body armored suits that protected the gunners from the intense heat generated by the weapon. He remembered a kid in Watanabe's platoon named Grant who had suffered extensive burns in the last big battle on Hanuman after firing on enemy troops with a salvaged onager and no protection.

He could also remember a time or two on Hanuman when delays in deploying the heavies had damn near cost him a fight.

Fraser shook his head slowly. Memories of Hanuman wouldn't help him here. He had to deal with the present, not live in the past.

Like Hawley.

He glanced at the captain. Hawley had strapped on chest armor and a holster with a rocket pistol, and he looked alert enough now. But since the start of the fighting his only comment had been the question on Fraser's decision to hold back the reserves from Bravo Company. Otherwise he had seemed content to leave Fraser in command.

"Pass the word to the Armory to send out the Fafnir gunners as soon as they're ready. Lances aren't to wait until everyone is equipped—we need troops out there *now.*"

"Yes, sir," Garcia responded, reaching for the channel selector. "Sir—behind you!"

He spun in time to see the sapper, MacAllister, reeling back from the rampant with a bolt embedded in his shoulder. The other legionnaire swung his FEK and fired downward.

A *whoosh* and a thunderclap silenced the FEK as an explosive-tipped rocket projectile caught the second sapper square in the chest. The man flew backward, trying to save himself, but he slipped and fell. He landed in the mud below and lay still.

A dozen bulky, inhuman shapes clambered onto the parapet, their ill-assorted weapons gleaming in the light. One of them pointed a rocket rifle at Fraser and fired.

Karatsolis sprayed autofire into a cluster of nomad soldiers and shouted encouragement to the handful of legionnaires still on the wall nearby. The defending force was shrinking fast as the enemy advantage in numbers began to be felt. The duty section at the gate was down to six unwounded men—more than half of the original force dead or seriously injured—and the handful of reinforcements Karatsolis had brought from the motor pool was simply not enough to make a difference.

He wondered how Narmonov's men were faring. They'd

been pinned by heavy weapons fire for a while, and the last time Karatsolis had managed a look down into the compound the Alphas were still working their way forward to take out the position, a heavy multi-barrel gatling gun firing rocket-assisted projectiles.

It didn't help that most of the legionnaires had been caught unready. Karatsolis, Legionnaire Sandoval, and Narmonov's men had been in battledress after the riot in Ourgh, but most of the rest of the troops inside the Sandcastle had been in light duty fatigues or even, like Reynolds, in dress uniforms. Many of the men wearing battledress didn't have their helmets.

Karatsolis wished for the armored security of a magrep APC, or at least a veeter. He found himself grinning sourly at the thought of Selim Bashar, safe back in Ourgh. Bashar was probably putting some moves on the girl they'd pulled out of the riot.

The corporal was missing one hell of a fight.

With a wild scream a native flung himself over the wall, crashing into Karatsolis before the legionnaire could react. The FEK clattered across the fusand rampart while Karatsolis gasped for breath. Brandishing a wickedly curved sword, the nomad rose over him, the eyes on the end of their stalks wild with battle.

The legionnaire lashed upward with one foot, catching the nomad on his intricately tattooed stomach. It was like kicking a solid wall, but the nomad recoiled with a hoarse, wordless cry.

Then Sandoval was there, his FEK whining as he pumped round after round into the nomad. Dark blood splashed across Karatsolis as the wog fell.

"Thanks, Sandy," Karatsolis gasped, as he groped for his rifle.

*"De nada,"* Sandoval answered, turning his fire on another clump of nomads. "Hey, man, how long until somebody decides to help us out?"

Karatsolis grunted. It seemed like they'd been fighting for hours, but he knew the battle had started only a few minutes ago.

Three nomads were wrestling a bulky object—another of the gatling launchers, from the looks of it—into position on the roof of the gatehouse. From there it would command most of the compound . . . and put Narmonov's men in a crossfire.

He fired again, but the FEK chattered once and fell silent, the magazine empty. He checked the ammo readouts. The needle rounds were exhausted, and none of the legionnaires in the Sandcastle had been issued any rifle grenades.

Karatsolis swore and reached for a fresh magazine before he remembered that he'd already used up all the reloads O'Donnell had carried. With a final curse he flung the weapon aside. "Sandy! Come on!" he shouted, sprinting toward the nomads and their weapon.

Lieutenant Susan Gage tapped the side of her helmet as the command channel to Fraser's position went silent. Were those explosions she had heard over the commset? It was hard to separate the radio sounds from the noise of battle around her.

She was crouching behind a pile of cargomods with two squads from Third Platoon Alpha huddling under cover close by. Withering fire from the walls was keeping her troops from getting together an organized assault, and she was painfully aware of each passing second. There couldn't be more than a handful of men left around the gate. Unless they could mount an effective attack soon, the legionnaires were in danger of being drowned once the nomads flooded the compound.

Now Fraser was out of touch. *Damn!* she thought. *If he's gone, so is Captain Hawley. That makes me senior. . . .*

If only Hawley had been able to direct that battle himself! Then the two captains wouldn't have been together, and she wouldn't be stuck holding the bag. Her past experience had been confined to administration, not combat, and Gage wasn't sure she could come up with the right answers. Not like Fraser, who seemed to know exactly what to do.

Seconds ticked by as she studied the walls, searching for a weak spot, a flaw in the nomad position she could exploit. There were other Alpha Company troops pinned down nearby, she knew. Narmonov's men were right up against the wall, but they couldn't reach a ladder or stairway without taking fire from those gatling launchers.

They needed a break in the action, a distraction that would let her force-rush the enemy.

Reluctantly she gestured to her $C^3$ tech. "Patch me

through to Bravo Company,'' she said with a tired sigh. ''We need backup.''

''Follow me! Come on, you strakks, you want to live forever?''

Gunnery Sergeant Trent moved to block Lieutenant DuValier. ''Sir, our orders were to stay in reserve until the captain—''

''Fraser's out of touch, Sergeant. Probably dead.'' DuValier's expression was hard to read. Was that triumph in his eyes, or just the excitement of battle? ''Lieutenant Gage needs help at the gate, and she's in charge now.''

Trent felt a chill run through him. Fraser dead? After everything they'd gone through on Hanuman, could the captain really have died?

He'd lost his last CO in the massacre that triggered the fighting on that primitive world, and he had always felt secretly ashamed that he hadn't been there when it had really counted. Fraser had seemed a poor replacement for a man who had been his commanding officer and friend for nearly a decade, but as the long jungle march went on Trent had recognized the younger man's potential. By the time of the final battle, Fraser had been able to handle the company on his own, without the Gunnery Sergeant's advice and encouragement.

Trent didn't want to think he'd lost Fraser so soon.

''Sir,'' he said levelly. ''If the captain has been attacked, we have a security threat on the western perimeter. I submit we should respond there as well.''

DuValier frowned at him. ''Damn it, Sergeant, I said—''

''We can't turn our back on a gap in the defense, sir!'' Trent persisted.

The lieutenant hesitated for a moment, then nodded. ''Very well, Sergeant. Take the two recon lances and check it out. Coordinate with Warrant Officer Kelly—she's in charge back there. Now, move!''

''Pascali!'' Trent shouted. ''Braxton! Your lances with me! Let's go!''

He wouldn't believe that Captain Fraser was dead. Not until he saw a body.

Meanwhile, he knew that Fraser was counting on him.

# Chapter 7

With the bayonet, *mes enfants.* It's nothing but shot!
—Captain Arnaud-Jacques Leroy Constantine
French Foreign Legion, 1837

Karatsolis pulled his knife from its forearm sheath and slashed at the nomad in front of him. The native tried to parry with the cumbersome crossbow he carried, but Karatsolis reversed the direction of the attack at the last moment and thrust the weapon straight for the face. It sank to the hilt just below the left eyestalk, and the wog jerked back so hard that it tore the weapon from the legionnaire's grasp.

Behind him he could hear Sandoval's FEK whining. The sound cut off abruptly.

"*Caracoles!*" the Hispanic legionnaire swore. "I'm dry!"

Karatsolis snatched his knife from the dead wog's body and sprang forward, ducking to avoid a pike-thrust. He stabbed one tattooed torso, twisted to one side, then slashed again. The native was bellowing in pain or rage. A curved sword missed the legionnaire's head by centimeters.

Then Sandoval was beside him, swinging his FEK. The high-tech club took out the native with the sword, while Karatsolis finished off the pikeman with another knife thrust.

Only two more natives stood between the legionnaires and the nomads setting up the rocket launcher.

And one of them was already drawing a bead on Karatsolis with a pistol. . . .

Corporal Mike Johnson dropped prone behind the cover of one of the massive struts that supported the complex cradle in the center of the Sandcastle. The structure was designed to hold the *Seafarms Cyclops* when she docked for maintenance or repairs, but at the moment it was the perfect place for the legionnaires of Bravo Company to take shelter as they gathered for their assault.

His duraweave battledress didn't quite keep out the ubiquitous mud. The interior of the compound was usually muddy, especially after vehicles had come in while the tides were rising. Johnson ignored the wet goo that seeped in through his boot tops and focused his attention on the job at hand.

He peered cautiously around the bulky pillar and chambered a mini-grenade in his FEK. At least the troops from the barracks had been able to get grenade clips. If the poor devils out on the perimeter had only been issued the explosive ammo, the natives might never have reached the ramparts.

"What's it look like, Corp?" Legionnaire Delandry asked.

He glanced at her. In battledress, with an FEK in her hand, Elise Delandry didn't look much like a medic, but in the Legion every soldier, no matter what specialty they were trained for, was a rifleman first and foremost. "Hell, Delandry, what does it always look like?" he asked sarcastically. "Swarms of wogs, and not enough of us!"

She grinned at him. "Good. Place was getting too damned dull."

Johnson chuckled. He and Delandry had both lived through Hanuman, and at least twice they'd come close to buying it in a hopeless fight to the death. Both times Colin Fraser had pulled off a miracle and got them out. "You'd rather get in another scrape and make the Captain rescue us again? What's the matter, Delandry, are you trying for a spot on his personal staff? You'll have to do something about his Navy bitch first!"

"Didn't you hear, Corp?" Legionnaire Abban spoke up. "They're saying the Captain's bought it! Old Do-This-n-That's in charge now."

Delandry crossed herself. "*Merde,*" she said softly. "No . . . I don't believe it. Not Captain Fraser . . ."

"I heard it from Maxton, and he said he got it from somebody who was talking to Dubcek," Abban insisted. "The Exec's C-cubed boy should know, huh?"

The corporal opened his mouth to reply, but a crackle in his earphones cut him off.

"First Platoon Bravo, go left, Second Platoon right," DuValier's voice was saying coldly. "Make as much noise as you can. The idea's to distract the wogs so Alpha can take them down. Move! Move!"

Johnson rolled out from behind the strut and scrambled to his feet, firing a spray of needle rounds. Legionnaires shouting battle cries and hoarse-voiced obscenities followed him.

Rocket fire and a few crossbow bolts probed toward the attackers. An explosion less than a meter to the left made Johnson swerve and stagger, but Delandry steadied him and he kept running.

Nearby, Abban went to one knee and fired a three-round burst of grenades at the wall. He started forward again, but a rocket caught him square in the face.

Delandry started toward Abban as the legionnaire fell, then turned away as she saw what the round had left of the man's head. She looked sick.

Johnson kept firing until his magazine ran dry, then ejected the spent clip and slapped a fresh one into the FEK's side-mounted receiver, all without breaking stride. A crossbow bolt clattered harmlessly off his plasteel chest plate.

His foot slipped in the mud, and this time he went down. The landing was enough to knock the wind out of him. He groped for his FEK and tried to take stock of the battle.

There were a lot of other legionnaires down, many of them not moving at all, others moaning, writhing, or trying to crawl toward safety. Not that there was much of that on this killing ground. At least Alpha Company was in close to the walls where they had some cover. Out here there was nothing to hide behind.

He heaved himself to his hands and knees and found the FEK in the mud. The rugged little weapon would stand up to a lot worse treatment than that.

Johnson checked the barrel of the grenade launcher to make sure it was clear, then fired a burst of the lethal 1-cm rounds. The explosions went off in a tight cluster near the closest of the nomad heavy weapons positions.

But not close enough. Johnson saw the multi-barrel monstrosity swinging toward him, streaks of flame spouting from each aperture in turn.

The explosions approached him in an uneven line, like the footfalls of a predatory beast.

He tried to rise, lost his footing again, and fell back into the sticky mud.

Then a flash, a roar, and a searing pain lancing up his leg . . .

Elise Delandry's face bent over his. He saw her mouth moving, heard the sounds, but nothing seemed to connect. "Leave me . . . leave . . . here . . ." he croaked, knowing she wouldn't, knowing what a target they made, knowing . . .

Then blackness consumed him.

Karatsolis flinched as the grenade burst hit the wall just below the native with the rocket pistol. The nomad staggered, and Karatsolis gathered himself and sprang forward. A moment later Sandoval was with him, holding off the other enemy soldier while Karatsolis grappled with the massive wog.

The native swung a powerful arm, and the impact against his wrist made Karatsolis drop his knife. With his left hand he gripped the rocket pistol and tried to wrench it free.

The wogs had powerful arm muscles designed for swimming and climbing, which made them stronger than a man, but their hands were weaker and less versatile. Karatsolis strained, forcing the alien's fingers back. Suddenly he had the gun.

He continued the motion to bring it smashing into the wog's face just above the writhing feeding tendrils once . . . twice . . . and again. The nomad staggered back, dark blood welling from the ruined features. Karatsolis raised the awkward weapon and pressed the firing stud, but the range was too short. The projectile dipped as it left the barrel before the rocket cut in, but it didn't have time to build up much momentum.

Sandoval pushed past him, a knife in one hand, his clubbed FEK in the other, and finished off the stunned native. Karatsolis fired at the nearest of the three wogs manning the gatling launcher, saw the explosive round blow a hole in his abdomen.

The other two leapt from their weapon, eyes burning, hands drawing curved swords. Paralysis gripped Karatsolis for an instant. He wasn't used to soldiers who kept coming the way these wogs did. Any human soldier would have run from a foe who had charged them the way he had. These monsters didn't just stand their ground, they attacked. And kept attacking, again and again.

One of the swords sliced deep into Sandoval's arm, and he dropped the FEK as he reeled back. Karatsolis fired twice more, then lunged sideways to avoid another fierce slash. He rolled against a wog body as he hit the ground, and something long and hard prodded him. His fingers closed around one of the long pikes many of the nomads had carried. Grabbing the weapon, he thrust it upward as his attacker rushed him again.

Even in his death-throes the nomad was still trying to reach Karatsolis.

The legionnaire staggered to his feet, hardly able to believe that there were no more natives close by. He ran to the heavy gatling launcher and studied it for a moment. Somewhere nearby he heard a groan.

"Sandy? How is it, Sandy?"

The Hispanic's voice was weak. "I'll live, I think. Hey, man, are we winning?"

Karatsolis grinned. "Could be, Sandy. Least we don't have to play with those damned popguns any more!"

The explosive round hit the $C^3$ pack, and Fraser returned fire with his FEK on full auto. Half a dozen natives toppled backward off the wall under the hail of needle-thin slivers, but more kept on coming. He backpedaled, still firing, trying to reach the stairwell.

Garcia was sprawled near the shattered terminal. She stirred, rolled over, and raised her own weapon, firing from her prone position. Close by Hawley crouched beside the sapper MacAllister, his rocket pistol drawn and all trace of vagueness gone from his eyes. The captain fired twice, hitting his targets. Then he was grappling with another nomad armed with a sword.

Fraser switched to single-shot and placed a high-velocity needle round squarely through the native's forehead. He toppled, and Hawley grabbed MacAllister and started pulling him back toward Fraser and Garcia.

More natives were climbing over the wall, screaming, brandishing weapons, a seemingly unstoppable living tidal wave. Fraser kept his weapon on the single-shot setting, conserving ammo, but Garcia's FEK gave off the continuous whine of full-auto fire. She had a grim smile on her face as she sprayed the attackers with lethal slivers.

"Look out, Captain!" Fraser shouted, as a nomad swung his legs over the wall just behind Hawley. He tried to line up a shot, but the captain blocked it.

Hawley let go of MacAllister's shoulders and turned, but not quickly enough. A backhand blow knocked Hawley backward, sending him sprawling over the injured legionnaire. The nomad drew his sword.

With a hoarse shout Houghan!! leapt into the fight, moving fast for a creature of his bulk and age. The Elder had picked up a sword from one of the dead nomads, and with a deft movement he parried the killing blow aimed at Captain Hawley.

Houghan!! was no match for the nomad warrior, though. The Elder fell back under a flurry of blows, barely able to fend off the attack. Fraser squeezed off a shot, cursed, fired again. The nomad fell.

And an instant later an enemy bullet exploded in Houghan!!'s back. The Elder fell forward across the body of his opponent.

Hawley was up again, still not abandoning MacAllister. "Cover us, Garcia!" Fraser yelled, leaping to help the captain.

Between them they were able to half carry, half drag the sapper back to the door that led to the stairs. The fusand corner of the stairwell gave some cover, at least.

Fraser flipped the FEK's selector switch to full-auto. "Get him inside, sir!" he said, leaning around the corner and opening fire. He shouted over the battle rifle's whine. "Garcia! Fall back!"

The $C^3$ operator kept firing until her magazine ran dry, then rolled, scrambled to her feet, and sprinted for the door, running in a zigzag pattern that stayed clear of Fraser's line of fire.

Hawley had the door open and was maneuvering MacAllister's limp body inside. As nomads continued to try to mass on the rampart, Fraser kept up his automatic fire, painfully aware of how fast he was using up his only magazine. The FEK ran dry just as Garcia rounded the corner. She dropped to one knee and hastily switched magazines in her own rifle.

She paused to pull out an extra clip and pass it to Fraser. "That's my last, skipper," she said.

"Take the other side, Garcia," he replied. "Make 'em count. "Captain, I recommend you get MacAllister downstairs and then go find some backup."

Hawley's voice was gruff. "I should stay and fight. I don't like running." It was a tone Fraser had never heard from the older man.

"Then think of it as gathering reinforcements for a tactical envelopment," he said. "We'll keep their attention until you get back."

Hawley's chuckle was dry and no less startling. "Hang on, then, son. I won't let you down." More softly, as if to himself, he went on. "I *won't*. Not this time."

Gage shuddered as another rapid-fire salvo of rockets poured down into the ragged Bravo Company skirmish line. The nomad heavy-weapons positions were maintaining a devastating fire against the legionnaires, and she'd already seen at least twenty men go down under that withering barrage.

But the diversion had been useless after all. When Narmonov's men tried to break from cover and attack the wall, the rockets had turned on them, breaking the attack before it had really started. A similar attempt by the troops with her had fared no better.

Every man dead or wounded out there had fallen because of her foolish orders. And soon the nomads would have control of the gates. Then it would be over.

"Massire!" she snapped to her $C^3$ tech. "General signal to Bravo Company. Disengage and fall back!"

"That'll leave us useless," Gunnery Sergeant Valko said. He was bleeding where shrapnel had sliced open a savage gash in his left cheek.

"Damn it, Sergeant, I can't just let them keep dying out there!"

"Ma'am—" Valko didn't finish. "What the hell?"

A rocket launcher near the gatehouse had opened fire again, but not down into the compound. Rockets streaked through the air, probing at the nomads closest to Narmonov's men. The ripple of explosions was the most beautiful sight and sound Gage had ever witnessed.

"Goddamn!" Subaltern Carnes shouted. "One of our boys is still kicking!" Other legionnaires started to cheer.

"Cancel that disengage order, Massire!" Gage shouted. "Come on, boys, let's kick those strakking wogs back into the ocean where they belong! Come on!"

She led thirty yelling legionnaires across the muddy ground.

Karatsolis swung the heavy launcher, gasping at the effort, and fired again. Rockets lanced toward another nomad position, and natives on that section of the wall dived for cover.

Beside him, Sandoval was trying to figure out how the feed mechanism worked. "You're down to ten more rounds, Spear," he said. "Damned if I can reload this sucker."

"Damn," Karatsolis swore. "I hope it was enough. . . ." He could see Narmonov's troops swarming among the nomads who had kept them pinned down for so long. There were more legionnaires crossing the compound down below. All they needed was a little more time, a little more confusion in the enemy ranks, and the Legion could get up close and personal with the wogs. Those rocket pistols were almost useless at short ranges, and duraweave and plasteel armor would stop most of the other nomad weapons.

He fired again, aiming for another gatling launcher that was swinging to cover the nearest group of human troops. The shots weren't very accurate, but the natives' aim went wild as well.

Sandoval grabbed his arm and pointed. "Over there, Spear!" he shouted.

Karatsolis swore again and tried to turn the launcher in the direction the wounded Hispanic legionnaire had indicated. But the bulky launcher wouldn't turn fast enough.

Three nomads were wrestling their own launcher into line to get off a shot at Karatsolis and Sandoval. . . .

He hauled at the multi-barreled weapon desperately until Sandoval shoved him away bodily. He fell and rolled over the edge of the parapet, landing with a heavy thud on the gatehouse roof a meter below.

Fire streaked through the twilight, and a dozen rockets impacted around the launcher. Karatsolis hauled himself to his feet and started forward, then caught sight of the wreckage of the launcher and the shattered body of Legionnaire Enrique Sandoval.

* * *

Captain David Hawley was feeling really alive for the first time in years. Adrenaline pumped in his veins, and the weight of the FE-PLF in his hand brought back memories long lost in a fog of implant addiction and drink. The fight on the HQ roof had left him eager for more.

He knelt beside MacAllister and felt for the sapper's neck pulse. It was weak and thready, but the man was still alive. Satisfied, Hawley rose and turned away from the unconscious man, anxious to find reinforcements and get back to the fighting.

Down the corridor a swinging door banged open. Sigrid Jens and a handful of men in Seafarms coveralls were there, some carrying FEKs, others improvised clubs.

"We heard there was a breakthrough up there," Jens said. "I brought as many people as I could."

Hawley gaped at her. Jens and her assistant had been a thorn in his side since the moment Demi-Battalion Elaine had arrived on Polypheme. Somehow he'd never expected the Seafarms people to lift a finger in their own defense.

Not that they'd be much use in the fighting. But the weapons they'd scavenged . . .

"Thank you, Citizen," he said, the words seeming inadequate to convey his feelings. "Thank you." He hesitated, trying to decide on the best course.

Decisions always came so hard these days. Young Fraser could snap out orders with barely a pause, like everything was perfectly clear from the moment he first saw it.

Once David Hawley had been able to do that. Once, but not anymore.

"Ah . . . look, Citizen, ah . . . I'll take the men with rifles back to the roof. I need you . . . I need you to find some legionnaires and get them to back us up. Can you do that?"

She nodded quickly. "Got it. Anything else?"

He grappled with the question a moment. "Ah . . . get someone to the Armory and turn out the heavy-weapons lances. Tell them . . . tell them . . ." He tried to remember the order Fraser had been about to pass when the nomads had first attacked on the roof. "Tell them lances shouldn't wait to be fully equipped before they deploy. Get the Fafnir gunners out as soon as they're ready."

"Fafnir gunners. Right." Jens gave another curt nod. "Good luck, Captain."

"Follow me, citizens!" he said, waving the PLF and urging them toward the stairs.

He felt like a leader for the first time in many, many years.

Warrior-Scout !!Dhruuj croaked a complex, wordless message in his farspeaking voice, reporting the news Clan-Warlord Khroor! had ordered him to send.

The Strangers-Within were winning the fight. Their warriors were counterattacking the walls in strength, and the attack on the gates had already been turned away. The Clan would fight to the end, of course, but it was clear now that even the clever two-pronged attack had not been enough to keep the Strangers from rallying in defense of their mysterious domain.

Perhaps the War-Leader-of-Clans would have an answer, or could get one from the Strangers-Who-Gave-Gifts. !!Dhruuj felt a thrill of certainty within himself. The War-Leader-of-Clans was the mightiest warrior ever to swim free, mightier than any nomad, any city-dweller . . . mightier than the Strangers-Within.

Long minutes went by as !!Dhruuj listened for the Voices to reply. Then, faintly, he heard the distant sounds.

!!Dhruuj hesitated for a long moment before interpreting the Voices for the Clan-Warlord clinging to the wall beside him. It seemed unthinkable . . . unnatural. . . .

But it was the order of the War-Leader-of-Clans, and the Reef-Swimmers had sworn to obey him as they would their own Clan-Leader.

"The attack to end," he said at last. "The swimmers to retreat. The scouts to watch and await new orders."

The Clan-Warlord grunted understanding. He seemed to sense !!Dhruuj's unease with the orders. "Wisdom there is in this," he said slowly. "Withdraw now, and we can renew the attack later to our advantage. Stay, and we destroy the Clan to no gain."

!!Dhruuj studied the Clan-Warlord with a feeling of sudden comprehension.

The battle wasn't really over. The Swimmers would return to finish it—when the time was right.

# Chapter 8

I can refuse nothing to men like you!

Colonel Combas, Mexican Army,
to the survivors of Camerone
French Foreign Legion, 30 April 1863

"They'll be back," Fraser said flatly. "Count on it."

They were back in the conference room, now that the fighting was over, but it was far more subdued than the wrangling of their previous meeting. Even Barnett seemed a little less inclined to pick unnecessary fights. The man looked jumpy now, as if he were afraid that nomads might burst through the door any time.

He spared a glance for Captain Hawley. The older officer had lapsed back into apathy now that the immediate danger was over. The comparison between Hawley bending over the fallen legionnaire with pistol in hand and this more familiar figure slumped carelessly in his chair aroused strong emotions in Fraser, but he wasn't sure which was more powerful, pity or disgust.

Fraser closed his eyes, remembering the captain leading the armed civilians back onto the roof. They had come just in time, as Garcia and Fraser had been running out of ammo. By the time the defense was weakening again, Gunnery Sergeant Trent and two lances of recon troops had reached the building. Not long afterward, the natives had retreated.

But they'd left their mark on the Sandcastle. Medical teams were still counting the casualties and treating the injured, while the rest of the Legion checked damage to the walls and strengthened the defenses. He'd ordered Kelly to take charge of the work instead of returning to the meeting, but now he regretted not being able to bounce ideas off her.

She was one of the few people in the Sandcastle he could use as a sounding board.

"The measures we are taking now should prevent a recurrence," DuValier was saying. He alone of all the officers in the room seemed unaffected by the native attack.

"Here, perhaps," Fraser said, looking at the cold, self-contained lieutenant. The contrast with Hawley's Exec, Susan Gage, was startling. She had come back from the fighting with a haunted look in her eyes, and she had contributed nothing to the discussion. "Deploying heavy-weapons lances with the troops on watch and rigging up some strongpoints on the walls should keep the wogs at arm's length. But we have two other problems to address." He turned to study Sigrid Jens.

She shifted uncomfortably. "We had no idea the nomads could field that kind of a force," she said. "Obviously this puts a whole new complexion on the Project. I will issue orders for the recall of the *Cyclops.*"

"You can't!" Barnett said sharply. "It'll finish the Project."

She shrugged. "Maybe. And us with it, as far as Seafarms is concerned. But the safety of the Terran personnel on Polypheme is my responsibility, Edward, and I'm not putting those people at risk. We may still be able to salvage the Project, but only after we've figured out a way to deal with the nomad threat."

"I'm glad you feel that way, Citizen," Fraser said, cutting off whatever reply Barnett had been about to come back with. "But at this point *Cyclops* is only part of the problem."

"How do you mean?" she asked, lifting one eyebrow in surprise.

"I think you should pull out of the Seafarms facilities in Ourgh as well," he said. "Everything should be centered here at the Sandcastle. The danger in the city is probably far worse than aboard the ship."

"This is ludicrous!" Barnett exploded. "We can't possibly relocate our entire operation. And there's no reason for it! The nomads won't attack Ourgh, even with rocket guns. Damn it, there's enough militia in town to handle any nomad clan without even calling up the off-duty reserves!"

Fraser leaned forward and rested his elbows on the table. "First of all, Citizen Barnett, those nomads could go through the Ourgh militia faster than a nova takes out planets. They damn near beat us, and the Legion isn't some useless loke mob. Second, don't assume the nomads are operating with the same clan structure as they used to have.''

''Now, wait a moment, Captain Fraser,'' Jens said. ''I understand your concern, but our studies have shown that the nomad clans cannot work together. They are simply incapable of accepting leadership from outside the Clan grouping, and the concepts of a committee or ruling council are completely foreign to them.''

''The city-dwellers understand them well enough,'' Trent commented.

''Yes, Sergeant, they do,'' Jens said. ''But land- and sea-dwelling cultures on Polypheme are totally different, almost like they were separate species.''

''The point is,'' Fraser said, ''That they *aren't* completely different. The city-dwellers were an offshoot of the nomads, and they evolved new cultural standards to respond to different needs. Mr. Koenig, my Native Affairs specialist, has been studying the wogs for a long time, and his feeling is that the nomad cultures could learn to work together if they found it necessary, particularly if a charismatic warlord were to unite them against an outside threat.''

''Like the city-dwellers,'' Gunnery Sergeant Valko said. ''Or us.''

''This is all pure speculation,'' Barnett protested. ''Theory. The tribal tattoos on those natives were all the same. I don't know which Clan—''

''Reef-Swimmers,'' Susan Gage said softly. It was the first time she'd spoken, and the comment was offered diffidently.

''All right, the Reef-Swimmers Clan,'' Barnett said. ''One group. No sign of some kind of coalition.''

''No direct proof, yet,'' Fraser agreed. ''But consider this. Just a few hours ago the *Seafarms Cyclops* was attacked by nomads. Watanabe's report didn't include the name of the Clan—it isn't one of the ones we've studied like the Reef-Swimmers—but the follow-up should have more information. Point is, it's a different tribe, but using the same weaponry.''

Trent looked up. ''And even more important, the same tactics,'' he added.

''Exactly,'' Fraser said with an approving nod. ''The

same tactics. Up until today no nomad Clan would break off an attack while there was still a perceived threat to other Clan members. Today two different groups, hundreds of kilometers apart, suddenly demonstrated this new idea. No way it was independently developed, Citizen . . . no way at all.''

''So you suspect an overall leadership,'' Jens summed up.

''Right. One that has made contact with an off-planet source of armaments. I don't know if the tactics are a local innovation or something these helpful suppliers suggested, but I'll bet damned near any stakes you want that there's a central authority, probably a group of lokes, behind these attacks. And several native Clans working in harness together could wipe out Ourgh without even bothering to stop for a breather afterwards.''

''Not all of them carry the high-tech stuff,'' Barnett pointed out.

''That's about all that saved us today. They attacked before they were fully equipped. Probably the nomads are over-eager. Even if the Semti were controlling them, I doubt the nomads would be very easy to control. They've got new toys.''

''So they want to use them,'' Jens said.

Fraser nodded. At least she was getting it. Her assistant still looked stubborn.

''How can you be sure the nomads would attack us in the city? Aside from the slaving raids, the nomads haven't tried to take on the city culture openly before. Their interests don't coincide.''

''Right now nomad interests seem to involve us,'' Trent pointed out. ''And if we've got people in Ourgh . . .''

''That's not the only factor,'' Fraser said quietly. ''You all heard what Houghan!! had to say before the battle. The city-dwellers think we're dealing with both sides, and cutting them out of the weapons deals.''

''But that's nonsense,'' Barnett protested.

''Sure. But look at it from their point of view. The emissary they sent to protest about the weapons isn't coming back. And they only have our word that he was killed by a nomad while trying to help Captain Hawley.'' Fraser paused, steepled his fingers, and rested his forehead on them wearily. ''We lost a lot of good men today, but Houghan!!'s death really turns what should have been a victory into a major defeat. The Council in Ourgh won't trust us again, and the mood in the city is already swinging against us because we won't provide protection."

"Meaning?" Hawley asked, finally seeming to be aware of the discussion.

"Meaning, Captain, that in one stroke we've lost our last chance to recruit ourselves some sepoys to build up our troop strength, and also lost Ourgh as a safe haven. That riot I was in will look like a picnic when the lokes really start getting organized." He turned to Jens. "Once again, there just aren't enough legionnaires to cover your facilities and people in town. We have to concentrate out here, where we won't be overextended."

"You make a convincing case, Captain Fraser," Jens said with a trace of a smile. She glanced at Barnett. "Perhaps if I'd been given advice like this from the start we wouldn't be in this mess now."

"You're not going to buy this?" Barnett was out of his chair, his face flushed. "We've got to keep the port and the warehouses open!"

"That's enough, Edward," Jens said flatly. Her tone made it clear she wasn't listening to any more arguments. She turned back to Fraser. "If you'll assign an officer as liaison, we'll try to work out an evacuation plan that will meet all our needs. Military as well as corporate."

Fraser leaned back in his chair, relief draining the tension from his shoulders. He hadn't been sure anyone connected with Seafarms would listen to reason. "Thank you, Citizen Jens. Your cooperation will make this a lot easier."

He looked down the table for a moment. "Captain Hawley, if you can spare your Exec for a while I think she'd be a good choice for this."

Hawley shrugged. "If you think she can do the job, by all means, Captain."

"All right, then. Citizen, if you and Lieutenant Gage can get on this right away, we'll start the evacuation as soon as I'm sure the Sandcastle is secured. And I'll also need you to give the orders for the *Cyclops*. . . ."

"I know you have a low opinion of us, Captain," she said with another smile. "But please don't worry. We really are on your side, and when I say we'll cooperate, I mean to follow through."

As the meeting broke up Fraser remained in the chair, frowning, his eyes focused somewhere past the far wall. For now Seafarms would go along with what he said, but there was no guarantee that Jens would keep cooperating once the immediate threat had passed.

If this turned into a long siege, the civilians were likely to be the weak link in the chain. He wondered if their enemies, whoever they were, realized that time was as valuable to their cause as all the rocket guns on Polypheme?

If the Legion was forced entirely on the defensive they were all as good as dead.

The blackness was like a lake, deep and cold, and Mike Johnson was at the bottom of it. He struggled against unseen forces, fighting his way to the surface, back to light and warmth and air.

His eyes snapped open suddenly, relieved to see the harsh artificial glare of floodlights against the darkening sky.

He was on a stretcher, his arms and legs strapped down firmly. A large, bulky regen unit was attached to his left leg, humming faintly and making the skin tingle. He couldn't feel anything else, and when he tried to move the foot nothing happened.

Panic welled up inside. A regen unit accelerated the natural healing process, but its effectiveness in cases of major nerve damage was limited, and no one had found a way yet to regrow a lost limb.

A rich Terran who lost a leg could have a cyberlimb fitted, but a poor legionnaire on a backwater like Polypheme would be lucky to get an old-fashioned prosthetic job. Johnson knew ex-legionnaires missing arms and legs who had never received the therapy and retraining it took to use an artificial limb. They ended up as penniless beggars hanging around colonial street corners or systerm bars.

He tried to sit up, but the straps held him down. "Hey! Help me, dammit!' he shouted. "For God's sake . . ."

"Calm down, my son," a soothing voice answered. It was Father Fitzpatrick, known throughout Bravo Company simply as "the Padre," the unit's chaplain. More than half of the legionnaires stationed on Polypheme were Catholics, and although Fitzpatrick's branch of the Church—based on Freehold, a world which had been cut off from all contact with Terra during the Shadow Centuries—did not recognize the primacy of the Pope in Rome, he took care of their spiritual needs quite well.

Johnson was technically a Protestant and paid little enough attention to religion anyway, but the Padre's easy smile and gentle voice were reassuring nonetheless.

"Father . . . my leg. I can't move my leg. Is it . . . Will it be. . . ?"

Fitzpatrick knelt beside him and examined the diagnostic readout on the front panel of the regen unit. He necessarily spent a lot of time helping the company's medical specialist, Dr. Ramirez, and he knew his way around Legion medical gear and facilities. "It's all right, my son," he said in his quiet voice. "The unit has administered a local nerve block for the pain. You can feel a tingle, can't you?"

Johnson nodded.

"Then you're fine, my son. You'll be off your feet for a while, but you'll still have both of them when you recover." A smile creased the round, open features. "I've seen soldiers who did more damage tripping over each other after a rough night on the town."

Forcing himself to relax, Johnson sighed gratefully. "Thanks, Father. I . . . I was afraid . . ."

"No need to tell me, my son. Fear is not on any of the lists of sins I've seen."

"Have you . . . have you seen Legionnaire Elise Delandry, Father? She's a medic. She was helping me after . . . after I was hit."

Fitzpatrick nodded gravely. "She has been helping Dr. Ramirez with triage. I'll tell her you asked for her." He was gone before Johnson could thank him again, moving among the other wounded men who surrounded him. He tried to count the litters, but by the time he reached twenty he felt himself slipping back into oblivion.

Lieutenant Antoine Duvalier spotted the Padre kneeling by one of the wounded and crossed the open ground to join him. Fitzpatrick bowed his head in prayer, sketched the Cross, and straightened up slowly.

After a long moment the chaplain signaled to a medic. "Private Conneau is dead," he told the man. The soldier nodded, but didn't show much emotion. In the middle of all this suffering, one more death didn't cause much of a stir.

But DuValier felt the pain. Quietly, from behind the Padre, he said, "Conneau was a good man. He told me once that his parents were from Toulon before they emigrated to Devereaux."

Fitzpatrick gave a start, surprised by his silent approach. Then he recovered. "Toulon was where you were born, was it not?"

He nodded. "How bad is it?" he asked, his gesture taking in the casualties.

"Not good. A lot of men will be taking the dirt today." Many legionnaires took the soil from the graves of comrades, carrying a few grains of dirt from each planet on which they'd left brothers-in-arms. "I haven't heard a full count yet."

"This should never have happened," DuValier said harshly. He paused to rein in his emotions, further irritated that he had allowed his control to slip in the sight of the Padre. But Fitzpatrick just nodded solemnly and moved toward the next casualty in the line, leaving DuValier alone with his bitter thoughts.

For two years he'd been locked in a downward spiral, his career ruined. No one but the Legion would accept an officer with his record, so it was to the Legion he had come for his last chance to change his luck. DuValier had vowed that this time, *this* time he would not let himself give in to weakness. He would do what he had to do, no matter what stood in his way. But it wasn't easy.

And his superior, the man who commanded Bravo Company, just made the struggle that much harder. Colin Fraser . . .

The fighting in the compound had brought DuValier face to face with all the old memories again, and he knew the nightmares would start again tonight. The horrors of Fenris were never far below the surface in any case, but being under fire again had brought back every terrible moment.

Two years now since the rebellion on Fenris, two years since the orders to the 33rd Mobile Response Regiment to search out the suspected nest of rebels in Loki Province. They'd been issued detailed intelligence reports describing specifics on rebel strengths and probable deployments, and the Colonel had worked out the sweep in detail. It should have been routine.

But the reports were based on faulty data and sloppy interpretation, and the rebel strength had been nearly twice what they'd been led to expect. And they had far more anti-air and anti-armor capability than the 33rd planned on.

DuValier could still remember that day. He had been a

freshly promoted lieutenant then, in charge of the rear guard. That was what had saved him—along with less than eighty soldiers out of a regiment of over eight hundred men. All because of the intelligence screw-up.

All because of one Colin Fraser, then also a lieutenant in the regulars but now, ironically, a hero, a captain, and Antoine DuValier's new CO.

He viewed the accounts of the court-martial in a vidmagazine, both the initial stories where Fraser put the blame on his superior, Major St. John, and the later interviews with Senator Warwick, that uncovered the plot to hurt the senator through St. John, all hinging on Fraser's testimony. Warwick's opponents had protected Fraser from the blame, then swept him under the table afterward. Why else would he be in the Legion now? If he was blameless, he'd still be in some comfortable staff job.

DuValier had suffered for two years, messed up too many assignments because of his personal problems. He had transferred to the Legion in hopes of making a fresh start, but somehow he'd been tapped to fill the vacant Exec's position in Fraser's company after the Hanuman campaign. He was sure Fraser knew nothing of his record, and so far he'd kept a tight lid on his feelings.

For a few minutes it had looked like Fraser had died, and it had been a shock to find out that he was alive after all. Thoughts of killing Fraser had crossed his mind once or twice, but he couldn't give in. He'd never accomplish his goal if he murdered a superior officer.

But if the man died in battle . . .

He pushed the thought away. A time or two he'd come close to sharing his doubts with Fitzpatrick, but it was something he couldn't bring himself to talk about. He was probably closer to the chaplain than he was to any other man in Bravo Company, but his past wasn't something he wanted to share . . . and neither was his hatred of Colin Fraser. Fitzpatrick wouldn't understand that, anyway. He'd been on Hanuman, regarded Fraser as a hero. Just like the others who'd served with the man before.

DuValier looked at the bodies littering the compound. If the Padre knew how he felt about Fraser he'd be shocked, and DuValier would lose a friend. That was one casualty he wasn't going to give up to the murderer who'd destroyed the 33rd on Fenris.

# Chapter 9

Superb men, but the scrapings of every nation, an amalgam of every state, of every profession, of every social calling who have come to join one another and many of them to hide.

—Lieutenant Arnaud-Jacques Leroy Constantine
French Foreign Legion, 1837

"Feels good to be back where we belong, huh, Spear?" Corporal Selim Bashar asked, as he powered up the magrep fields aboard the M-980 Sabertooth FSV. "I mean, those veeters are okay, but I'd rather be in the *Angel* any time, wouldn't you?"

The voice in his headphones grunted a distracted response, and Bashar frowned. Spiro Karatsolis was the best friend Bashar had in the Legion, maybe the best friend he'd ever had, and he was sensitive to the Greek legionnaire's moods.

They'd met during basic training on Devereaux, two nubes surprised to find that they came from the same homeworld, New Cyprus, though everything else about them was different. Bashar had come from a city background, his father a wealthy merchant shocked by his only son's desire to join the Colonial Army. His father's resistance and a desire for adventure had driven Bashar to the Legion, where he could start fresh, beyond even his father's long reach.

But Karatsolis had come from a poor background, growing up on a farm raising the sheep that were the only Terran livestock that had adapted to New Cyprus. For the Greek kid's family, military service was a way for the boy to better himself, and the Legion the service of choice because other family members had served with the unit in times past. From background to ethnic heritage to goals and desires, the two young soldiers hadn't shared much in common, but still they'd gravitated toward one another.

Since earning the *kepi blanc,* Bashar and Karatsolis had managed to stay together, first in a regular infantry unit, then through specialist training and assignment to a Legion Transport Company. They'd soldiered together on more planets than Bashar cared to recall. On Hanuman they'd lost the battle-scarred Sabertooth Karatsolis and christened *Angel of Death,* but they had weathered the long march. The Greek had even saved Bashar's life. That was nothing unusual, of course; they'd been pulling each other out of danger since the first day of recruit training. Danger was something Bashar and Karatsolis thrived on, though of course like any veteran legionnaire neither would admit it.

Now they had a new Sabertooth, the *Angel II,* and enough danger on the horizon to keep a whole division of bored legionnaires happy. But Karatsolis had been withdrawn ever since Bashar had returned to the Sandcastle in response to orders recalling the Transport Section to prepare a major convoy to carry out the evacuation of offworlders from Ourgh. Since the riot in town, something had happened to disturb the normally cheerful Greek.

Karatsolis had been in a battle, of course, and by all accounts he'd been as close to death as he'd ever been. Rumors were already flying around the unit that the Greek was being recommended for the Commonwealth Legion of Merit for seizing an enemy rocket launcher and turning it on the wogs at the critical moment in the battle, and Bashar believed what he'd heard. Captain Fraser would be quick to recognize any legionnaire who deserved it.

What was bothering Karatsolis, then? Bashar wasn't sure, and that realization worried him almost as much as his friend's all too obvious pain.

"Roundup Escort, Roundup Escort, this is Alpha Two," a new voice crackled in his headphones. "Status check."

"Alpha Two, Roundup Escort," Bashar replied, using the call sign selected for the FSV for Operation Roundup, the evacuation mission. "Receiving you five by five. Power at maximum charge. All diagnostics nominal."

"Confirmed, Roundup Escort." Lieutenant Gage sounded tired and worried. Bashar shrugged the thought off. The responsibility of putting together the entire mission, and the problems of making several hundred civilians cooperate once it was ready, would be enough to make anyone sound frayed. "Estimate time of departure at 1730 standard."

Bashar entered the time on his computer terminal. "On the board, Lieutenant," he replied. "You set 'em up, we'll knock 'em down."

"Standby, Escort," was Gage's flat response. The command circuit went dead. Bashar could picture her in the command APC, a variant on the ubiquitous Sandray design filled with computer and communications gear, running through a careful check of each vehicle's status before giving the orders to depart the Sandcastle. She was a competent, careful Exec.

But he couldn't help but wish that Captain Fraser or Gunny Trent was in charge. He still remembered Hanuman. Gage was a good officer, but Bashar had trouble envisioning her handling a hannie attack in the middle of the jungle.

He leaned back in the driver's seat and cut in the intercom circuit. "Hey, Spear," he said carelessly. "If we're pulling an evac maybe we'll get to carry Katrina. She was real grateful for the ride on the veeter yesterday. I mean, *real* grateful." Actually the girl from the riot, Katrina Voskovich, hadn't said more than four words from the time she got aboard, but Bashar needed something to get the banter started up.

Karatsolis didn't rise to the bait. "I got a fault on my tracking scope, Basher," he said. "Give me another diagnostic on sensors, will you?"

Bashar sighed and punched the appropriate orders into the computer. Between the Greek and Lieutenant Gage, his own morale was starting to crack.

Floodlights held back the darkness and glinted harshly off the hulls of the vehicles parked in the center of the Sandcastle's open courtyard. Looking around at the preparations for the convoy into Ourgh, Colin Fraser felt a tug of guilt. He would have preferred to take charge of the evacuation himself. The idea of letting someone else take responsibility for such a difficult undertaking was still hard to deal with.

He almost smiled at the memory of a similar problem back on Hanuman. That time he had wanted to take command of a rear-guard party, but Gunny Trent had convinced him that his duty lay in organizing the Legion's withdrawal from a beleaguered fort. Now, just when his experience would have counted for something, he was stuck back here in the Sandcastle.

This time it had been Kelly, not Trent, who pointed out where his responsibilities were. For all intents and purposes he was in command—Captain Hawley, despite the flash of energy he had chosen rescuing the old sapper during the battle, was obviously unable or unwilling to exercise his authority—and the CO had to remain in the command center and coordinate the overall operation.

There were Sandcastle defenses to put into order, recon drones to watch, contingency plans to be made, and though these could be done from the Sandray command van if necessary, they required his full attention.

But knowing that she was right didn't make it any easier to accept.

The convoy didn't inspire much confidence. When the legionnaires had been assigned to Polypheme, no one had envisioned much need for mobile operations. The transport section attached to the demi-battalion, sixteen men and ten vehicles before the nomad attack, wasn't even sufficient to lift out a full company of a hundred and ten soldiers. There was only one Sabertooth fire support vehicle, a command van, two veeters, four standard Sandray APCs, and a pair of cargo vans. Those would carry fifty passengers in reasonable comfort, or perhaps twice that number under emergency conditions.

To make up the difference between the hundred people the Legion vehicles could hold and the estimated eight hundred plus workers, technicians, dependents, and other Commonwealth civilians in Ourgh, they would need to press every Seafarms vehicle into service, right down to the starport's magrep forklifts. Jens had also promised that a barge-like contraption used in outfitting the *Cyclops* would have magrep modules fitted in time for the evacuation. It would be able to hold cargo and perhaps ninety more people, but it would have to be towed. That could be dangerous, especially if there was trouble in Ourgh.

For all of that it would still require at least two trips to get everyone out, especially since they'd have to take up some of the available passenger space with troops to guard the civilians and whatever equipment and personal effects they brought out. Edward Barnett had argued against sending legionnaires—apparently he was more afraid that they'd decide to loot the Terran Enclave than he was of native intervention—but Jens had overruled him. It looked like the woman really was ready to let the Legion take charge now.

That made him think of the *Seafarms Cyclops.* True to her word, Jens had ordered the ship's captain to head for the Sandcastle, but it was a trip that would take several days. When Fraser had spoken to Watanabe, he'd come away with the feeling that the young subaltern was relieved to be on the way back. Hopefully, the nomads wouldn't try any more attacks on the extractor ship, but Fraser knew he couldn't count on it.

Those nomads were showing enough of a grasp of tactics to know that they'd be best served by picking the Terrans apart while they were separated. The next few standard days would be the most dangerous.

Gunnery Sergeant Valko was outside the command van, nodding sagely as he reviewed a compboard with a worried-looking civilian in a Seafarms coverall. The NCO looked up at Fraser's approach and saluted smartly.

"What's the word, Gunny?" Fraser asked him, forcing an encouraging smile.

The sergeant didn't smile back. "On schedule, sir," he said slowly. Valko was a man who weighed his words and his decisions before he committed himself. "I see no major problems as long as the civilians hold their end up."

The Seafarms man flushed and looked away. Like many of the more hard-bitten legionnaires, Valko didn't bother to hide the fact that he had as much contempt for civilians as people like Barnett had for the Legion.

But friction between the military and civilian organizations could undermine the security of the Sandcastle in the days ahead.

"I'm sure everything will be ready, Gunny," he said firmly. "And if not, I'm sure that you'll be able to work things out." He nodded toward the van. "Is Lieutenant Gage aboard?"

"Yes, sir," Valko replied. He rapped on the rear door, then moved off with the civilian in tow as the ramp dropped. A young legionnaire, probably fresh out of the training center on Devereaux, blinked at Fraser in surprise. "S-sir?"

"I'd like to see the lieutenant, son," Fraser said. As the soldier disappeared into the bowels of the APC he suppressed a smile. He wasn't really that much older than the legionnaire, but lately he'd been feeling distinctly paternal. *A few more years and I'll sound just like any other gruff old officer,* he thought.

Lieutenant Gage came out of the command van's center compartment, where the $C^3$ gear was housed. Her face was creased into a dark frown. "You wanted to see me, Captain?" she asked.

Fraser nodded, feeling distinctly uneasy. Concern was plain on her face, in her voice, and that sort of thing could be contagious. "Just to see you off, Lieutenant," he said, trying to sound confident and at ease. "Valko tells me everything's going smoothly."

"So far, sir," she said. "But I'm still not certain how to handle things if the Council in Ourgh gets nasty. If you or Captain Hawley were along . . ."

"Let Citizen Jens worry about the Council," Fraser told her. "She's been dealing with them since before we got here, and I think you can trust her judgment. You stick with handling the technical side of the evacuation. Captain Hawley and I have full confidence in you."

A flicker of anger clouded her features. Fraser wondered if he was sounding too patronizing, or if she was reacting to his reference to Hawley. No doubt she knew that Hawley hadn't expressed any such sentiment. Alpha Company's captain hardly noticed what his Exec did to keep the unit running. Fraser had never heard him utter a word of praise—or of reproof, for that matter. Hawley simply didn't care.

"Keep a close eye on your people," he went on, changing the subject. "We can't afford a lot of conflict with Seafarms, so don't let anybody decide the civilians are being uncooperative if it's really just a case of a murphy getting out of hand."

She nodded. "I'll do my best, sir."

"Good." Fraser hesitated before going on. "And if you need help, we'll do everything we can from this end."

"Thank you, sir," she responded, voice carefully neutral.

"Is Citizen Jens on board?"

"No, sir," Gage said. "She took a floatcar back to Ourgh to start putting things in motion there. Her assistant's with her, too."

He fought back a twinge of irritation. It would have been better if Jens and Barnett had stayed to coordinate the civilian side of the operation more closely with the Legion, but probably that had been too much to expect. Although Jens now seemed willing to go along with his suggestions, she was still the same decisive executive she'd been all along, and her temperament wasn't well suited to waiting when there was something she could be doing.

As she gave Gage a final salute and let her return to work, Fraser found himself thinking how much he and the Seafarms Project Manager had in common. He still wished he could join Operation Roundup himself.

Sigrid Jens cocked her head to one side and focused on the information coming in from the floatcar's computer by way of the tiny implant in her brain. It was a curious sensation to be hurtling through the dark night, only a few centimeters above the angry water, in the small magrep vehicle, with her full attention focused entirely on statistics, progress reports on the dismantling of the corporate office in Ourgh, and dozens of other pieces of highly technical information.

The unaided human mind could never have juggled so much data even without the distraction of the floatcar's high-speed motion. With the computer implant linking her to the onboard terminal and, via microwave link, to the master computer system at the corporate office building near the starport, she had complete access to everything in the files, from personnel records to specs on all Seafarms equipment. The computer could turn her thoughts into voice communications by way of any computer terminal or portable compboard or wristpiece hooked into the Seafarms network.

An implant was power, real power on a frontier world, not just the fashionable status symbol it had become on Terra. They were scarce out here—the only other one on Polypheme belonged to Captain Hawley—and they were valuable in direct proportion to that scarcity.

Thinking of Hawley made her grimace in distaste. How could a man have an implant and waste its potential on pointless games? Hawley was as bad as the addicts who sold their souls for some pornographic dreamchip. Too bad Fraser didn't have an implant: He was a man who would know how to use it.

Beside her, Barnett spoke for the first time since they'd left the Sandcastle, evidently taking her grimace as a sign that she'd finished her computer work. "I still think this is a bad move," he said.

"You've made that clear, Edward," she told him. "But I think the legionnaires made some valid points, and I have the final say."

She glanced at him. Barnett looked pale, nervous, as if he were afraid of something. What?

"We're perfectly safe in Ourgh," he insisted. "Why uproot everything and everyone, because some paranoid legionnaire wants to play at being some kind of big hero?"

She cut the mental connection with the main computer and sighed. "I'm not going to keep having this argument with you, Edward. The evacuation goes through, and so does the recall order on *Cyclops*. If you want a future with this company, you'll stop trying to second-guess me. Got it?"

Barnett subsided, suddenly meek. "Yes, ma'am." He paused. "But this mess could mean the end of the company anyway."

Silence followed. Jens contemplated her assistant with a trace of guilt. She knew his background: his parents killed in a border clash with the Ubrenfars, raised in an orphanage on New Atlanta, apprenticed to the Reynier Industries work-training program at age sixteen. Barnett had worked his way up to a position of responsibility despite a lack of formal education and all the attendant handicaps that had conspired to keep him back. His whole life centered on the drive to find security, and the company meant everything to him. Her threat must have cut deep.

She opened her mouth to apologize, but at that moment her implant signaled urgently for her attention. Although it was entirely computer-generated and quite inaudible, her brain interpreted the input as a tone as loud and clear as the whistle of the wind past the floatcar.

Jens focused her mind on the implant and mentally pronounced the code that established the computer link. At once she seemed to hear a voice, the dispassionate words of the computer system back at the Sandcastle. "Departure of Legion convoy at 1730 standard hours. Estimated time of arrival, Ourgh, 1815 standard hours."

So it had started. She acknowledged the signal but kept the computer link intact. There was still a lot of work to do if this evacuation was going to be carried out smoothly.

* * *

Warrior-Scout !!Dhruuj listened to the sound of rushing water and extended his eyestalks above the surface to investigate. The tide was ebbing slowly, but that had nothing to do with what he was hearing.

He remembered the Strangers-Who-Brought-Gifts telling the Warrior-Scouts about the huge mechanical pumps that drew water into the center of the Built-Reef. They created an artificial tide that could flood or empty the interior of the Built-Reef at will, allowing the Strangers to enter or leave without sending an uncontrollable rush of water through the gates as they opened.

Then the Strangers-Within were preparing to leave! Surely that was important.

He waited.

The sounds died away, and then a harsh, mechanical noise filled the water: grating, wholly unnatural, and alien. The gates rolled slowly apart.

As !!Dhruuj had expected, there was water inside the Built-Reef now. He watched expectantly for swimmers to leave, but instead saw an ungainly shape riding on—no, actually it was *above*—the waves. More followed, each large enough to hold many swimmers. Some carried devices that looked much like the far-reach weapons the Clan was using, and one mounted a pair of deadly-looking rocket shapes.

Weapons. The Stranger-Warriors were leaving the Built-Reef in force, well armed.

That might create opportunities the War-Leader-of-Clans would want to exploit.

!!Dhruuj croaked two signals, one to the other Clan scouts who waited among the rocks closer to the land, the other directed at the War-Leader-of-Clans himself.

He felt a burning pride. The Clan would be that much safer for his actions . . . and the Strangers-Within far more at risk.

# Chapter 10

Make every shot count. Each one you kill now will be one less to fight tomorrow.

Commandant Jean-Michel Soubiran,
to the guerrillas on Devereaux
Fourth Foreign Legion, 2729

Subaltern Leonid Narmonov flipped down the faceplate of his helmet and called up the light intensifier display. Details of the dark streets of Ourgh suddenly became as clear as if he had switched on a searchlight.

The planet's slow rotation made the nights seem endless. More than fifteen hours had passed since the nomad attack on the fort, and that had been just after sunset. It was still night, and would be for several more hours.

Nights that lasted close to a full standard day were just another petty irritation of life on Polypheme under normal circumstances, another strangeness that drove men to *le cafarde*. But this night was worse, far worse.

"Sergeant," Narmonov said, keying in his private comm channel to his platoon NCO. "I want the recon lance to check out those lights on the northeast perimeter."

"Sir!" Platoon Sergeant William Carstairs always sounded like the stereotypical noncom from an old historical holovid. Rumor in the platoon claimed he had been an actor before joining the Legion, a victim of the decline in live-action entertainment now that dreamchips and other computer-generated diversions had taken over such a large share of the market. Narmonov could believe the stories. Carstairs had a flair for the dramatic gesture. But he made an efficient platoon sergeant nonetheless.

He studied the flickering lights through the image-intensifier, but the range was too great to allow the system to resolve many details. He thought the light was coming from torches, and it looked like a large number of wogs were moving around. Hopefully his recon specialists could give him a better estimate of the threat, if any.

The evac had already run into more than enough glitches. Seafarms people had been ready enough to move out, but it had turned out that they had a lot more equipment and cargo to send to the Sandcastle than anyone originally had planned for. Two full loads of evacuees had already left Ourgh, and the third was gathering on the starport field in anticipation of the convoy's return. The extra time meant exposing legionnaires and civilians alike to the dangers posed by the natives.

And those dangers were getting stronger with each passing hour. An angry delegation of Elders had come to the port making demands. Narmonov hadn't been present during the meeting, but the rumors spreading through Alpha Company hinted that the city-dwellers were accusing the Legion of withdrawing and leaving Ourgh at the mercy of the nomads. Apparently there were questions about the fate of their earlier envoy, too.

The Project Director and her assistant had gone to meet the Council face-to-face, over the objections of Lieutenant Gage. Despite the guarantees of safe-conduct offered by the lokes, the Lieutenant had been afraid it was a trap to take valuable hostages, but by all accounts she'd been unwilling to force the issue and risk friction with the civilians.

It sounded like an unwarranted risk to Narmonov. He wondered how Captain Fraser would have handled it.

If the Elders were turning hostile, how much longer would the dwindling human population be safe? He thought about the riot that had nearly killed Fraser, and shuddered.

Behind him Narmonov heard a low-pitched whine. He turned as the Toel shuttlecraft lifted off from the landing field, the only ship in port. Apparently they'd finally given in to arm-twisting by the Seafarms people to cut their commercial mission short. That was one less problem, at least. No one would have welcomed the Toels as refugees inside the Sandcastle. The Toels were a long way from popular in Commonwealth circles.

"Sir?" Carstairs said over the comm channel. "Sir, Corporal Haddad is in position. Do you want a verbal report or a vidfeed?"

Narmonov thought for a moment before replying. "I'll

take a vidfeed," he said at last. He motioned to Legionnaire Mattea, his C³ technician. "Link to Haddad," he ordered.

Seconds passed. Then, suddenly, his view of the spaceport faded as the helmet display switched over to showing the screen relayed by Corporal Haddad's camera.

Unlike Narmonov, Haddad was using infrared imaging, and the sudden shift was disorienting. Even processed through helmet-mounted microcomputers, the IR view was distinctly different from an LI display.

Torches flared bright over the mass of wogs. They were not obviously armed, nor did they appear especially agitated. Haddad's radio picked up their shouts and chants, but not clearly enough to allow Narmonov to translate.

It looked like nothing so much as a protest march, heading from the center of town in the general direction of the starport.

For now it was orderly enough, but a mob like that could easily turn violent.

"Corporal," Narmonov said. "Withdraw your lance to the port at once."

"Yessir," Haddad responded. The image on the faceplate display lurched abruptly, and Narmonov knew the corporal was turning to organize the five men in his unit.

Narmonov flipped up the faceplate. "Discontinue, Mattea," he ordered. Then, switching back to the command channel, he said "Sergeant Carstairs!"

"Sir!"

"Pass the word to the platoon to prepare for riot control."

"Yes, sir!"

"How's the work going along the perimeter fence?"

"Three more minutes," Carstairs replied. Narmonov had ordered some of his men to jury-rig a connection between the fence and the port's generator facilities. It wouldn't work for long, but in an emergency they could electrify the perimeter and buy some time.

But that would have to be a last resort. If there was an accident, the native reaction would be to turn actively hostile.

"Tell them to make it two minutes, Sergeant," he said. "But they're not to switch on until Lieutenant Gage or I give specific orders."

"Sir!"

Narmonov cut the transmission and turned back to Mattea. "Get me the Lieutenant," he said.

It would be a relief to let someone else start making the decisions.

"All right, Subaltern," Susan Gage said slowly. "You've done well. Keep monitoring the situation and report to me if anything changes. But do not engage the rioters unless absolutely necessary for the safety of the port or the evacuees. Understood?"

"Understood, Lieutenant," Narmonov's grave voice replied. She thought she could detect a trace of his native Russian accent. There was a joke in Alpha Company's officer's mess that Narmonov spoke better Terranglic than anyone else in the unit. He only showed traces of his Ukrainian boyhood when he was especially worried or distracted.

She thought he had every right to be worried. With the exception of Gage, Valko, and their $C^3$ specialist, Massire, Narmonov's platoon was the total Legion force available in Ourgh right now. And it was understrength, too, from the casualties they'd taken in fighting at the Sandcastle. If there was trouble now, twenty-six soldiers wouldn't buy the civilians much time.

"Good," she said at length. "Roundup Command, clear." She glanced across the command van at Legionnaire Massire. "ETA on the convoy?"

"Ten minutes, Lieutenant," the $C^3$ specialist told her. "Longer, if they have more trouble with that barge contraption." His teeth showed very white against his dark skin in the dim-lit compartment.

The barge that Seafarms had improvised had all the promised capacity, but one of the magrep generators was faulty. It had already broken down once, during the first trip out to the Sandcastle.

*Damn* the Seafarms people and their "extra equipment." If they'd been properly prepared, everyone would be safe back in the Sandcastle now. She'd been tempted to tell Jens to ditch the gear, but Fraser's instructions on keeping Seafarms happy had held her back. Now she was regretting the decision.

She remembered her feelings in the battle inside the Sandcastle, her horror as Bravo Company had been pinned.

If there were more casualties today, it would be her fault again.

*Damn* Seafarms!

That reminded her of Jens and Barnett. They had opted to stay with the Elders as long as possible in hopes of convincing them to stick with the Commonwealth. It was time to get them back to the port so they could come out with the rest of the evacuation.

"Get me the Project Director," she told Massire abruptly. As he bent to work at his communications console, she swiveled her seat to face Gunnery Sergeant Valko. "What do you think of putting up a recon drone to keep an eye on that crowd, Sergeant?" she asked.

"Good idea," Valko replied, nodding. "I'll get on it." He paused. "You may want to reroute the convoy through either the east or the south gate, Lieutenant. Just to keep them clear of the lokes."

Gage gave a nod. "Yeah. That makes sense." The first two convoys had come and gone through the main gate, the one that faced north toward Ourgh. It was larger, and with most of Narmonov's security concentrated on that side it made it easier to use. Now, though, there was too much chance of trouble. "We'll use the east side for now, but keep the south gate for a bolt-hole. Massire, I'll talk with Sergeant Franz while you're trying to raise Citizen Jens."

It didn't take long to update the Transport Section commander on the situation and order the change of route. When Franz acknowledged the orders, Gage leaned back in her chair, tapping her fingers on the armrest. The two executives were taking their time about answering Massire's call.

Damn them!

The commlink shrilled again, but Jens ignored it as she listened to the Elder with the missing eyestalk.

"Unsatisfactory! Unsatisfactory! None of your answers can be proven!" His words were echoed in English by a whisper only she could hear. Although she'd chipped advanced courses in the city-dweller dialect, Jens felt safer letting the computer translate.

The Elder sat down, and Jens formed the reply she wanted to make in her mind. The implant fed her a sentence that took into account not only the literal meaning of her reply, but subtleties of emotion and mood.

"Please, Reverend Ancient !Broor!, this is not fair. We have dealt in good faith from the beginning, Reverend Elders," she said slowly. "The Reverend Ancient Houghan!! accepted our words before he died. Fighting for us, for the safety of one of our people." Actually, Houghan!! had never said that he believed the Terrans, but Fraser's account of what had happened during the nomad attack made it clear that the Elder had recognized the Terrans as friends in the end.

"We have only your word for this," another council member said. "And for the hostility of the nomads to your kind, for that matter!"

Jens felt the anger surge inside her. "Then come to the Sandcastle and see the dead, damn it!" she flared, not bothering to wait for the computer to provide suitable words.

"And walk into a trap," !Broor! said flatly. He rubbed the scar where his missing eyestalk should have been. "Nomads did this to me thirty winters ago. I'm not giving you a chance to turn me over to them now, the way you did with Houghan!!."

The commlink shrilled again, and Jens looked down at it irritation. *Damn the legionnaires!* she thought. Couldn't they carry out the evacuation without bothering her with petty details every ten minutes?

"Your pardon, Honored Elders," she said with a sigh. She picked up the commlink. "Jens. What the hell do you want this time?"

Lieutenant Gage sounded as annoyed as Jens felt. "Pack it up and get back to the port, Citizen. The last load mags out of here in less than half an hour."

"That's not convenient," Jens said. "Can't you hold it up for a while longer?"

"There are rioters assembling outside the perimeter fence," Gage replied. "The longer we stay, the more likely we get involved in an incident nobody wants. We pull out as soon as everything's loaded."

"Then I'll follow in my floatcar with Edward when I'm done here."

"Negative, Citizen," the lieutenant said sharply. "My orders say everyone comes out now." There was a pause. "Please, Citizen, don't complicate this any further."

"If I leave now, we may never get the Elders to cooperate

again.'' She tried to keep a reasonable note in her voice. ''I'm sure Captain Fraser—''

''Lieutenant!'' someone's voice interrupted her, faint but distinct. ''Lieutenant, we have trouble on the north perimeter. Shots fired!''

''All right, that's it,'' Gage said firmly. ''We've got hostiles outside the port, Citizen. Get back here right away. No arguments!'' The channel went dead before Jens could frame a reply.

She glanced up at Barnett, then looked at the Elders arrayed at their semicircular table facing the two Terrans. ''Reverend Ancients,'' she said slowly, trying to find the most diplomatic way to end the meeting. ''I assure you again that the nomads are as much our enemies as they are yours. But it is clear that we cannot convince you of this tonight. As you know, my people are withdrawing to the old Toel base. We believe . . . We believe that the presence of Terrans in Ourgh may have much to do with the nomad attacks in this area. Perhaps once you have seen that they are concentrating on us instead of you there will be a chance to reach a new agreement.''

''They shouldn't be allowed to leave!'' one of the council members, somewhat younger than the rest of the Elders, shouted, slamming a fist on the table. ''Once the Terrans are safely out of the city they can launch the nomads against us without fear! Keep them here!''

!Broor! answered. ''No, Traur!, no. Let them leave. We will not be the ones to start hostilities, Terran, but we will be ready for any tricks you may use against us.'' He paused. ''I hope that you are telling the truth. But even if you are not helping our enemies, you have been poor friends. Any new agreement we make with you will have to redress the wrongs your people have done. Now go, before there is further trouble.''

Jens rose slowly, grateful that the old councilman was honorable despite his obvious distrust. ''I thank you, Reverend Ancient,'' she said. ''And I hope those wrongs can indeed be redressed.'' She looked at Barnett. ''We have to get back, Edward. Right away.''

As they left the Council Chamber Sigrid Jens wondered if there would be any way to make a fresh start with the natives on Polypheme. It was plain that Seafarms had underestimated the problems of dealing with the locals—perhaps fatally.

"Switch power to the fence!" Narmonov shouted. "Now, goddamn it! Now!"

Something whooshed in the distance, capped by a small thunderclap. "That sounded like a Fafnir, Sub," Corporal Haddad said.

"Yeah, or like one of those strakking rocket guns the wogs were using at the Sandcastle," another legionnaire added.

Narmonov keyed in his helmet commlink. "Chandbahadur! Are any of your men firing?"

Corporal Chandbahadur Rai, the little Gurkha who commanded one of the platoon's two heavy-weapons lances, answered promptly. "No, sir. We've had no orders to fire."

He knew that Chandbahadur's lance was the only unit that could have been using Fafnir missile launchers. The other heavy-weapons lance, commanded by Legionnaire First-Class Lynch, was helping to sort the Seafarms people among the convoy vehicles that had set down in the compound only a few minutes earlier.

"Maintain status," he ordered the Gurkha. Switching off the commlink, he shot a look at Carstairs. "It's not our people, Sergeant."

Carstairs had his faceplate down, so it was impossible to see his features. He was facing toward the sounds of the rockets, his whole body tense, straining. "Sir," the ex-actor said softly. "I've got a party of what look like nomads on the city wall, bearing three-five-four. They're firing into the crowd."

"Into the crowd!" Narmonov flipped to image-intensification and lined up on the bearing Carstairs has indicated. Several natives were clustered on top of the mud-and-stone wall. In the magnified firelight their tribal tattoos showed up plainly. As he watched, one raised a rifle and fired.

The projectile dipped before its rocket engine ignited, sending it into the civilian mob below.

"What the hell are they doing, Sub?" Haddad asked.

"Getting the townies to do their dirty work for them," Narmonov said slowly. He raised his faceplate. "If the city wogs don't know who's attacking, they're going to assume it's us. . . ."

"God," Carstairs breathed, his role forgotten for once.

"Where's your sniper, Haddad?" Narmonov asked the recon lance commander.

Haddad grinned wolfishly. "Killer! Time to go to work!"

Legionnaire Second-Class Arnold Kelso looked more like a scholar than a legionnaire, slender, almost meek, despite his battledress and field kit. But his deadly accuracy with the Whitney-Sykes HPLR-55 laser rifle had earned him his nickname. "What's the target, Corp?" he asked, as he joined the others at Narmonov's makeshift command post.

Haddad pointed out the nomads and Kelso nodded. Unfolding a bipod on the front of the laser rifle, he set it up carefully on an upended, empty cargomod and carefully scanned the nomad position through his helmet II gear. Then he plugged a lead into the rifle sights and into his helmet, feeding an electronic image directly to his faceplate display. Narmonov dropped his own faceplate back down.

It seemed to take forever before the man finally squeezed the trigger. There was a crackle, a tang of ozone as the laser beam ionized the air, but no flash or telltale beam. But a nomad on the wall suddenly fell, with a neat centimeter-wide hole punched directly through his braincase. An instant later a second nomad went down, then a third. The remaining natives scrambled for cover.

"Carstairs! Get to the vehicle park. I want spotlights turned on that position now. Got it?"

"Sir!" The sergeant left at a flat-out run. Searchlights might dazzle the wogs up there . . . and they might draw attention to the nomads, and defuse the mob before it got ugly.

Shouts echoed through the night, then crashes and a harsh crackling noise. A stench of burning meat made Narmonov choke on his rising gorge.

The rioters were attacking the fence. It was too late to turn them aside now.

"Forget the rest of the equipment," Lieutenant Susan Gage said. "Get everyone else on board the convoy now."

"I'll tell them, Lieutenant," Massire replied. "But I hope the Seafarms people don't screw it up."

Gunnery Sergeant Valko cleared his throat. "Would you

like me to explain it to them, ma'am?'' he asked with a predatory smile.

''Do it,'' Gage said shortly. The sergeant left the APC hurriedly. ''Massire, what's the status on Jens?''

''On their way, Lieutenant,'' he told her. ''But with that mob in the streets, they'll have to be careful.''

She rubbed an eye as she thought. ''Order Bashar and Karatsolis to break through the mob with their Sabertooth. Find Jens and get her party out of town. Abandon their floatcar—we don't need it for the evac now.''

''Got it, Lieutenant,'' Massire said, reaching for the communications panel again.

She turned to the monitor displaying the recon drone's view of the city. Viewed from above, the mob looked like some bizarre single-celled organism flowing hungrily toward the perimeter fence. So far the generators Narmonov had hooked up were still feeding power, and it was holding them back.

The southern side of the port was still clear of lokes. She hoped that the FSV could get out that way and circle around the worst of the mob. The alternative was unthinkable: letting the Legion vehicle cut through the rioters. It would be a massacre.

Gage prayed she wouldn't have to give the order that would trigger that bloodbath.

The south gate swung open to allow the Sabertooth to exit, and a legionnaire at the gatehouse leaned through the window to wave the vehicle through. Bashar gunned the rotors, raising a dust cloud as the FSV sped through.

They were out of the port.

The Terran enclave nestled on the south side of Ourgh, with the starport on the very edge of town. Beyond were farmlands leased by Seafarms, where local workers grew Terran foodstuffs under contract to the company. Bashar was happy to have some maneuvering room. On Hanuman, the last time he'd driven a Sabertooth in a combat situation, the dense jungles had been a major problem. Here, at least until he had to move back into the city, he could push the vehicle to the limit.

''Look sharp, Spear,'' he said over the intercom. ''The Lieutenant said there are nomads out here, and I don't want to tangle with them if I can help it.'' So far, their arsenal hadn't included anything that could threaten the Sabertooth, but if they had kept something more lethal in reserve . . .

"I'm watching on IR," Karatsolis replied. "And I've got a fix on the floatcar. Feeding to your terminal now."

"Thanks, man," Bashar said. That was the most the Greek had said since the start of the operation.

The trace for the floatcar lit up on a computer display map of Ourgh. Bashar nodded approvingly. The Seafarms vehicle was moving well, and it was headed for a gate in the city wall well clear of the fighting. That would make things easier.

"Targets! Targets!" Karatsolis warned sharply. "Straight ahead—range fifty meters!"

Bashar cursed as he wrenched the Sabertooth hard to the left. "Fifty meters! How the hell did you miss them?"

"They just popped out of nowhere!" Karatsolis said. "Damn it! More targets. Straight ahead at seven-five meters."

"Allah!" Bashar turned again and cut the vehicle's speed. "Go to LI and pop a flare, Spear."

The image on his external monitor changed subtly as the light-intensifier setting cut in. "Flare!" Karatsolis announced. The launcher at the rear of the FSV thumped.

A second later the flare glowed, not a harsh or particularly bright light, but a soft, steady radiance that was just enough to illuminate for the LI gear.

Bashar used a joystick to manipulate the external camera view. As he swung through a full circle around the Sabertooth, he heard a sharp intake of breath through his headphones. Karatsolis had seen the same thing he was looking at.

The farmlands were riddled with long, shallow pits, each one deep enough to conceal several wogs . . . and each one a potential obstacle to a magrep vehicle.

# Chapter 11

But I've a rendezvous with Death
At midnight in some flaming town.
—Legionnaire Alan Seeger
French Foreign Legion, 1916

Legionnaire Second Class Lin Wu-Sen raised his faceplate and nudged his lancemate in the ribs. "Hey, Reese, got a 'stick?"

"Come on, Lin." Legionnaire Third-Class George Reese sounded annoyed. "You know we're not allowed to smoke, man. We're on duty."

"Quit talking like a nube, Reese," Lin sneered. "Who's going to report me. You?"

"Convoy'll be coming out soon. . . ."

"Yeah, so this is my last chance. Come on, kid, hand 'em over."

With seeming reluctance, Reese slung his FEK and dug in his belt pouch for a packet of narcosticks. Lin took one and put it in his mouth.

"How about a light, kid?" he mumbled around the 'stick.

Reese produced a lighter, punched the recessed button, and waited a moment for the coil to heat up. As it started to glow red he held it up to the narcostick. Lin took a few trial puffs, savoring the heady taste of the smoke. They were against regs, of course, but narcosticks were popular with soldiers on boring garrison duty. They gave a man a lift without dulling his reactions. . . .

A bright streak cut through the night with a soft *whoosh*, and Reese flung the lighter away. But it was too late. The rocket projectile hit him squarely in the stomach and exploded. Reese staggered back, doubled over, and fell.

Lin flung himself to the ground, groping for the FE-MEK lance-support weapon he'd left leaning on the gatehouse wall. Another explosive bullet hit just behind where his head had been a moment before.

He spat out the narcostick and flipped his faceplate down, trying to assess the situation on IR. As he scanned the night, he hit the general comm channel. "First Platoon Alpha! East gate is under attack. Repeat, east gate under attack, probable nomad force!"

He thought he caught movement, and swung the MEK to cover it. He squeezed the trigger, hearing the deep-throated hum of the heavy kinetic-energy rifle as it spat needle rounds into the darkness.

Legionnaire Lin never saw the rocket that killed him.

"Nomad attack on the eastern perimeter, Lieutenant," the $C^3$ technician reported coolly. "No details. Sergeant Hooks is deploying First Platoon to check it out."

Susan Gage frowned. Subaltern Reynolds, First Platoon's CO, had been one of the first casualties in the Sandcastle fighting, and his platoon had taken the worst of Alpha Company's casualties. She hoped Hooks could handle the unexpected fighting without further support. There weren't enough legionnaires to go around.

"Tell Franz to leave by the south gate," she ordered. "And order Hooks not to get too heavily engaged. When we pull out, we're pulling out *fast.*"

As the $C^3$ tech turned back to his console, she swung the aerial recon drone around to the eastern side of the port to get a better look at the threat. The nomads had struck a little bit early, she thought with a grim smile. If they'd just waited a few minutes longer, they would have caught the convoy. But this way the Terrans had some warning, and the south gate was still open . . . at least, so far. And it would only be a few more minutes before they had the civilians ready to move.

Massire broke her train of thought. "Sergeant Valko says everything's ready, Lieutenant. He says, uh . . . he says, 'Let's mag the Topheth out of here.' "

She smiled at that. Valko was never hesitant about letting his superiors know what he thought. "Okay. General order, all units. Legionnaires to disengage and fall back. We'll keep the APCs back to pull them out. All other vehicles to move through the south gate. Once they're clear, top speed back to the Sandcastle."

She smiled again. Maybe, just maybe, she could pull off this operation after all.

"All units. All units. Convoy departing via south gate immediately. Legionnaires disengage and fall back on assembly point three. Roundup Two, Roundup Three, hold at assembly point to embark rear guard."

Bashar cursed as the voice crackled in his headphones. The nomads were thoroughly dug in down here, with traps and forces that would carve up the convoy with barely a pause. They couldn't withdraw this way.

He stabbed the comm button. "Roundup Leader, this is Escort. South gate exit is blocked, repeat blocked. Estimate three hundred nomad warriors with extensive fieldworks and traps in place. Do not use south exit."

Cutting the comm channel without waiting for a reply, Bashar spun the bulky Sabertooth in just over its own length and gunned the turbofans. "This is going to be bumpy, Spear," he said on the intercom. "Keep a watch for bad guys."

The fans roared, a sound that filled the cramped driver's compartment and threatened to drown out the attention signals from his control console. The light of the flare had faded, and Bashar shifted back to infrared.

"Targets ahead. Sixty-five meters." Karatsolis might have been a computer for all the emotion in his voice.

"Let 'em know we're not here to play around."

"Yeah." Barely a second passed before the Sabertooth's plasma cannon spoke. Superheated metal traced a blur across his forward monitor and hit the far edge of the wog pit. The natives still moving after the explosion were scattering. Karatsolis fired again.

The bow of the Sabertooth dipped suddenly as the leading edge of the magrep field hit the pit, but Bashar was ready for it. He increased the magrep field and stabilized the vehicle with a deft sweep of fingers over the control console. A moment later he made another adjustment as the vehicle climbed out of the other side.

It was easy enough for a driver ready for the problem. For the hodgepodge of vehicles and drivers in the convoy all trying to flee the port compound at high speed, though, it would have been a sure recipe for disaster.

For that matter, it could still be disastrous for the *Angel of Death II* if Bashar didn't stay alert. Or if Karatsolis didn't keep the wogs off-balance.

Something struck the side of the vehicle's hull and exploded, but the hull sensors reported minimal damage. Bashar fought the urge to relax and swerved to avoid another pit ahead.

He hoped his warning about the trap had come in time for the rest of the convoy.

Gage stared at the monitor in horror, seeing the pits, the small groups of nomads, and the trail of devastation left in the Sabertooth's wake. If it hadn't been for Bashar and Karatsolis the whole unit would have blundered into that trap, and damned few of them would have escaped it.

She'd committed one of the cardinal sins of command by not scouting out the escape route in advance.

*Now what?* she asked herself.

"Lieutenant?" Valko was back aboard the command van and looking at her quizzically. It took her a long moment to realize that she must have voiced her thoughts out loud.

"We have to get the hell out of here," she said. "But it looks like they've got us blocked. Any recommendations?"

Valko looked thoughtfully at the monitor. "The mess on the south side's too strakking thick to break through. I say we go for the east gate, like we originally planned."

"Even though it's under fire already?"

He stroked his thick mustache with hooded, thoughtful eyes. "It's all been too pat," he said slowly. "They stirred up the riots on the north side. Then we have an attack from the east, but I haven't seen much more than a few periodic rockets and a lot of noise. It looks to me like they're trying to herd us, Lieutenant. They want to encourage us to go out the south side."

Gage looked down at her console. "If they're really mounting an attack on the east gate, though . . ."

"They wouldn't waste all that strength to the south if their main thrust was coming from another direction," he argued. "Not even if they had extra troops to burn. If they had that kind of strength they'd launch simultaneous attacks, not play coy with the trap."

"We could knock down the fence and go out an unexpected direction. . . ."

"Some of the terrain out there is pretty rugged. Especially the west side, and that's the only place we haven't seen much activity. We'd lose that damned barge for sure.'' He paused. ''At least that would be better than trying the southern route.''

''But you're in favor of an east-side breakout.''

''Yes, ma'am,'' he said, suddenly formal. ''Perhaps on a broad front, like you suggested, instead of just pushing through the gate. Hit 'em hard enough and we'll punch right out.''

She wrestled with the choices, all too aware of how bad her judgment had been so far. Valko seemed convinced, and she trusted his instincts. . . .

''All right. That's what we'll do. But hold up the convoy until we can mount up most of our troops. We'll need them for firepower, since the Sabertooth's already busy.''

''That'll throw a lot of responsibility on whoever gets picked for rear guard,'' he pointed out.

''I know,'' she admitted. ''Do you think Narmonov's up to it?''

He nodded.

''Then let's get on it. And pray we don't run into anything else we didn't expect.''

''Fall back! Fall back!'' Narmonov was shouting, even though his commlink carried his words clearly to everyone in the platoon. He ducked as a crossbow bolt skimmed just over his head and scrambled toward the last line of defense

*''Hold as long as you can,''* his orders had said. In the face of the native mob, though, those orders were easier given than carried out.

The electrified fence had held them for a while, of course, and if the withdrawal had gone according to the original instructions the platoon could have disengaged easily. But with the delays and the sudden changes in plan, the platoon had been left hanging in air as the lokes smashed through the fence. Many natives had died, but the rest were just more inflamed than ever. And this wasn't just an unarmed crowd, either. There were a fair number of city militiamen mixed in, armed with crossbow, spears, and an assortment of melee weapons. Not much against Legion technology, but sheer weight of numbers and the absolute fearlessness of the wogs made the results inevitable.

What the hell was Lieutenant Gage doing, anyway? These sudden reversals of orders were screwing up everything.

He dove over a cargomod and rolled. The last line of resistance had been improvised from the equipment and supplies abandoned when the pressure had started to mount. Now fifteen legionnaires waited, crouched behind the barricade with a wall of alien flesh closing in on them. Narmonov didn't even have any heavy weapons left. Gunnery Sergeant Valko had pulled the two heavy lances out of the fighting line to give the breakout an extra punch. But that left the remaining defenders with precious little firepower . . . and their ammo stocks were starting to run low.

"Command reports the convoy's making its move on the east fence," Mattea reported. An MEK purred nearby, joined by the higher-pitched whine of an FEK.

"Where's our APC?"

"On the way. Sergeant Valko had it making a demonstration down by the south gate."

"Wonderful," someone nearby muttered.

"Legionnaires, ready to fire!" Carstairs shouted. Narmonov and Mattea joined the rest of the defenders along the barricade, leveling their weapons as the natives rushed forward. "Fire!"

The entire line opened up simultaneously, their sustained fire tearing through the first ranks of the natives. The pressure from the rear caused confusion, as more wogs became entangled in the carnage.

"Grenades!" Narmonov called, switching from needle rounds to grenades on his FEK. The four MEKs lacked the integral grenade-launchers and kept up automatic fire, but the rest of the legionnaires opened fire with the lethal little explosive rounds, raining more death and confusion into the enemy.

With a roar of fans a Sandray APC suddenly burst out of the darkness, setting down near the end of the barricade with a flourish. The kinetic-energy cannon in the vehicle's remote turret mount chattered, keeping the mob busy while the ramp dropped in the rear of the Sandray. "Come on!" a legionnaire in the back of the APC shouted, waving urgently.

Legionnaires sprinted for the safety of the Sandray. Narmonov stayed where he was and kept firing, along with Haddad and the men of the recon lance. Nearby Kelso was firing with calm, cool deliberation, picking off one wog after another with precise laser fire.

But the wogs kept pushing forward. Any professional army Narmonov had ever heard of would have broken by now, but these disorganized rioters kept on coming.

"Hurry!" someone shouted. "Before they get to the ramp!"

"Recon lance, move!" Narmonov shouted, abandoning his position at last.

By the Sandray, Carstairs and a handful of legionnaires were laying down extra covering fire of their own, but still those wogs showed no sign of wavering. Narmonov ran, desperate to reach the APC.

"They're gonna beat us to it!" Haddad shouted.

Carstairs must have come to the same conclusion at the same time. He waved his four companions forward and they ran straight at the rioters, firing from the hip as they went.

The humans plunged straight into the first rank, still firing, but now the mob was pressing in from all sides. Narmonov saw the ex-actor fall, as a wog clubbed him repeatedly from behind. Nor were the others faring any better.

But the threat they posed was causing the natives to concentrate on that handful of legionnaires. Narmonov and his men reached the ramp as the mob started to lurch forward again. By then it was too late to stop the platoon from escaping. The APC was stirring on magrep fields and turning away before the ramp had even started to rise.

Narmonov collapsed on a bench, hardly realizing that they were clear.

In his mind, all he could see was Carstairs playing out that last and most dramatic scene of his career.

Corporal Chandbahadur Rai smiled with satisfaction and patted the comfortable bulk of his onager plasma gun. He was a Gurkha from New Victoria, where a small settlement of his people kept alive the old ways and supplied troops for the Gurkha Regiment of the Commonwealth's Colonial Army. He would have still been among them, if he hadn't disgraced himself during the uprising against Terra on Tienkuo. In the fighting he had been separated from his unit, and lost all of his weapons while eluding the enemy. Although his superiors had seen nothing wrong with his actions, Chandbahadur had not been willing to remain among his fellow Gurkhas thereafter. Instead he had joined the Fifth Foreign Legion.

There wasn't much chance of losing his weapons today. The onager was attached directly to his armor by the ConRig harness that assisted targeting and control.

Now, crouched on top of one of the two manta-shaped cargo vans towing the laden barge, Chandbahadur was ready for action.

The barge would have to go out over the relatively level ground around the east gate, where enemy activity had been reported. That was fine by Chandbahadur. There was nothing like a good fight—nothing.

He saw legionnaires from First Platoon climbing onto the nearest vehicles. They'd been holding this position since the first attack on this side of the port, but now they had to mount up fast or be left behind.

"Clear the fence," Sergeant Valko's voice said quietly in his helmet speakers.

Chandbahadur raised his onager and activated his ConRig system. The harness slaved the movements of the gun to a sighting reticle, which picked up motions of his eyes and translated them to power-assisted movement of the weapon's barrel. He sighted carefully on the nearest portion of the fence, then opened fire. The onager moved smoothly along the line of the fence, sending round after high-energy round into the posts. Up and down the line other onagers, Fafnir rockets, and grenades were doing similar damage.

Seconds later the APC lurched forward, gathering speed. It rammed into what was left of the fence and plowed over the twisted metal wreckage.

Nomad rocket guns opened fire out of the night. With each telltale flash Chandbahadur sighted a nomad gunner and returned fire. In seconds their barrage fell silent.

The convoy sped through the darkness.

The FSV swerved to avoid another obstacle, and Spiro Karatsolis clung to the trigger mount of the plasma cannon.

"That's the last of them, Spear!" Bashar's voice rang loud and cocky in his headphones. "I think we're through!"

He glanced at his sensor screen. "Confirmed," he said shortly. "Looks like everything's behind us now."

"Hey, man, what else did you expect?" the Turk shot

back, his tone bantering again. "When you ride with the Basher you don't need a gunner!"

That should have been the signal for a typical comeback, something like "That's because you run into all our targets and bash them flat." But Karatsolis didn't answer. He didn't feel up to banter anymore.

It had started with the battle at the Sandcastle. First the nube, O'Donnell, had been cut down, and then Sandoval had saved Karatsolis and died from a shot that should have killed the Greek. Why were all these men dying?

He'd lost comrades before, even a few he'd called friends. You expected that in the army, especially in the Legion. Less than a quarter of all the soldiers who signed on with the Legion lived to complete a five-year enlistment. Hanuman had killed a lot of good legionnaires, but he'd come through it all without thinking about it much.

But this time was different. Part of it was the feeling of helplessness that came with any sort of garrison duty on a hostile planet. Karatsolis was a magger, a vehicle crewman, and though on the one hand he was used to sitting inside the cramped confines of the FSV, on the other he was used to a mobile war, where you didn't just sit and wait for the next attack. When men died, at least it wasn't just more attrition with nothing to show for the deaths.

It felt like O'Donnell and Sandoval had died such useless deaths. Who would be next? Bashar? Karatsolis himself? He'd joined the Legion because he felt that a soldier could make a real difference defending the Commonwealth, and not be just another statistic in the casualty reports.

He realized that Bashar had called his name again.

"Come on, Spear, look alive up there!" the corporal was saying. "Get me a range-and-bearing on that damned float-car."

He checked the instruments and read off the figures.

"Right," Bashar said. "Heading right for us. Get that oversized narcostick lighter of yours warmed up. We'll punch through the wall up here and head 'em off before they try for one of the gates."

Karatsolis acknowledged the order gruffly and ran a quick diagnostic on the plasma cannon. As he went through the routine motions, his mind was still wrestling with the overriding question. *Why am I a legionnaire?*

* * *

Edward Barnett fingered the small handgun in its hidden pocket and tried not to betray his fear.

*Everything is going wrong. . . .* The thought seemed to echo over and over again in his mind. From the moment the nomads had launched the attack on the Sandcastle, everything had gone wrong, and it would take desperate measures to regain control of the situation.

He darted a glance at Jens, sitting beside him in the back seat of the floatcar. If she'd just stayed tough with the thrice-damned legionnaires . . .

It might be too late even if he could take control now. Once they were cooped up inside the Sandcastle, would Fraser let any of the Terrans leave again?

He had to. Once the nomads started in on the Sandcastle there would be no stopping them, and Edward Barnett had no intention of being caught in the middle of that battle.

That supposed, of course, that they ever got out of this rabbit warren of a city. They had finally reached the walls of the Old Town, but getting to a gate and then making it through were starting to look like risky propositions at best. The damned legionnaires must have really stirred things up down by the port. Rioting had spread through a huge chunk of the city. Fires were burning only a few blocks away, and it was at least two kilometers to the port.

Help was supposed to be coming, but Barnett doubted the Legion could do much for them.

An explosion rocked the floatcar. A large section of the city wall erupted inward, showering the street with shattered masonry. The driver swerved to avoid rubble and skidded to a halt.

Framed in the gap opened up in the wall was a big armored vehicle, floating less than a meter off the ground on a magrep cushion. The Legion rescue party!

"Seafarms floatcar!" a PA announcer boomed. "Abandon your vehicle! We're here to take you back to the Sandcastle!"

Jens was looking as relieved as Barnett felt. She turned away from him, reaching for the door release.

Barnett pulled the rocket pistol out of his pocket. It was similar in design to the ones the nomads were using, but smaller, concealable, with a four-round magazine. An ideal holdout weapon, or so he'd been told when he'd been given the pistol and the secure comm unit hidden in his briefcase.

He waited until she had the door open and was halfway out before he shot her in the back. Then he palmed the weapon and rolled out of his side of the vehicle. "Snipers! Nomad snipers!" he shouted. "Caldwell, help the boss! Quick!"

The driver tried to scramble to where Jens had sprawled on the street. With a glance to make sure no one aboard the Legion vehicle could see him, Barnett fired twice more. Caldwell collapsed over the body, unmoving.

Barnett tucked the weapon into a hidden pocket in his left sleeve, grabbed his briefcase, and ran toward the hole in the wall, still shouting warnings of nomad snipers. The vehicle turned, dropping a ramp.

He held his breath. If there were troops there, they might examine the bodies, even collect them, and that might reveal too much. But no one came out.

He ran up the ramp in feigned panic.

Now Sigrid Jens was out of the way. Now he could take charge of the Project, and put right everything that had gone wrong.

# Chapter 12

The Legion has no friends.
—Commandant Michel DuValier
Third Foreign Legion, 2419

Subaltern Toru Watanabe entered the bridge of the *Seafarms Cyclops* feeling like a gladiator on his way to confront a hungry lion. The captain's summons had come before Lieutenant DuValier had finished telling him about the latest problem over the Legion's secure commlink.

He took a deep breath and tried to control his expression, as Captain Ian MacLean turned from the navigation table and frowned at him.

"Ah yes, Watanabe," the ship's captain said gruffly. "I imagine your headquarters people have already updated you on our orders, hmm?"

Watanabe nodded curtly. "I've been told. But I don't think I understand, Captain."

"Not much to understand, is there?" MacLean asked with a shrug. "Acting Project Director Barnett has ordered us to resume normal operations."

Watanabe lowered his voice so that only MacLean could hear him. "Look, Captain, I thought you agreed with the last batch of instructions—the ones from Citizen Jens. We were on our way back to the Sandcastle."

"I agree, Mr. Watanabe, with whatever orders the company sees fit to hand me. Right now those orders are to keep the *Cyclops* at sea, so that's what we're doing."

"And what about the nomads? That attack happened, and no set of orders is going to erase the fact that they're still out there."

"The nomads are your problem, Watanabe. You and your men are on board to deal with any further attacks."

"Captain Fraser isn't very happy about this, sir," Watanabe said carefully. "I fully expect him to invoke Section 34 and require Seafarms to submit itself to military authority."

Maclean laughed. "Section 34, eh? Martial law? Your precious Captain Fraser had better be damned sure of his grounds before he starts playing games with civil authority. The Commonwealth doesn't take kindly to military men overriding local government, especially when it has the kind of connections Seafarms can bring to bear at the hearing. A lot of promising careers have been wrecked on Section 34, kid."

Watanabe scowled at him. "I still think this is ill advised," he said angrily.

"And I still think this is my ship, Watanabe. And my bridge. You've got your instructions . . . now get off it."

Watanabe turned and stalked out, not trusting himself to answer the man.

Legionnaire John Grant kept one eye on the computer's sonar display and the other on his two lancemates. Since the attack, standing orders required three men on watch in Operations at all times, but usually there wasn't enough to keep three men occupied. Normally the most junior would have been on watch while his betters amused themselves, but not this time. Slick had the job, so that Dmitri Rostov could use the opportunity to further the education of the Recon Lance's newest member in the basics of poker. The game was completely new to Legionnaire Third-Class Myaighee, who less than a year before had been a low-caste worker on Hanuman.

Myaighee stood a meter tall, with the dark olive skin, powerful arms, hairless head, and quilled neck-ruff of the species humans usually referred to as "monkeys" or "hannies." That species was hermaphroditic, without any gender distinctions; since words like "he" and "she" didn't apply, the hannie term "ky" was used to refer to members of the race. Ky wore a uniform specially tailored for the hannie frame, leaving most of the neck-ruff uncovered. Myaighee would wear a plate of plasteel armor over it in combat, but the quills were sensitive enough to make that sort of covering too uncomfortable for routine use.

The alien had helped warn the Terrans of the treachery that sparked off the rebellion on Hanuman, and ky had joined in Bravo Company's long march to safety. Ky had learned Terranglic from chip lessons on the way, and developed a real bond with the Terrans. At the final battle at the end of the march it was Myaighee who had helped Colin Fraser spring a crucial ambush that saved the survivors of the unit.

Ky had chosen to join the Legion after that rather than try to return to kys own kind, who probably would have viewed the hannie as a traitor anyway. Although ky had never been to Devereaux for formal Legion training, Myaighee had demonstrated considerable skill, and Watanabe had assigned ky to the Recon Lance to replace Legionnaire Auriega.

The hannie was showing equal skill in mastering the nuances of poker.

"How many cards?" Rostov was asking.

The alien's neck ruff twitched like a cornfield in a stiff breeze. Movements of those slender, poisonous spines were supposed to convey emotional content, but so far no one in Bravo Company fully understood the complexities of reading them. "One, Corporal," Myaighee said, in kys customary diffident tone.

"One, eh?" Rostov said, watching the movements of the neck ruff speculatively. As the hannie looked at the card, the ruff continued to move. Grant couldn't tell if it changed at all, if there were new emotions at work, and he was fairly sure Rostov couldn't either. Certainly Myaighee's face betrayed nothing.

"Dealer takes two," Rostov said, still eyeing the alien. His own emotions were plain enough. Was Myaighee excited because ky held a good hand, or because ky was trying to bluff? "What say we raise . . . ten?"

Myaighee didn't even look at kys cards again. "Ten . . . and twenty more, Corporal."

"Twenty more?" Rostov shook his head. "You're out for blood, aren't you?" He paused. "That's too steep for me. You take it."

Myaighee tossed kys cards down and raked in the pot without any apparent change in expression, though Slick noticed the neck ruff was no longer so agitated. Rostov reached out to pick up the cards.

"Hell, I don't believe this," he said. "A pair of deuces?

This blasted monkey just bluffed me out of a week's pay with a pair of deuces."

"Serves you right, Corp," Slick said. "About time you found out what it was like to be a sucker!"

"That's enough out of you, kid," Rostov told him, laughing. "Hell, it's violating that natural order of things. Third-Classes were put in this universe for the express purpose of filling the pockets of First-Classes and Corporals, not the other way around."

"And where does that leave me?" Slick asked, looking up and grinning. "What are Second-Classes supposed to do?"

"When we know that, kid," Rostov shot back, "I'm pretty sure we'll have solved the basic mystery of life."

At that moment the computer cut the conversation short by sounding a shrill warning tone. Slick cursed as he looked down at the sonar display. "Multiple targets, Corp. Heading this way. Range about half a klick and closing."

"A school of fish, maybe?" Rostov suggested hopefully, as he joined Slick at the Operations console. The corporal cut the computer's insistent buzz.

"Only if we're talking about goddamned big fish that learned how to swim in a military academy," Slick said sourly. He pointed to the monitor. The targets were arrayed loosely, but they were certainly in formation. And the computer was reading the echoes as man-sized or larger.

"Looks like more company," Rostov said. He settled into the chair beside Slick and slapped the general alarm button, then picked up a mike. "Condition Three, condition three," he announced. "Natives spotted. Subaltern Watanabe, report to Operations."

Slick and Rostov exchanged a grim look. It looked like another attack was on the way.

As the insistent clamor of the alarm filled the corridor, Watanabe shoved past a startled crewman and into the ship's sensor center. Two more crew members looked up from their consoles.

"Intercom!" Watanabe snapped. One of the sailors pointed to the panel. "Check your sonar," he continued. "I want a display."

He stabbed the three-digit code for the Operations Center. "Watanabe here. What have you got?"

"Corporal Rostov, Sub," came the reply. "Bearing three-four-one, range four hundred meters. They're on a converging course, and the computer is scanning them as man-sized biologicals."

Watanabe watched as the crewman brought up the display on a wall-screen monitor. "I'm looking at them, Corporal. Looks like a major attack from here."

"Yes, sir," Rostov said. There was a pause. "Computer's estimating a hundred and fifty targets. There could be more, though."

"Yeah." Watanabe studied the screen. "Judging from the reports we had from the Sandcastle, these wogs might be planning some kind of ambush or surprise. Wait one, Rostov." He rubbed his forehead, trying to concentrate. "You—what's your name?"

"Brown, sir . . . "

"What kind of bottom are we passing over, Brown?"

The crewman superimposed a high-resolution chart on the sonar display. Watanabe felt the familiar sensation of having pieces of a puzzle fall into place as he examined the monitor. He hit the intercom button again.

"Rostov, the charts up here in the sensor room say we're over rocky ground. Concentrate scans on the bottom. I have a feeling we may have some friends waiting for us down there."

"Yes, sir," the corporal acknowledged.

"Next, alert Gessler. It'll take me a few minutes to get aft, but I want the platoon mustered and deployed right away. Cover all four docking platforms. Recon and one heavy-weapons lances on mobile reserve." Watanabe paused. "Have Sergeant Muwanga take over for you . . . and send for Forbes, too." Legionnaire Warren Forbes had taken over Trousseau's duties as the platoon's $C^3$ technician, though he remained part of Radescu's rifle lance.

"That will mean Radescu will only have two other men in his lance, Sub," Rostov pointed out.

Watanabe cursed under his breath. He had forgotten that Myaighee, the legionnaire he'd assigned to the Recon Lance, had transferred from Radescu's unit. "All right, Rostov, put Radescu on the entrance nearest the ready room. Understood?"

"Got it, Sub. We'll get things moving down here."

"Do it. I'll be down as soon as I take care of something

up here.'' Watanabe cut the intercom, then punched in the Bridge combination.

''Bridge,'' a sailor responded.

''This is Subaltern Watanabe. I want the captain.''

There was a pause before MacLean came on. ''What the hell's going on, Watanabe?'' he asked gruffly.

''We're tracking what we believe is an enemy formation off the port bow, less than a half kilometer away now. There is also a chance of a second force concealed somewhere nearby. I want a change of heading. We can outrun those bastards and avoid a fight.''

''Run from a bunch of savages?'' MacLean sounded incredulous. ''Nonsense! Anyway, we still have to go this way sooner or later. The Scylla Passage is the only convenient way into the Polar Ocean, and that's where we're going. Your legionnaires will just have to deal with any of the wogs stupid enough to attack us.''

Watanabe slapped the cutoff switch, unwilling to waste more time arguing. Obviously nothing was going to turn MacLean from the path his orders had set down.

As he left the sensor room, he remembered the uncertainties he'd been feeling on the day of the first nomad attack. Now his doubts about his ability were taking second place to his concern over the foolishness of the Seafarms people.

If the Terrans on Polypheme were defeated, it would be because Seafarms refused to look beyond their narrow interests or to accept the locals for the threat they were.

Corporal Dmitri Radescu kept his eyes on the surface of the Sea of Scylla, watching for any sign of the nomads. It was morning at last, the first planetary morning since Trousseau and Auriega had died, though thirty-six hours had passed by Terran reckoning.

He shrugged off the thought. Better to concentrate on the ocean.

Beside him Legionnaire Hoyt checked the magazine of his MEK and spat over the side of the docking platform. ''Wish something would happen,'' he said, his growl of a voice matching his bearlike appearance.

''Yeah,'' Legionnaire Steiner agreed. He looked deceptively relaxed, with his FEK slung under his arm. Radescu had seen Steiner swing the battle rifle up and pick off a target at three hundred meters with barely a pause. "We missed out on the fun last time. Rostov's glory boys got all the action, as usual."

Radescu shrugged. "Luck of the draw, man. You want the truth, I wish they were out here now."

"Losing your nerve, Count?" Hoyt asked with a laugh. Radescu sprang from Transylvanian peasant stock, and though his family had been forcibly relocated to the colony world of Hecate when he was only ten, he had kept the accent of his youth. His lean build, dark hair, and pale complexion combined with that accent to make him the butt of endless Dracula jokes.

"Just wishing we had a full lance," Radescu told him. "Three men against an army isn't my idea of good odds."

"Hell, it's like Steiner said. The glory boys get all the best. They take a casualty, somebody else transfers in."

"Yeah, but look what they got," Hoyt said. "I'm glad to lose that little ale creep." He wasn't known for liking nonhumans, even the ones who joined the Legion.

Radescu knew how Hoyt felt. He'd fought the monkeys on Hanuman, and he could still remember what it was like to watch a horde of the little creatures drop out of the trees in ambush or swarm over the walls of a Legion outpost.

Right now, though, even Legionnaire Myaighee would have been a comforting addition to his depleted lance.

Steiner pointed suddenly, "Hey, Count, what's . . ." The words trailed off in an all-too-familiar gurgle as the legionnaire slumped to the deck. There was a crossbow bolt protruding from his throat, bare centimeters above the collar of his duraweave battledress.

Dropping prone on the deck, Radescu trained his FEK on the ocean, squinting against the dazzle of sunlight on the water. Beside him Hoyt was on one knee. The big gunner swept his MEK in an arc, firing on full automatic and keeping up a running stream of curses that nearly drowned out the hum of the weapon's gauss-generator.

Then there was an explosion and the MEK fell silent. Hoyt was down, too, with a ruined mask of blood and torn flesh for a face.

Radescu keyed in his commlink and swallowed, tasting fear. He opened fire as he mouthed an incantation his grandmother had taught him, a chant that was supposed to ward off the servants of evil.

* * *

"Attack on Docking Platform Two! Rostov, take your lance."

"On it, Sarge," Rostov acknowledged Platoon Sergeant Gessler's order. "Let's do it, Recon!"

"Recon!" the rest of the lance echoed in unison. Rostov felt a surge of pride. It was a good team.

They ran out of the ready room, with Slick on point and the hulking Gwyrran, Vrurrth, just behind. Rostov was third, backed up by Myaighee and the sniper, Judy Martin, bringing up the rear. It was a formation the lance had drilled in countless times, with the hannie taking the place of young Auriega as if ky had been with them all along.

Slick rounded the last corner, crouching low. Vrurrth stopped, flattened himself against the wall, and held up his hand to signal a stop. Rostov and the others halted as well.

"Hatch is still open," Slick's voice sounded softly in Rostov's ears. "Explosions outside . . . I hear an FEK."

"Someone's still alive, then," Rostov said. "Back him up, kid. Let's go!"

Slick had stopped by the hatch and was firing through it as the rest of the lance sprinted down the corridor. Through the opening Rostov could see glimpses of battle: the dead body of a big legionnaire with an MEK, a wog sprawled nearby, another nomad grappling with Corporal Radescu. More wogs were climbing out of the water.

A burst from Slick's FEK cut down the native fighting with Radescu. "Get inside, man!" Rostov shouted, joining Slick on the firing line. "Vrurrth, get ready to dog the hatch."

The Gwyrran nodded ponderously.

Rostov, Slick, and Myaighee were all firing now, covering the Rumanian corporal's retreat. Radescu stopped to retrieve Hoyt's MEK, then maintained steady fire as he fell back.

They all stopped firing as Radescu dived through the hatch. Then Vrurrth slammed the hatch shut.

"Will the hatches hold them?" Martin asked. She didn't seem to be speaking to anyone in particular.

"Not against explosives," Rostov, who was trained as a demolitions specialist, said quietly. "We'd better set up a barricade and let Sarge and the Sub know what's happened."

* * *

"Both entries on the port side were attacked. Platform Two was lost; the boys on Number One drove back the wogs."

"What happened on Two?" Watanabe asked.

Sergeant Muwanga shrugged. "That was Radescu's lance. Rostov says they were short-handed to start with. Apparently two of them were taken out right away, but Corporal Radescu made it back inside after the Recon Lance started laying down some cover."

Watanabe glanced across C-cubed at Legionnaire Forbes. The man was looking sick.

No wonder. Half his lance gone in a matter of seconds, and Forbes hadn't been there to help them. A five-man lance in the Legion was closer than most civilian families.

"Any further activity from Two?"

"Rostov reported hearing some noises through the hatch, sir. He believes they'll try to blow it and break in. Sergeant Gessler wants permission to deploy more men there."

Watanabe sat down heavily. They didn't have very many reserves left, and if there was another attack somewhere else they'd be hard-pressed to respond.

But if Rostov wasn't backed up and the natives broke through, they'd be damned close to the engineering spaces. Assuming the enemy knew something about the layout of the *Cyclops*—and that was an assumption the legionnaires had to make, even if it erred on the side of caution—they could render the huge ship helpless if Rostov couldn't hold.

Either way the legionnaires would be in trouble.

"Sir . . ." Forbes broke in suddenly, looking up from the monitor with a look of horror on his face. "Sir, I've got targets on the bottom scan . . . at least two hundred. They're hiding in the rocks, but there's enough motion for the computer to pick them out of the clutter."

"Motion? What kind?"

"Ship's passing over them now, sir, and they're starting up toward us."

"Where the hell are they going to hit?" Muwanga asked, his big fist slamming the corner of the console. "Where?"

"Wherever it is," Watanabe said, "I'm not sure we can stop them. There's just too damned many of the bastards."

He turned away, staring at the wall. The only way to head

off disaster was to break up the attack in a big way. Something unexpected. Something clever . . .

*You're the one everyone says is the clever tactician,* he told himself.

And an old memory surfaced slowly, a memory from his boyhood on the watery world of Pacifica, and the commercial fishing vessel his older brother had worked on the summer before Watanabe had left for the Academy.

He found himself smiling as he turned back to explain his plan.

The banging and scraping had stopped, and now the corridor off Docking Platform Two was as quiet as a graveyard.

Slick crouched behind the barricade they'd improvised out of a dozen cargomods filled with spare parts from a nearby storeroom halfway down the passageway, hardly daring to breathe. Myaighee and Rostov waited on either side, with the others poised further back, at the intersection.

"What are they waiting for?" Slick muttered.

"Probably scared of you, kid," Rostov said with mock cheerfulness. "Maybe they're waiting for you to die of old age before they rush us." His FEK never wavered, and he kept all of his attention focused on the hatch.

Slick hated the waiting. He'd never liked enclosed places or static defense; he was more at home on a recon patrol in the open or a sudden ambush where he set the pace of the fighting.

Back on Hanuman he'd nearly broken a time or two, in situations like this. He'd learned to deal with it, but he still didn't like to be pinned down this way.

The seconds dragged by interminably.

"Maybe the Old Man knew what he was doing when he decided against sending any help," Rostov commented, "Maybe the attack here was just a diver—"

And at that moment the hatch erupted inward in fire, thunder, and hurtling fragments, and alien shapes appeared through the smoke, their rocket weapons held at the ready.

# Chapter 13

> I am asking for six hundred men of the Foreign Legion who are able, if need be, to die decently.
>
> —General Joseph Gallieni
> French Foreign Legion, 1896

"All right, are you clear on what we're doing?" Watanabe paused in his restless pacing in front of the six legionnaires who made up his only reserve. They were the men of the platoon's two heavy-weapons units, but they had put aside their onagers and Fafnir rocket launchers in favor of FEKs. Instead of regular battledress or plasteel armor, each member of the strike force, including Watanabe, was clad in a Legion-issue hardsuit, the only type of diving gear practical for use on Polypheme.

"We're ready, sir," Sergeant Gessler answered for all of them.

"Then it's time. . . . Let the games begin." He forced a smile before lowering the faceplate on his diving helmet and checking the seals.

As the other legionnaires followed his example, Watanabe keyed in his commlink. "Muwanga? Communications check. Alpha, Bravo, Charlie . . ."

"Read you five-by-five, sir," Muwanga replied. He and Forbes would continue coordinating the legionnaires from C-cubed. "Zeigler's ready on Platform Four."

"Good. We're moving out now. Tell him to drop the first charges in one minute . . . mark! Channel clear." Watanabe cut the commlink and picked up the FEK, feeling constricted by the stiff armor of the hardsuit. The diving gear was constructed as full-coverage protection for underwater combat, though on Polypheme it had always been considered more important that the suits resisted the highly corrosive effects of the ocean. Ordinary materials didn't last long in that environment.

He followed the others down the corridor toward Docking Platform Four. This plan would put his team into serious danger, challenging the wogs in their own native environment with a considerable disadvantage in numbers.

Watanabe could only hope that the surprise he had planned would keep the nomads off balance long enough to give the legionnaires a chance to hit hard.

These natives had been showing a flair for unorthodox tactics. Now it was time to even the score.

Sergeant Ralph Zeigler watched the digital countdown on the inside of his faceplate and raised his arm. On either end of Docking Platform Four a member of Vane's Rifle Lance braced a foot on a canister and turned a young, worried face to look for Zeigler's signal.

Four . . . three . . . two . . . one . . .

The sergeant dropped his arm and the two riflemen kicked their tubes. They hit the water so close to simultaneously that Zeigler heard only one splash.

"Get ready, Vane," Zeigler ordered. He saw Corporal Vane tighten his grip on the remote-control box that would detonate the explosives in the two improvised depth charges.

Putting explosives into the water to take out the wogs . . . the subaltern had really outdone himself this time. The canisters were the standard buffered transport containers for stocks of PX-70, the obsolete military demo charges used by the company for survey works and other scientific and engineering applications. A few minutes' work dismantling the buffers and slapping detpacks into the explosives had transformed safe shipping modules into very large, very lethal underwater bombs.

A new countdown was ticking off on his faceplate, the time left to detonation. Watanabe wanted those charges to go off fairly deep, partly to protect the *Cyclops*, partly to catch as many of the wogs still on the bottom as possible.

"And three . . . and two . . . and one . . ."

One of the legionnaires went down as a barrage of rocket fire opened up from the forward end of the platform. A large tattooed shape heaved itself onto the deck, brandishing a heavy mace studded with wicked-looking spikes. Legionnaire Bergmann fired, killing the wog, but another was climbing out of the water to take the dead nomad's place.

"Hit it, Vane!" Zeigler shouted, bringing his own FEK into action.

The corporal hit the button.

Then Vane was down, clutching at the stump of his wrist where a rocket had exploded. The remote-control box skittered across the deck. Everything seemed to be moving in slow motion. Surely the canisters should have detonated? Had something gone wrong?

Just then twin geysers erupted aft of the ship, one close to the rear end of the platform, the other further astern. Water surged across the open deck, knocking Bergmann down and sweeping him toward the edge.

But the legionnaires had been expecting the blast, while the nomads had not. Zeigler and the other riflemen clung to nearby handholds and kept firing, clearing the rest of the natives off the platform.

No others appeared, though a number of bodies were rising to the surface, either stunned or dead.

Zeigler grabbed Bergmann and helped him to his feet. "First aid for Vane, then get him to sick bay," he ordered. "The rest of you stay on your toes. If you see a wog, shoot him. . . . Even the ones that look dead."

FEKs whined.

Then Sergeant Gessler, ungainly in a hardsuit, came through the hatch. Zeigler flashed him a thumb's-up.

Now it was time for the counterattack.

Slick shouted a colorful curse he'd picked up from Rostov and held the trigger of the FEK down, spraying full-auto fire into the nomads crowding through the blown hatch. An analytical part of his mind was thankful that Rostov had placed the barricade far enough back to avoid the worst effects of the blast when the hatch blew. Any closer and they would have been too stunned, too blinded by smoke, and the nomads would have overrun them.

It was lucky the natives didn't use hand grenades. They weren't very practical underwater weapons, but a single grenade would have cleared the corridor easily.

Unfortunately these wogs were too bloody adaptable. One of them would think of using their explosives as a satchel charge soon enough.

All they could do, though, was keep on pouring fire into that hatchway, keeping the natives from shooting rockets down the corridor and praying that Subaltern Watanabe was right in assuming that this wasn't going to be the main enemy drive.

Suddenly there were no fresh targets. "Goddamn!" Rostov said. "They're not supposed to be able to disengage that way!"

Something moved in the hatch, and Legionnaire Martin shouted "Look out, Corp!" She fired, the laser beam crackling invisibly over Slick's head. A wog toppled through the hatch onto the bodies of several of his comrades, but not before something bulky bounced and slid partway down the passageway.

"Satchel charge!" Rostov called. "Get back!"

Myaighee was a blur of motion, leaping over the barricade and running toward the sack. The hannie grabbed it with both hands and threw it back with a strength anyone that didn't know kys race would never have believed possible.

A crossbow bolt struck the alien near the base of the throat, and Myaighee fell.

"Cover me, Corp," Slick said, starting over the barricade to retrieve his lancemate. He heard a staccato *thunk-thunk-thunk* from Rostov's FEK as the corporal fired a three-round burst of grenades.

Just then the satchel charge detonated, and Slick used the confusion to sprint to the fallen hannie. He stooped, picked the small body up, and ran for the barricade.

There was no enemy fire from the hatchway.

"Explosion must have cleared the platform," Radescu said from the corridor intersection. "We can take it back now."

"No way," Rostov said. "Sub said we let 'em stay put until he does his thing. That's what we do."

Slick carried Myaighee to the intersection and lowered the alien to the deck.

"Get back on the firing line, kid!" Rostov called from the barricade. "Martin, first aid!"

Slick hesitated, unwilling to leave the hannie. Martin knelt beside Myaighee, then looked up at him. "It's bad," she said. "But I'll do what I can until we can get a real medic."

* * *

Water closed around Watanabe's head, murky and somehow hostile. An alien sea, completely unlike the clear blue waters of Pacifica.

This ocean was home to the wogs, not to Mankind, and Watanabe was all too aware of being an intruder in this unfriendly realm.

He checked his gauges. The artificial gill mounted on the back of his helmet was drawing well, and his suit was maintaining integrity. Watanabe touched a stud on his forearm control band and the backpack waterthruster hummed to life. It was no substitute for the mobility the lokes enjoyed underwater, but impellers in the pack would push him along substantially faster than he could swim.

The water was cloudy, filled with mud—and other things Watanabe preferred not to think about—churned up by the depth charges. He hit another control and his faceplate turned into a small-scale sonar display, less accurate than the computer-enhanced shipboard system, but adequate.

With luck the legionnaires would actually be able to "see" better than the opposition, at least for a while. Transponders in the hardsuit commlinks would tag friends; everything else would be a foe.

"Stick close," he ordered. "Let's go!"

He dived, keeping close to the hull of the *Cyclops*. The sonar display showed a few drifting bodies nearby, but nothing that looked like living targets.

Maybe the charges had taken all of them out . . .

As he reached the bottom of the vessel, though, he could see that his hope had been vain.

A knot of perhaps thirty wogs was swimming along the keel, moving toward the bow of the huge ship. They probably had been partially screened from the shock waves.

So far, the legionnaires had apparently gone unnoticed. Watanabe signaled for a halt, cut his thruster, and watched. What were they doing?

Then he saw it. And if the wogs reached their objective, *Seafarms Cyclops* and everyone aboard her would be helpless against the nomad attackers.

Ghrookwur!-Huntmaster clutched his head, still dizzy from the force of the explosions the Strangers-Above had set off in the water. The shock wave had knocked him out for a time, and now, as he recovered consciousness, his head and ears ached. He swiveled an eyestalk to examine his ear and saw that it was oozing blood.

*May the offworlders find nothing but dry land and choking dust,* he thought as he groped for his spear. It was floating close by, tangled with the body of Dur!ghur-Fartrader.

The Stormriders Clan had suffered many losses today, far more than War-Leader-of-Clans Choor! had said they would lose. Perhaps Choor! was wrong about the Strangers-Above. He claimed they were no match for the Clans United, that even without the Strangers-Who-Brought-Gifts the nomad tribes could drive away these foreign devils and save the seas for the Free Swimmers.

The War-Leader-of-Clans had brought the most powerful tribes of these seas together, bound by a common purpose instead of being separated by constant strife. He was wise in the ways of war, and he had the support of the Strangers-Who-Brought-Gifts. But so far this war on the Strangers-Above had brought little gain at high cost . . . and that cost mostly in the lives of Stormriders. Perhaps Choor! really was above all Clan ties and rivalries . . . or perhaps the Stormriders were being expended here so that some other Clan—the Wavesingers, perhaps, or the Reef-Swimmers—could gain that much more power among the Clans United.

That was disturbing. If Ghrookwur!-Huntmaster lived through the day, he would have much to say to the Clan-Leader and the Clan-Warlord.

If he lived.

He sensed movement in the water close by and swiveled his eyestalks. Strange shapes moved through the murk, grotesque parodies of the Free Swimmers. The Strangers!

His hands and feet closed tight around the spear, and he thrashed his tail, gathering speed. The Strangers had to be stopped. . . .

Watanabe barely had time to react to the sudden movement from a target that had seemed dead moments before. He kicked his legs hard and dodged the wog's first rush, but the alien was fast as a striking snake. Before Watanabe could turn the wog was attacking again. His spear struck the subaltern's backpack.

Then Gessler was there, striking the alien from behind with the butt of his FEK. "Prisoner," Gessler grunted, hitting the still form one more time to be sure. He produced an inflatable buoy, secured it to the nomad, and triggered it. As the captive rose toward the surface the Platoon Sergeant informed Zeigler to expect the package.

Watanabe nodded in satisfaction. Captain Fraser would be pleased if they could get worthwhile information out of a prisoner or two, and so far it had been so damned hard to stop one of the bastards without killing them. . . .

He studied his sonar scan again. "C-cubed, this is Bravo Two One. I need a computer feed."

"Bravo Two One, acknowledged," Forbes's voice responded. "What do you need?"

"Ship schematics for the lower decks," Watanabe told him.

"Roger that. Wait one." A moment later the sonar image faded out, replaced by a diagram showing the underside of the *Cyclops*.

And there, right where he'd thought it should be, was the intake for the largest of the ship's three main impeller tunnels.

Like the backpack thruster units, the *Seafarms Cyclops* relied on water sucked in through inlet ducts forward and forced out under high pressure aft for propulsion. The largest of these was located directly over the keel, with the intake located fifty meters from the bow.

It was an efficient piece of engineering, but if that master intake was damaged badly enough the ship would have to limp along at less than half its usual slow speed, easy prey for multiple attacks.

Probably the natives lurking along the bottom had planned to take out all three impeller tunnels, but after the explosions they were concentrating on the main one.

That meant they knew a hell of a lot about the layout of the ship. . . .

Watanabe pushed the thought aside. It wasn't important now. For the moment the problem was stopping those wogs before they struck. They had perhaps three hundred more meters to swim before they reached the intake.

He cut the computer feed and signaled his men to follow. With backpacks on full thrust, the legionnaires started after their targets.

* * *

"Here they come again!" Rostov shouted, opening fire. The legionnaires pumped round after round into the hatch, with Radescu spraying three-round grenade bursts past the barricade.

The nomads weren't pressing this attack home nearly as hard as before. It was just as Slick had said that first day, when Auriega had bought it. They seemed to have learned something about tactics. It felt as if they were mounting a diversion, pushing just hard enough to attract attention.

The subaltern had been right, then. But just now Rostov wished Watanabe had fallen for the trick, at least enough to send some backup. Myaighee was out of action, and sooner or later the attackers would score more hits.

Beside him Slick stopped firing and glanced his way. "I don't like the feel of this, Corp," he said. "Those bastards are up to something new this time."

Rostov nodded; it matched the feeling he'd been getting. "Yeah, but what do you think it is?"

"If they've got more explosives, they could try to open another hole."

"Hull's a lot stronger than the hatches are, kid," he said.

"Yeah, but if they're serious . . ."

Rostov switched on his commlink. "Hey, Sarge, do we have any outside cameras left by Platform Two?" he asked.

"Cameras?" Muwanga responded, sounding uncertain. "Uh . . . yeah. What are you looking for?"

"We think the wogs are up to something out there. Maybe planning to blast themselves a new hatch. Can you see anything?"

"Wait one." There was a long pause. "Goddamn it, Rostov, they're setting charges about ten meters aft of your position, and right along the waterline. Get the hell out of there!"

"Radescu! Cover us! Come on, kid, we're making some tracks!"

As they sprinted up the passageway, crouching low to leave the Rumanian a clear field of fire, a blast shook the corridor. Lights flickered overhead.

And they could hear the rush of water, mingling with the triumphant shouts of wog soldiers, from the storage compartment aft of their defensive position.

"Negative, C-cubed, negative!" Watanabe gasped as he kept swimming. "If you weaken any of the other platforms, the wogs'll just have that many more places to try to break in. Rostov has to hold as well as he can. If they run true to form, they'll cut their losses if we stop them here."

He switched the commlink to the lance tactical frequency, shifted from sonar to direct-vision viewing, and raised his FEK. "Legionnaires!" he called, squeezing the trigger.

Water boiled as the gauss rifle hurled deadly needle rounds at the enemy. The fantastic muzzle velocity of the FEK was hampered very little by the thicker medium of underwater combat, though the range was sharply restricted. Nomads died in the storm of metallic slivers.

But some were quick enough or lucky enough to take cover behind the ship's keel. Rockets streaked toward the legionnaires like tiny torpedoes. Legionnaire Erlich let go of his FEK and clutched at a gaping hole in the torso section of his hardsuit. His scream echoed in Watanabe's headphones for what seemed like an eternity. Then he was dead.

"Sergeant," Watanabe ordered crisply. "Take two men. Drop deeper and get an angle on those wogs. We'll keep them busy."

Gessler stabbed a blunt finger at two of the legionnaires and pushed off from the bottom of the ship, striking out for the depths. One of the men following him took a rocket hit in one leg but kept right on going, a trail of blood marking his passage like the ink sprayed by a Terran squid.

Watanabe tried to concentrate on firing. His magazine ran dry, and he slapped a fresh clip into the receiver. Beside him Corporal Dmowski switched to grenades. They weren't quite as effective underwater as the needle rounds, but the pattern of bursts around the keel flushed one of the nomads. The remaining legionnaire killed him.

Then more of the nomads were breaking from the cover of the keel as Gessler's men opened up. They seemed ready to swim straight for Watanabe's position, obeying their drive to overwhelm the enemy at any cost.

Moments later they were fleeing, all the fight gone out of them.

Watanabe watched as the legionnaires picked off a few of the fugitives, wondering once again what it was that made these natives tick. Their battle plans were elaborate, but they still had trouble fighting their own reflexes in combat. Something was guiding them, that much was sure . . . but what? And how?

Watanabe knew that the answers to those questions could be the solution to the whole native threat. He only hoped they could find them in time.

Rostov was favoring his left shoulder, bruised in the confusing minutes before the end of the battle. They had split up as they retreated, with Radescu, Martin, and Myaighee falling back to the nearest watertight door forward, while the other three cut their way through the wogs to secure the aft end of the corridor. It wouldn't have been enough—there was still a rabbit warren of compartments and passageways uncovered, and with explosives the wogs could have broken out at will, but the legionnaires had kept them tied up just long enough.

Then, just as C-cubed had said, the nomads had retreated. Apparently once their attempt on the intakes was compromised, they were unwilling to press on with the all-too-successful diversion.

The platoon was drawn up in Hold Two, the ready room, except for the ones like Myaighee who were confined to the ship's sick bay.

Or the legionnaires like Hoyt and Steiner, who wouldn't be attending muster again.

Watanabe had put on a dress uniform that looked out of place among the battledress fatigues. ''You've done good work today, men,'' he said. ''More than anyone had a right to expect. But I'm afraid the day's work isn't done yet.''

There was a stir through the ranks.

''I've made a decision, one that will probably cost me my bar. I need your support to carry it out.'' He paused. ''Seafarms has ordered Captain MacLean to continue the cruise. If he follows those orders, what we went through today is going to keep on repeating, over and over, until we make a mistake or we're just too worn down by attrition to fight the wogs off. I will not subject this command to those conditions.''

This time the legionnaires were muttering audibly among themselves. Rostov heard Martin whisper to Slick. ''Why doesn't someone at the Sandcastle take charge, huh?''

Watanabe must have heard a similar comment. ''I have decided to take action without reference to higher authority. Captain Fraser can't invoke Section 34 without running the risk of bringing Seafarms down on his back, and apparently that's about the only thing that would get them to change their orders. I can't convince MacLean to play it smart, either. But the best chance for everyone is to rejoin the rest of the demi-battalion at the Sandcastle, instead of letting the wogs wear us down separately."

He drew his PLF pistol. "This leaves it to us to deal with the situation. Who's with me?"

Rostov's voice joined with the rest of the platoon in roaring out his approval.

The Legion would stand together.

# Chapter 14

Not by blood inherited, but spilled.
—Legionnaire Pascal Bonette
French Foreign Legion, 1914

"I insist that you order this man Watanabe to return control of the *Cyclops* to Captain MacLean!"

Fraser frowned at Edward Barnett. "Citizen, I'm getting tired of these arguments," he said quietly. "Before you took charge, the question was settled. It was your reversal of policy that started this nonsense, and frankly I'm more than satisfied with what Mr. Watanabe has done."

"Then he's acting under your orders?" Barnett challenged.

Leaning back in his chair, Fraser looked around the conference room before he answered. It was a lean staff meeting, with Fraser, DuValier, Gage, and Kelly, plus Garcia in one corner recording the minutes.

And Barnett. Since his rescue from Ourgh, Barnett had stepped into the role of Seafarms Project Director as if he had been born to the job. In a matter of hours he'd undone most of what Jens had agreed to do.

Fraser had blocked his hopes of returning to Ourgh, though. That had mostly been Gunny Trent's doing; it was the NCO's suggestion that Fraser agree to allow the Seafarms people to leave any time they wanted, provided they realized that there would be no Legion help on the return trip. Impounding all the vehicles inside the Sandcastle, even that ramshackle magrep barge, had driven the point home even further.

So Barnett and his people remained in the Sandcastle . . . but they weren't even pretending to cooperate now, here or aboard the *Cyclops*. If it hadn't been for Watanabe's bloodless mutiny, the ship would still be on course for the open sea—or more likely, drifting helpless in the wake of fresh nomad attacks.

Kelly met his gaze with a warning look. She had a knack for reading him. He ignored the cautionary note in her eyes and answered Barnett.

"The fact is, I didn't issue any such orders," Fraser admitted. He paused. "But I wish I had, and my own report is going to indicate my full support for the subaltern's action."

That much was certainly true. He should have forced the issue long since, but instead he'd avoided confrontation with Barnett. The legalities of the situation on Polypheme were cloudy, and he'd told himself that caution was best, but the choice had nearly cost Watanabe and his platoon—and the crew of the *Cyclops*—their lives.

He'd almost allowed concern for his career to override his plain duty. Luckily Watanabe had taken the initiative.

Barnett leaned forward, scowling. "I'll make sure you and he both get what you deserve," he said, standing abruptly. "Your career's going to make your precious Captain Hawley's look impressive by comparison."

Fraser laughed. "If any of us live through the next couple of weeks, Barnett, you're welcome to whatever revenge you want." He hardened his tone. "Meanwhile, starting now, this base is under military authority. Seafarms has no further say in any decisions that get made here."

"You can't make that kind of decision!" DuValier exploded. "You're not even the ranking officer!"

"Captain Hawley will back me up, I think, Lieutenant," Fraser said mildly. "I discussed my views with him before the meeting, and he agrees that we can't keep letting Seafarms wreck everything we try to accomplish."

"That doddering old fool agrees with whoever's talking with him," Barnett said angrily. "You won't hide behind him when it comes to taking the blame for this—not like you did over Fenris!"

Captain David Hawley's voice cut through the room like a knife. "The 'doddering old fool' doesn't agree with *you,* Citizen. And whether you try to spread the blame or not, I'm ultimately responsible for everything that happens in this command."

Heads swiveled. Hawley's entrance had gone unnoticed,

but his words brought instant attention. He was wearing issue battledress, and he seemed straighter and firmer than any of them had seen him before.

Fraser stood up. "Ten-hut!" he barked, and the other legionnaires followed suit.

"As you were," Hawley said with a vague gesture. He took his seat at the head of the table. "Arguments about who's in charge or who should be blamed aren't going to keep us alive. Citizen Barnett, I support Captain Fraser's position regarding military authority inside the Sandcastle. Inform your people, and then stay the hell out of our way."

Barnett seemed about to reply, but instead he stormed out of the room. There was a long silence.

"Thank you, Captain," Fraser said quietly. "I'm afraid that as long as there was any doubt about where the orders were coming from, he'd find more ways to obstruct us."

Hawley smiled. "I'm not good for a whole lot anymore, son," he said. "I've had too many light-years and too little practice to be much of a CO. But I'm *damned* if some puffed-up civilian is going to shove the Legion around!"

"Well, whatever the reason, it's good to have you in charge," Fraser said. He was surprised at the change in the man. It was like the spark that had started in the first battle had finally ignited a flame.

"Don't expect miracles, Captain," Hawley said, as if he were reading Fraser's mind. "As far as I'm concerned, you're in command of the defense here. Like I said, I'm not much of a CO anymore, but I'll do everything I can to keep up my end."

Fraser started to protest, but the older man held up his hand. "I said it before—arguing isn't going to help us now. If you want to take orders from me, take these. You're in tactical command, son. I know you've already got some pretty good ideas, so let's get them in place."

"Yes, sir," He swallowed and punched in a combination on the keyboard in front of him. "We've started installing heavy-weapons positions on the wall. My first idea is to build on these with several additional emplacements. . . ."

As he started to lay out the plans he and Trent had been working on since the first attack, Colin Fraser was conscious of a glow of pride within. Hawley was no longer simply dodging his responsibilities, but he still respected Fraser's opinions. Hawley, the hero of Aten.

And Fraser realized just how much Hawley's good opinion meant to him.

Lieutenant Antoine DuValier left the conference room and started toward his own office. He was confused and uncertain, and he needed some time alone to reexamine his feelings.

What Barnett had said in there about Fraser hiding behind Hawley had hit close to home. It was easy to see the similarities between this situation and what must have happened between Fraser and Major St. John after the Fenris situation. Of course Fraser would use the excuse that the senior officer carried responsibility for the decisions. . . .

Yet Fraser hadn't really acted like he was trying to use Hawley as a scapegoat. On the contrary, it had been Barnett who had suggested the idea—and Hawley, for that matter. But Fraser had fought his own battle until the older captain's appearance.

Had he misjudged Fraser? Or was Hawley even more of a puppet than anyone had thought, trotting out whatever help Fraser needed on command?

DuValier would have a lot to think about.

The meeting had broken up, but Fraser remained in the conference room, hunched over one of the computer monitors, studying one of the enclosures in Watanabe's report. He paused and rested his head in his hands, frustrated, tired. Every lead, every new scrap of information, seemed to complicate things.

"Don't let it get to you, Col," Kelly's soft voice made him look up.

"I didn't know you were still here," he said. "Sorry."

She smiled and sat down next to him. "I just wanted you to know you've got people on your side."

"Thanks. Between Barnett and Antoine DuValier I'm starting to think I've got more enemies inside the walls than outside. Lieutenant Gage won't say anything unless you prod her. Thank God for Hawley . . . and for your moral support, too."

Kelly frowned. "Are you sure you can count on Captain Hawley, Col? I mean, as long as he's in command, Barnett could still get to him. He's not the most strong-willed man I've ever seen."

"That's like saying Hanuman was a trifle unpleasant," Fraser chuckled. Then he turned serious. "The captain's had it tough, Kelly. Too damned tough."

"It doesn't answer the question, though, does it? Barnett could force him to back down."

"What do you want me to do, Kelly? Relieve him on grounds of mental incapacity?"

"You could, you know. Ramirez would back you up."

He shook his head, angry. "I'm not going to do it! Damn it, he deserves better than that!" Fraser looked away. When he went on he had control of his temper. "Sorry . . . that came out pretty strong. But it's the way I feel. David Hawley got the short end of the stick. A good career turned sour . . . the kind of thing I keep picturing for my own future. He could have retired, probably should have, years ago. But the army's all he's ever had. Hell, when he goes off to Dreamland it's usually a military fantasy, a battle story or a wargame. Well, I'm not going to be the one who takes it away from him, Kelly. He deserves a chance to keep whatever dignity he can."

She nodded slowly. "I see what you mean. So if Barnett goes over your head . . . ?"

"I'll take it as it comes. Anyway, I don't think Barnett will play around with politics much more. I'm a hell of a lot more concerned with figuring out what the next move from our fishy friends will be."

"What were you working on there?" she asked, gesturing toward the terminal.

"Watanabe pulled a prisoner out of the fighting around the *Cyclops*, but the wog suicided."

"Damn," Kelly said softly.

"Yeah, that's pretty much what Trent and I said, though the Gunny put it a lot more eloquently and carried on for a few minutes longer. All we got out of the nomad was the slogan 'Long live the warriors of Choor!' and a couple of nasty epithets. Then he grabbed a knife from one of the guards and killed himself."

"Choor! . . . A Clan chief?"

"Unlikely," Fraser answered. "Personality cults aren't very common in nomad society. Their loyalty is to the Clan. The individual is not as important as his role within the clan hierarchy."

"What have our native scouts come up with?"

"It's that kind of question that makes me wish you were my Exec instead of friend Antoine," he said with a smile. "The Gunny's down having a chat with them now. If we get a handle on just who or what Choor! is, maybe we'll have a shot at figuring out what to do about the nomads."

"How much reliance can you place on our wogs?" she asked.

He grinned. "You're starting to sound like Barnett. No offense intended." Fraser paused. "You know, I haven't been in the Legion much longer than you, but I'm finally starting to understand some of the mystique. Shared dangers, shared adventures . . . hell, the shared miseries of eating rapacks . . . It's the cement that binds these people together, Kelly. None of them are Citizens by birth, but they earn it by shedding blood together. You've seen it cross species lines—your little friend Myaighee, for instance—and it's just as powerful. The nomads who volunteered as auxiliaries had a lot of the same motives that drive our regulars. I think they're trustworthy, and I think they're going to do everything they can to help us. If only because they're in the same fix we are once the nomads hit us again."

"And if they don't know anything useful?"

"Then we'll just have to keep on fighting in the dark. Sooner or later something's got to give."

She looked grim. "Just hope it isn't us."

Gunnery Sergeant John Trent exchanged looks with the unit's Native Affairs specialist and shook his head. "You take this one, Hermann. I'm getting a sore throat from all this damned gargling."

*"Ja,"* agreed Warrant Officer Fourth-Class Koenig. He was a tall, gangling man who looked too young to hold a specialist's commission, but Trent knew the kid had two degrees in xenostudies and another in linguistics. Like a lot of the specialists who served as Warrant Officers in the Colonial Army, he had agreed to serve a five-year hitch with line troops, giving advice and analysis to pay off his tuition. It helped combat units to have experts on hand in areas like medicine, sciences, or engineering.

Right now Koenig was helping him question the native auxiliaries. If any of them could throw more light on the nature of the opposition . . .

Unfortunately, all of these nomads had been recruited out

of Ourgh. They were mostly failed merchants from distant clans who had taken service with the Legion as an alternative to a long journey home and the disgrace of failure at the end of it. That meant they knew little about the local situation—or at least they were claiming ignorance.

Trent wished they had the facilities at the Sandcastle for a proper Intelligence setup. With a little patience, and access to a computer implant, an Intel officer could conduct direct, mind-to-mind examinations that were far more reliable than any of the old drug or conditioning techniques. Of course it was physically and mentally tough on both the subject and the interrogator, but the results were worth it.

Well, it wouldn't have mattered much. The only implant in the Sandcastle belonged to Captain Hawley, and Trent doubted the old man had the willpower or mental agility to handle the stress of that kind of questioning. If Captain Fraser had remained in Intelligence longer, or had been born on Terra, he might have had an implant. Fraser knew how to set up the whole procedure—he'd explained it to Trent once during the last stages of the Hanuman mop-up campaign—but the captain wasn't capable of handling it himself.

Which left verbal questioning of the nomads to try to ferret out useful information. He just hoped the auxiliaries would have something worthwhile to offer.

Trent leaned back as Koenig beckoned the next auxiliary to the chair in front of the desk they'd set up in the Alpha Company ready room. He checked the fit of the language chip behind his ear. He wasn't going to trust himself to translate; the computer could give it to him a hell of a lot faster, and that would help him concentrate on trying to sift useful information out of the session. A one-task chip was nowhere near as useful as an implant, but it was still a handy tool to have.

"Your name and clan?" Koenig asked the new nomad in his native tongue. Trent felt a twinge of jealousy as he realized that the warrant officer had no chip and hadn't even seen the need to take a refresher course before the session. The man's skill with alien languages was uncanny.

Then again, Trent thought Koenig knew next to nothing about laying an ambush or setting up a defensive perimeter.

"Oomour am I, of the clan of the Seacliffs," the native replied, the Terranglic words a soft whisper in Trent's ear.

"Where does your clan swim, Oomour-of-the-Seacliffs?" Koenig asked formally.

The native's feeding tendrils writhed. "Few of the Seacliffs swimming are," he replied. "Those that do . . . scattered to the far waves."

"His clan was destroyed?" Trent asked Koenig in Terranglic.

The specialist nodded thoughtfully. "Doesn't happen much. Usually their interclan conflicts are like their fights with the city-dwellers—raids, skirmishes, that sort of thing. The Free-Swimmers don't have much concept of territorial possession or property rights, and it's a big ocean. Usually if a dispute arises, one side or the other just moves on."

Trent tugged thoughtfully at the corner of his sandy mustache. "The nomads have been doing a lot of funny things lately. Follow it up."

Koenig nodded. "How was your clan lost, Oomour?"

The native's gills vibrated, an expression of anger or great emotional stress. "By Choor! was the Clan attacked. Because join his tribe-of-tribes we would not."

"Orbit," Trent said softly. They had a lead.

"All right, let's run through what we know." Captain David Hawley leaned forward across the desk as he focused on Fraser's report. "This Choor! is a nomad leader who is trying to band together a coalition of clans—sort of a tribal empire. I thought that sort of cooperation was impossible. Something about sublimated territorial instincts, or some such."

From the corner of Hawley's office WO/4 Koenig spoke up. "Strictly speaking, you're right, sir," he said, a touch of pedantry in his tone. "The nomads have very little sense of physical territory, but a highly developed sense of the proprieties of their tribal hierarchies and allegiances. No Clan leader is likely to take orders from another Clan leader."

The warrant officer paused to consult a compboard note. "Apparently what we have here is a special exception. This Choor! seems to have been virtually orphaned when his Clan was ambushed by raiders—it had already fallen on hard times, and when bigger neighbors pounced on them they couldn't escape. A few survivors, including Choor!, but no more."

"So?" Hawley was getting impatient with the man's slow, deliberate presentation. "Where is this going?"

Fraser took over. "From what we've learned, sir, Choor! hooked up with another tribe. They do that, sometimes, but they're always regarded as outsiders. It's rare for a nomad tribe to fully adopt a stranger. Unfortunately for us, this Choor! is some kind of military genius. Literally. Even discounting a lot of what our natives fed us as the beginnings of a cult-legend, this guy revolutionized the way his new friends fought. They started coordinating their actions and using real tactics—the stuff we've seen in action—and that meant they could score big on their rivals."

Hawley suddenly understood. "Genghis Khan," he said aloud. "A goddamned Genghis Khan!"

Fraser nodded, clearly appreciating the comparison. "Yes, sir. Choor! seems to have discovered the same scheme Genghis Khan used with the Mongols. When he beats a tribe, they have the choice between joining up or getting squeezed out entirely."

"And they'll take his orders?"

"His *advice*, more like it," Fraser said. "In theory, he's still just a poor orphan boy without a tribe . . . but the chiefs and warlords in the coalition all regard him as a trusted advisor. As long as he keeps on winning, they keep getting all the benefits of their new empire. Fewer disputes, less competition, a genuine chance to challenge the city-dwellers . . ."

"And apparently, some big-time friends running guns and other high-tech gear in," Hawley added. "How much of this comes from Choor!, and how much from our unknown troublemakers?"

"Hard to say," Fraser said. "What we've learned comes from three nomads out of our auxiliaries, two of them refugees from tribes that ran away instead of knuckling under to the coalition, and the other one an ex-merchant repeating market-place gossip. There's no hint of any outsiders involved, but it's possible that this Choor! has been fed all of his 'innovations' from the word go." He shrugged. "If the Semti are involved, I'd say that's what happened. You know how they like to guide things from the shadows. But until we have more proof, I wouldn't make any definite judgments."

"Doesn't matter much in any case," Hawley said. "Either way, we've got a warlord running a coalition of tribes and getting technical help from the outside." He paused, thinking hard. "But it does give us an angle. Choor! has to keep winning to keep his hold over the Clans. Once they start figuring he's lost his touch, his advice means nothing and he loses his whole power base."

"Right," Fraser nodded. "They've already had a couple of failures . . . which means that Choor! is further out on a limb than ever."

"So if we can just hold out . . ."

"Easier said than done, sir," Fraser said. "When he hits us again, he won't be fooling around. This guy is good, Captain, and you can bet he'll take stock of previous failures and apply what we've taught him."

"You've got a knack for turning good news inside out, son," Hawley said with a dry, humorless chuckle.

"There's something else to consider, sir. Risky, but worth aiming for."

"And that is?"

"Friend Choor! really is the indispensable man where the nomads are concerned. All we need is a crack at him, and we've got a shot at breaking the coalition for good."

Hawley allowed himself a frown. "How do we spot him? Is he even going to hazard himself?"

"I don't know, sir," Fraser admitted. "But at least we've got a couple of angles to work on now. That puts us a couple of moves further ahead than we were this morning."

"Yeah." Hawley looked across the office at the painting that depicted the Fourth Foreign Legion's last stand on Devereaux. "All we have to do is avoid pulling a Devereaux until we can exploit them."

# Chapter 15

Heroes of Camerone and model brothers,
Sleep in your tombs of peace.

—From *Le Boudin,*
official marching song
of the French Foreign Legion

"By the standard calendar, today is the thirtieth of April. Today is Legionnaires' Day." Gunnery Sergeant Trent paused, surveying the upturned faces in the compound. It seemed odd to be making this address in a darkness relieved only by the glare of the floodlights, but it was 0800 by Legion timekeeping, despite the fact that the sun had gone down four hours ago and wouldn't rise again for nearly twenty more. Except for the duty section manning the walls, a few of the more serious cases on the injured list, and of course the civilians, the entire garrison was formed up in the open area below the headquarters building, turned out in full dress uniforms and white kepis. It made him feel good, like a renewal of his faith in the Legion and everything it stood for, to see those ordered ranks taking part in the annual ceremony that was at the very core of the unit's tradition.

He cleared his throat and continued. "One hundred and nineteen years ago today, in a cave in the highlands overlooking the Great Desert on Devereaux, Commandant Thomas Hunter and seventy-eight survivors from the Fourth Foreign Legion made the decision to attack the Semti garrison at Villastre. This was the culmination of the eight-month resistance to the Semti invasion, which had destroyed the rest of the Legion as a fighting force. The Semti Conclave's Ubrenfar and Gwyrran military forces on Devereaux at that time numbered in excess of sixty thousand, and the garrison at Villastre alone was known to be nine thousand strong.

"The Legion's resistance had already bogged down the Semti offensive into Terran space, buying months of valuable time. With the legionnaires so badly outnumbered, Hunter and his men might have considered surrender, or they might have remained in hiding out of reach of enemy forces until help arrived. Instead Commandant Hunter organized a final raid on the port control facilities at Villastre. The choice of the thirtieth of April was a deliberate one, for it marked the anniversary of the heroic stand by the First Legion on Terra at the village of Camerone. That happened nearly a thousand years ago, before the discovery of starflight.

"Hunter and his men boarded several VTOL transports and flew in low, under the Semti sensor umbrella, while their orbital watch was below the horizon. They caught the garrison at Villastre completely by surprise and destroyed the port control facilities and several warehouses loaded with the plunder of Devereaux. In the fighting Hunter and forty-one of his troops were killed. Lieutenant Eric Kessel took command of the thirty-six survivors as an Ubrenfar rapid-response unit deployed near the port.

"After an hour of sniping and two enemy assaults, the Legion force had been reduced to twelve men under the command of Chief-Sergeant Guy Marchand. The Semti governor and the leader of the Ubrenfars sent a demand to the legionnaires offering safe-conduct if they would surrender, but Marchand turned the envoys away. One hour later he and his men charged the Ubrenfar lines. Two men survived the fighting and were taken prisoner. The rest died in the service of the Legion."

Trent paused. "Their final gesture caused the Semti to shut down Devereaux as a supply port for another two months, and resulted in another ten thousand troops being added to their garrison against the chance that more legionnaires might have been lurking in the hills. But there were no more. Hunter and his seventy-eight were the last. By their stand, the last unit of the Fourth Foreign Legion may have saved Terra at a critical juncture of the Semti War. More important, though, they reconfirmed the lessons of Camerone and set an example for all their successors in the Legion to follow."

There was a stir among the men. Trent knew what they were thinking. On this Legionnaires' Day these men knew they could be facing the same kind of odds as the defenders of Devereaux . . . or of Camerone. But Trent stuck with the traditional close to the speech. "I don't know if any of you apes will ever really get what it's all about. But maybe, just maybe, one of you might understand Devereaux some day." He paused again, then went on in a brisker, more authoritative tone. "All personnel will draw an extra ration of wine tonight to toast the heroes of Camerone and Devereaux. Due to the nature of the threat to this garrison, Captain Hawley has been forced to suspend the usual celebrations." There was a groan at that. Usually Legionnaires' Day was treated as a three-day holiday. "Duty rosters are posted in the computer files. Don't get so busy remembering the past that you forget the present. Now . . . dismissed."

He turned and saluted smartly to the knot of officers standing nearby on the balcony that was serving as a reviewing stand. Captain Hawley returned the gesture with stiff formality.

Devereaux and Camerone . . . When the Fifth Foreign Legion was formed in the wake of the destruction of Hunter's unit, the two names became the core of the fledgling organization's mystique. "To do a Devereaux" was to face enormous odds with no hope of success, only the intention of upholding the Legion's honor.

If they did a Devereaux here, on Polypheme, it wouldn't have the same value as that stand by Hunter's troops. The wogs wouldn't go on to threaten the whole human sphere, and stopping them at the cost of the entire unit wouldn't be hailed as one of the great military victories of history.

But the Legion would know . . . and remember.

Leonid Narmonov leaned on the parapet and stared out into the darkness. It was approaching high tide, and that meant the danger from the nomads was reaching its peak. They could swim right to the walls, the way they'd done in the first assault.

They'd have a harder time launching a surprise attack now, though. A full platoon—six lances—was deployed along the wall at all times, with the others ready to provide backup at short notice. There were nomad auxiliaries patrolling the waters outside the Sandcastle when the tides were in, and a

Sandray or Sabertooth when the waters receded. And today Lieutenant DuValier had been supervising some electronics technicians, Legion and civilian, in fitting sonar transducers around the outer perimeter. After the next low tide gave them a chance to finish, the Sandcastle would have a full set of underwater sensors that would warn of any approach.

> So it's wine all around for these fine gentlemen,
> As I sing the refrain of these heroes again,
> The seventy-nine who died long ago,
> But live on in our memory of Devereaux!

Narmonov left the parapet to walk toward the source of the singing, a small knot of legionnaires clustered around a dim camp light. He recognized Haddad and Kelso from the Recon Lance, sitting together with a bearded sapper and a soldier whose collar tabs marked her as a Bravo Company medic. Kelso had a musynther, set now to reproduce a guitar, and played it with the same skill he showed lining up a laser shot.

Haddad looked up at his approach. "Ten-hut!" he said.

"As you were," he replied quickly.

The corporal sat down and produced a canteen. "Join us in the Legionnaires' Toast, Mr. Narmonov?" he asked.

Narmonov accepted it and drank to the heroes of Devereaux and Camerone. Then he paused, and instead of returning the canteen he held it up. "Let's drink another one to Sergeant Carstairs and the other good lads we've lost," he said quietly. "They kept the faith with the ones who made the Last March before."

The others drank with him. He saw the pride on the faces of Haddad and Kelso, both obviously pleased with the way their subaltern thought of his people. He thought it was easy to win the loyalty of these soldiers. And once earned, that loyalty would make them follow a man to Hell and back.

Something splashed in the distance, and searchlights swung to scan the water.

Narmonov handed the canteen back and hurried toward the nearest guard post. The moment of rapport was broken.

Oomour-the-Lost knew fear, the same fear that had gripped him the day the Clan of the Seacliffs had been hunted down and destroyed by the Clans United. He had been separated from the others that day, too far away to come to their aid in time, though the death agonies of his people had echoed clearly through the sea.

Then the Voice of the Clan, the repetitive signals that identified them over vast distances and provided a sense of identity even to those who foraged far from the Clan, ceased. Oomour had reached the scene of the last battle to find the attackers gone, his clanmates dead and stripped of the tribal property, the young vanished. His whole life had gone with the Clan, leaving him a husk, empty, useless.

No one had really believed that Choor! would follow through with his threat to exterminate any Clan that resisted him. But the massacre had been Choor!'s work. He'd seen bodies he knew belonged to tribes in the Clans United.

Another Clan, the Far-Wave-Hunters, had taken him in for a time. Not as a part of the Clan, of course, but they had treated him well enough and given him the chance to join their trading expeditions among the land-dwellers.

Then Choor! had come again, to demand the Far-Wave-Hunters join his Clans United. The Clan-Warlord had talked of fighting, the Clan-Chief of moving somewhere out of reach of Choor! and his allies. All the same discussions the Clan of the Seacliffs had held . . .

And Oomour had simply fled, too much afraid of seeing his new friends slaughtered as his old brothers had been. He'd fled to Ourgh, lived for a time as a beggar, then joined the Strangers-From-The-Skies to be a part of their "Legion."

Now he swam the long circuit outside the walls of their Built-Reef, a scout for the Legion-Clan, watching for signs that Choor! would attack.

He was afraid, and had to fight the urge to flee once again. Where could he swim, though, that Choor! and his Clans would not some day catch up?

Oomour started toward the surface, distracted by his thoughts. He never saw the looming figure waiting behind and above him, a figure who lashed out savagely with a nomad spear.

Pain lanced through Oomour's side, biting, searing.

Then there was nothing.

Narmonov ran to the watch post as a legionnaire pointed and shouted. "Something moving down there!"

Another soldier raised his FEK, but Narmonov knocked it aside. "Hold your fire, dammit!" he said sharply. "That might be one of our wogs down there!"

Lights knifed through the darkness, probing the waves. Dropping his faceplate and setting it on infrared vision, the subaltern scanned the area. Nothing . . . Nothing . . .

Something warmer than the water bobbed to the surface, a fuzzy bright patch on his display. Narmonov switched quickly to LI and the image shifted, becoming clearer, plainer. A native, floating facedown, either unconscious or dead. He recognized the tattoos on the nomad's back. It was one of the auxiliaries . . . Oomour, that was the name.

Blood stained the water around the unmoving form.

"Send one of our other wogs out there," Narmonov ordered. "That's one of our scouts."

He caught a movement out of the corner of his eye and swung to face it.

Dark shapes were crawling up the wall of the Sandcastle near the HQ building.

"Sound the alarm!" he shouted, unslinging his FEK. "Get some men to the wall over there!"

"Fire! Pour it on, you sons of strakks!" Trent bellowed the order as he ran, still buckling on a piece of plasteel chest armor. He'd been checking over the next day's duty roster with Sergeant Valko and Legionnaire Garcia in the base's operations center when the klaxon sounded. Now Valko was rousing the off-duty troops while Trent headed for the wall.

The compound was ablaze with light, and searchlight beams were playing across the eastern side of the base as gunners searched for targets. Trent ran past a small, gaunt legionnaire wearing corporal's stripes on his gaudily painted armor. The man was stripping the cover off of an onager that had been rigged on a pintel mount overlooking the ocean. Further on, several Legion riflemen were leaning over the parapet and pumping full autofire into the restless waves below.

Subaltern Narmonov was directing troops nearest the threatened sector. The young Ukrainian looked harassed.

"Gunny!" he shouted as Trent approached. "Glad you're here. Take charge of getting the reinforcements on the line. And try to get our friendly wogs reeled in. We've got at least three out there, and one poor devil who's probably had it." He paused. "I'll be over there," he concluded, with a wave in the direction of the fighting. A few dark nomad shapes were mixed in among the legionnaires flocking to defend the wall, and more were climbing rapidly.

The wogs had chosen a good spot to launch a strike. The walls at that point projected outward at an angle that shielded the attackers from the legionnaires' fire. That allowed the natives to climb virtually unmolested.

So far the troops at the top were holding them, but as more attackers added their weight to the assault the legionnaires would be in trouble.

"Yes, sir," Trent acknowledged the subaltern's order. He doubted if Narmonov heard; the officer was already running for the thick of the fight, shouting encouragement punctuated by fierce oaths in Russian.

A lance from Alpha Company came up the stairs from the center of the compound. It was a heavy-weapons unit, and Trent directed the corporal in charge to deploy around the gatehouse in case of another assault in that sector. "Get those Fafnirs ready, but don't fire them until you get orders . . . or until the wogs are threatening to overrun you," he finished. "Explosions in the water will screw the wogs up, but some of our scouts are still out there."

"We're on it, Sarge," the corporal told him cheerfully. He was grinning. "Come on, you sandrats, let's bag us some polliwogs!"

"What's the situation here, Sergeant?"

Trent spun as Lieutenant DuValier and Bravo Company's two recon lances appeared, with the unit's junior $C^3$ technician, Legionnaire Dubcek, bringing up the rear. As usual the Exec was impeccably turned out, managing to make even battledress look elegant and stylish, though he looked tired. "Nomad assault, sir," the sergeant said formally, touching his helmet. "So far it appears confined to Sector One, but I've posted extra men by the gatehouse. I saw Subaltern Bartlow mustering some troops by the main pumping station, too."

DuValier nodded curtly. "I ordered him there. Why aren't you bombing the bastards in the water?"

"Sir our wogs are still out there," Trent responded, spreading his hands. "Mr. Narmonov says he saw one of them either killed or badly wounded, but the rest are unaccounted for."

The lieutenant scowled. "Damn stupid putting them out there," he muttered. "Score another for the boy genius." He seemed to recover himself. "All right, Sergeant. Continue here."

"And you, sir?"

"Since we can't blast them out of the water, I'm going to try something else. What we need is to get a better angle on those damned wogs as they climb. Some troops out there will do the trick." His gesture took in the water beyond the wall.

"That's suicide, sir!" Trent protested. "The wogs'll be all over you. Anyway, by the time you get on your hard-suits . . ."

"The hell with suits!" the Frenchman snapped. He touched a device hanging from his neck, and Trent realized for the first time that all of them were wearing oxymasks. They were usually used in riot-control situations, but they'd work for a short time underwater. "Come on, you misbegotten misfits! Let's do it!"

They pushed past Trent, heading for the parapet and fitting their masks in place. Dubcek started shedding his C³ terminal. The computer and communications terminal wouldn't stand much exposure with those corrosive waters below. But that wouldn't stop Dubcek from following DuValier into action.

Trent's eyes followed them. Part of him wanted to stop the lieutenant, while another part wished he were following the man.

Then he turned. "Mr. Wijngaarde!" he shouted, catching sight of the First Platoon CO. "Can I have some riflemen for the walls here? We have to cover Lieutenant DuValier!"

In the back of his mind Trent felt a twinge of regret. It was too bad that Lieutenant DuValier had taken such a dislike to the captain. Fraser and DuValier had a lot in common.

Starting with bravery . . .

Fraser burst into the command center, still cursing the alert that had awakened him from the first good sleep he'd enjoyed in three standard days. *Just when you let your guard down,* he told himself bitterly. *That's when trouble always starts.*

He didn't like the coincidence of this attack on the evening of Legionnaires' Day. Had they just been lucky, or had Choor!'s clans learned that a Legion garrison usually declared it a holiday? Extra rations of wine and a wild night of celebrating would have made an attack easy. . . .

Hawley, Garcia, and one of Alpha Company's C³ technicians were already in the room. The senior captain looked up. "Looks like a commando job, Fraser," he said casually. "They picked a protected approach up the walls, and seem to be confining the attack there."

"Recon drones?" Fraser asked.

"Up and circling, Captain," Garcia told him. "Very little sign of activity. I think that supports Captain Hawley's theory."

"A good move, I'd say," Hawley said approvingly. "Looks a bit like the Imperial French op against the terrorists on Ys. The Ysan Freedom Brigade's garrison didn't have much perimeter security, of course. I'd say we've got a much better position than the YFB . . . and the wogs aren't anything comparable to the French, no matter how good this Choor! is."

"With all due respect, sir," Fraser said, "I'm afraid this isn't a wargame. We've got a fight on our hands."

Hawley didn't answer. He seemed entranced by the view on the monitor as the recon drone circled beyond the walls.

"What the hell. . . ?" Fraser whispered, as he caught sight of humans in the water.

"Lieutenant DuValier, sir," Garcia broke in quickly. "He's got Pascali's and Braxton's recon lances."

"They're not even in hardsuits!" he said, sitting down beside Garcia. "What the hell are they playing at out there?"

"Sergeant Trent says they're trying to clear the attackers off the wall. He's deployed riflemen to cover them from the nomads."

Fraser looked away. It was a good plan, but damned risky. If nothing else, those men would be sick by the time they were fished out of the sea. Polypheme's oceans weren't quite lethal to unprotected humans, but even short-term exposure caused some nasty allergic reactions.

That was assuming the wogs didn't get them first.

"What reserves do we have left?" he asked.

The Alpha Company technician—Fraser vaguely remembered that his name was Jurgensen—checked a computer display. "Sergeant Reynolds, sir. First Platoon Alpha. Twenty-one effectives."

"All right. Pass the word for Reynolds and his men to suit up and relieve Lieutenant DuValier out there." Fraser leaned back in the chair and closed his eyes. He only hoped the backup wouldn't come too late.

# Chapter 16

> Go and tell your general that we're not here to surrender.
>
> —General Pierre Koenig,
> during the siege of Bir Hakeim
> French Foreign Legion, 1942

The water stung DuValier's face and hands, and the FEK slung across his back felt heavier than the four kilograms claimed in the technical stats, but he ignored the discomfort as he pushed away from the Sandcastle's wall and fell into a slow, steady breaststroke. Behind him the rest of the legionnaires kept pace.

On the wall behind them DuValier could hear FEKs whining, laying down covering fire. That must have been Trent's work. The Gunnery Sergeant was a good man, except for his obvious attachment to Colin Fraser.

Or was that just further proof that Fraser wasn't as bad as he'd first thought?

DuValier thrust the question from his mind. What mattered now was getting men in position to clear those walls and keep them cleared. Fraser could wait.

Stopping and treading water, DuValier signaled for a halt. "Pascali, keep an eye out for bad guys," he said. The oxymask made it hard to talk clearly, but Corporal Pascali nodded and signaled her lance to disperse in a loose perimeter. "Braxton, your people concentrate on those wogs." He pointed at the wall, where at least twenty nomads were using their sucker-lined limbs to climb toward the parapet.

Braxton kept his head and shoulders out of the water by using powerful kicks, and raised his FEK. As he fired, DuValier turned away to study their surroundings. Were any of the wogs taking an interest in them yet?

From the wall, shouts and screams attested to the deadly

effect of the legionnaires' fire. They reminded DuValier of the cries he'd heard that day on Fenris.

It took all of his will to shut the sounds out of his mind.

"Sir!" That was Vaslov Dubcek, touching his arm and pointing to the left. "Over there!"

He followed the gesture and saw the bobbing figure thirty meters away. A wog, apparently unmoving.

Trent had mentioned a wounded or dead scout. DuValier started toward the figure, knowing that the $C^3$ technician was following close behind.

He reached the body and rolled it over. Blood was oozing sluggishly from two stab wounds in the native's chest, but the gills were moving slowly and there was a pulse in the big artery on the front of the throat. DuValier wasn't familiar with wog first aid, and thought it would be wisest not to meddle with what he didn't know. He turned the wounded scout over again to get a better water flow past the gills, then started back toward the Sandcastle.

Something thrashed in the water nearby. He released his burden and turned in time to see a nomad driving a pike through Dubcek's chest. The legionnaire struggled at the end of the lance like a fish on the end of a spear, then went limp.

With a curse DuValier started to fumble for his FEK, then gave it up and drew his PLF rocket pistol instead. The wog wrenched the spear out of the dead $C^3$ tech's body with a deep-throated shout and raised himself halfway out of the water, brandishing the weapon.

DuValier squeezed off a round and threw himself sideways. The spear missed him by inches. He surfaced again, ready to fire, but the wog was drifting now, as helpless as the injured scout.

He dived, squinting through the dark water, searching for fresh signs of pursuit. Something that he felt more than heard made him shake his head. Sounds, but at the very lowest limit of a human's range of hearing. They were nothing like wog speech, but there was something . . . *intelligent* about that noise. *Organized.*

He surfaced again beside the floating scout and wiped uselessly at his stinging eyes. Corporal Pascali was swimming toward him, another legionnaire close behind. "They're retreating, sir," she said. "And Captain Fraser's sent some hardsuited troops to take over."

He got a grip on the wounded native and nodded. "Get Dubcek's body," he said tiredly.

But although he was suddenly feeling exhausted from the short but intense clash, Antoine DeValier's mind was still racing, trying to piece together the whirling fragments of a half-formed idea.

"All right, Gunny, what's next?" Fraser asked wearily. The attack had ended less than six hours before, but routine had reasserted itself inside the Sandcastle. The administrative side of running a military unit had never appealed to him, but even in the face of the native threat the work had to go on.

"Four men for company punishment," Gunnery Sergeant Trent said stiffly. "Unfit by reason of intoxication."

Fraser glanced at the four prisoners lined up just outside the office door. They were flanked by a pair of guards from Alpha Company. Antoine DuValier, looking none the worse for his swim the night before, was with them as well, presumably as the officer filing the charges.

Softly, to Trent, Fraser asked, "What's the story, Gunny?"

"They're from Wijngaarde's platoon, skipper," Trent replied in the same quiet tones. "Apparently Legionnaire White, there, had a still set up down in the maintenance tunnels by the pumping station. They decided to celebrate Legionnaires' Day with something stronger than wine, and were passed out cold when the fun and games started last night."

Fraser frowned. There was no rule to prevent legionnaires from drinking, even on duty, but stiff penalties were imposed on men who rendered themselves unfit. Still, in their current situation, he was reluctant to put these four in cells. "Any way we can look the other way on this one, Gunny?" he asked.

The sergeant shook his head. "Lieutenant DuValier found them sleeping it off behind the docking cradle after the battle. He threatened them with cells in front of witnesses."

"Well, let's get to it, then," Fraser said, rubbing the bridge of his nose and wishing he could do something easy, like face another native raid.

The prisoners were brought in, and he went through the formalities of hearing their stories, and DuValier's. When the testimony was over he nodded gravely. "Sounds straightforward enough. One week in cells." Fraser paused. "White, your hobby has endangered the security of this command, so I'm ordering your still dismantled. You'll have an extra week in cells to think about, too."

The legionnaire glared at him. "Nothin' in regs about runnin' a still, sir."

"Ordinarily, I wouldn't care if you were brewing homemade rat poison to drink," Fraser told him bluntly. "But I need men who can see straight and put up a fight. Gunny, see to the punishment." He waved a hand in dismissal.

They started to leave. "A moment, Mr. DuValier," he said to the Exec.

"Sir?" As usual, the Frenchman managed to turn the polite formality into thinly concealed contempt.

Trent closed the door, leaving the two officers alone. "What the hell were you thinking of, Lieutenant?" Fraser asked.

"I don't understand, sir," DuValier said.

"The last thing we need is to throw those men into cells. They might not do us much good when they're drunk, but they don't do us any good when they're locked up, damn it!"

"Then why didn't you let them off?" DuValier challenged. "It's your decision."

"Because, Mr. DuValier, I am obligated to back up my officers even when they pull a damn-fool stunt. You threatened them publicly with punishment, and I had to hand out that punishment or undermine your authority."

"I'm not asking for your support, sir," DuValier said harshly.

Anger welled up inside Fraser. "I've had it with this goddamned posturing, Lieutenant! If you can't start playing on the team, at least quit pulling the other way!"

"At least I don't let my men down," DuValier shot back, flushing. "Not like you did on Fenris!"

Fraser stood up slowly, fighting for control. "What happened on Fenris, and my part in it, doesn't make a strakking bit of difference here, Lieutenant. Do what you want to after we've got the nomads under control, but until then you can forget about Fenris. It's ancient history, and by God you'll keep it that way! Do you get me, Lieutenant?"

The Exec drew himself up stiffly. "I'll never forget Fenris, Captain,'' he said slowly. ''Never. I lost too many friends there . . . and too much of myself.'' He paused. ''Am I dismissed?''

Fraser sank back in his chair. He hadn't realized DuValier had been part of the fighting on Fenris. No wonder he'd been so hostile.

But there still wasn't room for a personal vendetta now. ''I meant what I said, Lieutenant,'' he told DuValier quietly. ''About the past . . . and about the present. Every man in this compound is needed if we're going to get off this planet alive.'' When the other man made no response, Fraser added a curt ''Dismissed.''

DuValier left the office. A moment later, Gunny Trent returned. ''Rough, skipper?''

''Yeah,'' Fraser thought about Fenris. ''Yeah, rough. What else do you have for me, Gunny?''

''Warrant Officer Kelly has some ideas she wants you to look over, skipper,'' Trent said. ''She says she has a way to keep those wog bastards off the walls.''

''Send her in,'' Fraser said, forcing a smile. ''If she can do that, I'll put *her* in charge of this circus and go fishing.''

DuValier slammed the door to the Headquarters building behind him and stalked across the compound, seething inside. For once he didn't care how much of his anger showed through.

*Damn* Fraser! The man was so smug, so superior, with his fatherly pretensions and his sham concern over the men. Fraser hadn't cared about the soldiers on Fenris!

He knew, now, that his first judgment had been right, that the captain really was to blame for everything. What had Fraser done last night during the attack? Nothing. But the man would probably grab the credit when the time came.

DuValier had planned to broach his ideas on the nomad coordination techniques this morning, but it was clearly useless to try now. He'd work out the rest of the puzzle on his own, then present Fraser with the finished product later, when the time was right.

Sergeant Mohammed Qazi, Third Platoon's senior NCO and the noncom in charge of Supply, hurried across the compound to intercept him. ''Lieutenant?'' he began, saluting.

''What is it, Qazi?'' DuValier responded curtly.

The sergeant seemed to recoil from him. "Begging your pardon, Lieutenant, but you wanted to know when the sonar installation was complete. We've got all the transducers in place. I put Legionnaire Sinora in charge of the electronics end of things, since Dubcek bought it." Sinora was Third Platoon's $C^3$ specialist.

DuValier nodded. "Good job," he said. "How soon until it's on-line?"

"Sinora said four hours. Less, if he can get some help from the Seafarms technical people."

"You light a fire under the civilians, Qazi," DuValier ordered. "I've got another project I need to get on."

Qazi looked unhappy. "Sir . . . C-cubed just called. I've got a meeting with Captain Fraser and Miss Winters—er, Miss Kelly, that is. Supply problems."

"Then tell Bartlow to take care of it!" he flared. "Just get that sonar system up and running!"

DuValier turned away, conscious of Qazi's eyes following him as he headed for the Sandcastle's hospital section.

"The main problem will be jury-rigging the power system. If we can nail that down, I think we'll be home-free."

Fraser nodded as Kelly finished, looking down at the terminal screen on his desk. He couldn't find anything wrong with the technical side of her scheme. If they could make this work . . .

"Any opinions, Gunny?" he asked.

Trent spoke up from the other side of the office. "It won't be perfect, skipper. Magrep's been tried for antipersonnel work before, and there are always problems with it. But anything that makes it hard for those bloody wogs to get at us is a good idea."

"That's the way I see it, too," Fraser said. "Thanks, Kelly. That was good work."

She smiled. "Actually, the idea came from one of my sappers—MacAllister."

"Is he back on duty already?"

Kelly nodded. "Yesterday. He says he remembered something similar to this being used during the campaign on Thoth. A mobile column got pinned down by lokes in an open valley, and the CO dismantled the magrep generators and set them up as a perimeter defense." She glanced at

Trent. "As you said, Sergeant, some of them got through. But it kept them alive until a relief column reached them."

The intercom on Fraser's desk buzzed. "Sergeant Qazi, sir." Garcia's voice came over the line.

"Send him in," Fraser said.

The dark, hawk-nosed sergeant always managed to make him feel uneasy. Qazi was the kind of NCO who regarded officers as a necessary evil at best, and didn't hesitate to let his feelings be known. Fraser waved him to a seat and started outlining Kelly's scheme. The noncom listened with a solemn expression to the plans for immobilizing the magrep vehicles in the compound and mounting their magnetic-field generators on the outer wall to hamper climbers.

"Have you worked out the spacing you'll need between modules to make this work?" he asked as Fraser finished.

Kelly answered for him. "It's on the computer," she said.

Qazi moved to a terminal and studied the specs. "Legion generators won't be enough," he said at last. "I don't have enough spares, and even ripping the guts out of all our MSVs won't give us enough."

"There's always the Seafarms vehicles," Trent commented. "And whatever spares they have in stock."

"Barnett will scream," Kelly said.

"Let him," Fraser told them. "Sergeant, get together a work party to dismount those modules. Kelly, your sappers can mount them. If you need help from anyone, Legion or civilians, they're yours. Do it."

As they left, Fraser turned back to study the schematics again. He told himself this was the kind of teamwork they needed. Not the kind of infighting DuValier was fostering.

If they could just stand together, they might pull through. . . .

The wounded scout was awake, but obviously in pain. As DuValier leaned forward trying to catch his low, labored voice, he found time to admire the work Dr. Ramirez had done to patch the native up. The doctor had chipped a study on native medicine when they brought Oomour in, and it looked like regen therapy would have the nomad up and around in a day or two.

Considering how bad those wounds had been, that was getting close to a miracle, even given Commonwealth medical technology.

"The Voice of the Clan . . ." the nomad said softly. "The Voice of the Clan you heard . . . but . . ."

His voice faded away and DuValier leaned forward, alarmed. "But what? Come on, Oomour, explain it to me! Come on!"

An eyestalk swiveled to fix on him. "Not . . . the same. Not a Clan Voice . . ."

Another half hour of patient questioning left the wog exhausted. Ramirez finally administered a sedative and chased DuValier out of the ward, but not before he had the answers he'd been looking for.

He wished he had someone else he could use as a sounding board. Dubcek would have been perfect for that, but now he was dead. It left the Exec feeling very much alone among the legionnaires. They were Fraser's people, and Hawley's, not his own.

The best he could do was locate Warrant Officer Koenig. The Native Affairs specialist was going over the reports from the *Seafarms Cyclops*. He seemed happy to turn off his computer terminal and listen.

At length Koenig nodded. "You may be on to something here, Lieutenant," he said. "The sophonts do indeed have a method of broadcasting what you might call 'territorial signals.' It is a very low-frequency sound, quite independent of normal speech. The actual information content it could convey would be quite small, however."

"But with considerable range, correct?" DuValier asked.

"Yes," Koenig confirmed. "Possibly several hundred kilometers. Before Mankind developed engine-propelled ships on Terra, whales could communicate across oceanic distances using much the same method. Very likely it was the disruption caused by these new sounds which contributed to the decline and extinction of the whale population."

"So the wogs send out signals that identify them by Clan."

"Yes," the specialist said again. "Members of the clan can track the main body as they forage, and other clans are warned away from waters a given clan is exploiting." He checked a computer reference. "I believe they also use these same sounds to herd the pre-sentient juveniles."

DuValier nodded. "Now, the big question. You say the information content is low. Could these messages be made to transmit enough information to coordinate a battle? Last night I heard something that might have been one of these signals, but one of our wog scouts says that what he heard wasn't anything like a recognized Clan Voice. Just after I heard it, the natives retreated."

"The missing link in how they're coordinating their activities, then. Yes." Koenig looked thoughtful. "If they'd prearranged it . . ."

"What?"

"A code. As long as they have a prearranged set of signals, they could handle a variety of evolutions with a relatively limited 'alphabet.' The British Navy in the Age of Sail could send dozens of specific orders, even before they developed a true alpha-numeric signaling system. It was rigid, but an intelligent officer could use it quite ingeniously when the need arose."

"We're dealing with a very intelligent officer in this Choor!," DuValier said. "But now that we know how he's giving his subordinates their orders . . ."

Koenig grinned. "We can make his life miserable."

"Exactly," DuValier said.

He wondered what Fraser's reaction would be when he discovered it was his despised Exec who had ended the native threat.

Low tide.

It left the open ground beyond the Sandcastle's dun-colored walls uncovered, a muddy plain dotted with tidal pools and the flotsam and jetsam left behind by the receding waters. From the parapet above the gatehouse, Colin Fraser surveyed the flat terrain through the image-intensifier of his battle helmet.

The handful of natives were plainly nomads, adorned only by harnesses and tattoos and carrying a variety of weapons. They walked toward the base with no sign of fear, secure under the blue-green banner that fluttered in the wind above them.

His chipped knowledge of nomad customs told Fraser that they were envoys. The Clans regarded land as neutral ground, ideal for holding parleys between rival parties—another reason for their hostility toward their land-dwelling cousins, no doubt, who claimed to own the tracts of land that had been ownerless in nomad eyes for aeons.

A red banner would have signaled an intent to negotiate a blood-feud; yellow would have summoned all comers to trade. Blue-green, the color of the oceans, was the color of a truce between warring clans.

Beside him Trent had his FEK out. "It could still be a trick, skipper," he said quietly. "Remember, they lump us with the city people, and I've heard of cases where nomads broke a parley to attack land-dwellers. They don't regard them as real people."

"Just the kind of trick friend Choor! would try, too," Fraser said. "He may figure that our leadership is as vulnerable as his."

"Not if his intel is as good as it's been so far. But anything that would upset morale would be a good move. After last night . . ."

"He needs a victory now," Fraser finished. "By whatever means he can get it. All right, Gunny, we'll talk to them from here."

They waited for the natives to advance to within earshot. "Clansmen!" Fraser said at last, through an amplifier mike hooked up to Legionnaire Garcia's $C^3$ pack. "You seek a parley? State your mission."

Nomads exchanged looks as if taken aback by having to talk from a distance. Then one of them responded.

"In the name of the Clans United," he began, proceeding through a litany of eighteen individual nomad tribes before reaching the heart of the message. "In the name of these, who are the voice of the Free Swimmers, the Terrans who have intruded into our world are called upon to surrender themselves or face death. We are many times your numbers, Terrans, and we swim free while you crouch within your stone reef. We pledge that you shall be allowed to leave our world in peace should you surrender, but should you choose to resist further the Clans United shall not rest until the last of your people has been killed."

Fraser switched off the amplifier. "They learn fast," he commented. "But I doubt that whoever's been feeding them this stuff is really serious about letting us go."

"Yeah," Trent agreed. "This isn't quite the same thing as taking in a recalcitrant tribe and turning it into part of the organization."

He nodded to Garcia and spoke into the mike again. "No surrender," he said shortly. "You'll have to come in here and dig us out."

He turned away from the parapet. There would be no turning back from here.

# Chapter 17

> Getting bounced from the Legion? They don't bounce people from Hell.
>
> —attributed to an unknown legionnaire of the French Foreign Legion

The nomad scout was better after more regen therapy, and DuValier found him sitting up and looking alert, even restless. Aside from the steridressings on his chest and side, Oomour looked almost fully recovered.

"You I thank for bringing me back?" the scout asked DuValier as the lieutenant entered the ward.

He nodded, then remembered that among the natives it was a side-to-side movement that indicated assent. "I found you," he told Oomour. "It was luck, mostly."

"Then to you my life I owe," the nomad said. "To you a debt I would repay."

DuValier shrugged. "We don't abandon our own," he told the wog, wondering if the native would understand.

"Yes . . . yes, your Clan is mine now." Oomour seemed more grateful at being accepted as part of the Legion than at having his life saved.

"Well, your Clan is going to need you, Oomour," DuValier said. "When Dr. Ramirez discharges you tomorrow, see me. I want you to help me with a little project I have in mind."

"Project?"

He smiled. "Yeah. I'm going to make a Voice for the Legion Clan that'll give Choor!'s bastards a headache."

A footfall behind him made DuValier turn. Edward Barnett was standing just inside the door. "Lieutenant, I need to see you," the civilian said. He shot a look of distaste at Oomour. "When you're done here."

DuValier finished with the native quickly and joined Barnett. The civilian wouldn't speak until they were out of the medical center and out in the open. When he finally did talk, it was in hushed, conspiratorial tones.

"Lieutenant, you've struck me as the only voice of reason in this entire unit," Barnett began. "Between that incompetent Hawley and your boss Fraser, they've flouted everything Seafarms has tried to do on this planet, damn it, and neither of them seems to realize the damage they've done."

DuValier studied the civilian with distaste. He knew how Barnett felt about the Legion. He wouldn't be here, talking to a Legion officer, without some ulterior motive. "It isn't for me to criticize my superiors," he said guardedly. *Not to the likes of you,* he added to himself.

"You heard about the nomad peace offer yesterday, didn't you?"

"Yeah. A sham."

"So your Captain Fraser claims. But what if it isn't? The nomads may be giving us a way out. With negotiation, Seafarms might even find a way to deal with this warlord, Choor! or whatever his name is. But Fraser won't even think of exploring a peaceful settlement, and of course Hawley backs him up."

"The nomads, by themselves, could be offering terms, Citizen. But whoever's backing them, human or ale, knows enough about the Commonwealth to know Terra won't back down that easily. I can't see them letting the wogs arrange a peace that's liable to break down in a few months anyway. They'll want a solid victory, something to prove this place is too expensive to try and civilize."

"You seem to forget, Lieutenant, that Seafarms is the government here. As things are going now we'll probably drop the Cyclops Project and cut our losses. We can give these people exactly what they want, if that's what it takes, without any more loss of life. We can get out of this without any more battles, man. But Fraser seems determined to sit tight and take the whole planet on if he has to. And all that's going to do is get a lot of good people killed. Like he did on Fenris. You know about that, don't you?"

DuValier nodded tightly. "I . . . know." He thought about what Barnett had said. It seemed reasonable enough. What did they have to lose by negotiations?

Nothing but pride. Rumor had it that Fraser was likely to be investigated by the Warwick Commission, and giving in to the locals would be damning enough to get him into hot water even Warwick's well-connected enemies couldn't rescue the captain from. He might just take the whole unit down, if the alternative was watching his career be ruined. Like Hawley's.

"I can encourage them to take another look at negotiations, Citizen," he said carefully. "But beyond that . . ."

"Beyond that, there's something else to be concerned about," Barnett broke in. "Fraser and his girlfriend have cooked up some scheme to mount magrep generators on the walls. To pull it off, he wants to rip them out of Seafarms vehicles!"

"Planning a trip, Citizen?"

Barnett snorted. "Look, quite aside from the fact that these are company assets that I don't want to see destroyed, we don't know that we won't be needing those vehicles again. What if we do strike a deal with Choor!? Hell, what if the natives pound us so bad here that we have to run for it? We could be needing those vehicles, damn it, but Fraser plans on stripping all of them down."

DuValier studied him again. It was clear that Barnett had his own reasons for preserving those vehicles intact. Was it worth it to help him?

They didn't really need the generators. As soon as he finished his work with Oomour they'd have a weapon that would be just as effective, maybe more so. And if Barnett was right about negotiating their way out . . .

A friend at Seafarms was a friend inside Reynier Industries, and that wasn't a bad thing for a legionnaire to have. If getting Fraser to back down on the magrep generator idea would cement an alliance with Barnett, it might be worth his while to get involved.

"Just what do you want me to do?" he asked slowly.

"Why, I thought that was obvious," Barnett said. "Relieve Hawley and Fraser of their commands, and take charge of the garrison yourself."

"Tide'll be coming in soon," Fraser said, glancing at the display of his wristpiece computer to confirm the tide table data. "Is that going to interfere with your work?"

Beside him Kelly was crouched by the parapet, checking a power lead. "Not unless the nomads attack again when the water's high,'' she said. ''I'm more concerned about getting the magrep generators out of Seafarms.''

''Trouble?''

''They said they'd take care of it, but I think Barnett told them to pull a go-slow. MacAllister said that their people were evasive this morning when he asked them when they'd have some generators for us.''

''I'm getting damn tired of hearing about trouble with Seafarms,'' Fraser said. ''If I get any more of this nonsense I'll throw Barnett into cells. And any of his little helpers who want to back him up.''

''Careful, Col,'' she said quietly, hooking her circuit-tester to another lead. ''Every time you back that bastard into a corner you run the risk of having him bring you up on charges. You know Warwick's just waiting for an excuse like that.''

''Yeah. But if it's a choice between my career and our chances of getting out of here alive . . .''

''Let's try to pull off both,'' Kelly said with a grin. ''Come on, Col. If you get kicked out of the Legion now, where will that leave me? I didn't sign on for the glamour, you know.''

He wondered if she was serious. Sometimes she seemed to want nothing more than friendship, but there were other times . . .

Fraser wasn't about to complicate either of their lives further by pursuing that line of thought. Instead he tried to match her light tone. ''Don't worry. No one's figured out a way to drop someone from the Legion yet. There's nothing lower on the social scale to drop *to*. And I could always sign on as an enlisted man if they don't want me as an officer.''

She laughed. ''I'd love to see Sergeant Trent cuffing you on the ear and calling you 'nube.' ''

''So would he.'' Fraser paused. ''Seriously, though, I'd better go see what Seafarms is doing. If we can get those generators in place, I think we'll even be able to hold a major assault. And with *Cyclops* due back here in another couple of days, that'll finally put time on our side.''

Seafarms had taken over a disused part of the base. With more than eight hundred civilians from Ourgh now installed inside the Sandcastle, living quarters were cramped and the workshops and offices were necessarily squeezed for space, but that hadn't stopped Barnett from insisting on maintaining services that duplicated some of what the Legion was responsible for, like the motor pool.

If only Sigrid Jens had lived . . .

He cut across the center of the Sandcastle on his way to the Seafarms motor pool. A block of legionnaires from Alpha Company was drilling on open ground below the Ops center, supervised by Gunny Valko and Subaltern Narmonov. Some Bravos from Bartlow's platoon were working with Kelly's sappers, using the makeshift magrep barge to haul the first of the generators cannibalized from Legion vehicles toward the wall near the gatehouse. There was also a gang of Seafarms people, some armed, but most of them not, checking over the struts of the cradle that would support *Seafarms Cyclops* when Watanabe brought her in. Corporal Bashar was piloting a veeter and operating a winch to lift the heavy generators into place on the wall. The corporal gave Fraser something between a wave and a salute as he hovered over the barge.

He was glad to see the work going on. It was a big improvement over the way things had been before the crisis, when *cafarde* had been threatening to ruin them all. But it was a damned high price to pay to relieve a little boredom.

Fraser stopped as he saw Barnett crossing the compound from the direction of the Seafarms section. Several armed civilians were with him, almost a bodyguard. Lieutenant DuValier and some legionnaires from Wijngaarde's platoon were with them.

"Is there some kind of trouble here, Lieutenant?" he asked as the party approached. Had Barnett caused some kind of trouble?

Something wasn't right. . . .

"Captain Fraser," DuValier said formally. "I regret to inform you that I am relieving you of your command of Bravo Company under Article Two-oh-seven of Colonial Army Regulations. I hope it will not be necessary to place you under arrest."

"What the hell are you talking about, Lieutenant?" Fraser asked, stunned by the flat, emotionless statement. DuValier didn't sound triumphant, or defiant, or even concerned. Just cold and aloof, as always. "Two-oh-seven is relief by reason of incapacity. . . ."

"And in my judgment, sir, your recent decisions have

been proof of mental incapacity,'' DuValier shot back. ''Perhaps the strain of having to assume so many of Captain Hawley's duties in addition to your own . . .''

''It'll never stick, man!'' Fraser insisted. ''A junior officer can't relieve a superior when someone senior to both is available. You have to go through channels . . .''

''Face it, Fraser,'' Barnett said harshly. ''Hawley is even more obviously incompetent than you are. As a matter of fact, it's your coddling of the old fool that's going to be the basis of Mr. DuValier's case when it comes up.''

Fraser looked from one to the other, incredulous. Behind them, their men were a study in contrasts, the civilians grinning, the legionnaires more subdued. But they seemed ready to obey DuValier. The Legion expected obedience to authority, and in a case like this they'd obey DuValier as long as he kept quoting regulations.

If any of them had been Hanuman vets . . . But they were all from First Platoon, Wijngaarde's. They were almost all new men, legionnaires he didn't know very well. DuValier was right in one respect. He'd been so busy trying to help Hawley do his job that he'd neglected Bravo Company. He didn't even know these men by name.

''This is a mutiny, Mr. DuValier,'' he said, trying to buy time. What could he do? ''You won't succeed.''

''That's enough,'' Barnett said. He gestured to one of his Seafarms bodyguards. ''Disarm him. We'll take care of Hawley next.''

He thought of fighting, but rejected it. All he'd do by fighting was give DuValier and Barnett an excuse to kill him. They would be happiest if he did. . . . Fraser, alive, was dangerous to their cause, at least until they were in full control. But they'd have to obey the legalities if they wanted to keep the support of the legionnaires.

He raised his hands slowly and allowed the civilian to unbuckle his gun belt. For now, he'd have to play along. There were people in the Sandcastle who knew him, from Hawley and Kelly and Sergeant Trent down to soldiers like Bashar or Garcia. Barnett and DuValier would find it hard to win over or arrest all of them. . . .

Bashar cut back on the power and held the veeter in place as the work party below wrestled with the harness on the fourth of the magrep generators. It was one of the units out of the *Angel II,* and the thought made him wince. He hoped they'd be able to put the old girl back together again after the siege was over.

He glanced around the compound to take his mind off the *Angel.* Captain Fraser was talking to a cluster of civilians and legionnaires. He thought the captain had come a long way since Hanuman. From first to last he'd taken charge here at the Sandcastle, and so far they'd stopped the wogs cold.

Fraser raised his hands, and a civilian was advancing to take his gun. What . . . ?

"Allah!" he said aloud. "MacAllister, look over there. Four o'clock."

Legionnaire MacAllister from the sapper platoon was riding in the veeter's front seat today, helping him with the placement of the generators. The old veteran's head swiveled, and Bashar heard a string of low-voiced oaths in his headphones. "What the hell are those de'ils doing?"

"I don't know," Bashar said. "But I don't like it."

He tapped his radio mike thoughtfully. This looked like a mutiny. Who could he call? Who could he trust?

Karatsolis was back at the motor pool. Like all Transport specialists the Greek was cross-trained as a general mechanic, and he'd been drafted into the party that was dismounting generators from the other vehicles. He felt the same way about Captain Fraser as Bashar did.

Bashar changed radio channels. "Repbay, repbay, this is Veeter One."

"Repbay," the bored voice of Sergeant Franz replied. "What's the problem, Basher? The little bitch acting up on you?"

"Naw . . ." He paused, thinking fast. "Look, Sarge, can you put Spear on for me? I forgot my strakking wristpiece, and I can't remember what I did with it. Spear'll know where I had it last."

"And you can't wait until you're off-duty?" Franz complained.

"Ah, hell, Sarge, give me some boost here. My dad gave me that 'piece." That was a lie, but Franz didn't know it. "And you know those thieving civilians'd just love to rip one of us off."

There was a long pause. Then Karatsolis came on the

line. "What've you got, Basher?" he asked. His voice was flat, brooding.

"I've got a Veitch problem up here," he said, using the personal code that went back to their days in training on Devereaux. Veitch had been the worst of the NCOs in their recruit unit, a sadist and a bully who liked to uncover secrets his men wanted left hidden. Ever since those days, the name had been their way of hinting that private information was coming.

There was another pause before Karatsolis answered. "I'm on headphones. What's going on?"

Bashar explained the situation. "It looks like Lieutenant DuValier and that strakk Barnett," he finished up. "We've got to do something, Spear."

"I'll get Gunny," Karatsolis replied, considerably more animated than before. "He'll know what to do."

MacAllister was listening to the exchange. "Pass the word to Warrant Kelly, too," he suggested. "I dinna think she will stand for this."

Bashar grinned. "You're right about that. I'll keep an eye on them, Spear. Let me know what's going down."

Karatsolis didn't even bother to sign off.

The civilian guards closed in around Fraser at Barnett's command, and the little procession headed for the Ops center. As they passed the ship cradle the Seafarms executive rounded up the workers there and added them to his force. Fraser estimated forty of them, perhaps three-quarters with outdated FEKs—the Mark-24 model that lacked the grenade launcher and had been obsolete when Hunter led his men into battle on Devereaux—plus ten legionnaires and DuValier. Substantial odds . . . especially as long as the Legion loyalists they met weren't prepared for an encounter.

Perhaps he should have put up a fight after all. At least it might have attracted some attention, given Hawley a chance to muster a defense.

As if reading his thoughts, the nearest guard dug his FEK/24 into Fraser's back. "Don't give us any trouble," he hissed. "I don't want to have to kill you, Captain, but I've got my orders."

Fraser nodded, his fists clenching in frustration. He darted glances left and right, trying to size up the situation. There had to be something he could turn to his own advantage in all this.

Narmonov's men were still drilling, apparently oblivious to the mutineers. Or were they in it? No . . . neither Narmonov nor Gunny Valko was likely to be involved, and if the mutiny was that well organized the subaltern and the NCO would have been neutralized by now.

He noticed that Bashar's veeter wasn't hovering anymore, and it looked like the generator work party had thinned out. Unless they were just out of sight, blocked from Fraser's angle by the ship cradle and the barge. Wishful thinking . . .

"Halt!" The voice that boomed out of the portable amplifier was Trent's. Like the men around him Fraser searched desperately to spot the sergeant, then saw him on the balcony overlooking the compound. Garcia was beside him, along with a pair of soldiers in full armor carrying onagers. Behind them Fraser thought he could see Hawley giving orders to his own $C^3$ tech. "You people are covered," Trent continued. "Halt, or be fired on!"

There was a moment's hesitation among the mutineers before DuValier pushed his way forward. "Sergeant Trent! I order you to stand down at once!"

Trent drew a pistol. "Release Captain Fraser and disperse," he said, ignoring DuValier.

"Come on, Sergeant," Barnett sneered. He gestured to his men, who had spread out into a loose semicircle. "One volley and you people are dead."

The sergeant shook his head. "Not all of us, Citizen," he corrected.

Loud in the tense silence, dozens of *snick-snicks* were clearly audible. Fraser turned his head. Legionnaires, some of them sappers, were leveling FEKs from behind the shelter of the cradle. And from the other side Narmonov's platoon was moving toward the mutineers with weapons held at the ready.

A third group was trotting from the direction of the motor pool, the big figure of Spiro Karatsolis out in front of them.

"Give it up, Barnett," Trent continued, still ignoring DuValier entirely. "I'd rather save our ammo for the wogs, but if you force us to we'll wipe your little revolution out. I mean it."

"Damn it, Sergeant," the lieutenant said, sounding desperate. ''Seafarms can negotiate with the wogs! Fraser and Hawley just want a heroic stand. They don't care what happens to us!''

Fraser shoved past two of the civilian guards into the open. He didn't have an amplifier, but he raised his voice enough so that everyone would hear him.

''Listen to me! It's true the wogs are making an offer to let us surrender, but we rejected it because we know they will not honor any agreement that leaves us alive! You've seen how they fight, how they think. They don't let threats to their tribes survive. If these nomads can't absorb an enemy, they crush him. There aren't any other alternatives!''

He paused. ''Maybe you don't believe that. It's true enough, but that doesn't mean you'll buy it. Well, buy this.'' Fraser's gesture encompassed the mutineers. ''These men think they'll get off this planet safely if they put Captain Hawley and myself out of the way and negotiate. Maybe they will, too. But anyone who supports this mutiny had better be ready to spend the rest of his life a long way outside the Commonwealth. The Colonial Army doesn't like mutineers, you know.''

There were a few laughs among the loyalists. A stir went through the civilians.

''Think about what mutiny means,'' Fraser went on. He had every man's attention now. ''After the garrison on Talbot's Rock mutinied, the Commonwealth went on tracking them down for ten years. Now normally you could hide out by joining the Foreign Legion. We take care of our own. . . . But of course since the mutiny was in the Legion, I guess that would be hard to manage, wouldn't it?''

More laughs. Barnett raised his voice, trying to break the spell. ''Nonsense! This isn't a mutiny. You're all working for Seafarms! If there's a mutiny here, it started when my orders were ignored. No one will be prosecuted for helping Lieutenant DuValier's legal relief of two incompetent officers.''

''Does anyone want to take that risk?'' Fraser asked loudly. ''Any legionnaire who mutinies has bought a hot shot for sure. And you civilians are looking at treason charges. All it would take is one man going to HQ and claiming this was an armed uprising.''

Kelly appeared on the balcony beside Trent and took the amplifier. ''How many of you are going to feel safe after all this?'' she chimed in. ''Look at the guy beside you. Can you trust him not to turn you in? Can you trust him not to slip a knife between your ribs to keep *you* from turning *him* in? That's the kind of life you can expect if there's a mutiny here!''

''Lay down your weapons now,'' Fraser ordered. ''For God's sake, this thing is almost over! We can hold off those wogs, just as long as we're all fighting on the same side. Every man has a part to play in this, and I need every one of you to make it work. That's how we can beat them, by standing together. By each of us doing what he knows how to do. But if you don't believe what I'm telling you . . .'' He paused. ''Then fire the first shot now and get it over with. Or else get back to work and save the shooting for the wogs!''

There was silence. Then, slowly, the ten legionnaires put down their FEKs. The civilians were a little slower, but, ringed in by armed soldiers, they had no other option.

Fraser let out a sigh. ''Karatsolis! Mr. DuValier is relieved of duty immediately. Escort him and Citizen Barnett to cells. The rest of these . . . protesters . . . may go back to their normal duties.''

He turned away, unwilling to let them see his face.

And Edward Barnett slipped one hand into the secret pocket in his left sleeve, drawing out the tiny rocket pistol he'd used to kill Sigrid Jens. At least he'd have Fraser. . . .

# Chapter 18

Abnegation is the spirit of the legionnaire.
—Lt. Colonel Paul Rollet
French Foreign Legion, 1917

Karatsolis started forward, his FEK trained on DuValier. The lieutenant would be the more dangerous of the two prisoners, with his Legion training. Now that Barnett's thugs were disarmed, the civilians wouldn't be much of a problem. . . .

"Look out!" Kelly screamed from the balcony. "He's got a gun!"

He caught Barnett's movement out of the corner of his eye and whirled, feeling that everything, himself included, was moving in slow motion. The tiny pistol was coming up in line with Fraser's back. . . .

Karatsolis fired almost by instinct even as someone—was that Trent?—shouted "Don't kill him!" The FEK was set for a three-round burst, but even the short whine of the gauss fields seemed to stretch on forever.

The civilian spun away from the blast, dropping the pistol and clutching at his arm. The high-velocity rounds had torn through flesh, probably shattered the bone, and blood was spurting from the wound. Barnett stared at the arm for a long moment, then collapsed.

"Medic! Medic!" someone shouted. A legionnaire was beside the injured man already, applying emergency first aid. A moment later Legionnaire Delandry pushed through the crowd and joined him.

"Someone get the Doc," Delandry snapped, producing her medkit. "Hurry!"

Karatsolis lowered the FEK. He realized that one of his men already had DuValier covered. Everything had happened so fast that it had hardly registered on him.

Then Fraser was beside him. ''Good shooting, Spear,'' the captain said. ''Thanks. If it hadn't been for you . . .''

He nodded automatically. ''Yes, sir. I'll . . . take charge of the lieutenant for you.''

Slinging his FEK, Karatsolis joined the soldiers flanking DuValier. After the tense confrontation with the mutineers, the sudden action had drained him completely.

It took all his willpower to keep from stumbling as he led the detail toward the Legion's cell block.

''Skipper? I think you'd better see this.''

Fraser looked up from his desk at Trent. ''What is it, Gunny?'' he asked. It was hard even yet to keep his voice level, although more than an hour had passed since the abortive mutiny.

Trent laid a small weapon and another unidentifiable object in front of him. ''The pistol's the one our friend Barnett tried to use on you,'' the sergeant told him. ''Narmonov picked it up while they were policing all the other weapons.''

Picking up the small pistol, Fraser turned it over in his hands. It had a familiar look to it. . . .

''Good God!'' he said suddenly, as he recognized the workmanship. ''This is the same technology as the nomad rocket guns!''

''Right down the line,'' Trent agreed. ''Koenig looked it over and said the same. Barnett got this from the nomads . . . or from whoever's been supplying them.''

Fraser leaned back in his chair, still looking at the pistol. ''This isn't an infantry weapon,'' he said. ''It was designed for concealability.'' He remembered the questions that had crossed his mind during the first meeting in the conference room. ''You think Barnett was a spy?''

The sergeant nodded. ''I had his quarters and office searched,'' he said. Trent prodded the other device. ''Pascali turned this thing up. Transmitter.''

''Pretty lightweight job,'' Fraser commented. ''Not much range . . .''

''More than you'd think. Koenig says it's a Toel job, and they've got some pretty sophisticated electronics.''

''And a technology designed for underwater use, like these guns!'' Fraser finished the thought, angry that he hadn't made the connection sooner. ''Not to mention a lot of experience dealing with the natives here, to know the best weapons designs to manufacture!''

''That's the way we figure it,'' Trent said. ''The Toels have the biggest stake in all this. If Seafarms fails on Polypheme, the Toels might just pry it loose from the Commonwealth and set up their old operation all over again.''

''Pry it loose? Hell, Gunny, if Seafarms backed off of this dump, the politicians would be glad to unload it on the Toels. Especially with a massacred garrison and a lot of nasty hostiles complicating things. The Elders in Ourgh would disown Terra if we were wiped out, and anybody trying to come back here later would have to start from scratch. It all fits.''

''Gives us something to go on, at least,'' Trent said. ''I wonder how much Barnett knows about the whole operation. . . .''

''Maybe we can find out,'' Fraser said. ''Have you checked with Ramirez lately on his condition?''

''He'll be all right,'' the sergeant said with a look of distaste. ''A week or so in regen and he'll be ready for a hot shot.''

''Good. Tell Garcia to turn over her duties to the other $C^3$s. I've got some special work for her. We'll get some answers out of Barnett. You can count on it.''

''You figure DuValier was in on the whole thing?''

''I don't think so, Gunny,'' Fraser said slowly. ''He had a personal grudge against me, but I think he really thought he was doing the right thing. There were too many ways DuValier could have sabotaged us. He didn't. . . . Not until Barnett conned him with this negotiation nonsense.''

''I guess you're right. Looks like Barnett was just doing his best to keep Seafarms off-balance while the bad guys did their thing.''

''Yeah,'' Fraser said. He laughed as a thought struck him. ''God, he worked so hard to keep us from bringing the civilians in here. He must have had it figured that his friends would stay clear of Ourgh and concentrate on us! No wonder he didn't like the idea of a move!''

Trent nodded gravely. ''And when his boss ovrruled him . . .''

''She died, and he started screwing around, keeping his people from cooperating with us. He's probably been passing intel to them ever since he moved in. But I'll bet the surrender bit was his own idea, to get the hell out of here before the nomads hit us."

"If they know our timetable . . ."

"Then they know we'll have the magrep generators up about the same time *Cyclops* gets back, fifty hours at the outside!" Fraser pounded the desk with a clenched fist. "They'll attack before then, damn it! We'll have to step up everything."

"With Barnett gone, the Seafarms bunch'll cooperate a little better," Trent said. "I'll get their tech people out on the perimeter to help with the generators."

"Good. And while you're at it, find out how many have had some kind of military training and start issuing weapons. And let's have every legionnaire ready. We'll need all the troops we can get."

Trent raised an eyebrow and stroked nervously at the corner of his mustache. "Is that a good idea? We've already had one mutiny. . . ."

"Gunny, the next time Choor! hits us it's going to be with every nomad in his whole army. If the perimeter isn't secure by then, there's no way we can hold them off without some more troops. No way at all. We *have* to trust those people. Either that, or surrender now and let Choor! and his Toel friends win without a fight."

"God help us all," the sergeant said. He headed for the door.

Fraser looked at Barnett's pistol and radio on the desk. "Amen to that," he said softly.

Sparks crackled, and acrid smoke coiled from the makeshift power hookup on the magrep generator. Kelly shouted "Cut it off!" into her throat mike. She started to curse as she knelt by the housing to recheck the leads, then realized the mike was picking that up as well.

As the power cut off, she thought she could hear someone chuckling over the commlink. Kelly ignored it and reconnected the lines. Not for the first time—or the last, she suspected—she found herself wishing that the assortment of magnetic-field generators they were using wasn't quite so assorted. The equipment represented at least twenty different makes and models, some of them fifty years old or more. Some of the Legion vehicles had mounted four different units in the same chassis, many of them obsolete by any sane standards.

Kelly was beginning to believe that the mechanics who kept Legion APCs running were either geniuses or madmen, but she wasn't yet prepared to choose which.

This was a Stellectric Products Mark XVIII, probably off of the FSV Bashar and Karatsolis were so proud of. She'd hooked it up as if it were a Mark XXX, like the last one. No wonder it hadn't been working right!

"Try it again," she said aloud. Power hummed, and the improvised check light came on to indicate that the generator was up and running.

That made exactly half of the generators in place and running now. Fraser wouldn't be happy at the slow pace of the work. Ever since he'd begun to suspect that Barnett had been feeding information to the enemy, Fraser had been determined that the defenses had to be finished as soon as possible—preferably about a week ago. But it was a time-consuming job to install and hook up the magrep modules. At least they were ahead of the schedule Kelly had expected to manage.

As she gathered up her tools and moved down the line to the next unit, Kelly hoped again that they'd be fast enough.

A pair of civilian technicians was working on this one already, but Kelly wasn't planning on taking their work on faith. The mutiny was still too fresh in her mind to let her trust anyone from Seafarms, even though Fraser seemed prepared to do so.

She'd protested when he had briefed her on the situation. "You can't just ignore it, Col," she had said. "Letting everyone go back to work except Barnett and DuValier . . . You're asking for more trouble with them, you know."

"I can't lock up eight hundred civilians just because they might sympathize with Barnett," he'd replied wearily. "Or all the legionnaires who might've known and trusted DuValier more than me."

"I'm not saying you should, Col," she had shot back, angry. "But the ones who were with those two bastards in the mutiny . . ."

"Not even them," he'd said, looking away. "Those kids from Wijngaarde's platoon were just following DuValier's orders. I expect that's true of the Seafarms people as well. Once I can question Barnett I'll know for sure, but until then my main job is to get these boys and girls together. It's got to be a team effort from here on out, Kelly. Because if Seafarms really did decide to take us out and surrender, there's no way we'd stop them. We've less than two hundred legionnaires in this base now. That's the real tip-off that Barnett was improvising all this. If he'd been in a position to expect all of his people to support an uprising, he could have taken over easily, with or without DuValier."

"Yeah . . . maybe. But—"

"No more arguments, Kelly. Please. Just get those generators up. And pray."

He'd looked so tired, so dispirited . . . less confident than she'd ever seen him before, even in those rocky first days of the march on Hanuman.

That had been almost eighteen hours ago. Susan Gage and the two gunnery sergeants had been taking charge of the preparations in the fortress since that time, while Fraser, Hawley, and Angela Garcia concentrated on another project in the medical section, working with Dr. Ramirez on something no one was talking about.

Whatever it was, she hoped it would work.

"It's as ready as it's ever going to be, sir."

At Garcia's words Fraser looked up from the computer terminal. "Any problems?" he asked.

"You mean aside from the fact that I've never worked on a setup like this before, don't have all the right gear, and don't really believe in it anyway?" Garcia shrugged and grinned. "Not a one."

He wished he felt like joking about it. Garcia had summed up all the problems with his scheme in a nutshell, but it was their only hope of getting the information they needed.

Fraser looked past her at the two examining tables that had been set up side-by-side in the extra operating theater of the Sandcastle's medical center. The setup looked primitive compared to what he'd seen in service with regular Intelligence units, but it was the best they could improvise under the circumstances.

Most military personnel and Intel operatives were routinely conditioned against chemical methods of persuasion; that was standard procedure. In light of the dangers of modern corporate espionage, a lot of senior executives got similar workovers. Odds were that Barnett wouldn't be broken that way. If Seafarms hadn't seen to it, the Toels—if they were indeed his employers—would surely have done so.

Physical and psychological interrogation techniques would have worked eventually, but they took a long time, and time was something the Terrans didn't have right now.

That left Fraser's idea, unlikely as it was. They'd have to improvise the direct mind-to-mind questioning process that was SOP in Army Intelligence. Both theoretical and practical information were easy to come by in the files of the demi-battalion's master computer, but translating them into working interrogation equipment had taken hours of labor and all of Garcia's ingenuity. And there was still no guarantee they could make it work.

Looking through the glassed-in wall at the triage room where Ramirez was finishing a medical examination of Captain David Hawley, Fraser couldn't help but be pessimistic. Everything, literally, rode on the old man's slender shoulders this time.

At first he'd hoped that they could come up with a usable substitute for the computer implant usually used for this sort of interrogation. Externally worn adhesive chips—adchips—could do many of the same things as computer implants, and certainly the subject in one of these questioning sessions didn't need an implant. But as he'd studied the computer files, Fraser had realized that this was one place where shortcuts weren't going to work.

The interrogator and the computer had to work together on an almost instinctive level when interrogating a subject. Fraser might have been able to do it if they'd rigged up an adchip and given him several months to practice with the computer, but once again there just wasn't time. Only someone who had long experience with brain-computer interfacing could handle the nuances of mind-to-mind interrogation.

That meant there was only one candidate for the job in the Sandcastle, Captain David Hawley.

But it took a strong mind to handle the pressures of literally ripping information out of another man's memories—strong, and agile as well. Could Hawley break Edward Barnett? Or had he been retreating from reality, avoiding responsibility, for too long to be able to get the job done?

He cut the terminal, rose, and crossed to the door. Sticking his head into the triage room, he asked, "What's the verdict, Doctor?"

Ramirez glanced down at his compboard. "Physically, I see no problems," he said slowly. "Captain Hawley is in good condition. But this is certainly . . . unfamiliar work. Lacking formal training or experience in interrogation proceedings, I would say ten-minute sessions, at least until we see how the captain will hold up under the strain."

Hawley finished putting on his uniform blouse and favored Ramirez with an angry look. "Don't talk around the problem, Ramirez," he said harshly. "You don't think the old man can cut it, do you? Afraid I'll end up letting Barnett dominate me, instead of the other way around. Right?"

Before Ramirez could answer, Fraser intervened. "Sir, you know better than I do how much damage you can do to your mind through misuse of an implant. It takes a strong will to maintain control during an interrogation. And the doctor is right to be concerned. None of us want to see you burn out your mind fighting Barnett."

Hawley looked like he was about to flare, then nodded and sat down on the examining table. "And you're right to be concerned that I'm not up to it," he admitted. "My record's not exactly something to inspire confidence, is it?"

"Sir, your record's got nothing—"

"Don't interrupt me, Captain!" he barked. Then he smiled. "I was trained to command, son. Once. And I think I can safely say that I have more experience with this implant than most regular interrogators. If I can find my way back to reality from Dreamland as often as I do, surely I can do it this time." He paused, still smiling. "Anyway, if you're looking for a man with a strong will, what else would you call an officer who won't give it up even after twenty years of being told that a quiet resignation would be the best thing for everyone, hmm?"

Fraser forced a smile in return. "I'd call him stubborn, sir. Or perhaps 'pigheaded' would be a better term."

"There you have it. I'll have this bastard Barnett for lunch. I've been wanting a crack at him ever since the first time I heard a snide remark about how I wasn't fit to be a security guard at the Seafarms warehouse, much less the CO of the garrison. I was getting comments like that even before you got here, Fraser, and I'm getting damned sick of them!"

"You'll have your chance, sir," Fraser said. He nodded to Garcia. "Have an escort fetch Citizen Barnett from his cell. It's time he started helping us as much as he's helped the wogs."

Karatsolis leaned against the rampart, staring down at the restless waters of high tide. There was no more work for him in the repbay, now that all the magrep units had been dismounted. He had another twenty minutes of free time left before he was due to relieve Sergeant Franz, who was now operating the unit's second veeter on the south wall.

He couldn't get his mind off the mutiny. When Bashar had first called him, he had still been dwelling on O'Donnell and Sandoval, on the whole question of his place in the Legion. And he'd been no nearer to resolving it.

Then the mad rush, warning Kelly and Trent, then organizing the Transport Section at Trent's orders to help close the trap on the mutineers. Even Franz had taken his orders. Trent had made it clear that he wanted none but Hanuman veterans in charge of the operation, and to Topheth with rank.

When Fraser had started talking, his first reaction had been one of frustration. Why try to reason with the bastards?

But what he'd said about every man playing a part had hit home. And Barnett's assassination attempt . . .

He'd saved Fraser's life. Twice, maybe, since he'd helped organize the resistance to the mutiny. And if they held off the wogs and got off of Polypheme, it would be because Colin Fraser was alive to do it. Karatsolis had no doubt of that. None of the other officers inside the Sandcastle had Fraser's flair for tactics, or the ability to inspire the legionnaires the way he could.

One man like Fraser could really make a difference. And so, it seemed, could Karatsolis, when he guarded Fraser's back or did his part in combat.

A siren pulled him forcefully out of his reverie. "Attention! Attention!" the PA blared. It sounded like Gunny Trent himself making the announcement. "Sonar has detected large groups of targets approaching the base! All personnel to defense posts!"

Karatsolis ran for the nearest stairway. For the first time in days, he was eager to come to grips with the enemy.

To do his part.

# Chapter 19

Death before surrender!
—Lt. Clement Maudet, at Camerone
French Foreign Legion, 30 April 1863

David Hawley jerked upright on the examination table, his link to Barnett suddenly cut off. Sweat soaked his shirt and matted his hair, and he couldn't remember the last time he'd felt so totally exhausted.

No . . . he *could* remember. The last time had been on Aten, years ago, the day he'd led his men into the last terrible battle against the Ubrenfars. His clash of wills with Barnett was as close as he had ever come to the strain of that fight. Memories he'd buried for years were rushing to the surface now, memories like the ones that had driven him to seek refuge in Dreamland in the first place.

But at the same time there was something exhilarating about fighting and winning. He'd forgotten that feeling, too, even though he'd lost himself in chip wargames hoping to recapture it without having to face the darker side of the struggle. Now he realized it was that darker side that made the feeling so intense.

The flood of thought and emotion was over in an instant, and Hawley opened his eyes. Fraser and Ramirez were on either side of his table, both wearing worried expressions.

"The . . . the computer terminated the session," he said haltingly. It was hard to talk out loud, after relying on the machine-induced telepathy of the interrogation.

Fraser nodded. "We're on alert, sir," he said. "Large numbers of nomads on the way in. The doctor and I need to get to our posts. Garcia, too."

"Right. Just let me get my bearings. . . ." He tried to get up, but the room was swimming around him.

"No, sir," Fraser said. "Doctor Ramirez has a sedative for you. You need some rest, sir."

He started to protest, but Fraser held up a hand. "Captain, even trained interrogators take some crash time after a session. SOP." He paused. "We haven't seen all the transcripts yet. How'd it go?"

Hawley winced at the memory. "He's a stubborn bastard, Fraser. I didn't get much. But he *was* working for the Toeljuks and the nomads. Seems he was selling out for money. Security. He comes from a pretty bad background. . . . Wasn't getting very far with Seafarms, for all his strutting."

"And they call us mercenaries," Garcia muttered darkly from the corner by the computer equipment.

"I was on the track of their headquarters when the computer cut the link," Hawley went on. "He knows where they're set up—the Toels and Choor! too. But I'll need another session or two to get it."

"You'll have it," Fraser promised. "But right now you need to rest . . . and we have a fight to get to." He nodded to Ramirez, who advanced with a hypo.

As the doctor applied the spray injector to his arm, Hawley felt the fatigue washing over him. "Wish I . . . could be out there with you . . . son . . ." he heard himself saying.

He was surprised when he realized that this time he really meant it.

"Grenades!" Narmonov shouted.

All along the parapet the legionnaires of his platoon switched from conventional ammo to mini-grenades, firing single rounds into the water below the east wall of the Sandcastle. The individual explosions weren't much, but they'd keep the wogs off-balance.

He still couldn't believe the size of the nomad army. Every estimate they'd been able to make so far showed there were at least ten thousand warriors out there. The ordinary clan numbered less than a few hundred. Choor! must have sent every able-bodied swimmer in his confederation against the fort.

With the magrep generators still not fully installed, it would take a lot of killing to stop this attack.

"Sir!" That was Sergeant Zold, acting as platoon NCO

in place of Carstairs. "Permission to fire Fafnirs? Or would you rather use the charges?"

He glanced at the stack of explosive canisters piled nearby, then shook his head. "Save the explosives for when we know they're at the walls," he said. "Make it Fafnirs. One round each. Just to keep them guessing."

Zold gave him a gap-toothed grin. "Yes, sir!" He turned away, shouting orders despite having his helmet radio on. "Weapons Lances! Fafnirs ready! Timed detonation, thirty seconds. Launch!"

Nearby, one of the Fafnir gunners quickly programmed the instructions into the computer targeting system. The Fafnir was supposed to be a selectively targeted anti-vehicle missile, equally useful against ground or air targets, which were matched by silhouette in the missile's on-board brain. But it could also be programmed for area effect with a timed detonation, as Zold had ordered.

The legionnaire lifted the launch tube to his shoulder and squeezed the trigger. With a brilliant flare of burning propellant the missile leapt into the air, then arced downward and lanced into the water. Elsewhere along the wall other missiles followed.

Seconds passed. Then a ripple of underwater explosions followed.

Each missile, by itself, could kill a Sabertooth or a Sandray. Going off underwater like that, they'd disrupt the nomad attack.

Too bad the stock of Fafnirs in the Sandcastle was so low. No one had anticipated much call for anti-armor missiles, on a planet where the crossbow was still considered an advanced weapon system, and there were no more than five missiles per gunner on hand. Those would have to be hoarded.

At least some of their weapons weren't hampered by ammo concerns.

"Sergeant!" he called. "Fafnirs to cease fire. Order the onagers to engage at will."

"Onagers front! Onagers fire!" Zold sounded a lot like Carstairs, barking those orders with the same crisp precision. Maybe the actor hadn't been playing a part after all. It seemed like the job shaped the men, not the other way around.

Now the fully armored onager gunners were taking position on the parapet. Narmonov saw one, armor emblazoned with colorful emblems, checking the balance on his ConRig harness and running through a quick series of tests. That would be the Gurkha, Chandbahadur Rai. He remembered warning the corporal to repaint the armor in standard camouflage a few weeks back, before the crisis had blown up. When he'd told Gunny Trent he thought the man was getting a dose of the *cafarde*, the sergeant had just laughed and said, "With a Gurkha you can't tell. They're crazy all the time."

Chandbahadur chambered a round and fired. The plasma bolt was like a controlled bolt of lightning stabbing into the sea, raising a cloud of hissing steam as the superheated metal hit the surface of the water. The onager—officially the *fusil d'onage*, or "storm rifle"—deserved its name . . . and its fierce reputation.

Narmonov fired another grenade at the seething water. This was the strangest battle he'd ever fought in, with opponents who didn't show themselves and who hadn't, at least so far, started shooting back. There was no way to tell how much damage the legionnaires were doing, except by inference from the reports passed on from time to time from the civilian sonar operators in C-cubed.

Sooner or later the nomads would strike back. As he pulled the trigger yet again, Narmonov couldn't help but wonder whether the legionnaires were having any real effect on the enemy . . . and whether it would make any difference to their battle plans.

Fraser entered C-cubed at a run, Garcia following close behind. "Status!" he snapped as the door closed behind her.

A civilian technician looked up from a computer monitor. "Sonar shows five major groups out there now, Captain Fraser," he said. "So far they just keep feinting in and out, like they're testing our defenses. The fire from the walls seems to be discouraging them."

Fraser bent over the display. "I wish this thing was designed for computer imaging," he said. The sonar systems used aboard most ships and submersibles in the Commonwealth included programs allowing a computer to interpret signals as actual images, but the improvised detectors they'd installed around the perimeter were more like the primitive devices of Terra's pre-spaceflight era. All they registered was the presence and approximate size of objects underwater, without showing any real detail.

And detection wasn't completely accurate. Targets near the sea bottom or close in to the wall probably would be obscured by clutter.

If Barnett had been feeding the nomads information, they would surely know about the sonar. And Barnett could have told them about its limitations. . . .

So why were they limiting themselves to these highly visible demonstrations?

Beside him, Garcia stiffened. "Sir . . ." She hesitated, then went on, "Sir, I helped calibrate the system, with some of our wog scouts as sample targets. Some of those . . . don't look right."

"Decoys!" Fraser crossed to the communications desk and grabbed a microphone. "General call! General call! Natives are using decoys as sonar targets. Watch out for infiltration attempts! Repeat, watch for infiltration by nomad forces!"

Warrior-Scout !!Dhruuj looked up as another shock wave washed over him. So far the Strangers were focusing their fire close to the surface of the water, and their explosives were having little effect on the band of elite warriors who crept along the sea floor. Some of the big explosions had been dangerous, but they had come this far without casualties. A few more minutes and their job would be finished.

War-Leader-of-Clans Choor! had anticipated the Strangers once again. Their underwater sight was imperfect, limited in its ability to distinguish one object from another and nearly blind to anything that kept close to the bottom. So the Stranger-Who-Betrayed had reported, and the War-Leader-of-Clans had been quick to see how those weaknesses could be exploited.

What would the Strangers-Within think if they knew that most of what they were seeing now were not Swimmers at all but *woojoork,* the Swimmer-sized beasts of burden the Clans used to carry heavy loads on long treks? And would they realize that many of the Swimmers interspersed among the animals did not belong to the Clans at all, but were actually prisoners from Ourgh taken in a big raid two Tides ago? Only a few warriors of the Clans were actually among the many targets they would be seeing now, a handful who were responsible for keeping the captives and animals threatening the Built-Reef.

And while the Strangers allowed prisoners and beasts to distract them, the Clans would strike!

The Built-Reef loomed ahead, the walls made of the sand-that-was-harder-than-sand an impenetrable barrier. The first Clan assault had aimed for the gates, the second had relied upon Swimmers going over the walls. This time they had more accurate information, transmitted by the Stranger-Who-Betrayed before the Clans had arrived in force. !!Dhruuj followed Warrior-Superior Ghoodoor along the wall of the Reef until they found the gaping hole, the *intake pipe* that the Betrayer had described. It was wide enough for two Swimmers to pass through abreast, and the barriers within were said to be much weaker than the walls themselves.

Ghoodoor signaled !!Dhruuj to summon the others, and the Warrior-Scout swam out of the hole and waved to the rest of the party. The Swimmers approached slowly, three of them heavily burdened by the explosives they carried slung in a net between them.

!!Dhruuj clung to the wall and began speaking in the Voice-Without-Words, informing the Clans of their progress. When Ghoodoor finished placing the explosives, the party would withdraw to safety and set them off. Then, as water rushed into the center of the Built-Reef, the Clans would launch their attack.

Victory floated within a tendril's grasp . . .

"The Sandcastle's calling, Sub."

Toru Watanabe looked toward the comm station on the other side of the ship's bridge. Dmitri Rostov had the position this watch, and his lancemate, Legionnaire Martin, was keeping an eye on the civilian pilot at the helm. Since the day he'd ordered the platoon to seize the *Seafarms Cyclops* and turn back for home, the key Bridge and Engineering posts had either been staffed or watched by legionnaires. For the most part even the most stubborn civilians, Captain MacLean included, had accepted the situation long ago.

He crossed to Rostov's console and held a headphone to

one ear. Rostov keyed in his mike at Watanabe's nod. "Sandcastle, *Cyclops.* Watanabe here."

"*Cyclops,* be advised of sitrep update," Angela Garcia's voice came back. "Hostile forces around base may include decoys, repeat, decoys. Intentions of hostile command not known. Captain Fraser advises you be ready for possible attack."

"Acknowledged, Sandcastle," Watanabe answered. He gestured to Rostov, who hit the general alarm and began passing the warning to the rest of the ship's company over the PA system. "Revised ETA is now one hour, thirteen minutes."

There was a long pause at the other end. Then Fraser came on the line, sounding worried. "Toru, you could be sailing right into a major battle here," he said. "We still don't know which way the wogs are going to jump. If you want to hold off until things are settled here, it's your discretion. You know how vulnerable that monster of yours will be coming in."

Watanabe didn't need to think the decision through. "Sounds like you're going to need a hand there, Captain," he said. "We're coming in. I'll see if I can't shave some time off that ETA, too, so we don't miss the party."

Fraser sounded relieved. "Thanks. These bastards are playing for keeps, and I'll feel a hell of a lot better with the Second backing us up. Sandcastle clear."

He set down the headphones and turned away from the comm station. "Impellers to full thrust," he ordered.

"Sir!" The civilian helmsman turned in his seat to deliver his protest. "We're already pumping at the maximum safe level. . . ."

"I said full thrust, damn it! Even if you tear the guts out of her! Do it!"

The helmsman looked ready to argue, until he caught sight of Legionnaire Martin as she stepped toward him, her laser rifle a vivid reminder of just how far the platoon was willing to go to see that the civilians carried out Watanabe's orders. The man swallowed twice, turned back to his console, and advanced the throttle to the maximum thrust setting.

Watanabe could feel the vibrations as the impellers churned, driving the *Seafarms Cyclops* toward her goal.

* * *

The wall shuddered under Narmonov's feet, throwing him off-balance. He grabbed at the parapet to steady himself, dropping his FEK with a metallic clatter. *"Bojemoi!"* he exclaimed in Russian. "What the Topheth was that!"

"Explosion," Zold said curtly. "Must've been pretty deep. . . . Christ! Look at that!' He was pointing behind Narmonov, into the interior of the compound.

Narmonov followed the gesture and felt his mouth go dry.

Water was pouring through a gap below the gatehouse, an unstoppable torrent rushing into the compound.

"The intakes!" Narmonov shouted. "They've blown the main intakes!"

Zold waved his FEK over his head. "Chandbahadur! Haddad! Sinclair! Your lances with me!" The sergeant looked at Narmonov. "I'll try to set up an overwatch on that entrance, sir. Slow them down when they start coming through."

He nodded. "Do it. I'll stay here." He paused. "Good luck, Sergeant."

They'd all need luck before this was over.

"Breach in the wall, sir. Main intake pipe, below the gatehouse."

Fraser swore under his breath. They should have been expecting that, as soon as they'd realized the wogs were using decoys. A few commandos infiltrated along the bottom . . . Explosives like the ones Watanabe had reported the nomads carrying in the attack on the *Cyclops* . . .

"We'll need more troops out there, Garcia," he said. "What's the state of our reserves?"

"We can draw off troops from the perimeter if those really are decoys out there," she said. "Subaltern Narmonov's already deployed half his platoon to the gatehouse area on his own initiative."

Fraser looked away. Choor! had already proven himself a shrewd tactician. The nomad—and his Toeljuk backers—would probably know that the defenders' first reaction would be to weaken the outer wall in response to the threat of an attack into the center of the Sandcastle.

Which meant that there would be other native soldiers waiting to take advantage of that weakening. . . .

"Anything else?" he asked.

"Just the armed civilians," Garcia told him. "About a

hundred, with a mixed bag of weapons. Sergeant Trent's been keeping them back."

"We'll need them now," he said. "Pass the orders." He paused, rubbing his forehead. "I wish I knew how much we can rely on them. . . ."

"Just because Barnett was a traitor doesn't mean we all are, Captain," a technician spoke up from the other side of C-cubed. Fraser looked up. With a shock he recognized her. It was Katrina Voskovich, the technician he and Kelly had saved from the rioting in Ourgh the day of the first nomad attack. "We'll fight. All of us, if that's what you need. And if you have weapons for us."

One of the other technicians nodded, and another said, "That's right. Tell him, Kat."

"All right. Garcia, get together any civilian who wants to volunteer and break out more weapons from the Armory. I'll need . . . three volunteers to stay here with me."

"Yes, sir," Garcia said, a smile that could have been anticipation lighting up her face.

"You're in charge until I find an NCO or an officer to take over. Move!"

The technicians were talking among themselves in low, urgent tones. Finally Voskovich and four others joined Garcia, leaving Fraser his team.

As they started out the door, Voskovich turned back and caught Fraser's eye. "Don't worry, Captain. We may not be legionnaires, but we'll show the wogs a thing or two!"

"Fafnirs! One round each!" Narmonov shouted the order, all too well aware that they might need the missiles later. But if there were natives closing in on the hole under the gatehouse, they had to be discouraged from getting any closer. "Forty-five-second fuse delay!"

The two remaining Fafnirs in his section of the wall opened fire. The others were with Zold. There had already been some firing from that direction, probably against the commandos who had blown the intake. How many men had the wogs infiltrated while the Legion sniped at decoys?

"Some bodies there, sir!" someone called, pointing.

He let his FEK hang on its sling from his shoulder and flipped down his faceplate, hitting the image-intensifier setting. The distant objects suddenly filled his vision, bobbing in the waves.

One of them wasn't even vaguely humanoid. He recognized it as the beast of burden Terrans had dubbed "sea camel." Next to the animal another body, a wog this time, was lying facedown, staining the sea with blood. *So we got one of the bastards, at least,* Narmonov thought.

But something wasn't quite right. . . .

No tattoos, that was it. The wog wasn't tattooed, and all the nomads wore Clan tattoos.

"Damn them," he muttered. The wogs were using prisoners as well as animals for decoys. Probably a city-dweller from Ourgh or another nearby city.

A dark, sucker-lined arm snaked over the parapet, grabbing at Narmonov. He stumbled backward, surprised. They'd reached the walls!

He snapped his visor up just in time to see the nomad clamber over the top, swinging one of their strange crossbows into line. Narmonov fumbled for his rifle, bringing it up as the crossbow fired. His finger twitched reflexively on the trigger, and a full-auto burst nearly tore the alien in half.

Then pain was lancing through his left shoulder. He looked down, saw the bolt, the red stain on his battledress. Even the duraweave cloth hadn't been able to stop the weapon at such close range.

More nomads were appearing on the ramparts, climbing out of the angry sea below. They'd counted on the intake explosion to weaken the wall and further confuse the defenders . . . and they'd got just what they counted on.

He ignored the pain spreading through his arm and upper chest as he crossed to the pile of explosive ten-kilogram canisters, then cursed as he remembered that one of Haddad's men had the detonator box for this batch. The Recon Lance was with Zold. He should have realized it. . . .

"Look out, Sub!" a legionnaire shouted.

He spun around in time to see another nomad looming close behind him, wielding a curved sword and shouting some unintelligible battle cry. Narmonov tried to block the wog's swing with his FEK, but the deflected blow still cut deep into his injured arm. The native wrenched the blade free and raised it for another strike, then fell as a legionnaire pumped a dozen needle rounds into his back.

Dizzy, Narmonov staggered back against the parapet, trying to fight off the fog of pain and shock closing in around him.

They *had* to blunt this attack, now. . . .

Gathering his strength, he grabbed one of the canisters and jerked open the detpack wired to one end. Manually he set the timer, dropped it over the wall, then reached for another of the improvised depth charges.

A rocket-assisted bullet struck the wall half a meter away. He flinched but finished the setting on the second timer, throwing the bomb over the wall.

As he staggered under the weight of the third bomb, another bullet slammed into his back. The duraweave fatigues kept it from penetrating, but the impact rammed him against the parapet. He clung to the canister, fumbling with the timer.

A wog slashed at him with a bulky weapon like an outsized battleax as he finished making the setting. Narmonov rolled onto the top of the wall, kept rolling . . . until he was falling toward the hungry waves, the canister still clutched close to his chest.

He blacked out as he hit the water, and never felt the three explosions that killed him.

# Chapter 20

> Charge your rifles. You will fire on command, then we will charge with the bayonet. You will follow me.
>
> —Lieutenant Clement Maudet
> at the battle of Camerone
> French Foreign Legion, 30 April 1863

"Come on! This way!"

Karatsolis was knee-deep in swirling water as he ran across the open ground below the vehicle repbay. The orders for the Transport Section to assemble to defend that stretch of the wall had made him cut across the center of the base. Now, as the water rose, he was regretting the impulse that had taken him to the far wall before the attack.

Near the gatehouse he saw a pair of legionnaires wading through the raging water, firing at a group of wogs who had come through the hole they'd blasted. Three of the nomads fell, but the rest surged forward and brought them down with a hail of spear thrusts and sword cuts.

"Come on, Spear!" Bashar called again. The corporal was standing near the top of the ramp into the repbay, urging him on with frantic waves. "They're going to button up in a minute!" The heavy doors were already grinding shut.

Karatsolis dodged around the last APC lined up at the foot of the wide ramp. As each of the Legion vehicles had been stripped of its magrep generators, they had been towed out of the repbay and lined up in the open by a lumbering wrecker on treads to clear more space inside the motor pool. They stood in an orderly block, looking ready for a parade.

The *Angel II* was parked among them, her plasma cannon's barrel pointing at Karatsolis like an accusing finger. They hadn't finished putting in the generators, but none of the vehicles was mobile now. The Legion could really use some of them now. . . .

He stopped dead in his tracks, staring up at the FSV. The magrep modules were gone, and she couldn't move . . . but her power units were intact, and so was her weaponry. The Sabertooth might not be able to move, but she'd make a damned good pillbox. And after the water rose she'd be able to discourage wogs from swimming through the center of the Sandcastle.

"Basher!" he shouted, pointing at the *Angel II*. "We can still fight her! Give me a hand!"

Bashar didn't seem to understand right away, but as Karatsolis scrambled up on the chassis and opened the turret hatch the Turk ran down the ramp to join him. "You're nuts, farmboy!" he shouted.

"Not as nuts as the wog who tries to play games with our little bitch!" he yelled back happily.

The water was almost up to the level of Bashar's hatch by the time the Turk climbed in and started the power-up process. Up in the turret, Karatsolis ran through the weapon and sensor diagnostics, glad to have the chance of fighting out this battle doing what he did best.

"What the hell is that?" one of the technicians muttered.

Fraser crossed the Ops center and bent over the man's shoulder to study his board. He was monitoring the gate-side sensor readouts, sonar, radar, and motion detectors. "What've you got?"

The tech pointed to the radar screen. "This sucker just lit up. A big, surface-skimming target, like a magrep. Must've been hiding behind Haven Point, up here, or we would have spotted the bastard earlier. Closing fast, too . . . Must be a hell of a mover."

"Can the computer ID it?" Fraser asked.

The civilian looked blank for a moment, then punched in the code that called up the base's warbook files. Another computer monitor began running through comparison signal profiles faster than the human eye could follow, until it stopped at a probable match.

Fraser read the specs and let out a low whistle. "Good God. I didn't think the Toels would go this far helping them. . . ."

Legionnaire Angela Garcia knelt behind the parapet, her FEK braced on the fusand as she covered the rapidly flooding interior of the compound. Around her, Seafarms workers were dropping into similar positions.

"Down there!" Katrina Voskovich shouted, pointing. Garcia followed the gesture and saw a group of wogs slogging through the torrent.

"Fire!" she called, her finger tightening on the trigger. The gauss rifle whined and chattered. Then the noise swelled as the civilians joined in. The nomads thrashed and struggled, then flopped backward and floated with the rushing sea.

Adrenaline sang through her veins, making Garcia feel really alive for the first time since Hanuman. This was why she'd joined the Legion, to be a part of something larger than herself, to stand against the odds and fight back against a hostile universe. . . .

There was an explosion by the gates, and the inrush of water redoubled. Garcia saw wogs and Terrans alike being overpowered by the force of the water, but it wouldn't take long for the nomads to recover. For the humans, though, the torrent spelled death.

As the flow slacked off and the water levels inside and outside of the walls equalized, there were more explosions around the gate. The massive doors buckled and a large, menacing shape pushed through the wreckage.

It had the lean and deadly look of a shark, larger than a Sabertooth or a Sandray but riding, like them, on a magnetic cushion and propelled by powerful turbofans. Garcia had seen pictures of the Toeljuk assault vehicles known in Commonwealth parlance as "Gorgons," but this was the first time she'd seen one up close.

Wogs clung to the sides of the vehicle, brandishing weapons and shouting battle cries. They slid into the water as she watched, joining many more of their kindred who were already swimming through the shattered gates.

And a low bubble turret, mounting a pulse laser cannon, swung slowly to cover the gatehouse wall, where the fiercest fighting was still going on.

"Fall back! Fall back!" Gunnery Sergeant Trent shouted the orders, but he knew he was too late to save some of the defenders holding around the gatehouse.

He'd joined Bartlow's platoon to support the wavering Alpha Company troops, who were still demoralized by the loss of Subaltern Narmonov and the sudden two-front battle they'd been pressed into by the nomads. Subaltern Bartlow himself had been wounded in the first few moments of the fight, and Trent was in command now.

But it didn't look like he'd be in command of anything much, now that the Toel Gorgon had entered the fight.

"Weapons Lances!" he yelled. "Concentrate fire on that strakking thing! Burn every Fafnir you've got left if you have to!" Trent grabbed a retreating Alpha Company corporal. "Get your men under control, damn it! We've got to set up a fallback position and hold these wogs!"

The man nodded dumbly and pushed past Trent, but he was calling orders as he ran and looked like he was functioning again. Trent looked around wildly, saw the sappers moving a dismounted magrep generator into place across the parapet twenty meters behind them, using one of the small maglifts Seafarms normally used for bulk cargo handling. Kelly was there, too, waving for him to fall back to her position.

He cut in his commlink. "Task Force Gatehouse! Fall back on the sappers! Now!"

Then the Gorgon's laser cannon opened fire.

Garcia grabbed the handset of her $C^3$ pack, which was open on the rooftop beside her. "Ops! Ops! The gates are gone, and the Toels have brought in a Gorgon-class MAV. Come in, Ops!"

Fraser's voice came back, sounding worried but controlled. "Acknowledged, Garcia," he said curtly. "Bastards had it out of sight until a couple of minutes ago. What's your situation?"

Garcia looked back into the compound in time to see the laser cut loose with a string of rapid pulses that battered the fusand gatehouse, raising clouds of dust and debris with each strike. She saw a legionnaire caught in the beam, his head and torso vanishing in a flare of raw energy.

Then she saw the dark shapes in the water, swarming around the gatehouse wall and into the compound.

"We've got several hundred wogs in the compound now, Captain," she said, shivering. "That's *minimum*—there could be ten times that many too deep underwater for us to see from up here. The gatehouse is under fire from the Gorgon now, and Sergeant Trent is falling back. And I don't think there are any reserves left. . . ."

"Let me worry about that, Garcia," Fraser shot back. "Hold as long as you can. I'll find some more men for you . . . somewhere. Count on it."

As the comm channel went dead Garcia raised her FEK again and opened fire, knowing that she could rely on Colin Fraser to keep his word.

Fraser dropped the handset and turned to the technicians in the Ops center. "We can't do much more in here. Get out to the Armory and grab weapons, then report to Legionnaire Garcia."

One of the techs, an older man with a snow-white mustache, looked uncertain, "What about you, Captain?" he asked.

"I'm going to find some more reinforcements," he answered curtly. "Get moving. We need everyone we can get out there."

He followed them out the door, but turned left instead of right at the first branch in the corridor. Within minutes he'd descended two levels and crossed to the cell block section.

The four legionnaires he'd ordered confined for drunkenness were in one large holding cell together. Fraser unlocked the door and swung it open hurriedly. "Sentence suspended," he said, forcing a smile. "Lay up to the Armory and draw some weapons, boys. We've got a situation outside."

White, the one who'd operated the still, let out a whoop. "Come on! Let's get us some wogs!" They rushed past him.

"Captain!"

Fraser turned at the sound of DuValier's voice. The lieutenant was in a separate cell three doors down.

"Captain . . . let me fight too. Please."

Fraser shook his head slowly. "After the stunt you pulled? I couldn't trust you out there, Lieutenant. Forget it." He turned away.

"Wait . . . please, wait!" There was a note of desperation in that voice, usually so cool and controlled. "Captain, you need me out there."

"What I need is a couple of squadrons of Airsharks and an armored regiment," Fraser said harshly. "Not—"

"Listen to me, for Christ's sake! Before . . . before the mutiny I was working on an idea to screw up the nomad command and control setup. We can block the signals they've been using to pass orders. Believe me, Captain!"

Fraser hesitated. "I didn't see anything about this. . . ."

"Was I going to tell you about it? You know how I felt . . . before . . ." DuValier trailed off. "Damn it, Captain, ask Koenig about it. We talked about the options the other day. I was planning on telling you once I had the whole thing ready to go. Hell, I thought it would make the magrep modules unnecessary."

"You really think you can foul up their communications?"

"I'm sure of it. Just let me get to the med center, Captain. Put a guard on me if you have to . . ."

"I don't have the men to spare to guard you, dammit!" he said. Reluctantly he crossed to the cell and unlocked the door. "Your friend Barnett was a traitor. I hope I'm not making a mistake believing in you, Lieutenant."

"You aren't," DuValier told him. There was no trace of hatred in the man's eyes now, only a burning determination. "You aren't . . ."

"Firing!" Karatsolis called, hitting the stud on the console in front of him. The round chambered automatically, with a metallic clang that made his ears ring. An instant later the plasma cannon opened up with a screech of superheating ammo. The turret grew noticeably hotter, worse than usual because of the water boiling around the barrel and in the path of the searing plasma bolt.

Down in the driver's compartment Bashar was monitoring the commlink. "Spear! They've got an assault vehicle up there. Gorgon-class . . . one of those old Toel MAVs."

"Yeah, I know it," Karatsolis confirmed. "Remember? We ran into one of their export jobs on Embla."

"Sounds like it's got them running in circles up there," Bashar commented. "Two Fafnir gunners killed trying to nail the sucker, everybody else too busy with wogs. Can we get it?"

"Coords?"

Bashar reeled off a string of numbers. "Over by the gatehouse," he elaborated.

"This muck we're shooting through is screwing up the

plasma gun pretty bad,'' Karatsolis said, thinking hard. ''It's great for frying wogs, but I don't think it'll do much to the Gargon. . . . '' He swung in his seat, flipping a row of switches on one side. ''I've got the Grendels on line. Feeding target ID . . . firing!'' He slammed the red launch switch.

One of the Sabertooth's Grendel missiles slid off the launch rail behind the turret, slashing through the water like a predator in search of prey. Karatsolis fired the second missile.

Seconds passed. . . .

As the first missile cleared the water, Gunnery Sergeant Trent dropped flat behind the improvised barrier of magrep generators, shouting ''Get down! Get down!''

Around him legionnaires and civilians threw themselves to the fusand rooftop. The first missile struck the massive Gorgon assault vehicle squarely in the bow and exploded in a multicolored fireball. Showers of debris rained down on the compound.

The stern of the vehicle remained suspended on its own magrep fields for a moment, before the second Grendel finished the job. One of the sappers—the old man, MacAllister—raised a ragged cheer.

Then the rest of the legionnaires were taking up the call, and even a few of the Seafarms people.

Trent rolled, fired his FEK at a nomad climbing over the parapet, and got to his feet. ''Pascali!'' he called. ''Your lance to the inner wall! The Captain says Garcia needs some support in there!''

The battle went on.

Antoine DuValier burst into the medical center, pushing aside a burly medic in bloodstained battledress. Dr. Ramirez whirled, a look of shock on his face. ''Stop him! He's broken out of cells! Somebody cover Captain Hawley!''

DuValier stopped, holding out both hands. ''Captain Fraser let me out, Doctor,'' he said quickly. ''I need to see that wog scout . . . Oomour. Please!''

The doctor was joined by a pair of medics, with distinctly unmedical FEKs held at the ready. None of them looked ready to believe him. . . .

He didn't blame them a bit. It was miracle enough that

Fraser had trusted him, but in the confusion the word hadn't gone out yet. And who would trust a man who mutinied against the Legion? That was the only unforgivable sin in a unit well known as a haven for the worst humanity had to offer.

He caught sight of Father Fitzpatrick behind the others. "Padre! My word of honor . . . Before God, I'm telling the truth. Believe me!"

Fitzpatrick was frowning. He didn't want to accept DuValier's word any more than the others. But they'd been friends from the day DuValier had joined Bravo Company, and the lieutenant had always played it straight with the chaplain.

Finally he nodded. "Let him go, Doctor," the priest said quietly. With reluctance plain on their faces the others accepted the Padre's word. Not DuValier's, but the Padre's.

The shame of the Legion's hatred burned deep, but DuValier swallowed and pushed on.

Oomour was bending over a human casualty. Evidently the more lightly wounded patients were helping the doctor tend the seriously injured from the battle. "Lieutenant!" the native said, sounding pleased. "False Voice make we now?"

"Yes . . . yes, now. It's urgent." He urged the scout toward the door. "We have to move fast, Oomour!"

Together they ran for the broad stairs that led down to the lowest level. DuValier had laid out a hardsuit there, together with weapons, a hand-held amplifier for Oomour, and additional communications gear for himself. He was explaining his plan as he suited up with the clumsy help of the nomad.

Finally, his suit sealed and his FEK in one hand, DuValier checked the airtight inner door and then opened the outer one, the one that led to the compound. He had to cling to a stanchion as the water poured in.

They swam out side-by-side, the nomad clutching the amplifier in a dexterous foot and cradling his weapon in his arms, while DuValier held the FEK at the ready.

He gestured to the amplifier, and Oomour shifted it to his feeding tendrils. DuValier switched on the recorder function of his communications package. A few minutes of the nomad's live performance could be turned into a permanent jamming technique . . . if it worked.

Even amplified the Voice was at the very threshold of audibility, but judging from the way Oomour himself was cringing the sound must have been loud and clear to a native's ears.

DuValier swam past the alien and let himself sink slowly to the bottom. He waited, ready to protect Oomour, hoping he wouldn't have to.

Hoping he had a chance to redeem himself.

!!Dhruuj stopped dead in the water, baffled by the cacophony of sounds that suddenly filled the sea. Beside him Warrior-Superior Ghoodoor stopped as well. "What is that, Scout?" he asked.

"I . . . do not know, Warrior-Superior," !!Dhruuj admitted. "It is like the Voices . . . but different. Not the Voices of the War-Leader-of-Clans . . . not the Voice of any Clan I have heard."

Ghoodoor's feeding tendrils writhed in uncertainty. "Could it be some weapon the Strangers are using?"

The Warrior-Superior's concern was understandable, !!Dhruuj thought. The destruction of the Gift-That-Rode-Above-the Waves had unsettled them all. But it was not the way of the Swimmers to allow a setback to keep them from victory.

But these new Voices were something different. . . .

"Weapon or not," !!Dhruuj said at last. "I think we should withdraw."

"Retreat! We do not retreat! Not without the word of Choor!."

!!Dhruuj turned to face the Warrior-Superior. "How will we know what orders we are sent? How will Choor! hear our reports, to judge the next turning of the battle? Without the Voices, the Clans cannot work as one any more! We become a mob again, and Choor! has said that a mob cannot defeat the Strangers-Above!"

Ghoodoor hesitated, plainly torn between instinct and obedience to the War-Leader-of-Clans. "If we withdraw, the battle is lost. . . ."

"No! If we withdraw, we can see how far these new Voices reach, ask for advice from the War-Leader-of-Clans, mount a fresh assault when we are prepared!" !!Dhruuj knew his voice was edged with the unaccustomed fear he felt. Without the Voices he was no longer a Hand of the

Clan. He was cut off, like the only survivor of a dead tribe. He knew Ghoodoor was feeling it, too.

"Others might not be retreating. We cannot contact them."

"That is why we must retreat!" !!Dhruuj insisted.

The Warrior-Superior took a long time before he finally shook his head in assent. "Withdraw! Withdraw!" he shouted in the Voice-of-Speech. "Spread out in a skirmish line and urge others to withdraw as you meet them!"

They started back toward the hole in the Reef. !!Dhruuj fought the impulse to turn back and keep fighting, knowing that the Strangers would still be there when the Clans returned. This attack had hurt the Strangers, and they would not survive another such battle.

# Chapter 21

You have given the Legion too limited an objective.
It has assigned itself others.

—Lieutenant Colonel Paul Rollet
French Foreign Legion, August, 1917

DuValier emerged, dripping, up a ladder along the inside of the compound wall, with Oomour following close behind. The nomad had recorded almost ten minutes of random noises before DuValier had decided they had enough to work with.

He looked around as he climbed. There was still heavy fighting raging near the gatehouse, with legionnaires crouching behind barricades across the wall holding against fierce fire from nomads who had won a foothold. On the far side of the compound, near the motor pool building, there was more activity. That would be Lieutenant Gage with the bulk of Alpha Company, rallying against an assault which had hit soon after he'd gone underwater.

The center of the compound was growing quiet now. A mixed band of civilians and legionnaires were spread out along the rooftops of the Ops center and adjacent structures. They were still firing at random targets visible in the waters below, but on the whole it looked like Oomour's "Voice" had been enough to prompt a withdrawal.

At the top of the ladder DuValier stripped off the hardsuit and then crouched over the electronics module. He pulled out the chip that he had used to make the recording and tucked it into a belt pouch. Then he looked at Oomour. "You know what a remote speaker is?"

The nomad shook his head. "Yes. Used them I have, in training."

"All right, then. I want you to report to Lieutenant Gage. Tell her to have her $C^3$ technician drop a remote speaker over the wall where she is fighting.'' He pointed across the compound. ''She's over there. If you can't find her, find out who's in command and pass on the same order.'' He paused. They couldn't afford another round of arguments over whether or not DuValier could be trusted. ''Tell them you have Captain Fraser's authority on it. Understand?''

Oomour repeated the instructions back in his heavily accented dialect.

''Good,'' DuValier said. ''Get moving.''

As the alien hurried off, DuValier turned toward the nearer battle zone. He had to find a $C^3$ backpack to broadcast the message, and a remote of his own. Once they placed the speakers in the water, he could start broadcasting the jamming message. The relay units wouldn't last long in Polypheme's corrosive water, but if it bought them a respite now they could find a more permanent solution later. Hopefully that would turn the tide on the perimeter, as it evidently had inside the compound.

Hopefully . . .

''It's slacking off, Captain. Most of them are pulling back.''

Fraser slapped a fresh magazine into his FEK before he responded to Garcia. ''In here, maybe. They're still fighting on the outer wall.''

The $C^3$ tech took a moment to fire a long burst at half-seen shapes moving in the water below. ''What the hell's making them run?''

''Gunny says DuValier just reported in. This could be because of his jamming trick. I hope so.'' Fraser peered into the middle of the compound, searching for targets, but none was visible. Trent's last call had reported the situation as stabilizing now that the Gorgon had been destroyed, but the casualties by the gatehouse had been heavy. Maybe DuValier's bag of tricks would work, but Fraser didn't plan to lean too heavily on the lieutenant's scheme. He finally lowered his FEK and looked back at the $C^3$ tech. ''Garcia, I want you to stay here with half your people. I'll take the rest to help Gunny with the perimeter.''

She nodded. ''Take Hodges and the other legionnaires in your group, Captain,'' she suggested. ''I don't think we'll have much more fighting here.''

It took several long minutes to sort the civilians between

the two groups. Fraser heard more explosions near the gatehouse—grenades, from the sound of them—and silently cursed each wasted second. They had the wogs on the run . . . but it was still possible for the nomads to stage a comeback.

He had to win this fight before a new one started.

"Here goes, Sergeant," DuValier announced, pitching the speaker over the wall. "That'll keep the bastards from talking!"

The chip he'd made of Oomour was already broadcasting over a commlink from Legionnaire Tomlinson's C³ pack. Tomlinson wasn't alive anymore to operate it. He'd started on the Last March saving Subaltern Bartlow from a wog spear after the latter had been wounded, so DuValier himself had the bulky computer/communications unit slung across his back. With relays in place both inside the compound and at each corner of the perimeter, the wogs would be hard-pressed to communicate anywhere within a hundred meters of the walls, maybe further.

A rocket bullet hit the wall a few meters away and exploded, reminding him that many nomads hadn't chosen to run. At least their attacks were no longer coherent. With a little bit of luck, the legionnaires would have them cleared off the walls within another hour or so.

He crouched behind a temporary barricade of magrep modules the sappers had thrown up across the rampart, and checked the magazine on his FEK. Trent and the other men on the line were maintaining a steady fire, and so far Trent had been the only one even to acknowledge his presence.

DuValier squeezed off a round, shifted his aim, fired again. What the rest of the legionnaires felt no longer mattered as much as what he thought of himself.

Yells behind him made him glance over his shoulder. Fraser was running at the head of a disorganized mass of civilians carrying an assortment of weapons, mostly Legion FEKs. Those reinforcements would clean the nomads up even faster than he'd first estimated. . . .

Fraser saw DuValier, wearing a C³ pack awkwardly and holding an FEK. The lieutenant half rose from his crouching posture behind Trent's improvised barrier, shouting something Fraser couldn't pick out from the noise of the battle.

Suddenly the FEK came up into a firing position, and the blood turned cold in Fraser's veins. He'd *trusted* DuValier. . . .

He felt the hot breath of the burst, as needle rounds sliced past him. Then he heard the deep-throated wailing behind him, and spun around in time to see a trio of wogs reeling backward against the parapet. One of the Seafarms men was gaping at the natives, paralyzed.

DuValier was beside him a moment later. "Sorry about the near-miss, Captain," he said, leaning over the wall to pump some more rounds into the water below. "I didn't think your bunch of overnight heroes were going to take care of the bastards."

Firing a burst of grenades into the water where DuValier was aiming, Fraser let out a shuddering breath. "I'm the one who should be apologizing," he said quietly. "For doubting your word."

Somehow the Voice managed to convey anger and contempt, even though it was a simple arrangement of clicks and grunts that weren't supposed to hold any emotional content. !!Dhruuj strained to hear, trying to sort out the real Voice from the faint echoes of the false Voices around the Built-Reef-of-the-Strangers. A distant throbbing sound made it even harder to hear—probably another of the Strangers' weird weapons or devices off by the Reef.

Finally he turned in the water to face Clan-Leader Nuujuur!, the youngest of the clan leaders in the assembled army and hence the most revered for his fast rise to ascendancy. He was the Hand of Choor! here, responsible for translating the War-Leader-of-Clans' instructions into action.

"The War-Leader says we can still win, even without the lost Gift. He says that now is the time to allow the fighting madness to possess our troops, to let them attack and keep attacking until victory is ours. If we launch all of the remaining swimmers in the attack at once, he says our victory is assured."

"He's said that before," someone grumbled.

Nuujuur! silenced the offender with a glare. "If Choor! says to fight, we will fight," he said, but no one missed his pessimistic tone. The War-Leader-of-Clans had promised victory time and time again, but still the Strangers resisted.

"The Floating-Reef!" another scout called. "The Floating-Reef comes!"

The knot of officers started to scatter, and !!Dhruuj swam after Nuujuur! in case the Clan-Leader had any further messages to send. The throbbing of the water jets that drove the huge Floating-Reef, the thing the Strangers-Above called *"Cyclops,"* was suddenly loud as the massive structure drove toward them.

It had arrived sooner than anyone had expected . . . sooner than the Swimmers who had been assigned to watch it had predicted after many tides of seeing it travel. A hidden reserve of speed . . .

The bulk blocked the sunlight filtering through the waters, like one of the periodic passings of the moon across the face of the sun. Nuujuur! was diving, striking for the bottom as if he were being pursued by a hunting *woorroo.*

Something splashed into the water overhead and drifted lazily down. Suddenly !!Dhruuj remembered the reports of the explosives the Strangers had used to defend the Floating-Reef from an earlier attack, and he knew why Nuujuur! sought refuge in deep water. Another cylinder splashed, and another, and yet another. . . .

Long before the first explosion lashed through the water, !!Dhruuj knew neither he nor Nuujuur! would escape the blast. He doubted if any of the leaders would.

It would be a sad Tide for the Clans United when their leaders floated to the surface and led no more. !!Dhruuj wondered if their successors would be able to organize the final attack. . . .

Legionnaires cheered as the great bulk of the *Seafarms Cyclops* slid through the shattered gates and into the compound. Figures on the four boarding platforms waved in response. Some of them were capering like the overexcited monkeys Fraser remembered from Hanuman.

The jubilation was infectious. He felt like shouting or capering himself, now that Watanabe had brought the big harvester ship back. The subaltern had pushed her to the limit to get to the Sandcastle early, and on his way in had ordered that improvised depth charges be dropped every time his sonars reported contact with large groups of targets.

In combination with the defense the rest of the Legion had mounted inside the base, that would surely break up the wogs for a while. They'd bought yet another breathing space: time to regroup, reorganize . . . and count the dead.

High up in the small windows of the ship's bridge, Fraser saw Watanabe's slender, stiff figure. He waved, but the subaltern didn't respond.

The butcher's bill for the battle would be horrendous. He knew that much already. He also knew there was no way they'd be able to pay that price again, even with the full cooperation of the civilians and the arrival of Watanabe's men.

And much as he wanted to think that Choor!'s alliance had been broken by this defeat, there was no way to count on it. They had to expect the nomads to strike again, once they'd recovered from today's fighting. With their resources, they'd recover a hell of a lot faster than the Legion—especially if the Toels had more surprises like that Gorgon waiting in the wings.

As the *Cyclops* maneuvered slowly toward its cradle, Fraser turned away and stared out over the wall across the open sea.

Simple survival was no longer enough. The Legion had to seize the initiative now, before the enemy returned.

One way or another, the next battle would decide this campaign.

He was floating in a formless mist, stark, unrelieved by any detail or variation, different from any of the countless environments David Hawley had experienced in his past voyages into Dreamland. But he was not alone. He shared the mist with another soul, Edward Barnett's, and from somewhere in the distant corners of his mind the computer implant whispered to him.

"RESPONSE SHOWS RESISTANCE/BLOCKAGE AT PROBABILITY 86.5%."

Hawley thought of emptiness, of loneliness, and the computer translated his thoughts, magnified them, redirected them back at the link between Hawley and Barnett. The machine had identified this as one of Barnett's weaknesses, this fear of the void. It was part of the general psych profile, and it had already broken down many of the man's barriers. But Hawley was sharing in these induced feelings and dreams, and they were taking a toll on his spirit as well.

"Again, Barnett." He wasn't speaking, but he visualized the thoughts as words, "heard" them through the mist. "Again. The location of the Toeljuk base. Give me the location, and you won't be alone anymore. Give me the location. . . ."

It was an effective approach. Barnett was fighting him, of course, but Hawley was the only other entity in this private universe, the only link the traitor had to humanity. The poor colonial orphan inside Barnett needed that contact the way David Hawley needed his implant, needed the escape. . . .

He thrust the stray thought aside with an effort of will and repeated the question, holding out a lifeline to Barnett.

And after what seemed like an eternity, Edward Barnett began to answer.

The conference room held more people than it had at the last meeting, but even so Fraser was very conscious of the ones who were missing. Neither Jens nor Barnett was there this time, of course. Since Captain MacLean, the senior man in the Seafarms hierarchy now, had been confined to cells on Watanabe's recommendation, as too thoroughly committed to Barnett's policies to be trusted, it was Katrina Voskovich who represented the civilian viewpoint—not so much because of seniority as because she seemed genuinely ready to support the legionnaires and was respected by her own people at the same time.

DuValier was missing, too. He'd insisted on returning to his cell after the battle, even when Fraser offered to release him. "What I did today I did for the unit, Captain," he had said, stiff and formal. "My opinions on . . . other matters . . . haven't changed, and I didn't help you so I could earn some good-conduct prize." And Gunnery Sergeant Valko was dead, killed in the fighting around the motor pool in the tense moments before the destruction of the Toel Gorgon.

On the other hand, the remaining subalterns were present for this conference: Watanabe, looking remarkably fresh, despite the fact that he'd snatched only two hours' sleep since the *Cyclops* had berthed; Henck Wijngaarde, still managing to look embarrassed over the fact that the handful of Legion mutineers had all been from his unit; and Carnes, the only platoon leader from Alpha Company still alive. The demi-battalion's warrant officers were also present: Father Fitzpatrick, Dr. Ramirez, and Koenig, plus their opposite numbers from Hawley's outfit and, of course, Kelly.

That left the people clustered around him near the head of the table. Hawley, still looking pale and strained after his interrogation centers. Gunnery Sergeant Trent, who sported a large bruise on one cheek and a bandage on his left hand. And Susan Gage, who'd fought a stubborn battle by the motor pool but seemed as withdrawn and diffident as ever.

These were the men and women who would have to decide the fate of the Terrans on Polypheme. Tired people who'd been pushed to the limit . . . but were still determined.

"With the magrep generators and Lieutenant DuValier's tapes in place, we can sit here and laugh at the wogs," Subaltern Wijngaarde was saying. "We've won. I don't see what the problem is."

"The problem, Mr. Wijngaarde, is what it's always been," Kelly told him. "The nomads are smart. Especially this Choor!. We can't guarantee that our defenses are a hundred percent leak-proof."

"Especially with the Toels around," Trent added. "Last time it was a Gorgon, and odds are they only had the one or they'd have hit us with more during the assault. But they probably have a ship or some sort, and they have better weaponry than they've been giving to the wogs. The magreps won't hold against high-tech, and the wogs will come in expecting the jamming."

"What can they do about it?" Warrant Officer Simms, the Alpha Company chaplain, blinked owlishly at Trent.

"Lots of things, Chaplain," Trent said. "Me, I'd put together some simple attack plan ahead of time and ditch the fancy coordination. Win by strength of numbers and sheer wog guts. Or if they've figured out how we're doing it, they could send in commandos to shut our broadcasts down."

"The point is, we're still vulnerable," Kelly said. Trent and Watanabe both nodded at that. "Captain Fraser's right when he says we have to take the war to them for a change."

"How sure are we of their base?" Koenig asked. He

looked apologetic, but determined. "That jury-rigged questioning setup . . ."

"We're sure," Fraser said flatly. "It's another old Toel base like this one, about a hundred klicks down the coast. It was supposed to be abandoned, but when we ran through the Seafarms database it was pretty clear that Barnett had dummied up the survey reports to keep anyone from paying much attention to the place. Captain Hawley pried it out of the little strakk, and the computer puts a ninety-seven-plus probability on the accuracy."

There were a few skeptical looks around the table at the mention of Hawley's name. Ramirez cleared his throat. "I agree. Barnett wasn't holding anything back by the time Captain Hawley got through with him."

Fraser hid a smile. At least the doctor was convinced of Hawley's soundness now.

"What it comes down to, the way I see it, is whether or not we have the strength to mount an attack on the base." Heads turned as Lieutenant Gage spoke in a soft but clear voice. "We're talking about a compound just like this one, possibly defended by Toels and certainly full of wogs. If our chances of surviving another attack here are slim, what are the odds of winning there?"

"We're in bad shape," Fraser admitted. "We're going to have to break down one platoon out of each company to bring the other platoons up to something like fighting strength, and better than one-third casualties is not what I'd call sitting pretty. But Barnett's info suggests the Toels don't have much—probably no more than thirty or forty 'advisers,' and some of them would have gone up with the Gorgon. If we hit them hard, try for the element of surprise, we'll take them."

"But that sounds like you're abandoning the Sandcastle!" Gage exclaimed. "You don't seriously mean to use all the legionnaires on the attack?"

"All but the ones too badly wounded to serve as assault troops. Doc says we've got sixteen recovered enough to man the walls."

"Sixteen!" Carnes paled. "That's not enough to stand watch on the gatehouse!"

"Plus the civilians," Fraser said. "We'll take a few with us to operate the *Cyclops*, but the rest will be left here." He saw Voskovich opening her mouth to protest, and raised his hand. "I know your people are willing to do more, Katrina, but they aren't trained for a set-piece battle. Or a commando action. Or for combat in hardsuits, for that matter. Your people will have to flesh out our resources on this end."

"You're putting all the civilians at risk this way, sir," Chaplain Simms said quietly. "You've said yourself that another attack will overpower our defenses here, even with the legionnaires available. Isn't our first duty to protect these people? That's the way our orders read, isn't it?"

Hawley stirred. Even though he looked exhausted, haggard, there was a fire in his eyes. "This is the only way we can carry out these orders, Chaplain. Captain Fraser's right about this. It's the only move we've got left in this game."

DuValier looked up, surprised, as the cell door opened and Fraser entered the cramped, spartan room. "Is something wrong?" he asked, rolling out of his cot.

"Not exactly," Fraser said enigmatically. He motioned for DuValier to sit again. "We've decided on an assault on the nomad HQ. Barnett gave it to us."

"I heard," DuValier said. One of the guards who'd brought his dinner had shared the news. "You're taking the *Cyclops?*"

"Right. And every legionnaire who can fight. Fifty civilians as ship's crew, both veeters. It's all or nothing this time, Lieutenant."

He kept his response noncommittal. "Tough decision."

Fraser nodded vaguely. Suddenly he looked hard at his former exec. "We're damned short of officers, Antoine," he said. "Three subalterns, a lieutenant, one senior NCO. Captain Hawley, who might not be up to the long haul. It's bad enough we lost so many legionnaires, but it's officers we really need."

"You want me to come? After what happened?" DuValier laughed harshly. "Remind me to tell you sometime what I had to go through yesterday trying to get anybody to trust me. The kind of battle you're going into doesn't have room for hesitation like that!"

"I know. But I *do* need to leave someone in command here while we're gone. Bartlow's arm is coming off; he won't be much use. The senior NCO from the limited-duty bunch is a corporal, Johnson. And I can't spare any of the other officers to take charge of the Sandcastle. But you could.''

''You'd trust me with the base? With the civilians?''

''I did yesterday,'' Fraser said with a shrug. ''You did damned good work coming up with that voices thing, even if you did screw around on procedures and not tell anyone. And you've got the touch, Antoine. The wogs won't catch you napping.''

DuValier looked away. ''You're not going to stick me with some watchdog to keep me honest?''

''You'll be in charge. You're the best man for the job.''

He hesitated for a long moment, then nodded. ''All right. I'll take it.'' He laughed again. ''And God help us all.''

# Chapter 22

The Legion's in Magenta; the job is in the bag.
—General Patrice de MacMahon
French Foreign Legion, 1859

"Sorry you came, Kelly?" Fraser asked, joining Kelly Winters by the large observation window at the bow of the *Seafarms Cyclops*. The huge ship was laboring through rough seas on a course south and east from the Sandcastle, with three more hours to go until they were in position to strike at the enemy base. He'd ordered the legionnaires to rest while they could, but hadn't been able to relax himself. It looked as if Kelly was having the same problem.

She shook her head slowly but kept on staring at the water. A nasty storm was brewing out there, one of the powerful *bhourrkhs* spawned in the heat of the tropics that would spin north or south, with winds that could make a Terran hurricane look like a summer breeze. Another reason to finish this fight fast. Tides would be higher than usual for the next few days, and as long as the storms raged the wogs would have a huge advantage in any assault they mounted on the base.

If the legionnaires didn't finish this fight today, they probably wouldn't have another chance.

"I was just . . . thinking about this planet," she said. "The Toels kept the peace here for centuries, even though we always talk about how brutal they are. We let Seafarms take over here, and they drove the nomads to war in a couple of years."

"Seafarms had help," he said. "From the Toels, especially. They wanted the planet back, and they knew what buttons to push to make the nomads join them." He paused. "But you're right. I think sometimes that Mankind wasn't mature enough to take on a responsibility like the Commonwealth. The government needs commercial support to make it worthwhile to be out here at all, and the corporations are so busy with their profit margins they don't stop and think about the damage they're doing. So then the military gets called out to put things right, and there are times when the only way to do that is to smash the hostiles flat. . . ."

Kelly sighed. "When you put it like that, it sounds like you're one of those back-to-Terra people, ready to chuck it all and let the universe look after itself."

"Not really," he said. "You can't stuff the djinni back into the bottle. Terra has responsibilities we can't just ignore. We didn't know what we were getting into when we knocked down the Semti Conclave, but someone had to step in when they collapsed, and it looks like we were the ones who got picked for it. For every primitive native like Choor! and his people, there are ten who are benefiting from Commonwealth rule, one way or another. We'd create even more hardship by pulling out."

"So we just muddle through, then? That's not much of an answer."

"It's all I've got, anyway," he admitted. "We took oaths to uphold the Commonwealth and help spread civilization among the stars, Kelly. We can't stop idiots from screwing things up, and you know there'll always be idiots—politicians or bureaucrats or misguided business executives. All we can do is put things right when they do screw up, and try to leave the situation a little less volatile than it was when we found it."

"Do you think we can, here?"

"If we pull this off . . . maybe. Seafarms went wrong by assuming they could simply ignore the locals except where they were useful. They won't have that option again."

"But if we break Choor!'s confederation . . ."

He shook his head. "That's another djinni that won't fit back into the bottle. The nomads have found out that they can work together. It's only a matter of time before they realize it doesn't take Choor! to make cooperation work. And once the natives have a stable confederation this gaggle of independent city-states won't be viable anymore, either. Ideas spread fast here, thanks to the way the nomads move around. Mark my words, Kelly, whether Choor! wins or loses, Polypheme won't be the same again. Any offworld dealing with the locals will have to involve a global policy, not just focus on one favored city and ignore everybody else."

"I hope Seafarms sees it the way you do."

"I left a tape with DuValier before we left, told him to pass it on or make sure it's somewhere an expeditionary force will uncover it if things go sour for us. My recommendations are in there, and I'm pretty sure the Legion will persuade the Colonial Administration to go along with them. Polypheme's going to have to be a full Commonwealth protectorate after this. Even if Seafarms doesn't want it, we can't afford to let the Toels win and move back in. We're too close to some pretty important systems here to let the Toels build this into an advanced base."

"Well . . . I'd rather you delivered your recommendations in person, Col."

"Me too," he said with a faint smile. "I'm just covering all the possibilities, that's all."

"Can we really win this fight?" She turned from the window and looked him in the eye. "And don't give me the morale-building speeches you give to the others. I want it straight."

"Straight? I don't know. We don't have very many troops to pull this off with, and you know the state of our officer corps. There's a hell of a lot riding on unknowns."

"Finally having doubts about Hawley?" she asked. "He *seems* better. . . ."

He shrugged. "Him among others." The battle plan they'd drawn up required the bulk of the legionnaires to distract the nomads in a general engagement, while a smaller, more elite force attacked the enemy base. Fraser was taking charge of the latter unit, backed up by Kelly and her sappers and by Gunnery Sergeant Trent. But it left the main battle to Hawley, Gage, and the three surviving subalterns. It was a lot of responsibility to push onto David Hawley, no matter how dramatically he had changed. And Gage didn't inspire much more confidence. "Mostly, though," he continued, "I'm having doubts about me."

She looked at him with a questioning expression.

He didn't elaborate. But the doubts had been growing since the first time the natives had attacked. He'd underestimated them in the first battle, and after that he'd allowed first Jens and then Barnett to paralyze the defense of the Sandcastle with their interference. That near-mutiny should never have been allowed to happen, either. . . .

Now they were on the verge of being committed to a battle he wasn't sure the Legion could win. Was this how it had started for Hawley? The miracle on Hanuman had set Fraser up as a hero, but a debacle on Polypheme was looking more and more likely. If he lived through this, would he follow David Hawley's path, retreating from reality and trying to recapture the glory of that first lucky victory? Or maybe he'd be more like DuValier, searching for someone else to blame for his misfortunes and twisting his whole life out of shape as a result.

Kelly laid a hand on his shoulder. "Try not to lose that battle before we even leave the *Cyclops*, Col," she said softly. "You're the one who held things together this far. And without you in there doing your best, there's no way we'll win. Don't forget, you're supposed to be part of the Legion, so try following in the footsteps of all those Legion heroes. Go in swinging, do your best, don't give up. These people have a right to that, you know. They need you." She paused. "And I do, too. I don't want to lose you."

The observation bay was quiet except for the distant throbbing of the impellers. Fraser took her hand, and the two of them looked out at the endless ocean together.

David Hawley stood on the docking platform, feeling uncomfortable in the stiff hardsuit. The sun was low on the eastern horizon, just below a building mass of storm clouds. The colors of the sunrise were a spectacular mix of reds and pinks reflected from the dark and angry canopy. A bit of ancient doggerel from pre-spaceflight Terra ran through his mind. *Red sky in morning, sailor take warning. . . .*

Next to him Legionnaire Second-Class Jurgensen cocked his head to one side as he listened to a report over his $C^3$ network. "That's the last of them, sir," he said. "Subaltern Watanabe's platoon is in the water."

"Then I guess it's time," Hawley said slowly, feeling reluctant to commit himself. He'd thought he could do this, but now he wasn't so sure. A lifetime of dodging responsibility was a hard habit to break . . .

Fraser crossed the platform from the hatch, saluting smartly. "Good luck, Captain," he said formally.

"And to you," Hawley responded automatically. He started to lower his faceplate, then stopped and fixed his second-in-command with a hard stare. "Look, Fraser . . . Colin . . . thanks. Anyone else probably would have eased me out of the unit a long time ago, and I wouldn't have fought very hard. But you . . . you gave me what I needed. An example to remind me of what being a Legion officer is all about." He stuck out his hand. "It's been an honor to serve with you, Colin—and my personal privilege."

Fraser took his hand with a firm grip. "The honor and the privilege are both mine, sir," he said. "But thank you for the sentiment."

The reluctance was gone now. He closed his helmet and ran a quick diagnostic on the suit. Although Hawley still felt no real confidence in his ability to command the main body of the attack, he knew he'd at least go down trying. If only because he could do no less for Colin Fraser, the only officer he'd met in many long years who'd ever seen anything of value in the washed-out veteran of Aten.

With Jurgensen close behind, Hawley crossed to the edge of the platform and jumped into the water. Now it was too late to turn back. Right or wrong, he was in command.

The water was fairly clear, and with the vision-enhancement setting on his faceplate Hawley could see everything within fifty meters plainly. Beyond that they'd have to rely on sonar.

Below him, the bulk of the demi-battalion was drawn up loosely, divided by platoons. Fraser had five recon lances—the sixth, from Narmonov's shattered formation, had been broken up to provide replacements for the others—plus two heavy-weapon lances and all the surviving sappers. By breaking up Narmonov's and Bartlow's outfits and drafting most of the legionnaires from the transport section, Hawley's platoons were all close to full-strength, except for those missing lances. That gave him a total force of just under a standard paper-strength company. Not much to occupy the attention of whatever nomad forces were covering the enemy headquarters, especially when this fight would be taking place in an environment where the wogs would have all the advantages.

"Sergeant Franz!" he said sharply on the NCO channel of the commlink. "Switch to sonar, and keep me informed of what's out there."

"Clear for now, sir," the sergeant replied. He was probably unhappy at losing what amounted to autonomous command of the transport troops, but he was the best replacement they could find for Gunny Valko.

No one knew how many wogs were here. It was possible that the entire army had withdrawn from the Sandcastle once the Cyclops left, though Fraser had been fairly sure that Choor! would leave at least some of his forces to try another attack on the Legion base while it was shorthanded. But they could expect to be outnumbered, regardless, and in the water FEKs would be hampered a lot more than the rocket guns the nomads used. The legionnaires needed an equalizer. . . .

He found himself comparing the situation to simulations he had played over the years. Ambush and good use of terrain were the best equalizers in combat, but it was damned hard to mount an ambush in what amounted to an offensive role.

Unless the side that was on the offensive was able to stand on the defense tactically.

"Trebbia, 218 B.C.," he muttered. "Or F'Rujukh's counterattack on Ganymede."

"Sir?" Jurgensen sounded uncertain. Hawley hadn't realized he'd spoken out loud.

"Never mind," he said.

At Trebbia Hannibal's Carthaginians, exhausted and weak from the crossing of the Alps, had drawn the Roman legions into a fight by using light cavalry to goad them into a rash attack across an icy river. The Romans had never expected Hannibal to conceal a large force behind some low hills. The resulting rout had destroyed Rome's best hope of stopping the Second Punic War before it could really get started.

And Ganymede. Marshal F'Rujukh had lost two pitched battles to Alliance forces on Jupiter's moon, but that didn't stop him from laying a beautiful trap around Frenchport. Concealing the bulk of his forces in a series of caves, he'd used a brigade of the Third Foreign Legion as bait to encourage an Alliance landing, caught them from behind, and annihilated them, capturing sufficient transport to mount his brilliant counteroffensive, which prolonged the fighting on Ganymede by at least six months.

Or there was Second Manassas from the American Civil War, or . . .

He stopped himself. There were dozens of precedents, and he'd fought most of those battles himself, in simulation. A weak enough force retreating from the wogs should encourage a general pursuit, while another unit lying in ambush could exploit the confusion that was sure to follow. That was the key.

He started toward the bottom on full thruster. For the first time, he was beginning to feel that he could actually be an asset to this fight after all. . . .

"Sonar reports a large force of nomads leaving their compound. Stand by."

Selim Bashar glanced over the controls of the veeter, impatient for the order to begin the attack. Karatsolis looked anxious too, as he rechecked his weaponry.

They had to wait, though. Until the nomads were fully committed to responding to Captain Hawley, an assault on their fortress would be useless.

Minutes passed. Bashar turned in his seat, glancing first at the other veeter flying parallel to them, and then down and back at the barge hooked to the two flyers by tough flexsteel cables.

The barge had been reequipped with its magrep generators before the *Cyclops* had sailed from the Sandcastle. With the magrep fields operating, it rode uneasily just above the ocean surface. And when the time came the two veeters could tow it into action at a fairly high speed—faster, certainly, than *Cyclops* could have covered the distance to the old Toel complex. And even if they ran into trouble the ship would be intact to pull out the legionnaires when the battle was over, win or lose.

Two veeters, a makeshift barge, and sixty-seven legionnaires weren't much for an attack on the enemy headquarters. Bashar hoped they would be enough, Allah willing.

"CO Alpha reports the enemy has engaged the main body," the civilian communications tech aboard the *Cyclops* relayed.

"CO Strikeforce to all Strikers," Fraser's voice came on the line. "Commence attack!"

Bashar waited until Legionnaire Shapiro, piloting the second veeter, had signified his readiness. Then he hit the countdown button on the autopilot. Seconds later, the throttle began to advance automatically in the preprogrammed pattern that would keep the two veeters pulling evenly on their towlines. They gathered speed, slowly at first, then more quickly.

The enemy base came into view ahead, swelling as the veeters hurtled toward it. The complex was similar to the Sandcastle in overall layout and appearance, but this one hadn't been modified to accommodate Terrans. The gates on this one had never been repaired, and water filled the center of the compound. There were other differences, mostly of detail.

The large beehive shape that rose from the middle of the complex, gleaming in the morning sunlight, was the most noticeable difference of all. It had all the characteristics of a Toeljuk spacecraft, probably one of their smaller models. Fifty or sixty crew, perhaps, given the gregarious nature of the Toels. Less, with the ones that Karatsolis had taken out aboard that Gorgon.

The veeters pressed on, closer . . . closer . . .

"Gunners! Stand by!" Fraser shouted.

The barge was pitching in the rough water, and he wondered for the hundredth time if his plan had any hope of success. The heavy weapons needed a stable platform if they were going to succeed in this first crucial phase of the attack plan. If they couldn't do it, they'd have to circle and attack by way of the opening where the main gates should have been. That area would be heavily defended. . . .

They had to try. "Gunners, fire!"

Two Fafnirs leapt into the sky almost as one, and the harsh glare of four onagers outshone the sun. The onagers kept on firing, laying down four steady streams of superheated plasma at preselected points along the wall, while the Fafnir gunners reloaded their launchers with the last two missiles in their stockpile.

Kelly had mapped the stress points carefully back at the Sandcastle, and computer simulations had given them good odds of opening a breach of the required size with the arsenal they'd selected.

Maybe he should have assigned more heavy weapons to the strike force . . . but Hawley would need them, too, to help equalize the odds in *his* battle. These would have to do the trick.

He dropped his faceplate and switched to image-enhancement, as the first two Fafnirs struck the wall and exploded. Those hits, at least, had been right on target. And the onagers were taking a toll as well. Fraser held his breath, willing the attack to work. . . .

The second wave of Fafnirs hit, and part of the wall seemed to buckle, sagging under the impact. "Pour it on!" Fraser shouted to the onager gunners. More fusand exploded under the onslaught, while the bombardment superheated the entire target area. The fusand was glowing, running, melting.

And the wall loomed closer as the veeters pulled the barge on.

"Now!" Bashar shouted, hitting the release on the tow cable and jerking his joystick hard over and up. The wall flashed under the veeter, a few surprised-looking nomads gaping up at them from the rooftops. Karatsolis swung his MEK into line and opened fire as the veeter passed, and many of the natives were left staring at the sky with unseeing eyes.

Behind them there was a flash and the roar of an explosion. As he brought the veeter around in a tight turn, Bashar felt his breath catch in his throat. Shapiro hadn't made it.

Maybe he hadn't been able to release his towline in time, or maybe he'd been a fraction of a second too slow in climbing as he approached the wall. The veeter had almost cleared the rampart, but not quite. Now pieces of the shattered flyer littered the wall and the adjacent rooftops, and the hole Fraser's men had cut gaped a little wider near the top than it had before.

There wasn't time to mourn the two men from the other veeter, though. With a muttered appeal to Allah, Bashar swung around again and passed low over the compound, giving Karatsolis a chance to sow death and confusion in their path.

Drifting free, the barge continued to rush toward the wall under the momentum of the high-speed approach. Fraser studied the breach with a critical eye.

One of the veeters scraped the wall and lost control. He recoiled as the blast lit up the cloud-darkened sky and showered them with debris. Two more men dead. When would it end. . . ?

"Steady, boys!" Trent called out, as if unaffected by the explosion. "The old scow's a little too wide! Brace yourselves!"

Fraser grabbed a rail moments before the barge hit. As Trent had said, the gap wasn't quite wide enough for the barge to pass through, but that wasn't important. The jagged hole extended just below the waterline, and beyond, the enemy compound spread before them. "Let's move!" he shouted.

"Go! Go! Go!" Trent was yelling as legionnaires ran forward, closing the helmets of their hardsuits and springing over the rails, across the remains of the wall, and into the fort. Kelly was marshaling her sappers further aft.

"All right!" Fraser called. "Plan Tango! Kelly, you've got the Toel ship. Gunny, with me! Let's take 'em!"

He closed his hardsuit and followed the others.

The die was cast.

"Strikeforce is going in, Lieutenant."

Susan Gage barely noticed Massire's report, as she drew a bead on a wog and fired. The attacking force was larger than she'd expected, and it moved with a speed and discipline that were incredible to watch. It would take a miracle to keep her diversionary force out of reach until the captain sprang his trap.

A miracle she would have to pull off.

She had both of Alpha Company's platoons, less all the heavy weapons. Thirty-nine legionnaires all told, against hundreds of nomads . . .

Did Hawley really expect her to keep them together, keep them retreating without starting a rout? Over and over, the battle in the Sandcastle where she'd let Bravo Company get pinned down under withering fire kept replaying itself. If she made a single mistake now, her own outfit would be the one to suffer.

But another phrase also echoed in her mind, Hawley's last words as he gathered the ambush force and withdrew to the boulder-strewn terrain he'd chosen to hide them in. "Of course you can do it, Lieutenant," he'd said after she'd expressed her concerns aloud. "There's no one else I would entrust my Alphas to."

She'd always thought that Hawley was indifferent to his Exec. Now she knew he had confidence in her, and for the first time in a long time she realized that Hawley's confidence was all the respect she needed.

"Dalton! Hsien! Tighten it up!" she ordered, checking her sonar display again. "Keep it moving . . . keep it moving. . . ."

Susan Gage was going to bring off the miracle—or die trying.

# Chapter 23

Were you satisfied with my men?
—last words of Commandant Faurax,
killed at Dogba, Dahomey
French Foreign Legion, 1892

"Keep down! Wogs coming through!" the sapper called over his radio, and Kelly flattened herself behind the cover of a half-ruined fusand stairway, one that led up to the roof of the structure they used as the motor pool back at the Sandcastle. Moving and fighting underwater was awkward. She had thought her Navy training in zero-G operations would help, but so far she'd found it heavy going just to keep up with the rest of the sapper platoon. She was glad of the chance to rest while they waited for the band of nomads to swim past, heading for the fighting on the far side of the compound.

They had worked their way around the wall after leaving the breach, trying to avoid contact for as long as possible. Fraser and Trent were supposed to keep the defenders occupied while the sappers took care of the Toel ship. If that vessel got airborne it could cause a lot of damage, and now that the aliens had revealed themselves once they had no further reason for staying hidden. The Toeljuk Autarchy had never been slow to use whatever methods were necessary to achieve their goals. If anything, it was a surprise that they hadn't already used the ship for an attack on the Sandcastle. But the Toels probably preferred not to risk their ticket home, against the same Grendels that had knocked out their assault vehicle.

The last report from Fraser suggested he was doing his part of the job. Garcia had passed the word that the recon lances were under heavy attack from nomads, and Katrina Voskovich aboard the *Cyclops* had relayed a sonar report that suggested the wogs engaged with Hawley had dispatched most of their reserves to support the base.

That would make Hawley's situation a little less desperate, but it also meant that at least part of Fraser's battle plan was already unraveling. He'd counted on Hawley's main body to keep most of the enemy distracted.

At least they'd bought some time this way. But if the battle here lasted more than fifteen or twenty minutes the nomads would be getting reinforcements, and that would spell disaster.

Everything was balanced on a knife edge. . . .

Something hissed through the water from above them, striking Legionnaire Gordon squarely in his backpack thruster unit. The projectile exploded, and in the same moment the thruster controls shorted out. Gordon's body convulsed a few times.

Then Kelly was too busy to notice the casualty, as more shots plowed toward her unit like so many tiny torpedoes. She rolled in the water and fired a long burst from her FEK. As she cut in her thruster and raced for cover, she saw their attackers. Not the sleek, elongated figures of the wogs, these were squat, with a dozen thick tentacles and many more smaller ones, wearing uniforms with many of the same characteristics as her own battledress and carrying strangely-shaped weapons no human hand could have made or used.

The Toels had discovered them. And there was no way any of her sappers was going to run the gauntlet and reach the spaceship as long as the fighting went on. . . .

''Onagers forward!'' Fraser called. ''Stand clear!''

Four legionnaires took up positions in front of his ragged skirmish line. Unlike the rest of the legionnaires, they didn't have hardsuits. Their regular combat armor was sealed against all environments, including the incredible heat generated by their plasma weapons. Hardsuits were less effective, and it was wise to give the onager gunners a wide berth.

The Alpha Company corporal in the garishly decorated armor called out the order to fire, and the onagers flared bright in the water. They kept up a steady barrage, and after a few seconds there were no more nomads to threaten their position.

That wouldn't last long. This was the fourth wave of native soldiers that had been entirely wiped out. Choor! evidently wasn't worrying much about controlling his soldiers' fighting instincts when it came to the defense of his headquarters. And even with a sizable number facing Hawley's force outside the compound, there were plenty of wogs to expend.

"Casualties!" he snapped.

Garcia repeated the order, waited as she received replies from each lance, then responded. "Three killed. Valdez, Martin, and Llewellyn. And Vrurrth took some shrapnel in that last rocket attack, but Corporal Rostov says it's superficial."

That brought the total dead since the start of the assault to seven. "Tighten up the sonar watch," he ordered. "We've got to spot them before they launch another attack." It was getting to be a pattern. The wogs would get in the first shot by sneaking up on the legionnaires, and men would die. Then the Legion weaponry would shatter the enemy assault. He couldn't afford to keep on fighting a war of attrition, though. Not when the nomads had a seemingly endless supply of replacements, and more on the way from outside.

"Sir, Warrant Officer Kelly reports the Sapper Platoon has come under attack by Toels approximately seventy meters from the grounded ship. They are pinned down and requesting reinforcements."

Kelly . . .

Fraser fought the urge to snap out orders to split up his force and launch a relief mission. That would just give the nomads a better chance of defeating them all in detail. "Tell her to hang on as long as possible, Garcia," he said. "We've got problems of our own."

Even as he spoke, his sonar display showed movement to the left and down near the bottom. Another attack getting organized? Probably.

"We'll get her help as soon as we can," he finished. He shifted to the private channel that linked him to Trent. "Gunny. We're getting targets bearing two-five-seven, down."

"I see them, skipper," Trent replied.

"Let's make them uncomfortable. Take Rostov and Pascali. Call for backup if you need to." It took all his control to keep his impatience and anxiety from showing. He didn't like the thought of what would happen if Kelly was captured by those Toels. They were one of the few races that preferred slave labor to automation. . . .

Too many enemies, too few legionnaires to carry out his ambitious attack plan. Everybody else had been right. Now they were paying the price for his mistakes.

Hawley watched the sonar display, fascinated by the unfolding battle. It was so much like one of his simulations, this movement of tiny dots across his faceplate display. The legionnaires in Gage's force were falling back steadily, managing to stay just out of reach of the pursuing nomads. Just a few more minutes . . .

He welcomed the feeling that it was all just another elaborate simulation. When he thought of the battle in terms of a real conflict, with real casualties and an outcome that depended entirely on his own decisions, panic would scream within him.

Reality took him back to that day on Aten, to the fears of failure and the sickening realization of loss each time a man died. Far better to think of them all as units in a game, unfeeling, imaginary.

Perhaps if he could have done that, things would have gone differently all along. A few better breaks here and there and he'd be a brigadier now, ready to retire after a long and honorable career. Instead of being a failure whose single moment of glory had been lost in a lifetime of uselessness. . . .

No! He couldn't keep mourning a lost past. It was time to live in the present. His men needed him now.

Now . . .

It was time to act. ''Jurgensen! Start broadcasting the wog voice recording!'' He switched to the general transmission channel. ''Come on, boys, let's show those wogs what the Legion's made of!''

''Legion!'' half a hundred voices replied. Then someone else shouted ''Hawley! Hawley!'' and the others took it up. He had forgotten the thrill of it, the feeling of *belonging* that was part of being an officer of the Legion.

The legionnaires broke from cover, opening fire at the rear ranks of the nomads chasing Gage. The trap was sprung. . . .

* * *

"Now!" Gage shouted. "Turn and give 'em hell, Alphas!"

The two depleted platoons responded flawlessly, pivoting in the water and unleashing a murderous FEK barrage against the closest wog troops. Following so close upon Hawley's ambush, this counterattack destroyed the last of their cohesion. A moment ago the natives had been a disciplined fighting force. Now they were a mob, trapped in a deadly crossfire, unable to react quickly enough as the initiative suddenly shifted to the Legion.

But the confusion didn't diminish the individual bravery of the wogs. They still fought fearlessly, and they still outnumbered the legionnaires by a wide margin. If they got a chance to reorganize, they'd still be dangerous.

She gestured to Massire. "Make sure that wog noise is playing loud and clear," she ordered. They had to make sure that Choor! didn't start coordinating this battle again. There wouldn't be much chance of that, as long as the wogs were getting a double dose of DuValier's recording from each of the two Terran forces.

Massire gave a thumb's-up, but a moment later a native rocket bullet tore a hole through his chest. He was dead before Gage could reach him. . . .

"Tsiolkov!" she called to the nearest legionnaire. "Take the C³ unit." She paused to fire a long FEK burst before shouting again. "Hit them! Hit them hard!"

"Hit the bastards again!" Corporal Mike Johnson shouted. "No, not like that, you stupid son of a strakk!"

He grabbed an FEK out of a civilian's hands and snapped the selector switch from full-auto to the three-round burst fire setting. "Don't just pump out a whole strakking clip, for Chrissakes! We want some ammo for the next attack, too!"

A couple of the Seafarms people laughed, sounding relieved. If the legionnaire could talk about the next fight, maybe they really could come through this. . . .

The assault had been going on for close to half an hour now. Unlike the previous attacks against the Sandcastle, this one hadn't involved any finesse or maneuvering on the part of the wogs. They'd just come boiling out of the sea from all directions at once, trying to overwhelm the defenses.

Luckily, the magrep generators had slowed them down,

so that even the armed civilians could hold the walls. The worst weak spots were the shattered gates and a short section of the wall near the Seafarms office block, where one of the magrep modules had been removed to outfit the barge Fraser's men were using for their attack on the enemy base.

Lieutenant DuValier had the gate area. It was up to Johnson to take charge at this other danger zone. But it wouldn't pay to ignore the rest of the perimeter, either. If any of the generators failed, or if the nomads forced their way through despite them, the civilians wouldn't be much of a match for the wogs.

He thrust the battle rifle back into the man's hands and pointed at the crowded waters below. "Now let 'em know you mean business!"

Limping on his injured leg, stiff and tingling inside the regen cast still strapped there, Johnson moved back. It was hard to let the civilians do the fighting while he just looked on, but Lieutenant DuValier had told him that the best thing the legionnaires in the Sandcastle could do was stay back and direct the defense. An officer couldn't allow himself to be drawn so deeply into the fighting that he didn't pay attention to what was happening all across the battlefield. And for all intents and purposes Johnson was an officer now. With two other wounded legionnaires, he was in command of what amounted to two full platoons.

It was a responsibility he gladly would have traded for his old lance command, but he wasn't going to let Captain Fraser down. Or DuValier, who despite the abortive mutiny had been a powerhouse, organizing the defense since Hawley and Fraser had left aboard the *Cyclops*.

"Corporal! Corporal!" That was Legionnaire Myaighee, the injured alien from Watanabe's platoon who was operating Johnson's $C^3$ unit. "Trouble by the gatehouse, Corporal. A major attack this time. Wogs have penetrated the gates and are attacking the lieutenant's position from three sides now!"

"Pass the word to Wu," Johnson ordered. "Tell him to round up . . . five civilians from each unit and get over to the gatehouse right away. Grab five of our people to go, too!"

The hannie saluted and hurried off. Johnson scanned the sea again. If they could just keep holding until Captain Fraser smashed the enemy base . . .

* * *

DuValier crouched behind the rampart and slapped his last magazine into his FEK. He'd run out of grenades long since, and it wouldn't be long before he was out of needle rounds as well.

In which case, he told himself, he'd throw shards of fusand at any wog who tried to climb onto the gatehouse roof. If this was going to be another disaster like Fenris, he wasn't planning on surviving the massacre. This time he'd go out fighting, and he'd take as many wogs with him as he could manage. Antoine DuValier wanted an honor guard to escort him to Hell.

He leaned over the rampart and fired down, heedless of the questing rocket bullets and crossbow bolts that responded to his fire. There were only eleven Seafarms men left on the walls around him out of the fifty he'd started with, and four of them were wounded. The technician with his $C^3$ pack had tumbled off the roof a few minutes earlier, so he didn't have any way of raising the rest of the defenders now. Corporal Johnson would have to keep up the fight as best he could. . . .

He kept on firing until the clip ran dry, then threw the FEK at a nomad climbing slowly up the inner wall. Another rifle lay nearby where someone had dropped it. DuValier scrambled for it, checked the magazine, and brought it up to fire a burst into a wog climbing over the parapet. The nomad screeched and fell over backward, hitting the water below with a loud splash.

Panting, DuValier crouched for a long moment. If the Sandcastle fell, at least he'd die with a weapon in his hands. Captain Fraser had given him that much.

If he had worked with Fraser all along, instead of letting his hate blind him to the man's nature, perhaps none of them would be in this corner now. Or maybe this would have been the outcome no matter what.

All that really mattered anymore was the battle. DuValier raised the battle rifle again and thrust himself back into the fray.

"Here they come again!" someone shouted. Hawley braced the FEK in his hands and strained to see through the murky water. The battle had churned up mud and blood that made it hard to spot anything more than a few meters away.

That was giving the wogs an advantage, despite the Legion sonars. In this confused battle it was impossible to follow all the enemy targets successfully, and when a nomad erupted from a liquid fog at close range he had all the benefits of speed and familiarity with the environment. Most of the Legion casualties in this fight were coming from sword cuts and spear thrusts, not the high-tech weaponry supplied by the Toels.

There was an irony somewhere in there, but Hawley wasn't laughing.

Nearby, Subaltern Watanabe and a corporal named Radescu raised their weapons and fired almost simultaneously as a trio of wogs broke into view. Radescu screamed as a heavy-bladed sword drove downward through his shoulder and deep into his torso, but the nomads thrashed and bled under the subaltern's withering fire. More inhuman shapes appeared, and Hawley added his FEK's voice to the battle.

The nomads were broken as a fighting force, but they were still attacking anywhere they could. It looked as though this time they were going to keep on fighting until there were no wogs left at all. A lot more legionnaires would die as well.

The butcher's bill was going to hurt later, but for now Hawley had a battle to fight. He didn't even need the fiction of a game anymore. All that mattered was keeping these wogs tied up until Colin Fraser could win the fight inside the compound. And that was just what Hawley would do, no matter what the cost might be.

"Sir!" That was Jurgensen, sticking close beside him despite the double encumbrance of the thruster unit and his $C^3$ pack. "*Cyclops* reports that bunch of wogs heading back for the base has broken up. Some of them are heading for us again. Sounds like they're completely disorganized."

"Acknowledge the report," he said, his mind wrestling with the new information. It sounded like Choor!'s war machine was breaking down. Those nomads would want to rally around their own clans as the fighting became general. The wog commander would know that the defense of the base was most important, but in the long run his coalition was still weaker than the individual clan loyalties within it.

That would help Fraser. But the last thing he needed out here was more nomads. . . .

"Captain! Look out!" Watanabe yelled the warning too

late. A nomad spear seemed to come from nowhere, thrusting into the pit of his stomach. The pain was like nothing he'd ever felt before.

He tried to shoot at the wog, as the nomad yanked the spear clear and thrust again, but he'd dropped his FEK. The pain redoubled, and Hawley bent double, clutching his injured stomach and sobbing.

The wog shuddered and thrashed as a hail of needle rounds ripped through him. A moment later Watanabe was there, fumbling at his first aid kit. "Medic! Medic!" he yelled.

"Save . . . save it," Hawley gasped out. "Nothing . . . a medic . . . can do for . . . me. Not now . . ."

"Take it easy, sir," Watanabe was saying, as he moved closer to examine the wound. Even through his faceplate his grave expression was clear enough. The subaltern knew the wound was a mortal one.

"More . . . nomads . . . on the way . . ." Hawley forced the words out, trying to ignore the burning pain in his gut. "Must . . . unify. . . . Join Gage. . . . Hit them all together. . . . No defeat in detail . . ." It was all clear in his mind, but he didn't know if he was making sense to Watanabe. Marshal Vigny had allowed an Alliance relief force to smash into his troops while they were still dispersed after the first part of the Battle of Dijon, and the afternoon battle had ended with the rout of the French and the final collapse of the Imperial resistance in Metropolitan France at the end of the Grand Crusade.

The battle was clear in his mind, as clear as this fight against the wogs. But he couldn't find the words to explain it. . . .

Gage and Watanabe could handle the fight. They'd beat the wogs cold. With these legionnaires, they could do anything.

He rallied enough to go on. "Tell . . . tell the men . . . I'm proud of them all. . . ."

And blackness descended on him for the last time.

# Chapter 24

They're not men, they're wild beasts.
—a German major, speaking of
the French Foreign Legion, 1916

Katrina Voskovich held the receiver to her ear and listened to the chatter from inside the enemy base. Around her, the other civilians on the bridge of the *Seafarms Cyclops* watched her, waiting. She'd never expected to be a leader, but it seemed as if the role had been forced on her anyway.

"The sappers are still pinned," she said. "And it sounds like the captain's troops are running into heavy resistance." She looked across at Warrant Officer Koenig, the only legionnaire on the bridge. "Sounds like they're in trouble."

Koenig shifted uncomfortably. Aside from him, only Father Fitzpatrick and Dr. Ramirez remained on board the ship. "What about Captain Hawley's men? Can we get any of them free to support the strike force?"

"I don't think so," Voskovich told him. "The fighting down there is still pretty confused, and that new bunch is moving in."

The warrant officer let out a ragged breath. "Then there's no way of helping Fraser's people. They'll have to handle it on their own. . . ."

"We're available," Voskovich said flatly. "I say we go for it."

"Captain Fraser's orders—"

"Damn the orders!" she flared. "Look, he wanted the *Cyclops* safe so there was a way out if things went sour. Well, they're going sour, but none of those legionnaires will make it unless they get support fast. We may not be much, but we can turn up the heat on the wogs."

A spasm of indecision crossed Koenig's face. She pressed

on. "What do the rest of you say? We've disobeyed the military people before, right? Let's make it count for something, for a change!"

The bridge crew's reaction was mixed. The ones who'd been in the fighting at the Sandcastle were cheering, but the regular ship's personnel looked sullen. Their only experience of the Legion had been Subaltern Watanabe's takeover. . . .

Koenig looked around, then gave a curt nod. "Do it," he said shortly.

"You heard the man," Voskovich said loudly. "Get this monstrosity under way. And get everyone who has a weapon and isn't needed to operate the ship down to the boarding platforms. We'll show the legionnaires they aren't the only ones crazy enough to take on these wogs!"

Fraser swam past a knot of dead nomads, to join Gunnery Sergeant Trent beside one of the twisted struts that had been part of a harvester ship cradle near the center of the enemy compound. Steady fighting had pushed them deeper and deeper into the base, but they still had a long way to go to reach Kelly's position beyond the bulk of the Toel ship.

Fourteen dead and eight wounded, so far. More than half of his force were casualties now, and still the nomads kept on fighting. The wog coalition was larger than anyone had predicted, and there were still plenty of hostiles left inside their fortress. Enemy troops were closing in behind them now, and the next attack would probably come from all sides.

He was certain now that this final gesture against Choor!'s headquarters had failed. They hadn't seen anything yet that looked like it might be the native warlord's bodyguard or staff, just scores of nomad soldiers rallying to the defense. He had a good idea now of where Choor! was: The defenders were strongest in the direction of the gatehouse complex, and Fraser suspected that the lower levels there were probably flooded and occupied by the enemy leadership. But the gatehouse was even farther away than Kelly's beleaguered sappers. It didn't look like he was going to reach either target now.

Explosions erupted behind the legionnaires, a long way off but loud in his external audio pickups. They were coming from the direction of the breach, and they sounded like the depth charges the legionnaires had improvised. "What the hell. . . ?" he said aloud.

He kicked off from the bottom and broke the surface, ignoring the risk of being spotted. Looking across the compound, Fraser spotted the breach.

The huge shape of the *Cyclops* loomed behind the hole, and civilians were streaming off one of the boarding platforms onto the abandoned barge. He thought he saw Koenig . . . Voskovich . . . even the burly shape of the guard who had threatened him during Barnett's mutiny. None of them had hardsuits, but they were firing into the water and shoving explosive canisters through the gap to confuse the nomads.

Fraser dived again. They'd disobeyed his orders to stay clear of the fighting, but he was glad of the disobedience. With this new threat the nomads would have to regroup, and in the meantime he just might be able to turn the battle around. . . .

"Gunny!" he shouted. "Take two lances toward the breach. *Cyclops* is there, and we can catch some wogs in a crossfire if we hurry. Then go support Kelly."

"What about the rest of the men?" Trent asked. "You're not splitting us up?"

"Yes, we are. We'll smash through the nomads over there and hit the gatehouse! That should make Choor! rethink his battle plan!" He switched frequencies. "Onagers, form up in front and prepare to advance. Let's get this thing over with!"

He slapped a fresh magazine into the receiver of his FEK. This new plan still risked a defeat in detail, but the appearance of the *Cyclops* had opened up a window he couldn't afford to ignore.

Even if they failed, the nomads would know they'd been in a fight.

"Lieutenant!" Watanabe felt relief wash over him as he caught sight of Susan Gage in the middle of a cluster of legionnaires, advancing out of the swirling murk ahead. Since Hawley's death he'd been trying to hold his force together and close ranks with the other unit. Now, at last, he could pass the responsibility back to a superior.

Gage and her $C^3$ technician swam over to him. "Where's the captain?" she asked.

"Dead, Lieutenant," Watanabe told her. "You're in charge now."

"Damn," she said softly. "Just when he had a chance . . ."

"He died the way he would have wanted to," he said. "Let's concentrate on saving the living."

"Right," she nodded, visibly taking control of herself. "We've broken the back on the main body. Wish we had a better idea of what's going on with Captain Fraser. That's where the real action is." She paused. "Do you have a status on those reinforcements?"

"Lost them in the clutter a few minutes ago," he said. With the bodies so thick throughout the battlefield, the sonar units were having a lot of trouble distinguishing the live targets that were still out there. "They'll be here soon. . . ."

She brought up her FEK suddenly and fired past him, yelling "They're here now!" Watanabe rolled over and added his own weapon to hers. A cluster of nomads with mixed weaponry swam right into the kill zone and died.

Then there were more, swarming out of the murk. He maintained fire until his magazine ran dry, then drew his PLF rocket pistol.

Gage ran out of ammo at almost the same moment and fumbled for a fresh magazine. As she did, a wog raised a rocket gun and fired. Watanabe tried to shove her out of the way, but it was too late. Susan Gage was dead, too. That made him the senior surviving officer—maybe the only one. Wijngaarde had died in the early stages of the ambush, and he hadn't seen Carnes yet. . . .

"Close up, legionnaires!" he called on the comm circuit. "Throw the bastards back!"

He heard Sergeant Gessler shouting orders and encouragement, heard the grudging respect in the man's voice as he called, "Come on, you sandrats! The Sub needs us!"

Kelly flinched as another of her sappers died. The Toels had the whole position ringed in now, and there was precious little cover that wasn't exposed to one of the alien soldiers. Even the arrival of the *Cyclops*, reported by Trent over her commlink, hadn't slowed the Toels down. It looked like they were letting their allies go down, while they concentrated on protecting their ship.

Beyond their defensive positions she could see Toeljuk workers loading cargo through the open bay doors near the base of the vessel. If only she could get some explosives up there . . .

A Toel laser probed toward her. She could feel the water temperature going up each time the pulse passed overhead. Kelly clung more tightly to the fusand wall and returned fire, but the laser was shielded behind a plasteel barrier.

Without reinforcements from Fraser, there was no way the sappers were breaking out of this crossfire. And Fraser, she knew, was busy elsewhere. There was still no sign of Trent's two lances, either.

Suddenly the Toel laser position ceased firing as the gunner let go of his weapon and drifted toward the surface, no longer moving. Another Toel nearby did the same a moment later. Through her headphones she heard a whoop of triumph.

"Rydell to the rescue!"

"Knock it off and find a target." Trent's gruff voice overrode the exuberance of the laser gunner from Braxton's recon lance. "Miss Kelly? Are you still here?"

"Alive and kicking, Sergeant," she answered, firing again. More Toels were dying, as the two fresh lances took them from behind. Trent had circled around so that his attack had come from the direction of the ship, and the Toels had never even noticed. "How the hell did you sneak up on them like that?"

"Climbed out and used the walls. Basher and Spear have things pretty clear topside now, and the bad guys aren't paying much attention up there anymore."

She grinned inside her hardsuit helmet. For a change the Terrans had made terrain work in their favor.

"Let's move!" she shouted to her sappers. Kicking off from the bottom and cutting in her thruster, Kelly raced toward Trent and his men. A few random shots followed from other Toel positions, but at least for now the enemy was too busy to effectively cover the legionnaires.

Sappers followed, led by old MacAllister. The veteran trailed a large satchel of PX-90 behind him. "Dinna worry, lassie!" he called, as he caught up to her. "We'll blast yon bastards!"

Mbote, another of Braxton's men, passed her and dropped

toward the bottom, blazing away steadily with his FEK. "We'll cover you," he said. "But make it fast!"

Trent was already swimming ahead, with Pascali's lance spread out in a loose skirmish line on either side, cutting a swath through the unarmed Toel workers around the cargo door. Kelly and MacAllister were close behind, with a handful of other sappers in tow.

There was a savage gun battle at the door itself, with a pair of Toels armed with heavy laser rifles holding the recon lance. Finally Trent and Corporal Pascali rolled through, firing a volley of mini-grenades. In the confusion, the rest of the lance was able to break in and kill the two aliens. The cargo bay was clear—for the moment.

"Go! Go!" Trent called. Kelly and MacAllister split the explosives between them and started working their way around opposite sides of the cargo bay, slapping liberal quantities of the PX-90 in place. The other sappers followed behind, setting detpacks and programming them to Kelly's shouted orders. The recon troopers kept a wary eye on the two doors, ready for any Toel reinforcements.

Kelly planted her last charge and waited impatiently for the others to finish. "Let's mag out!" she said. The Terrans swam clear of the cargo bay, back into the battle outside. Braxton's lance was giving way slowly before a determined Toel attack. Now the legionnaires hit their thruster and angled away from the ship.

Pausing to draw out a remote control unit, Kelly hit the detonator. An instant later explosions erupted from the interior of the ship. The Toeljuks pursuing them broke off the fight and headed for the vessel.

"No way they'll be leaving now," Kelly said confidently. They'd planted the charges to breach the hull in several places, and it would be hours before they could patch the ship well enough to make her spaceworthy.

They'd done their job. Now if Fraser could carry off his . . .

Inside the Reef-of-the-Gift-Bearers, Choor! listened to the reports from his subordinates with mounting concern. All contact lost with the force sent outside the walls to face the Strangers there, no word on the progress against their fortress. And every force they'd mustered against the raiding party had been thrown back or destroyed.

How could these Terran-Strangers fight so well? The Gift-Bearers had said that Terrans were a weak race, indecisive, whose warriors ran from a losing battle and whose merchants would sell one another as slaves when they scented profit in the current. An easy victory, they had said, which would deliver Ourgh and eventually the rest of the land-dwellers into the tendrils of the Clans United with less effort then it took to subdue a hostile Clan.

But this had been anything but an easy victory. Even if they finished off these Terrans, the Clans United might never recover. Too many warriors lost, too much of Choor!'s prestige used up in useless assaults and stratagems the leaders of the Strangers had anticipated all too thoroughly. Even the Betrayer had proven useless to the Clans.

This ''Legion'' of Terran warriors was more tenacious in battle than any Clan, fighting, *winning* against impossible odds and never knowing when to give up. They were more like a blood-hungry *woorroo* following the scent of its prey. Animals . . .

But dangerous animals. Animals who had broken his dream of the Clans United.

''If you wish, you can still win free with the remaining guards,'' one Clan-Leader was saying.

''No!'' Choor! rejected the suggestion as automatically as the most instinct-enslaved Warrior-Inferior. ''No . . . Muster the last guards. Break these animals for me. Break them!''

The wogs erupted out of the gatehouse so suddenly that Fraser hardly had time to react. For a few minutes he'd thought the battle was over. But there were still nomads rallying to the defense after all.

Just one more battle . . . Surely this would be the last.

A native with a pike twice his own length charged straight at Fraser, but the huge Gwyrran named Vrurrth thrust past and grappled with the wog. The pike drifted away as Vrurrth wrenched it from the smaller alien's hands. Then the wog was thrashing, as those powerful fingers dug into the nomad's gills. A moment later the native stopped moving, and the Gwyrran pushed the limp body away with a contemptuous flourish. It floated toward the surface in slow motion, blood oozing from the gill-slits.

Fraser opened fire just as another nomad, this one wielding a sword, slashed at Legionnaire Grant. The boy flashed him a quick thumb's-up as he directed a steady stream of autofire at the gatehouse door. Corporals Rostov and Haddad were close by, also firing until it seemed that the water was growing black with needle rounds.

The Gurkha corporal commanding one of the weapons lances touched Fraser on the shoulder and pointed at the gatehouse wall a few meters from the door. Fraser gave him a quick nod, then he backed away fast as the onager came into play again. The other onagers joined in an instant later, and in seconds they had opened another breach in the inner wall. Fraser gathered up a handful of legionnaires and swam for the hole. The heat of the water near the gap was almost intolerable, but he squeezed through into the building, his men close behind.

And stopped at the sight of the lone figure waiting inside.

The nomad wore an ornate dagger at this side and cradled a rocket gun in his arms. His bearing made his identity plain, though he was nothing like what Fraser had imagined.

Choor!, the nomad warlord, was a young wog, probably younger than any of the leaders he had "advised." He was distinctly overweight, too, and looked more like one of the scholarly class from Ourgh than he did like a being who had single-handedly brought such terror to Polypheme.

Fraser hesitated. Suddenly it didn't seem right to kill this mild-looking wog.

But Choor! plainly didn't share that sentiment. He raised his rifle and fired.

A legionnaire shoved Fraser out of the way and took the round in his own arm. A moment later it was over, with half a dozen Legion soldiers pumping round after round into the nomad leader.

Gunnery Sergeant Trent climbed wearily onto the boarding platform of the *Cyclops*, opening his hardsuit helmet and taking a deep, satisfying breath of air. He could hardly believe it was over.

The civilian leader, Voskovich, hurried across the deck. "Did you hear the news?" she was asking, her eyes shining.

He shook his head wearily.

"The wogs attacked the Sandcastle again, but we held

them. Corporal Johnson called a few minutes ago to report that they were running. Someone must have sent word to them about Choor!. . . ."

"Johnson? Was DuValier. . . ?"

She shook her head. "He was wounded in the fighting, and Johnson's in charge, but the medical people say the Lieutenant will be all right."

If Fraser wanted to prefer charges over the mutiny, DuValier would be wishing the wogs had killed him. Death by lethal injection wasn't a pleasant way to go. . . .

"Everyone else aboard?" he asked, changing the subject. Another death was something he didn't want to think about just now. Not after all the killing Trent had seen today.

She nodded. "Captain Fraser brought the Toel prisoners aboard a few minutes ago. And Mr. Watanabe and the survivors of the main body are already down in Legion country." She smiled. "There was one named White who was talking about booze."

"They deserve it," Trent said. "Hell, *I* deserve it! You want to join us?" Voskovich had played no small part in getting the fight inside the base back on track.

She nodded hesitantly. "Yes . . . yes, I'd like that, Sergeant."

"Then give the orders to get us going, and come on down. I'm not going to stop celebrating until we sight home."

# Epilogue

> It is thanks to you, gentlemen, that we are here at all. If I ever have the honor to command another expedition, I shall ask for at least a battalion of the Foreign Legion.
>
> —General Charles Duchesne,
> commander, Madagascar expedition
> French Foreign Legion, 1895

Colin Fraser leaned on the rampart and looked out at the Navy lighter grounded outside the Sandcastle, his feelings a mixture of relief, pride . . . and not a little sadness. With the arrival of Commandant Miloradovich and his battalion, Demi-Battalion Elaine would be leaving Polypheme. But they would be leaving behind many comrades and many memories. That was a part of being a legionnaire.

The Commandant had escorted a new contingent of Seafarms executives, who were already busy trying to put the Cyclops Project back together. The carrier ship that had brought the legionnaires to the Polypheme system had also carried a contingent of government people, who would soon be putting together everything necessary to turn Polypheme into a full-fledged Commonwealth protectorate.

They'd have little trouble getting the natives to cooperate. The Elders in Ourgh had been more than just eager to resume their close ties with the Terrans in the wake of the battle at the enemy headquarters, and several of Choor!'s erstwhile confederates had approached Fraser asking for assistance in recovering now that the fighting was over. Choor!, they said, had been responsible for the conflict. Without him, and without the warriors lost in those desperate attacks, the individual tribes were almost helpless.

Down on the mud flats, he saw a guard detail escorting a gaggle of Toel prisoners aboard the ship. Sergeant Michael

Johnson was in command. Getting him that extra stripe for the way he'd held together the garrison after DuValier was wounded had been one of the small rewards that almost made the other side of the coin, the butcher's bill, tolerable. The Toels would be returned to their own people, but not before the Autarchy heard just how dim a view the Commonwealth took of interference in the affairs of worlds within the Terran sphere of influence. The Toeljuk Autarchy wasn't prepared for a full-scale war. Fraser was sure those Toels would be labeled "outlaws" by an embarrassed Autarch, regardless of what the real facts of the plot might have been.

"Captain?" The familiar voice sounded a little less cool and controlled than it usually did. Lieutenant Antoine DuValier had recovered from his physical wounds. Whether he had healed the scars in his mind was another question.

Fraser turned and examined him. The uniform was spotless as ever, and it was hard to tell the stiffness of his wounds from his usual straight-backed stance. "What is it, Mr. DuValier?"

"I . . . thought you might not have heard. Senator Warwick's cut his tour short and headed back to Terra."

He nodded. "The Commandant told me." Miloradovich had also told him, in strictest confidence, the reason for Warwick's abrupt cancellation of his witch-hunt on the Frontiers. Evidently Reynier Industries had been applying quite a bit of pressure on the commission to recognize a certain Captain Colin Fraser for his heroism in defending Commonwealth interests on Polypheme. Warwick wouldn't be a party to a medal for the captain, but he was in no position to block it. One of the other members of the Commission would be left to deal with an embarrassing situation.

The medal didn't matter that much, but it was good to know that Warwick wouldn't be hovering over his shoulder, at least for a while. He only hoped that Reynier Industries wouldn't lose sight of the other heroes of Polypheme. Like David Hawley.

DuValier seemed unwilling to go on, but finally spoke again. "Sir . . . Captain . . . I was wondering if you'd heard anything about . . . what happens now?"

"Alpha Company's being dissolved," he told him. "Most of them will wind up as Bravos. The Commandant says we're being posted back to Devereaux for a few months. After that . . ." He shrugged. "Who knows?"

They'd be taking some other recruits with them as well, including the nomad scout, Oomour, and Katrina Voskovich, who had resigned from Seafarms to look for adventure in the Legion.

DuValier looked away. "I . . . was hoping . . ." He trailed off. "You've done so much just by dropping the mutiny charges. . . ."

"You earned that," Fraser said harshly. "Several times over."

"I was hoping you'd reconsider keeping me on as Exec," DuValier blurted out. "I was wrong about you. And I'd be honored to keep on serving with you."

Fraser shook his head firmly. "I'm sorry, Lieutenant. That's out of the question. I need to know that my Executive Officer is someone I can rely on, no matter what. Someone who knows my mind better than I know it myself. Even though you've . . . changed a lot, I still could never give you the kind of loyalty you deserve. That's a two-way street that can't be put right by a few kind words and a little soul-searching."

DuValier looked unhappy. "I'm . . . sorry, sir. I hope you can find someone else who'll meet your standards."

"I already have, Lieutenant. The Commandant has already let me know that my recommendation for promoting Toru Watanabe's been approved. He'll be my new Exec."

"He's a good man," DuValier said, turning away.

Fraser followed the French lieutenant with his eyes. *So are you, my friend,* he thought. With a fresh start in a new outfit, without this hatred gnawing away at his guts, Antoine DuValier would find his feet again. He had the makings of a first-rate Legion officer. Someone Fraser would be proud to serve with again someday.

Someone even David Hawley would approve of.

# Glossary

**adchip:** Short for "adhesive chip," any of the button-sized minicomputers designed to hook directly into the human nervous system for total sensory interaction. A cheap alternative to computer implants.

**Airshark:** Ground support aircraft used in the Colonial Army.

**ale:** slang for "alien"; applied to any nonhuman.

**battalion:** Military formation which, in Commonwealth usage, fields 6–9 companies under the command of a commandant or major. Three or more battalions form a regiment.

**bhourrkh:** Native name for the fierce storms on Polypheme.

**C$^3$:** Command, control, and communication, used in referring to specialist technicians, to the computer/commo packs they carry and operate, or the larger control centers in bases or vehicles where these operations are performed. Also "C-cubed."

**CEK:** Cannon d'Énergie Kinetique; vehicle-mounted autocannon.

**chip:** Short for adchip; used as a verb, "to chip" means to take computer-induced instruction in a subject such as language.

**Citizen:** Citizenship in the Terran Commonwealth is universal on Terra but highly prized off-planet, and the title

"Citizen" is commonly used on Colonial and frontier worlds to denote someone who has inherited or been awarded citizenship. Legionnaires who have served for at least one five-year term receive Commonwealth citizenship as a reward for service.

**Colonial Army:** The military arm of the Commonwealth employed to defend and extend the Colonies. Unlike the regular Terran Army, the Colonial Army is raised entirely from the Colonies, seeing duty on worlds other than their home planet (usually along the frontier of Commonwealth space).

**commandant:** Commonwealth military officer commanding a battalion; equivalent to the rank of major.

**company:** Smallest independently-fielded fighting unit of the Terran Commonwealth. A standard Light Infantry company of the Fifth Foreign Legion comprises three platoons plus a command lance of five (CO, Exec, Company NCO, and two $C^3$ technicians), as well as any attached personnel such as warrant officers, transport units, sappers, etc. Typically a company will contain 109 officers and men.

**compboard:** A self-contained minicomputer used like a clipboard.

**ConRig:** A control harness which governs onager-aiming, in conjunction with helmet HUD sights.

**demi-battalion:** An ad-hoc formation of two or more companies, usually commanded by the senior company commander present. Demi-battalions are frequently fielded for long-term detached operations where a full battalion may not be appropriate or available.

**detpack:** A programmable detonator system used with PX-90 explosives. The operator may select remote, timed, or conditional detonation; without programming, the detpack/explosive combination is completely safe.

**Devereaux:** Frontier world, attacked 2729 by a Semti invasion fleet. Site of the heroic Fourth Foreign Legion resistance to an eight-month siege, which saw the destruction of that Legion as an effective fighting force. Now the homeworld of the Fifth Foreign Legion, and site of its extensive training facilities.

**dreamchip:** Originally a trade name, now generic, for adchips designed to impart game or fantasy sequences. Also used loosely for the similar programs run on implants.

**dreamland:** slang for the withdrawn state of someone using an adchip or implant.

**Fafnir:** man-portable rocket launcher issued on a section level to the Fifth Foreign Legion. The Fafnir rocket is "smart" (able to discriminate various target silhouettes pre-programmed by the operator) and is equally proficient in anti-tank and air defense roles.

**FE-FEK/27 (Fusil d'Énergie Kinetique Model 27):** kinetic-energy rifle manufactured by Fabrique Europa, standard longarm of the Fifth Foreign Legion.

**FE-MEK/15 (Mitrailleuse d'Énergie Kinetique Model 15):** kinetic-energy assault gun manufactured by Fabrique Europa, the standard lance-level support weapon used by the Fifth Foreign Legion.

**FE-PLF (Pistolet Lance-Fusée):** 10-mm rocket pistol manufactured by Fabrique Europa, a popular sidearm with officers of the Fifth Foreign Legion.

**floatcar:** an open-topped magnetic suspension vehicle used in both civilian and military applications. A staff car or jeep.

**FSV:** acronym for Fire Support Vehicle.

**fusand:** Derived from "fused sand"; a process developed by the Toels and used in the construction of their bases on Polypheme.

**Gorgon:** Commonwealth designation for a Magrep Assault Vehicle built by the Toeljuk Autarchy.

**Grendel:** large vehicle-mounted missile found on the Sabertooth FSV.

**implant:** Computer link surgically placed directly in the brain. Most upper-class Terrans and a few exceptionally wealthy Colonials have implants, as do certain military officers whose duties require their use.

**KEC:** A heavy kinetic-energy weapon found in a vehicle mount aboard Sabertooth and Sandray class vehicles. It is the kinetic-energy weapon equivalent of a contemporary Vulcan gatling cannon, with an extremely high rate of fire and muzzle velocities that will defeat almost any type of conventional armor.

**lance:** designation of the Commonwealth's basic military unit, either five infantrymen or a single tank or aircraft.

**last march:** Legion slang for death.

**legionnaire:** loosely, a member of the Fifth Foreign Legion (or any other "Legion" in the army, if there are such). Specifically, an enlisted soldier holding the rank of Legionnaire First Class, Legionnaire Second Class, or Legionnaire Third Class. Non-Legion units use the designation "Soldier" instead of Legionnaire.

**loke:** slang for "local"; applied to a native nonhuman.

**mag:** Slang derived from magnetic suspension technology, meaning "move." To "mag out" is to "move out" or "bug out"; a "mag-out" is a hasty departure.

**magger:** anyone who operates an MSV; a tank or APC crewman.

**magrep module:** Small semi-circular projection unit (linked to a generator) which produces a magnetic suspension cushion.

**MAV:** acronym for Magrep Assault Vehicle.

**MSV:** Magnetic Suspension Vehicle, official designation of any vehicle operating on a Magnetic Suspension Cushion.

**murphy:** Any unforeseen and potentially catastrophic occurrence.

**musynther:** Small musical instrument, much favored by soldiers, capable of reproducing the sounds of many different traditional instruments.

**nube:** A newcomer or rookie.

**onager (fusil d'onage; storm rifle):** plasma gun, originally invented during the French Imperial period (hence the French-derived name). The onager is one of the standard section-level heavy weapons used by the Fifth Foreign Legion (the other is the Fafnir rocket launcher). Onagers require soldiers to wear fairly cumbersome body armor to protect them from heat effects, but they are devastatingly powerful on the battlefield. A larger version of the weapon, the onager cannon, is found in a turret mount on the Sabertooth FSV.

**platoon:** Basic tactical unit of the Commonwealth's ground forces, containing either six tanks, thirteen APCs, or two infantry sections plus a sub-lieutenant as platoon leader and a Platoon Sergeant as unit NCO (for a total of 34 men).

**platoon sergeant:** NCO rank equivalent to the contemporary USA rank of Staff Sergeant. Serves as Platoon XO.

**PX-90:** explosive compound, packaged in 1-kg blocks. The explosive is a high-tech version of plastique, used with a detpack programmable detonator. PX-90 has both military and engineering applications.

**rapack:** ration pack; the 29th century equivalent of an MRE.

**regen therapy:** advanced medical technique for regrowth of damaged tissue.

**Reynier Industries:** Giant corporation in Commonwealth space that retains a monopoly on the manufacture of interstellar drive systems. The company's political influence is very extensive, and Reynier has been called "the forty-sixth Member" in the Commonwealth's forty-five member-worlds.

**Sabertooth (M-980 FSV):** Company-level Fire Support Vehicle employed by the Fifth Foreign Legion, mounting two Grendel missiles, an onager cannon in a turret, and a fixed-forward kinetic energy cannon. It can carry up to six men, plus a crew of two. Typically, a company mounted on thirteen vehicles will include two Sabertooths.

**Sandray (M-786 series):** Generic name for an entire family of armored personnel carriers and specialty variants used by the Fifth Foreign Legion. Typical vehicles include an APC, a command van, an engineering vehicle, a supply carrier, a medical van, and so on. They carry six men plus a specialty compartment (except the APC, which carries twelve men). Many of them mount kinetic-energy cannons in a remote-controlled turret; the engineering vehicle mounts a low-power laser cannon and various types of engineering hardware such as bulldozer blades or cranes.

**section:** designation for an infantry unit containing three lances, plus a sergeant as Section Leader. The section thus contains sixteen men.

**Semti:** An alien race, formerly rulers of the Semti Conclave but now subject (for the most part) to the Terran Commonwealth. Evolved from scavenger stock, they are bilaterally symmetrical, upright bipeds, basically humanoid in appearance but with dry, leathery skins and large eyes. Their ruthless pragmatism brought them into direct conflict with Terra during the Semti War, in which they lost control of the 200-world empire known as the Semti Conclave. Since that time the Conclave Sphere has been a wide-open colonial frontier, over which the Commonwealth and other interstellar powers have extended their control.

**strakk:** A small, repulsive animal native to Devereaux. It has been said to combine the worst features of the cockroach, the rat, and the lemming. The word has passed into Army (especially Legion) parlance as a general perjorative.

**subaltern:** lowest officer rank, commanding a platoon. Commonly "Sub."

**systerm:** "System Terminal," the major port facilities used for carriership operations near the fringe of a star system.

**Terran Commonwealth:** The human interstellar state that fields the Fifth Foreign Legion. Following the Semti War, the Commonwealth acquired virtual control over most of the Conclave Sphere, and thus became a colonial power in the old (19th-century) sense of the term.

**Toeljuk:** An alien race, another of the colonial powers exploiting former Semti space. The Toeljuks are a squat, low-grav race with tentacles, who like wet marshlands and coastal plains. They have a reputation for brutality and greed.

**Topheth:** Planet of the Procyon star system noted for rich metal deposits and hellish conditions. The name has passed into Commonwealth usage as a common synonym for Hell.

**Ubrenfars:** A saurian race with a growing empire along the fringe of the former Semti sphere. The Ubrenfars contributed to the downfall of the Conclave, which was engaged in a campaign to subdue them when the Terrans declared war. They are now widely considered to be the chief rivals for dominance in interstellar affairs. Heavily caste-oriented, the Ubrenfars field a dedicated and highly skilled military force.

**veeter:** A small VTOL aircraft used for recon work.

**vidmagazine:** A holovid entertainment device worn like glasses, which allows the user to experience the contents as if at first hand. Becoming largely obsolete as adchips spread, the vidmagazine is primarily found now in the role of 20th-century newspapers or infotainment magazines or programs.

**warrant officer:** A specialist officer in the Colonial Army, not in the regular chain of command but with many of the privileges and responsibilities of regular officers. There are four grades (WO/1 through WO/4); a WO/4 is equivalent to a sublieutenant and is found on a company staff. Ability as a warrant officer frequently leads to a full officer's commission. Typical specialties include medical, chaplain, sciences, intel/alien technologies, combat engineering, and others. Note that other branches of the armed forces do not use this system.

**Whitney-Sykes HPLR-55 (High-Power Laser Rifle Mark 55):** A laser rifle manufactured by the Australian small arms company Whitney-Sykes, commonly used as a sniper's rifle by the Fifth Foreign Legion.

**wog:** Derogatory slang term (derived from "polliwog") for the natives of Polypheme. Though not originally based on the perjorative "wog" of 19th-century Terra, usage is quite similar.

**wristpiece:** A computer terminal worn on the wrist and forearm. The wristpiece is now becoming largely obsolete on Terra (where computer implants are the cutting edge of technology), but are still quite common off Terra. They can perform a wide variety of functions, including calculation, data storage/retrieval, translation, and other jobs. Some are designed to link to implants or adchips worn by the operator, while others are voice-activated with a remote radio receiver worn behind the ear.

Commonly known as a " 'piece."